Sydney Brides

KANDY SHEPHERD

MILLS & BOON

GIFT-WRAPPED IN HER WEDDING DRESS
© 2015 by Kandy Shepherd
Australian Copyright 2015
New Zealand Copyright 2015
First Published 2015
Third Australian Paperback Edition 2024
ISBN 978 1 038 90864 3

CROWN PRINCE'S CHOSEN BRIDE
© 2016 by Kandy Shepherd
Australian Copyright 2016
New Zealand Copyright 2016
First Published 2016
Third Australian Paperback Edition 2024
ISBN 978 1 038 90864 3

THE BRIDESMAID'S BABY BUMP
© 2016 by Kandy Shepherd
Australian Copyright 2016
New Zealand Copyright 2016
First Published 2016
Second Australian Paperback Edition 2024
ISBN 978 1 038 90864 3

Published by
Mills & Boon
An imprint of Harlequin Enterprises (Australia) Pty Limited (ABN 47 001 180 918), a subsidiary of HarperCollins Publishers Australia Pty Limited (ABN 36 009 913 517)
Level 19, 201 Elizabeth Street
SYDNEY NSW 2000
AUSTRALIA

Printed and bound in Australia by McPherson's Printing Group

CONTENTS

Gift-Wrapped In Her Wedding Dress

Kandy Shepherd swapped a career as a magazine editor for a life writing romance. She lives on a small farm in the Blue Mountains near Sydney, Australia, with her husband, daughter and lots of pets. She believes in love at first sight and real-life romance—they worked for her! Kandy loves to hear from her readers. Visit her at kandyshepherd.com.

Books by Kandy Shepherd

The Summer They Never Forgot
The Tycoon and the Wedding Planner
A Diamond in Her Stocking
From Paradise...to Pregnant!
Hired by the Brooding Billionaire

Visit the Author Profile page
at millsandboon.com.au for more titles.

Dear Reader,

When it comes to Christmas, you'll never hear me say "bah humbug." I love the festive season with all its anticipation, joy and celebrations with family and friends. Each year, I revel in all the baking and decorating and filling the house with Christmas music. We usually have a party on Christmas Eve, lunch with family on the actual day, and then collapse in a heap the next day.

With my love of all things Christmas, you can imagine how much I enjoyed writing *Gift-Wrapped in Her Wedding Dress*.

It was such fun to bring together a billionaire Scrooge who hates Christmas (he's very much a "bah humbug" man!) and a vivacious party planner who loves everything about the season. Dominic Hunt has tragedy and secrets in his past. When he's forced to host a Christmas party for business purposes, lovely Andie Newman breezes into his life and his damaged heart starts to yearn for something more. But Andie has to overcome the pain of past loss before she can open her heart to Dominic—and Dominic has to learn to trust her. I so enjoyed helping these two realize the best Christmas present they could give each other was their love.

In my past life as a magazine editor, I edited magazines with December issues that were totally devoted to Christmas. I've given Andie a magazine background that helps her organize a magnificent party for Dominic that helps them reach out to each other and find their happy-ever-after. Dominic then has some party planning of his own up his sleeve...

I hope you enjoy reading Andie and Dominic's story as much as I enjoyed writing it—and I wish you a Happy Christmas and all the very best for the festive season.

Warm regards,

Kandy

To all my Christmas magazine colleagues,
in particular Helen, Adriana and Jane—
the magic of the season lives on!

CHAPTER ONE

SO HE'D GOT on the wrong side of the media. Again. Dominic's words, twisted out of all recognition, were all over newspapers, television and social media.

Billionaire businessman Dominic Hunt refuses to sleep out with other CEOs in charity event for homeless.

Dominic slammed his fist on his desk so hard the pain juddered all the way up his arm. He hadn't *refused* to support the charity in their Christmas appeal, just refused the invitation to publicly bed down for the night in a cardboard box on the forecourt of the Sydney Opera House. His donation to the worthy cause had been significant—but anonymous. *Why wasn't that enough?*

He buried his head in his hands. For a harrowing time in his life there had been no choice for him but to sleep rough for real, a cardboard box his only bed. He couldn't go there again—not even for a charity stunt, no matter how worthy. There could be no explanation—he would not share the secrets of his past. *Ever.*

With a sick feeling of dread he continued to read onscreen the highlights of the recent flurry of negative press about him and his company, thoughtfully compiled in a report by his Director of Marketing.

Predictably, the reporters had then gone on to rehash his well-known aversion to Christmas. Again he'd been misquoted. It was true he loathed the whole idea of celebrating Christmas. But not for the reasons the media had so fancifully contrived. Not because he was a *Scrooge.* How he hated that label and the erroneous aspersions that he didn't ever give to charity. Despaired that he was included in a round-up of Australia's Multi-Million-Dollar Misers. *It couldn't be further from the truth.*

He strongly believed that giving money to worthy causes should be conducted in private—not for public acclaim. But this time he couldn't ignore the name-calling and innuendo. He was near to closing a game-changing deal on a joint venture with a family-owned American corporation run by a man with a strict moral code that included obvious displays of philanthropy.

Dominic could not be seen to be a Scrooge. He had to publicly prove that he was not a miser. But he did not want to reveal the extent of his charitable support because to do so would blow away the smokescreen he had carefully constructed over his past.

He'd been in a bind. Until his marketing director had suggested he would attract positive press if he opened his harbourside home for a lavish fund-raising event for charity. 'Get your name in the newspaper for the right reasons,' he had been advised.

Dominic hated the idea of his privacy being invaded but he had reluctantly agreed. He wanted the joint venture to happen. If a party was what it took, he was prepared to put his qualms aside and commit to it.

The party would be too big an event for it to be organised in-house. His marketing people had got outside companies involved. Trouble was the three so-called 'party planners' he'd been sent so far had been incompetent and he'd shown them the door within minutes of meeting. Now there was a fourth. He glanced down at the eye-catching card on the desk in front of him. Andrea Newman from a company called Party Queens—*No party too big or too small* the card boasted.

Party Queens. It was an interesting choice for a business name. Not nearly as stitched up as the other companies that had pitched for this business. But did it have the gravitas required? After all, this event could be the deciding factor in a deal that would extend his business interests internationally.

He glanced at his watch. This morning he was working from his home office. Ms Newman was due to meet with him right now, here at his house where the party was to take place. Despite the attention-grabbing name of the business, he had no reason to expect Party Planner Number Four to be any more impressive than the other three he'd sent packing. But he would give her twenty minutes—that was only fair and he made a point of always being fair.

On cue, the doorbell rang. Punctuality, at least, was a point in Andrea Newman's favour. He headed down the wide marble stairs to the front door.

His first impression of the woman who stood on his porch was that she was attractive, not in a conventionally pretty way but something rather more interesting—an angular face framed by a tangle of streaked blonde hair, a wide generous mouth, unusual green eyes. So attractive he found himself looking at her for a moment longer than was required to sum up a possible contractor. And the almost imperceptible curve of her mouth let him know she'd noticed.

'Good morning, Mr Hunt—Andie Newman from Party Queens,' she said. 'Thank you for the pass code that got me through the gate. Your security is formidable, like an eastern suburbs fortress.' Was that a hint of challenge underscoring her warm, husky voice? If so, he wasn't going to bite.

'The pass code expires after one use, Ms Newman,' he said, not attempting to hide a note of warning. The three party planners before her were never going to get a new pass code. But none of them had been remotely like her—in looks or manner.

She was tall and wore a boldly patterned skirt of some silky fine fabric that fell below her knees in uneven layers, topped by a snug-fitting rust-coloured jacket and high heeled shoes that laced all the way up her calf. A soft leather satchel was slung casually across her shoulder. She presented as smart but more unconventional than the corporate dark suits and rigid brief-cases of the other three—whose ideas had been as pedestrian as their appearances.

'Andie,' she replied and started to say something else about his security system. But, as she did, a sudden gust of balmy spring breeze whipped up her skirt, revealing long slender legs and a tantalising hint of red underwear. Dominic tried to do the gentlemanly thing and look elsewhere—difficult when she was standing so near to him and her legs were so attention-worthy.

'Oh,' she gasped, and fought with the skirt to hold it down, but no sooner did she get the front of the skirt in place, the back whipped upwards and she had to twist around to hold it down. The back view of her legs was equally as impressive as the front. He balled his hands into fists by his sides so he did not give into the temptation to help her with the flyaway fabric.

She flushed high on elegant cheekbones, blonde hair tou-sled around her face, and laughed a husky, uninhibited laugh as she battled to preserve her modesty. The breeze died down as quickly as it had sprung up and her skirt floated back into place. Still, he noticed she continued to keep it in check with a hand on her thigh.

'That's made a wonderful first impression, hasn't it?' she said, looking up at him with a rueful smile. For a long mo-ment their eyes connected and he was the first to look away. *She was beautiful.*

As she spoke, the breeze gave a final last sigh that ruffled her hair across her face. Dominic wasn't a fanciful man, but it seemed as though the wind was ushering her into his house.

'There are worse ways of making an impression,' he said gruffly. 'I'm interested to see what you follow up with.'

* * *

Andie wasn't sure what to reply. She stood at the threshold of Dominic Hunt's multi-million-dollar mansion and knew for the first time in her career she was in serious danger of losing the professional cool in which she took such pride.

Not because of the incident with the wind and her skirt. Or because she was awestruck by the magnificence of the house and the postcard-worthy panorama of Sydney Harbour that stretched out in front of it. No. It was the man who towered above her who was making her feel so inordinately flustered. Too tongue-tied to come back with a quick quip or clever retort.

'Th…thank you,' she managed to stutter as she pushed the breeze-swept hair back from across her face.

During her career as a stylist for both magazines and advertising agencies, and now as a party planner, she had acquired the reputation of being able to manage difficult people. Which was why her two partners in their fledgling business had voted for her to be the one to deal with Dominic Hunt. Party Queens desperately needed a high-profile booking like this to help them get established. Winning it was now on her shoulders.

She had come to his mansion forewarned that he could be a demanding client. The gossip was that he had been scathing to three other planners from other companies much bigger than theirs before giving them the boot. Then there was his wider reputation as a Scrooge—a man who did not share his multitude of money with others less fortunate. He was everything she did not admire in a person.

Despite that, she been blithely confident Dominic Hunt wouldn't be more than she could handle. Until he had answered that door. Her reaction to him had her stupefied.

She had seen the photos, watched the interviews of the billionaire businessman, had recognised he was good-looking in a dark, brooding way. But no amount of research had prepared her for the pulse-raising reality of this man—tall, broad-shouldered, powerful muscles apparent even in his sleek tailored grey suit. He wasn't pretty-boy handsome. Not with that strong jaw, the crooked nose that looked as though it had been broken by a viciously aimed punch, the full, sensual mouth with the faded white scar on the corner, the spiky black hair. And then there was the almost palpable emanation of power.

She had to call on every bit of her professional savvy to ignore the warm flush that rose up her neck and onto her cheeks, the way her heart thudded into unwilling awareness of Dominic Hunt, not as a client but as a man.

She could not allow that to happen. This job was too important to her and her friends in their new business. *Anyway, dark and brooding wasn't her type.* Her ideal man was sensitive and sunny-natured, like her first lost love, for whom she felt she would always grieve.

She extended her hand, willing it to stay steady, and forced a smile. 'Mr Hunt, let's start again. Andie Newman from Party Queens.'

His grip in return was firm and warm and he nodded acknowledgement of her greeting. If a mere handshake could send shivers of awareness through her, she could be in trouble here.

Keep it businesslike. She took a deep breath, tilted back her head to meet his gaze full-on. 'I believe I'm the fourth party planner you've seen and I don't want there to be a fifth. I should be the person to plan your event.'

If he was surprised at her boldness, it didn't show in his scrutiny; his grey eyes remained cool and assessing.

'You'd better come inside and convince me why that should be the case,' he said. Even his voice was attractive—deep and measured and utterly masculine.

'I welcome the opportunity,' she said in the most confident voice she could muster.

She followed him into the entrance hall of the restored nineteen-twenties house, all dark stained wood floors and cream marble. A grand central marble staircase with wrought-iron balustrades split into two sides to climb to the next floor. This wasn't the first grand home she'd been in during the course of her work but it was so impressive she had to suppress an impulse to gawk.

'Wow,' she said, looking around her, forgetting all about how disconcerted Dominic Hunt made her feel. 'The staircase. It's amazing. I can just see a choir there, with a chorister on each step greeting your guests with Christmas carols as they step into the house.' Her thoughts raced ahead of her. Choristers' robes in red and white? Each chorister holding a scrolled parchment printed with the words to the carol? What about the music? A string quartet? A harpsichord?

'What do you mean?' he said, breaking into her reverie.

Andie blinked to bring herself back to earth and turned to look up at him. She smiled. 'Sorry. I'm getting ahead of myself. It was just an idea. Of course I realise I still need to convince you I'm the right person for your job.'

'I meant about the Christmas carols.'

So he would be that kind of pernickety client, pressing her for details before they'd even decided on the bigger picture. Did she need to spell out the message of 'Deck the Halls with Boughs of Holly'?

She shook her head in a don't-worry-about-it way. 'It was just a top-of-mind thought. But a choir would be an amazing use of the staircase. Maybe a children's choir. Get your guests into the Christmas spirit straight away, without being too cheesy about it.'

'It isn't going to be a Christmas party.' He virtually spat the word *Christmas*.

'But a party in December? I thought—'

He frowned and she could see where his reputation came from as his thick brows drew together and his eyes darkened. 'Truth be told, I don't want a party here at all. But it's a necessary evil—necessary to my business, that is.'

'Really?' she said, struggling not to jump in and say the wrong thing. A client who didn't actually want a party? This she hadn't anticipated. Her certainty that she knew how to handle this situation—this man—started to seep away.

She gritted her teeth, forced her voice to sound as conciliatory as possible. 'I understood from your brief that you wanted a big event benefiting a charity in the weeks leading up to Christmas on a date that will give you maximum publicity.'

'All that,' he said. 'Except it's not to be a Christmas party. Just a party that happens to be held around that time.'

Difficult and demanding didn't begin to describe this. But had she been guilty of assuming December translated into Christmas? Had it actually stated that in the brief? She didn't think she'd misread it.

She drew in a calming breath. 'There seems to have been a misunderstanding and I apologise for that,' she said. 'I have the official briefing from your marketing department here.' She patted her satchel. 'But I'd rather hear your thoughts, your ideas for the event in your own words. A successful party plan comes from the heart. Can we sit down and discuss this?'

He looked pointedly at his watch. Her heart sank to the level of the first lacing on her shoes. She did not want to be the fourth party planner he fired before she'd even started her pitch. 'I'll give you ten minutes,' he said.

He led her into a living room that ran across the entire front of the house and looked out to the blue waters of the harbour and its icons of the Sydney Harbour Bridge and the Opera House. Glass doors opened out to a large terrace. *A perfect summer party terrace.*

Immediately she recognised the work of one of Sydney's most fashionable high-end interior designers—a guy who only worked with budgets that started with six zeros after them. The room worked neutral tones and metallics in a nod to the art deco era of the original house. The result was masculine but very, very stylish.

What an awesome space for a party. But she forced thoughts of the party out of her head. She had ten minutes to win this business. Ten minutes to convince Dominic Hunt she was the one he needed.

CHAPTER TWO

DOMINIC SAT ANDIE NEWMAN down on the higher of the two sofas that faced each other over the marble coffee table—the sofa he usually chose to give himself the advantage. He had no need to impress her with his greater height and bulk—she was tall, but he was so much taller than her even as he sat on the lower seat. Besides, the way she positioned herself with shoulders back and spine straight made him think she wouldn't let herself be intimidated by him or by anyone else. *Think again.* The way she crossed and uncrossed those long legs revealed she was more nervous than she cared to let on.

He leaned back in his sofa, pulled out her business card from the inside breast pocket of his suit jacket and held it between finger and thumb. 'Tell me about Party Queens. This seems like a very new, shiny card.'

'Brand new. We've only been in business for three months.'

'We?'

'My two business partners, Eliza Dunne and Gemma Harper. We all worked on a magazine together before we started our own business.'

He narrowed his eyes. 'Now you're "party queens"?' He used his fingers to enclose the two words with quote marks. 'I don't see the connection.'

'We always were party queens—even when we were working on the magazine.' He quirked an eyebrow and she paused. He noticed she quirked an eyebrow too, in unconscious imitation of his action. 'Not in that way.' She tried to backtrack, then smiled. 'Well, maybe somewhat in that way. Between us we've certainly done our share of partying. But then you have to actually enjoy a party to organise one; don't you agree?'

'It's not something I've given thought to,' he said. Business-wise, it could be a point either for her or against her.

Parties had never been high on his agenda—even after his money had opened so many doors for him. Whether he'd been sleeping rough in an abandoned building project in the most dangerous part of Brisbane or hobnobbing with decision makers in Sydney, he'd felt he'd never quite fitted in. So he did the minimum socialising required for his business. 'You were a journalist?' he asked, more than a little intrigued by her.

She shook her head. 'My background is in interior design but when a glitch in the economy meant the company I worked for went bust, I ended up as an interiors editor on a lifestyle magazine. I put together shoots for interiors and products and I loved it. Eliza and Gemma worked on the same magazine, Gemma as the food editor and Eliza on the publishing side. Six months ago we were told out of the blue that the magazine was closing and we had all lost our jobs.'

'That must have been a shock,' he said.

When he'd first started selling real estate at the age of eighteen he'd lived in terror he'd lose his job. Underlying all his success was always still that fear—which was why he was so driven to keep his business growing and thriving. Without money, without a home, he could slide back into being Nick Hunt of 'no fixed abode' rather than Dominic Hunt of Vaucluse, one of the most exclusive addresses in Australia.

'It shouldn't have come as a shock,' she said. 'Magazines close all the time in publishing—it's an occupational hazard.

But when it actually happened, when *again* one minute I had a job and the next I didn't, it was…soul-destroying.'

'I'm sorry,' he said.

She shrugged. 'I soon picked myself up.'

He narrowed his eyes. 'It's quite a jump from a magazine job to a party planning business.' Her lack of relevant experience could mean Party Planner Number Four would go the way of the other three. He was surprised at how disappointed that made him feel.

'It might seem that way, but hear me out,' she said, a determined glint in her eye. If one of the other planners had said that, he would have looked pointedly at his watch. This one, he was prepared to listen to—he was actually interested in her story.

'We had to clear our desks immediately and were marched out of the offices by security guards. Shell-shocked, we all retired to a café and thought about what we'd do. The magazine's deputy editor asked could we organise her sister's eighteenth birthday party. At first we said no, thinking she was joking. But then we thought about it. A big magazine shoot that involves themes and food and props is quite a production. We'd also sometimes organise magazine functions for advertisers. We realised that between us we knew a heck of a lot about planning parties.'

'As opposed to enjoying them,' he said.

'That's right,' she said with a smile that seemed reminiscent of past parties enjoyed. 'Between the three of us we had so many skills we could utilise.'

'Can you elaborate on that?'

She held up a slender index finger, her nails tipped with orange polish. 'One, I'm the ideas and visuals person—creative, great with themes and props and highly organised with follow-through.' A second finger went up. 'Two, Gemma trained as a chef and is an amazing food person—food is one of the most important aspects of a good party, whether cooking it yourself or knowing which chefs to engage.'

She had a little trouble getting the third finger to stay straight and swapped it to her pinkie. 'Then, three, Eliza has her head completely around finances and contracts and sales and is also quite the wine buff.'

'So you decided to go into business together?' Her entrepreneurial spirit appealed to him.

She shook her head so her large multi-hoop gold earrings clinked. 'Not then. Not yet. We agreed to do the eighteenth party while we looked for other jobs and freelanced for magazines and ad agencies.'

'How did it work out?' He thought about his eighteenth birthday. It had gone totally unmarked by any celebration—except his own jubilation that he was legally an adult and could never now be recalled to the hell his home had become. It had also marked the age he could be tried as an adult if he had skated too close to the law—though by that time his street-fighting days were behind him.

'There were a few glitches, of course, but overall it was a great success. The girl went to a posh private school and both girls and parents loved the girly shoe theme we organised. One eighteenth led to another and soon we had other parents clamouring for us to do their kids' parties.'

'Is there much money in parties for kids?' He didn't have to ask all these questions but he was curious. Curious about her as much as anything.

Her eyebrows rose. 'You're kidding, right? We're talking wealthy families on the eastern suburbs and north shore. We're talking one-upmanship.' He enjoyed the play of expressions across her face, the way she gesticulated with her hands as she spoke. 'Heck, we've done a four-year-old's party on a budget of thousands.'

'All that money for a four-year-old?' He didn't have anything to do with kids except through his anonymous charity work. Had given up on his dream he would ever have children of his own. In fact, he was totally out of touch with family life.

'You'd better believe it,' she said.

He was warming to Andie Newman—how could any red-blooded male not?—but he wanted to ensure she was experienced enough to make his event work. All eyes would be on it as up until now he'd been notoriously private. If he threw a party, it had better be a good party. Better than good.

'So when did you actually go into business?'

'We were asked to do more and more parties. Grown-up parties too. Thirtieths and fortieths, even a ninetieth. It snowballed. Yet we still saw it as a stopgap thing although people suggested we make it a full-time business.'

'A very high percentage of small businesses go bust in the first year,' he couldn't help but warn.

She pulled a face that told him she didn't take offence. 'We were very aware of that. Eliza is the profit and loss spreadsheet maven. But then a public relations company I worked freelance for asked us to do corporate parties and product launches. The work was rolling in. We began to think we should make it official and form our own company.'

'A brave move.' He'd made brave moves in his time—and most of them had paid off. He gave her credit for initiative.

She leaned forward towards him. This close he could appreciate how lovely her eyes were. He didn't think he had ever before met anyone with genuine green eyes. 'We've leased premises in the industrial area of Alexandria and we're firing. But I have to be honest with you—we haven't done anything with potentially such a profile as your party. We want it. We need it. And because we want it to so much we'll pull out every stop to make it a success.'

Party Planner Number Four clocked up more credit for her honesty. He tapped the card on the edge of his hand. 'You've got the enthusiasm; do you have the expertise? Can you assure me you can do my job and do it superlatively well?'

Those remarkable green eyes were unblinking. 'Yes. Absolutely. Undoubtedly. There might only be three of us, but between us we have a zillion contacts in Sydney—chefs, decorators, florists, musicians, waiting staff. If we can't do it ourselves we can pull in the right people who can. And none of us is afraid of the hard work a party this size would entail. We would welcome the challenge.'

He realised she was now sitting on the edge of the sofa, her hands clasped together and her foot crossed over her ankle was jiggling. She really did want this job—wanted it badly.

Dominic hadn't got where he was without a fine-tuned instinct for people. Instincts honed first on the streets where trusting the wrong person could have been fatal and then in the cut-throat business of high-end real estate and property development. His antennae were telling him Andie Newman would be able to deliver—and that he would enjoy working with her.

Trouble was, while he thought she might be the right person for the job, he found her very attractive and would like to ask her out. And he couldn't do both. He *never* dated staff or suppliers. He'd made that mistake with his ex-wife—he would not make it again. Hire Andie Newman and he was more than halfway convinced he would get a good party planner. Not hire her and he could ask her on a date. But he needed this event to work—and for that the planning had to be in the best possible hands. He was torn.

'I like your enthusiasm,' he said. 'But I'd be taking a risk by working with a company that is in many ways still…unproven.'

Her voice rose marginally—she probably didn't notice but to him it betrayed her anxiety to impress. 'We have a file overflowing with references from happy clients. But before you come to any decisions let's talk about what you're expecting from us. The worst thing that can happen is for a client to get an unhappy surprise because we've got the brief wrong.'

She pulled out a folder from her satchel. He liked that it echoed the design of her business card. That showed an attention to detail. The chaos of his early life had made him appreciate planning and order. He recognised his company logo on the printout page she took from the folder and quickly perused.

'So tell me,' she said, when she'd finished reading it. 'I'm puzzled. Despite this briefing document stating the party is to be "A high-profile Christmas event to attract favourable publicity for Dominic Hunt" you still insist it's not to reference Christmas in any way. Which is correct?'

Andie regretted the words almost as soon as they'd escaped from her mouth. She hadn't meant to confront Dominic Hunt or put him on the spot. Certainly she hadn't wanted to get him offside. But the briefing had been ambiguous and she felt she had to clarify it if she was to secure this job for Party Queens.

She needed their business to succeed—never again did she want to be at the mercy of the whims of a corporate employer. To have a job one day and then suddenly not the next day was too traumatising after that huge personal change of direction she'd had forced upon her five years ago. But she could have put her question with more subtlety.

He didn't reply. The silence that hung between them became more uncomfortable by the second. His face tightened with an emotion she couldn't read. Anger? Sorrow? Regret? Whatever it was, the effect was so powerful she had to force herself not to reach over and put her hand on his arm to comfort him, maybe even hug him. And that would be a mistake. Even more of a mistake than her ill-advised question had been.

She cringed that she had somehow prompted the unleashing of thoughts that were so obviously painful for him. Then braced herself to be booted out on to the same scrapheap as the three party planners who had preceded her.

Finally he spoke, as if the words were being dragged out of him. 'The brief was incorrect. Christmas has some...difficult memories attached to it for me. I don't celebrate the season. Please just leave it at that.' For a long moment his gaze held hers and she saw the anguish recede.

Andie realised she had been holding her breath and she let it out with a slow sigh of relief, amazed he hadn't shown her the door.

'Of…of course,' she murmured, almost gagging with gratitude that she was to be given a second chance. And she couldn't deny that she wanted that chance. Not just for the job but—she could not deny it—the opportunity to see more of this undoubtedly interesting man.

There was something deeper here, some private pain, that she did not understand. But it would be bad-mannered prying to ask any further questions.

She didn't know much about his personal life. Just that he was considered a catch—rich, handsome, successful. *Though not her type, of course.* He lived here alone, she understood, in this street in Vaucluse where house prices started in the double digit millions. Wasn't there a bitter divorce in his background—an aggrieved ex-wife, a public battle for ownership of the house? She'd have to look it up. If she were to win this job—and she understood that it was still a big *if*—she needed to get a grasp on how this man ticked.

'Okay, so that's sorted—no Christmas,' she said, aiming to sound briskly efficient without any nod to the anguish she had read at the back of his eyes. 'Now I know what you *don't* want for your party, let's talk about what you *do* want. I'd like to hear in your words what you expect from this party. Then I can give you my ideas based on your thoughts.'

The party proposals she had hoped to discuss had been based on Christmas; she would have to do some rapid thinking.

Dominic Hunt got up from the sofa and started to pace. He was so tall, his shoulders so broad, he dominated even the large, high-ceilinged room. Andie found herself wondering about his obviously once broken nose—who had thrown the first punch? She got up, not to pace alongside him but to be closer to his level. She did not feel intimidated by him but she could see how he could be intimidating.

'The other planners babbled on about how important it was to invite A-list and B-list celebrities to get publicity. I don't give a damn about celebrities and I can't see how that's the right kind of publicity.'

Andie paused, not sure what to say, only knowing she had to be careful not to *babble on.* 'I can organise the party, but the guest list is up to you and your people.'

He stopped his pacing, stepped closer. 'But do you agree with me?'

Was this a test question? Answer incorrectly and that scrapheap beckoned? As always, she could only be honest. 'I do agree with you. It's my understanding that this party is aimed at…at image repair.'

'You mean repair to my image as a miserly Scrooge who hoards all his money for himself?'

She swallowed a gasp at the bitterness of his words, then looked up at him to see not the anger she expected but a kind of manly bewilderment that surprised her.

'I mightn't have put it quite like that, but yes," she said. 'You do have that reputation and I understand you want to demonstrate it's not so. And yes, I think the presence of a whole lot of freeloading so-called celebrities who run the gamut from the A to the Z list and have nothing to do with the charities you want to be seen to be supporting might not help. But you *are* more likely to get coverage in the social pages if they attend.'

He frowned. 'Is there such a thing as a Z-list celebrity?'

She laughed. 'If there isn't, there should be. Maybe I made it up.'

'You did say you were creative,' he said. He smiled—the first real smile she'd seen from him. It transformed his face, like the sun coming out from behind a dark storm cloud, unleashing an unexpected charm. Her heartbeat tripped into double time like it had the first moment she'd seen him. Why? Why this inexplicable reaction to a man she should dislike for his meanness and greed?

She made a show of looking around her to disguise her consternation. Tamed the sudden shakiness in her voice into a businesslike tone. 'How many magazines or lifestyle programmes have featured this house?' she asked.

'None. They never will,' he said.

'Good,' she said. 'The house is both magnificent and unknown. I reckon even your neighbours would be willing to cough up a sizeable donation just to see inside.' In her mind's eye she could see the house transformed into a glittering party paradise. 'The era of the house is nineteen-twenties, right?'

'Yes,' he said. 'It was originally built for a wealthy wool merchant.'

She thought some more. 'Why not an extravagant *Great Gatsby* twenties-style party with a silver and white theme—that gives a nod to the festive season—and a strictly curated guest list? Guests would have to dress in silver or white. Or both. Make it very exclusive, an invitation to be sought after. The phones of Sydney's social set would be set humming to see who got one or not.' Her eyes half shut as her mind bombarded her with images. 'Maybe a masked party. Yes. Amazing silver and white masks. Bejewelled and befeathered. Fabulous masks that could be auctioned off at some stage for your chosen charity.'

'Auctioned?'

Her eyes flew open and she had to orientate herself back into the reality of the empty room that she had just been envisioning filled with elegant partygoers. Sometimes when her creativity was firing she felt almost in a trance. Then it was her turn to frown. How could a Sydney billionaire be such a party innocent?

Even she, who didn't move in the circles of society that attended lavish fund-raising functions, knew about the auctions. The competitive bidding could probably be seen as the same kind of one-upmanship as the spending of thousands on a toddler's party. 'I believe it's usual to have a fund-raising auction at these occasions. Not just the masks, of course. Other donated items. Something really big to up the amount of dollars for your charity.' She paused. 'You're a property developer, aren't you?'

He nodded. 'Among other interests.'

'Maybe you could donate an apartment? There'd be some frenzied bidding for that from people hoping for a bargain. And you would look generous.'

His mouth turned down in an expression of distaste. 'I'm not sure that's in keeping with the image I want to…to reinvent.'

Privately she agreed with him—why couldn't people just donate without expecting a lavish party in return? But she kept her views to herself. Creating those lavish parties was her job now.

'That's up to you and your people. The guest list and the auction, I mean. But the party? That's my domain. Do you like the idea of the twenties theme to suit the house?' In her heart she still longed for the choristers on the staircase. Maybe it would have to be a jazz band on the steps. That could work. Not quite the same romanticism and spirit as Christmas, but it would be a spectacular way to greet guests.

'I like it,' he said slowly.

She forced herself not to panic, not to bombard him with a multitude of alternatives. 'If not that idea, I have lots of others. I would welcome the opportunity to present them to you.'

He glanced at his watch and she realised she had been there for much longer than the ten-minute pitch he'd allowed. Surely that was a good sign.

'I'll schedule in another meeting with you tomorrow afternoon,' he said.

'You mean a second interview?' she asked, fingers crossed behind her back.

'No. A brainstorming session. You've got the job, Ms Newman.'

It was only as, jubilant, she made her way to the door—conscious of his eyes on her back—that she wondered at the presence of a note of regret in Dominic Hunt's voice.

CHAPTER THREE

TRY AS SHE MIGHT, Andie couldn't get excited about the nineteen-twenties theme she had envisaged for Dominic Hunt's party. It would be lavish and glamorous and she would enjoy every moment of planning such a visually splendid event. Such a party would be a spangled feather in Party Queens' cap. But it seemed somehow *wrong.*

The feeling niggled at her. How could something so extravagant, so limited to those who could afford the substantial donation that would be the cost of entrance make Dominic Hunt look less miserly? Even if he offered an apartment for auction—and there was no such thing as a cheap apartment in Sydney—and raised a lot of money, wouldn't it be a wealthy person who benefited? Might he appear to be a Scrooge hanging out with other rich people who might or might not also be Scrooges? Somehow, it reeked of…well, there was no other word but hypocrisy.

It wasn't her place to be critical—the media-attention-grabbing party was his marketing people's idea. Her job was to plan the party and make it as memorable and spectacular as possible. But she resolved to bring up her reservations in the brainstorming meeting with him. *If she dared.*

She knew it would be a fine line to tread—she did not want

to risk losing the job for Party Queens—but she felt she had to give her opinion. After that she would just keep her mouth shut and concentrate on making his event the most memorable on the December social calendar.

She dressed with care for the meeting, which was again at his Vaucluse mansion. *An outfit that posed no danger of showing off her underwear.* Slim white trousers, a white top, a string of outsize turquoise beads, silver sandals that strapped around her ankles. At the magazine she'd made friends with the fashion editor and still had access to sample sales and special deals. She felt her wardrobe could hold its own in whatever company she found herself in—even on millionaire row.

'I didn't risk wearing that skirt,' she blurted out to Dominic Hunt as he let her into the house. 'Even though there doesn't appear to be any wind about.'

Mentally she slammed her hand against her forehead. What a dumb top-of-mind remark to make to a client. But he still made her nervous. Try as she might, she couldn't shake that ever-present awareness of how attractive he was.

His eyes flickered momentarily to her legs. 'Shame,' he said in that deep, testosterone-edged voice that thrilled through her.

Was he flirting with her?

'It…it was a lovely skirt,' she said. 'Just…just rather badly behaved.' How much had he seen when her skirt had flown up over her thighs?

'I liked it very much,' he said.

'The prettiness of its fabric or my skirt's bad behaviour?'

She held his cool grey gaze for a second longer than she should.

'Both,' he said.

She took a deep breath and tilted her chin upward. 'I'll take that as a compliment,' she said with a smile she hoped radiated aplomb. 'Thank you, Mr Hunt.'

'Dominic,' he said.

'Dominic,' she repeated, liking the sound of his name on

her lips. 'And thank you again for this opportunity to plan your party.' *Bring it back to business.*

In truth, she would have liked to tell him how good he looked in his superbly tailored dark suit and dark shirt but she knew her voice would come out all choked up. Because it wasn't the Italian elegance of his suit that she found herself admiring. It was the powerful, perfectly proportioned male body that inhabited it. And she didn't want to reveal even a hint of that. *He was a client.*

He nodded in acknowledgement of her words. 'Come through to the back,' he said. 'You can see how the rooms might work for the party.'

She followed him through where the grand staircase split—a choir really would be amazing ranged on the steps—over pristine marble floors to a high-ceilinged room so large their footsteps echoed as they walked into the centre of it. Furnished minimally in shades of white, it looked ready for a high-end photo shoot. Arched windows and a wall of folding doors opened through to an elegant art deco style swimming pool and then to a formal garden planted with palm trees and rows of budding blue agapanthus.

For a long moment Andie simply absorbed the splendour of the room. 'What a magnificent space,' she said finally. 'Was it originally a ballroom?'

'Yes. Apparently the wool merchant liked to entertain in grand style. But it wasn't suited for modern living, which is why I opened it up through to the terrace when I remodelled the house.'

'You did an awesome job,' she said. In her mind's eye she could see flappers in glittering dresses trimmed with feathers and fringing, and men in dapper suits doing the Charleston. Then had to blink, not sure if she was imagining what the room had once been or how she'd like it to be for Dominic's party.

'The people who work for me did an excellent job,' he said.

'As an interior designer I give them full marks,' she said.

She had gone to university with Dominic's designer. She just might get in touch with him, seeking inside gossip into what made Dominic Hunt tick.

She looked around her. 'Where's the kitchen? Gemma will shoot me if I go back without reporting to her on the cooking facilities.'

'Through here.'

Andie followed him through to an adjoining vast state-of-the-art kitchen, gleaming in white marble and stainless steel. The style was sleek and modern but paid homage to the vintage of the house. She breathed out a sigh of relief and pleasure. A kitchen like this would make catering for hundreds of guests so much easier. Not that the food was her department. Gemma kept that under her control. 'It's a superb kitchen. Do you cook?'

Was Dominic the kind of guy who ate out every night and whose refrigerator contained only cartons of beer? Or the kind who excelled at cooking and liked to show off his skills to a breathlessly admiring female audience?

'I can look after myself,' he said shortly. 'That includes cooking.'

That figured. After yesterday's meeting she had done some research into Dominic Hunt—though there wasn't much information dating back further than a few years. Along with his comments about celebrating Christmas being a waste of space, he'd also been quoted as saying he would never marry again. From the media accounts, his marriage in his mid-twenties had been short, tumultuous and public, thanks to his ex-wife's penchant for spilling the details to the gossip columns.

'The kitchen and its position will be perfect for the caterers,' she said. 'Gemma will be delighted.'

'Good,' he said.

'You must love this house.' She could not help a wistful note from edging her voice. As an interior designer she knew only too well how much the remodelling would have cost. Never in a million years would she live in a house like this. He was only a few years older than her—thirty-two to her twenty-eight—yet it was as if they came from different planets.

He shrugged those impressively broad shoulders. 'It's a spectacular house. But it's just a house. I never get attached to places.'

Or people?

Her online research had showed him snapped by paparazzi with a number of long-legged beauties—but no woman more than once or twice. *What did it matter to her?*

She patted her satchel. *Back to business.* 'I've come prepared for brainstorming,' she said. 'Have you had any thoughts about the nineteen-twenties theme I suggested?'

'I've thought,' he said. He paused. 'I've thought about it a lot.'

His tone of voice didn't give her cause for confidence. 'You... like it? You don't like it? Because if you don't I have lots of other ideas that would work as well. I—'

He put up his right hand to halt her—large, well sculpted, with knuckles that looked as if they'd sustained scrapes over the years. His well-spoken accent and obvious wealth suggested injuries sustained from boxing or rugby at a private school; the tightly leashed power in those muscles, that strong jaw, gave thought to injuries sustained in something perhaps more visceral.

'It's a wonderful idea for a party,' he said. 'Perfect for this house. Kudos to you, Ms Party Queen.'

'Thank you.' She made a mock curtsy and was pleased when he smiled. *How handsome he was without that scowl.* 'However, is that a "but" I hear coming on?'

He pivoted on his heel so he faced out to the pool, gleaming blue and pristine in the afternoon sun of a late-spring day in mid-November. His back view was impressive, broad shoulders tapering to a tight, muscular rear end. Then he turned back to face her. 'It's more than one "but",' he said. 'The party, the guest list, the—'

'The pointlessness of it all?' she ventured.

He furrowed his brow. 'What makes you say that?'

She found herself twisting the turquoise beads on her necklace between her finger and thumb. Her business partners would be furious with her if she lost Party Queens this high-profile job because she said what she *wanted* to say rather than what she *should* say.

'This party is all about improving your image, right? To make a statement that you're not the…the Scrooge people think you are.'

The fierce scowl was back. 'I'd rather you didn't use the word Scrooge.'

'Okay,' she said immediately. But she would find it difficult to stop *thinking* it. 'I'll try again: that you're not a…a person lacking in the spirit of giving.'

'That doesn't sound much better.' She couldn't have imagined his scowl could have got any darker but it did. 'The party is meant to be a public display of something I would rather be kept private.'

'So…you give privately to charity?'

'Of course I do but it's not your or anyone else's business.'

Personally, she would be glad if he wasn't as tight-fisted as his reputation decreed. But this was about more than what she felt. She could not back down. 'If that's how you feel, tell me again why you're doing this.'

He paused. 'If I share with you the reason why I agreed to holding this party, it's not to leave this room.'

'Of course,' she said. A party planner had to be discreet. It was astounding what family secrets got aired in the planning of a party. She leaned closer, close enough to notice that he must be a twice-a-day-shave guy. *Lots of testosterone, all right.*

'I've got a big joint venture in the United States on the point of being signed. My potential business partner, Walter Burton, is the head of a family company and he is committed to public displays of philanthropy. It would go better with me if I was seen to be the same.'

Andie made a motion with her fingers of zipping her lips shut. 'I… I understand,' she said. Disappointment shafted through her. *So he really was a Scrooge.*

She'd found herself wanting Dominic to be someone better than he was reputed to be. But the party, while purporting to be a charity event, was simply a smart business ploy. More about greed than good-heartedness.

'Now you can see why it's so important,' he said.

Should she say what she thought? The scrapheap of discarded party planners beckoned again. She could imagine her silver-sandal-clad foot kicking feebly from the top of it and hoped it would be a soft landing.

She took a deep steadying breath. 'Cynical journalists might have a field-day with the hypocrisy of a Scrooge—*sorry!*—trying to turn over a new gilded leaf in such an obvious and staged way.'

To her surprise, something like relief relaxed the tense lines of his face. 'That's what I thought too.'

'You…you did?'

'I could see the whole thing backfiring and me no better off in terms of reputation. Possibly worse.'

If she didn't stop twisting her necklace it would break and scatter her beads all over the marble floor. 'So—help me out here. We're back to you not wanting a party?'

She'd talked him out of the big, glitzy event Party Queens really needed. Andie cringed at the prospect of the combined wrath of Gemma and Eliza when she went back to their headquarters with the contract that was sitting in her satchel waiting for his signature still unsigned.

'You know I don't.' *Thank heaven.* 'But maybe a different kind of event,' he said.

'Like…handing over a giant facsimile cheque to a charity?' Which would be doing her right out of a job.

'Where's the good PR in that?'

'In fact it could look even more cynical than the party.'

'Correct.'

He paced a few long strides away from her and then back. 'I'm good at turning one dollar into lots of dollars. That's my skill. Not planning parties. But surely I can get the kind of publicity my marketing department wants, impress my prospective business partner and actually help some less advantaged people along the way?'

She resisted the urge to high-five him. 'To tell you the truth, I couldn't sleep last night for thinking that exact same thing.' *Was it wise to have admitted that?*

'Me too,' he said. 'I tossed and turned all night.'

A sudden vision of him in a huge billionaire's bed, all tangled in the sheets wearing nothing but…well nothing but a billionaire's birthday suit, flashed through her mind and sizzled through her body. *Not my type. Not my type.* She had to repeat it like a mantra.

She willed her heartbeat to slow and hoped he took the flush on her cheekbones for enthusiasm. 'So we're singing from the same hymn sheet. Did you have any thoughts on solving your dilemma?'

'That's where you come in; you're the party expert.'

She hesitated. 'During my sleepless night, I did think of something. But you might not like it.'

'Try me,' he said, eyes narrowed.

'It's out of the ball park,' she warned.

'I'm all for that,' he said.

She flung up her hands in front of her face to act as a shield. 'It…it involves Christmas.'

He blanched under the smooth olive of his tan. 'I told you—'

His mouth set in a grim line, his hands balled into fists by his sides. Should she leave well enough alone? After all, he had said the festive season had difficult associations for him. 'What is it that you hate so much about Christmas?' she asked. She'd always been one to dive straight into the deep end.

'I don't *hate* Christmas.' He cursed under his breath. 'I'm misquoted once and the media repeat it over and over.'

'But—'

He put up his hand to halt her. 'I don't have to justify anything to you. But let me give you three good reasons why I don't choose to celebrate Christmas and all the razzmatazz that goes with it.'

'Fire away,' she said, thinking it wasn't appropriate for her to counter with three things she adored about the festive season. This wasn't a debate. It was a business brainstorming.

'First—the weather is all wrong,' he said. 'It's hot when it should be cold. A *proper* Christmas is a northern hemisphere Christmas—snow, not sand.'

Not true, she thought. For a born-and-bred Australian like her, Christmas was all about the long, hot sticky days of summer. Cicadas chirruping in the warm air as the family walked to a midnight church service. Lunch outdoors, preferably around a pool or at the beach. Then it struck her—Dominic had a distinct trace of an English accent. That might explain his aversion to festivities Down Under style. But something still didn't seem quite right. His words sounded…too practised, as if he'd recited them a hundred times before.

He continued, warming to his point as she wondered about the subtext to his spiel. 'Then there's the fact that the whole thing is over-commercialised to the point of being ludicrous. I saw Christmas stuff festooning the shops in September.'

She almost expected him to snarl a Scrooge-like *Bah! Humbug!* but he obviously restrained himself.

'You have a point,' she said. 'And carols piped through shopping malls in October? So annoying.'

'Quite right,' he said. 'This whole obsession with extended Christmas celebrations, it…it…makes people who don't celebrate it—for one reason or another—feel…feel excluded.'

His words faltered and he looked away in the direction of the pool but not before she'd seen the bleakness in his eyes. She realised those last words hadn't been rehearsed. That he might be regretting them. Again she had that inane urge to comfort him—without knowing why he needed comforting.

She knew she had to take this carefully. 'Yes,' she said slowly. 'I know what you mean.' That first Christmas without Anthony had been the bleakest imaginable. And each year after she had thought about him and the emptiness in her heart he had left behind him. But she would not share that with this man; it was far too personal. And nothing to do with the general discussion about Christmas.

His mouth twisted. 'Do you?'

She forced her voice to sound cheerful and impersonal. Her ongoing sadness over Anthony was deeply private. 'Not me personally. I love Christmas. I'm lucky enough to come from a big family—one of five kids. I have two older brothers and a sister and a younger sister. Christmas with our extended family was always—still is—a special time of the year. But my parents knew that wasn't the case for everyone. Every year we shared our celebration with children who weren't as fortunate as we were.'

'Charity cases, you mean,' he said, his voice hard-edged with something she couldn't identify.

'In the truest sense of the word,' she said. 'We didn't query them being there. It meant more kids to play with on Christmas Day. It didn't even enter our heads that there would be fewer presents for us so they could have presents too. Two of them moved in with us as long-term foster kids. When I say I'm from five, I really mean from seven. Only that's too confusing to explain.'

He gave a sound that seemed a cross between a grunt and a cynical snort.

She shrugged, inexplicably hurt by his reaction. 'You might think it goody-two-shoes-ish but that's the way my family are, and I love them for it,' she said, her voice stiff and more than a touch defensive.

'Not at all,' he said. 'I think it…it sounds wonderful. You were very lucky to grow up in a family like that.' With the implication being he hadn't?

'I know, and I'm thankful. And my parents' strong sense of community didn't do us any harm. In fact those Christmas Days my family shared with others got me thinking. It was what kept me up last night. I had an idea.'

'Fire away,' he said.

She channelled all her optimism and enthusiasm to make her voice sound convincing to Sydney's most notorious Scrooge. 'Wouldn't it be wonderful if you opened this beautiful home on Christmas Day for a big lunch party for children and families who do it hard on Christmas Day? Not as a gimmick. Not as a stunt. As a genuine act of hospitality and sharing the true spirit of Christmas.'

CHAPTER FOUR

DOMINIC STARED AT Andie in disbelief. Hadn't she heard a word he'd said about his views on Christmas? She looked up at him, her eyes bright with enthusiasm but backlit by wariness. 'Please, just consider my proposal,' she said. 'That's all I ask.' He could easily fire her for straying so far from the brief and she must know it—yet that didn't stop her. Her tenacity was to be admired.

Maybe she had a point. No matter what she or anyone else thought, he was not a Scrooge or a hypocrite. To make a holiday that could never be happy for him happy for others had genuine appeal. He was aware Christmas *was* a special time for a huge percentage of the population. It was just too painful for him to want to do anything but lock himself away with a bottle of bourbon from Christmas Eve to Boxing Day.

Deep from within, he dredged memories of his first Christmas away from home. Aged seventeen, he'd been living in an underground car park beneath an abandoned shopping centre project. His companions had been a ragtag collection of other runaways, addicts, criminals and people who'd lost all hope of a better life. Someone had stolen a branch of a pine tree from somewhere and decorated it with scavenged scraps of glittery paper. They'd all stood around it and sung carols with varying degrees of sobriety. Only he had stood aloof.

Now, he reached out to where Andie was twisting her necklace so tightly it was in danger of snapping. Gently, he disengaged her hand and freed the string of beads. Fought the temptation to hold her hand for any longer than was necessary—slender and warm in his own much bigger hand. Today her nails were painted turquoise. And, as he'd noticed the day before, her fingers were free of any rings.

'Your idea could have merit,' he said, stepping back from her. Back from her beautiful interesting face, her intelligent eyes, the subtle spicy-sweet scent of her. 'Come and sit outside by the pool and we can talk it over.'

Her face flushed with relief at his response and he realised again what spunk it had taken for her to propose something so radical. He was grateful to whoever had sent Party Planner Number Four his way. Andie was gorgeous, smart and not the slightest in awe of him and his money, which was refreshing. His only regret was that he could not both employ her and date her.

He hadn't told the complete truth about why he'd been unable to sleep the night before. Thoughts of her had been churning through his head as much as concerns about the party. He had never felt so instantly attracted to a woman. Ever. If they had met under other circumstances he would have asked her out by now.

'I really think it could work,' she said as she walked with him through the doors and out to the pool area.

For a heart-halting second he thought Andie had tuned into his private thoughts—that she thought dating her could work. *Never.* He'd met his ex-wife, Tara, when she'd worked for his company, with disastrous consequences. The whole marriage had, in fact, been disastrous—based on lies and deception. He wouldn't make that mistake again—even for this intriguing woman.

But of course Andie was talking about her party proposal in

businesslike tones. 'You could generate the right kind of publicity—both for your potential business partner and in general,' she said as he settled her into one of the white outdoor armchairs that had cost a small fortune because of its vintage styling.

'While at the same time directly benefiting people who do it tough on the so-called Big Day,' he said as he took the chair next to her.

'Exactly,' she said with her wide, generous smile. When she smiled like that it made him want to make her do it again, just for the pleasure of seeing her face light up. *Not a good idea.*

Her chair was in the shade of one of the mature palm trees he'd had helicoptered in for the landscaping but the sun was dancing off the aqua surface of the pool. He was disappointed when she reached into her satchel, pulled out a pair of tortoiseshell-rimmed sunglasses and donned them against the glare. They looked 'vintage' too. In fact, in her white clothes and turquoise necklace, she looked as if she belonged here.

'In principal, I don't mind your idea,' he said. 'In fact I find it more acceptable than the other.'

Her smile was edged with relief. 'I can't tell you how pleased that makes me.'

'Would the lunch have to be on actual Christmas Day?' he said.

'You could hold it on Christmas Eve or the week leading up to Christmas. In terms of organisation, that would be easier. But none of those peripheral days is as lonely and miserable as Christmas Day can be if you're one…one of the excluded ones,' she said. 'My foster sister told me that.'

The way she was looking at him, even with those too-perceptive green eyes shaded from his view, made him think she was beginning to suspect he had a deeply personal reason for his anti-Christmas stance.

He'd only ever shared that reason with one woman—Melody, the girl who'd first captivated, then shredded, his teenage heart back in that car park squat. By the time Christmas had loomed in the first year of his marriage to Tara, he'd known he'd never be sharing secrets with her. But there was something disarming about Andie that seemed to invite confidences—something he had to stand guard against. She might not be what she seemed—and he had learned the painful lesson not to trust his first impressions when it came to beautiful women.

'I guess any other day doesn't have the same impact,' he reluctantly agreed, not sure he would be able to face the festivities. Did he actually have to be present on the day? Might it not be enough to provide the house and the meal? No. To achieve his goal, he knew his presence would be necessary. Much as he would hate every minute of it.

'Maybe your marketing people will have other ideas,' she said. 'But I think opening your home on the actual December twenty-five to give people who really need it a slap-up feast would be a marvellous antidote to your Scrooge…sorry, *miser*… I mean *cheap* reputation.' She pulled a face. 'Sorry. I didn't actually mean any of those things.'

Why did it sting so much more coming from her? 'Of course you did. So does everyone else. People who have no idea of what and where I might give without wanting any fanfare.' The main reason he wanted to secure the joint venture was to ensure his big project in Brisbane would continue to be funded long after his lifetime.

She looked shamefaced. 'I'm sorry.'

He hated that people like Andie thought he was stingy. Any remaining reservations he might hold about the party had to go. He needed to take action before this unfair reputation become so deeply entrenched he'd never free himself from it. 'Let's hope the seasonal name-calling eases if I go ahead with the lunch.'

She held up a finger in warning. 'It wouldn't appease everyone. Those cynical journalists might not be easily swayed.'

He scowled. 'I can't please everyone.' But he found himself, irrationally, wanting to please *her*.

'It might help if you followed through with a visible, ongoing relationship with a charity. If the media could see...could see...'

Her eyes narrowed in concentration. He waited for the end of her sentence but it wasn't forthcoming. 'See what?'

'Sorry,' she said, shaking her head as if bringing herself back to earth. 'My thoughts tend to run faster than my words sometimes when I'm deep in the creative zone.'

'I get it,' he said, though he wasn't sure what the hell being in the creative zone meant.

'I meant your critics might relent if they could see your gesture was genuine.'

He scowled. 'But it *will* be genuine.'

'You know it and I know it but they might see it as just another publicity gimmick.' Her eyes narrowed again and he gave her time to think. 'What if you didn't actually seek publicity for this day? You know—no invitations or press releases. Let the details leak. Tantalise the media.'

'For a designer, you seem to know a lot about publicity,' he said.

She shrugged. 'When you work in magazines you pick up a lot about both seeking and giving publicity. But your marketing people would have their own ideas, I'm sure.'

'I should talk it over with them,' he said.

'As it's only six weeks until Christmas, and this would be a big event to pull together, may I suggest there's not a lot of discussion time left?'

'You're right. I know. But it's a big deal.' So much bigger for him personally than she realised.

'You're seriously considering going ahead with it?'

He so much preferred it to the Z-list celebrity party. 'Yes. Let's do it.'

She clapped her hands together. 'I'm so glad. We can make it a real dream-come-true for your guests.'

'What about you and your business partners? You'd have to work on Christmas Day.'

'Speaking for me, I'd be fine with working. True spirit of Christmas and all that. I'll have to speak to Gemma and Eliza, but I think they'd be behind it too.' Securing Dominic Hunt's business for Party Queens was too important for them to refuse.

'What about caterers and so on?' he asked.

'The hospitality industry works three hundred and sixty-five days a year. It shouldn't be a problem. There are also people who don't celebrate Christmas as part of their culture who are very happy to work—especially for holiday pay rates. You don't have to worry about all that—that's our job.'

'And the guests? How would we recruit them?' He was about to say he could talk to people in Brisbane, where he was heavily involved in a homeless charity, but stopped himself. That was too connected to the secret part of his life he had no desire to share.

'I know the perfect person to help—my older sister, Hannah, is a social worker. She would know exactly which charities to liaise with. I think she would be excited to be involved.'

It was her. *Andie.* He would not be considering this direction if it wasn't for her. The big glitzy party had seemed so wrong. She made him see what could be right.

'Could we set up a meeting with your sister?' he asked.

'I can do better than that,' she said with a triumphant toss of her head that set her oversized earrings swaying. 'Every Wednesday night is open house dinner at my parents' house. Whoever of my siblings can make it comes. Sometimes grandparents and cousins too. I know Hannah will be there tonight and I'm planning to go too. Why don't you come along?'

'To your family dinner?' His first thought was to say no. Nothing much intimidated him—but meeting people's families was near the top of the list.

'Family is an elastic term for the Newmans. Friends, waifs and strays are always welcome at the table.'

What category would he be placed under? His memory of being a real-life stray made him wince. Friend? Strictly speaking, if circumstances were different, he'd want to be more than friends with Andie. Would connecting with her family create an intimacy he might later come to regret?

He looked down at his watch. Thought about his plan to return to the office.

'We need to get things moving,' she prompted.

'I would like to meet your sister tonight.'

Her wide smile lit her eyes. 'I have a really good feeling about this.'

'Do you always go on your feelings?' he asked.

She took off her sunglasses so he was treated to the directness of her gaze. 'All the time. Don't you?'

If he acted on his feelings he would be insisting they go to dinner, just the two of them. He would be taking her in his arms. Tasting her lovely mouth. Touching. Exploring. *But that wouldn't happen.*

He trusted his instincts when it came to business. But trusting his feelings when it came to women had only led to bitterness, betrayal and the kind of pain he never wanted to expose himself to again.

No to feeling. *Yes* to pleasant relationships that mutually fulfilled desires and were efficiently terminated before emotions ever became part of it. And with none of the complications that came with still having to work with that person. Besides, he suspected the short-term liaison that was all he had to offer would not be acceptable to Andie. She had *for ever* written all over her.

Now it was her turn to look at her watch. 'I'll call my mother to confirm you'll be joining us for dinner. How about I swing by and pick you up at around six?'

He thought about his four o'clock meeting. 'That's early for dinner.'

'Not when there are kids involved.'

'Kids?'

'I have a niece and two nephews. One of the nephews belongs to Hannah. He will almost certainly be there, along with his cousins.'

Dominic wasn't sure exactly what he was letting himself in for. One thing was for certain—he couldn't have seen himself going to a family dinner with any of Party Planners Numbers One to Three. And he suspected he might be in for more than one surprise from gorgeous Party Planner Number Four.

Andie got up from the chair. Smoothed down her white trousers. They were nothing as revealing as her flyaway skirt but made no secret of her slender shape.

'By the way, I'm apologising in advance for my car.'

He frowned. 'Why apologise?'

'I glimpsed your awesome sports car in the garage as I came in yesterday. You might find my hand-me-down hatchback a bit of a comedown.'

He frowned. 'I didn't come into this world behind the wheel of an expensive European sports car. I'm sure your hatchback will be perfectly fine.'

Just how did she see him? His public image—Scrooge, miser, rich guy—was so at odds with the person he knew himself to be. That he wanted her to know. But he could not reveal himself to her without uncovering secrets he would rather leave buried deep in his past.

CHAPTER FIVE

DOMINIC HAD FACED down some fears in his time. But the prospect of being paraded before Andie's large family ranked as one of the most fearsome. As Andie pulled up her hatchback—old but in good condition and nothing to be ashamed of—in front of her parents' home in the northern suburb of Willoughby, sweat prickled on his forehead and his hands felt clammy. How the hell had he got himself into this?

She turned off the engine, took out the keys, unclipped her seat belt and smoothed down the legs of her sleek, very sexy leather trousers. But she made no effort to get out of the car. She turned her head towards him. 'Before we go inside to meet my family I… I need to tell you something first. Something… something about me.'

Why did she look so serious, sombre even? 'Sure, fire away,' he said.

'I've told them you're a client. That there is absolutely nothing personal between us.'

'Of course,' he said.

Strange how at the same time he could be relieved and yet offended by her categorical denial that there ever could be anything *personal* between them.

Now a hint of a smile crept to the corners of her mouth. 'The thing is…they won't believe me. You're good-looking, you're smart and you're personable.'

'That's nice of you to say that,' he said. He noticed she hadn't added that he was rich to his list of attributes.

'You know it's true,' she said. 'My family are determined I should have a man in my life and have become the most inveterate of matchmakers. I expect they'll pounce on you. It could get embarrassing.'

'You're single?' He welcomed the excuse to ask.

'Yes. I… I've been single for a long time. Oh, I date. But I haven't found anyone special since…since…' She twisted right around in the car seat to fully face him. She clasped her hands together on her lap, then started to twist them without seeming to realise she was doing it. 'You need to know this before we go inside.' The hint of a smile had completely dissipated.

'If you think so,' he said. She was twenty-eight and single. What was the big deal here?

'I met Anthony on my first day of university. We were inseparable from the word go. There was no doubt we would spend our lives together.'

Dominic braced himself for the story of a nasty break-up. Infidelity? Betrayal? A jerk in disguise as a nice guy? He was prepared to make polite noises in response. He knew all about betrayal. But a *quid pro quo* exchange over relationships gone wrong was not something he ever wanted to waste time on with Andie or anyone else.

'It ended?' he said, making a terse contribution only because it was expected.

'He died.'

Two words stated so baldly but with such a wealth of pain behind them. Dominic felt as if he'd been punched in the chest. Nothing he said could be an adequate response. 'Andie, I'm sorry,' was all he could manage.

'It was five years ago. He was twenty-three. He…he went

out for an early-morning surf and didn't come back.' He could hear the effort it took for her to keep her tone even.

He knew about people who didn't come back. Goodbyes left unsaid. Personal tragedy. That particular kind of pain. 'Did he…? Did you—?'

'He…he washed up two days later.' She closed her eyes as if against an unbearable image.

'What happened?' He didn't want her to think he was interrogating her on something so sensitive, but he wanted to find out.

'Head injury. An accident. The doctors couldn't be sure exactly how it happened. A rock? His board? A sandbank? We'll never know.'

'Thank you for telling me.' He felt unable to say anything else.

'Better for you to know than not to know when you're about to meet the family. Just in case someone says something that might put you on the spot.'

She heaved a sigh that seemed to signal she had said what she felt she had to say and that there would be no further confidences. Why should there be? *He was just a client.* Something prompted him to want to ask—was she over the loss? Had she moved on? But it was not his place. Client and contractor—that was all they could be to each other. Besides, could anyone *ever* get over loss like that?

'You needed to be in the picture.' She went to open her door. 'Now, let's go in—Hannah is looking forward to meeting you. As I predicted, she's very excited about getting involved.'

Her family's home was a comfortable older-style house set in a chaotic garden in a suburb where values had rocketed in recent years. In the car on the way over, Andie had told him she had lived in this house since she was a baby. All her siblings had. He envied her that certainty, that security.

'Hellooo!' she called ahead of her. 'We're here.'

He followed her down a wide hallway, the walls crammed with framed photographs. They ranged from old-fashioned sepia wedding photos, dating from pre-Second World War, to posed studio shots of cherubic babies. Again he found himself envying her—he had only a handful of family photos to cherish.

At a quick glance he found two of Andie—one in a green checked school uniform with her hair in plaits and that familiar grin showing off a gap in her front teeth; another as a teenager in a flowing pink formal dress. A third caught his eye—an older Andie in a bikini, arm in arm with a tall blond guy in board shorts who was looking down at her with open adoration. The same guy was with her in the next photo, only this time they were playing guitars and singing together. Dominic couldn't bear to do more than glance at them, aware of the tragedy that had followed.

Just before they reached the end of the corridor, Andie stopped and took a step towards him. She stood so close he breathed in her scent—something vaguely oriental, warm and sensual. She leaned up to whisper into his ear and her hair tickled his neck. He had to close his eyes to force himself from reacting to her closeness.

'The clan can be a bit overwhelming *en masse*,' she said. 'I won't introduce you to everyone by name; it would be unfair to expect you to remember all of them. My mother is Jennifer, my father is Ray. Hannah's husband is Paul.'

'I appreciate that,' he said, tugging at his collar that suddenly seemed too tight. As an only child, he'd always found meeting other people's families intimidating.

Andie gave him a reassuring smile. 'With the Newman family, what you see is what you get. They're all good people who will take you as they find you. We might even get some volunteers to help on Christmas Day out of this.'

The corridor opened out into a spacious open-plan family room. At some time in the last twenty years the parents had obviously added a new extension. It looked dated now but solid—warm and comfortable and welcoming. Delicious aromas emanated from the farmhouse-style kitchen in the northern corner. He sniffed and Andie smiled. 'My mother's lasagne—wait until you taste it.'

She announced him with an encompassing wave of her arm. 'Everyone, this is Dominic. He's a very important new client so please make him welcome. And yes, I know he's gorgeous but it's strictly business between us.'

That was met with laughter and a chorus of 'Hi, Dominic!' and 'Welcome!' Andie then briefly explained to them about the party and Hannah's likely role in it.

There were so many of them. Andie's introduction had guaranteed all eyes were on him. About ten people, including kids, were ranged around the room, sitting in comfortable-looking sofas or around a large trestle table.

Each face came into focus as the adults greeted him with warm smiles. It wasn't difficult to tell who was related—Andie's smile was a strong family marker that originated with her father, a tall, thin man with a vigorous handshake. Her mother's smile was different but equally welcoming as she headed his way from the kitchen, wiping her hands on her apron before she greeted him. Three young children playing on the floor looked up, then kept on playing with their toys. A big black dog with a greying muzzle, lying stretched out near the kids, lifted his head, then thumped his tail in greeting.

Andie's sister Hannah and her husband, Paul, paused in their job of setting the large trestle table to say hello. His experience with social workers in his past had been good—a social worker had pretty much saved his life—and he was not disappointed by Hannah's kind eyes in a gentle face.

'I straight away know of several families who are facing a very grim Christmas indeed,' she said. 'Your generous gesture would make an immense difference to them.'

Andie caught his eye and smiled. Instinctively, he knew she had steered him in the right direction towards her sister. If all

Andie's ideas for his party were as good as this one, he could face the Christmas Day he dreaded with more confidence than he might have expected.

Andie's policy of glaring down any family member who dared to even hint at dating possibilities with Dominic was working. Except for her younger sister, Bea, who could not resist hissing, 'He's hot,' at any opportunity, from passing the salad to refilling her water glass. Then, when Andie didn't bite, Bea added, 'If you don't want him, hand him over to me.' Thankfully, Dominic remained oblivious to the whispered exchanges.

Her family had, unwittingly or not, sat Dominic in the same place at the table where Anthony had sat at these gatherings. *Andie and Ant—always together.* She doubted it was on purpose. Dominic needed to sit between Hannah and her and so it had just happened.

In the years since he'd died, no man had come anywhere near to replacing Anthony in her heart. How could they? Anthony and she had been two halves of the same soul, she sometimes thought. Maybe she would never be able to love anyone else. *But she was lonely.* The kind of loneliness that work, friends, family could not displace.

In the months after Anthony's death her parents had left Anthony's customary seat empty out of respect. Unable to bear the emptiness that emphasised his absence, she had stopped coming to the family dinners until her mother had realised the pain it was causing. From then on, one of her brothers always occupied Anthony's chair.

Now she told herself she was okay with Dominic sitting there. He was only a client, with no claim to any place in her heart. Bringing him along tonight had worked out well—one of those spur-of-the-moment decisions she mightn't have made if she'd given it more thought.

Dominic and Hannah had spent a lot of time talking—but he'd managed to chat with everyone else there too. They were obviously charmed by him. That was okay too. *She* was charmed by him. Tonight she was seeing a side of him, as he interacted with her family, that she might never have seen in everyday business dealings.

Her sister was right. *Dominic was hot.* And Andie was only too aware of it. She was surprised at the fierce urge of possessiveness that swept over her at the thought of 'handing over' Dominic to anyone else. Her sister could find her own hot guy.

Even at the dinner table, when her back was angled away from him to talk to her brother on her other side, she was aware of Dominic. His scent had already become familiar—citrus-sharp yet warm and very masculine. Her ears were tuned into the sound of his voice—no matter where he was in the room. Her body was on constant alert to that attraction, which had been instant and only continued to grow with further contact. On their way in, in the corridor, when she'd drawn close to whisper so her family would not overhear, she'd felt light-headed from the proximity to him.

It had been five years now since Anthony had gone—the same length of time they'd been together. She would never forget him but that terrible grief and anguish she had felt at first had eventually mellowed to a grudging acceptance. She realised she had stopped dreaming about him.

People talked about once-in-a-lifetime love. She'd thought she'd found it at the age of eighteen—and a cruel fate had snatched him away from her. Was there to be only one great love for her?

Deep in her heart, she didn't want to believe that. Surely there would be someone for her again? She didn't want to be alone. One day she wanted marriage, a family. She'd been looking for someone like Anthony—and had been constantly disappointed in the men she'd gone out with. But was it a mistake to keep on looking for a man like her teenage soulmate?

Thoughts of Dominic were constantly invading her mind. He was so different from Anthony there could be no comparison.

Anthony had been blond and lean, laidback and funny, always quick with a joke, creative and musical. From what she knew of Dominic, he was quite the opposite. She'd dismissed him as not for her. But her body's reaction kept contradicting her mind's stonewalling. How could she be so certain he was Mr Wrong?

Dessert was being served—spring berries and home-made vanilla bean ice cream—and she turned to Dominic at the precise moment he turned to her. Their eyes connected and held and she knew without the need for words that he was happy with her decision to bring him here.

'Your family is wonderful,' he said in a low undertone.

'I think so,' she said, pleased. 'What about you? Do you come from a large family?'

A shadow darkened his eyes. He shook his head. 'Only child.'

She smiled. 'We must seem overwhelming.'

'In a good way,' he said. 'You're very lucky.'

'I know.' Of course she and her siblings had had the usual squabbles and disagreements throughout their childhood and adolescence. She, as number four, had had to fight for her place. But as adults they all got on as friends as well as brothers and sisters. She couldn't have got through the loss of Anthony without her family's support.

'The kids are cute,' he said. 'So well behaved.'

Her nephews, Timothy and Will, and her niece, Caitlin, were together down the other end of the table under the watchful eye of their grandmother. 'They're really good kids,' she agreed. 'I adore them.'

'Little Timothy seems quite...delicate,' Dominic said, obviously choosing his words carefully. 'But I notice his older cousin looks after him.'

A wave of sadness for Hannah and Paul's little son overwhelmed her. 'They're actually the same age,' she said. 'Both five years old. Timothy just looks as though he's three.'

'I guess I don't know much about kids,' Dominic said, shifting uncomfortably in his chair.

She lowered her voice. 'Sadly, little Timothy has some kind of rare growth disorder, an endocrine imbalance. That's why he's so small.'

Dominic answered in a lowered voice. 'Can it be treated?'

'Only with a new treatment that isn't yet subsidised by the public health system. Even for private treatment, he's on a waiting list.' It was the reason why she drove an old car, why Bea had moved back home to save on rent, why the whole family was pulling together to raise the exorbitant amount of money required for tiny Timothy's private treatment.

But she would not tell Dominic that. While she might be wildly attracted to him, she still had no reason to think he was other than the Scrooge of his reputation. A man who had to be forced into a public display of charity to broker a multi-million-dollar business deal. Not for one moment did she want him to think she might be angling for financial help for Timothy.

'It's all under control,' she said as she passed him a bowl of raspberries.

'I'm glad to hear that,' he said, helping himself to the berries and then the ice cream. 'Thank you for inviting me tonight and for introducing me to Hannah. The next step is for you and your business partners to come in to my headquarters for a meeting with my marketing people. Can the three of you make it on Friday?'

CHAPTER SIX

ANDIE AND HER two business partners, Gemma and Eliza, settled themselves in a small waiting room off the main reception area of Dominic's very plush offices in Circular Quay. She and her fellow Party Queens had just come out of the Friday meeting with Dominic, his marketing people and senior executives in the boardroom and were waiting for Dominic to hear his feedback.

Situated on Sydney Cove, at the northern end of the CBD, the area was not just one of the most popular harbourside tourist precincts in Sydney—it was also home to the most prestigious office buildings. Even in this small room, floor-to-ceiling glass walls gave a magnificent close view of the Sydney Harbour Bridge and a luxury cruise liner in dock.

Andie couldn't help thinking the office was an ideal habitat for a billionaire Scrooge. Then she backtracked on the thought. That might not be fair. He hated the term and she felt vaguely disloyal even thinking it. Dominic was now totally committed to the Christmas Day feast for underprivileged families and had just approved a more than generous budget. She was beginning to wonder if his protestation that he was *not* a Scrooge had some truth in it. And then there was his gift to her mother to consider.

As she pondered the significance of that, she realised her

thoughts had been filled with nothing much but Dominic since the day she'd met him. Last night he had even invaded her dreams—in a very passionate encounter that made her blush at the hazy dream memory of it. *Did he kiss like that in real life?*

It was with an effort that she forced her thoughts back to business.

'How do you guys think it went?' she asked the other two. 'My vote is for really well.' She felt jubilant and buoyant—Dominic's team had embraced her idea with more enthusiasm than she could ever have anticipated.

'Considering the meeting was meant to go from ten to eleven and here it is, nearly midday, yes, I think you could say that,' said Eliza with a big smile splitting her face.

'Of course that could have had something to do with Gemma's superb macadamia shortbread and those delectable fruit mince pies,' said Andie.

'Yes,' said Gemma with a pleased smile. 'I thought I could describe until I was blue in the face what I wanted to serve for the lunch, but they'd only know by tasting it.'

Party Queens' foodie partner had not only come up with a detailed menu for Dominic's Christmas Day lunch, but she'd also brought along freshly baked samples of items from her proposed menus. At the end of the meeting only a few crumbs had remained on the boardroom's fine china plates. Andie had caught Dominic's eye as he finished his second pastry and knew it had been an inspired idea. The Christmas star shaped serviettes she had brought along had also worked to keep the meeting focused on the theme of traditional with a twist.

'I think they were all-round impressed,' said Eliza. 'We three worked our collective socks off to get our presentations so detailed and professional in such a short time. Andie, all the images and samples you prepared to show the decorations and table settings looked amazing—I got excited at how fabulous it's going to look.'

'I loved the idea of the goody bags for all the guests too,' said Gemma. 'You really thought of everything.'

'While we're doing some mutual backslapping I'm giving yours a hearty slap, Eliza,' said Andie. 'Their finance guy couldn't fault your detailed costings and timelines.'

Eliza rubbed her hands together in exaggerated glee. 'And I'm sure we're going to get more party bookings from them. One of the senior marketing people mentioned her daughter was getting married next year and asked me did we do weddings.'

'Well done, Party Queens,' said Andie. 'Now that the contract is signed and the basic plan approved I feel I can relax.' Her partners had no idea of how tight it had been to get Dominic across the line for the change from glitz and glamour to more humble with heart.

She and her two friends discreetly high-fived each other. The room was somewhat of a goldfish bowl and none of them wanted to look less than professional to any of Dominic's staff who might be walking by.

Eliza leaned in to within whispering distance of Andie and Gemma. 'Dominic Hunt was a surprise,' she said in an undertone. 'I thought he'd be arrogant and overbearing. Instead, I found myself actually liking him.'

'Me too,' said Gemma. 'Not to mention he's so handsome. I could hardly keep my eyes off him. And that voice.' She mimed a shiver of delight.

'But *he* couldn't keep his eyes off Andie,' said Eliza. 'You'd be wasting your time there, Gemma.'

Had he? Been unable to keep his eyes off her? Andie's Dominic radar had been on full alert all through the meeting. Again she'd that uncanny experience of knowing exactly where he was in the room even when her back was turned. Of hearing his voice through the chatter of others. She'd caught his eye one too many times to feel comfortable. Especially with the remnants of that dream lingering in her mind. She'd had to force herself not to let her gaze linger on his mouth.

'Really, Andie?' said Gemma. 'Has he asked you out?'

'Nothing like that,' Andie said.

Eliza nodded thoughtfully. 'But you like him. Not in the way I liked him. I mean you *really* like him.'

Andie had no intention of admitting anything to anyone. She forced her voice to sound cool, impartial—though she doubted she would fool shrewd Eliza. 'Like you, I was surprised at how easy he is to get on with and how professional he is—even earlier this week when I switched the whole concept of his party into something he had never envisaged.' That overwhelming attraction was just physical—nothing more.

'And you totally didn't get how hot he was?' said Gemma. 'Don't expect me to believe that for one moment.'

Eliza rolled her eyes at Andie. 'I know what's coming next. *He's not your type*. How many times have I heard you say that when you either refuse a date or dump a guy before you've even had a chance to get to know him?'

Andie paused. 'Maybe that's true. Maybe that's why I'm still single. I'm beginning to wonder if I really know what *is* my type now.'

Her friendships with Gemma and Eliza dated from after she'd lost Anthony. They'd been sympathetic, but never really got why she had been so determined to try and find another man cast in the same mould as her first love. That her first love had been so perfect she'd felt her best chance of happiness would be with someone like Anthony.

Trouble was, they'd broken the mould when they'd made Anthony. Maybe she just hadn't been ready. Maybe she'd been subconsciously avoiding any man who might challenge her. Or might force her to look at why she'd put her heart on hold for so long. *Dominic would be a challenge in every way.* The thought both excited and scared her.

Eliza shook her head. 'It's irrelevant anyway,' she said. 'It would be most unwise for you to start anything with Dominic Hunt. His party is a big, important job for us and we don't have much time to organise it. It could get very messy if you started dating the client. Especially when I've never known you to stay with anyone for more than two weeks.'

'In my eagerness to get you fixed up with a handsome rich guy, I hadn't thought of that,' said Gemma. 'Imagine if you broke up with the billionaire client right in the middle of the countdown to the event. Could get awkward.'

'It's not going to happen, girls,' Andie said. 'I won't lie and say I don't think he's really attractive. But that's as far as it goes.' Thinking of last night's very intimate dream, she crossed her fingers behind her back.

'This is a huge party for us to pull together so quickly. We've got other jobs to get sorted as well. I can't afford to get…distracted.' How she actually stopped herself from getting distracted by Dominic was another matter altogether.

'I agree,' said Eliza. 'Eyes off the client. Okay?'

Andie smiled. 'I'll try,' she said. 'Seriously, though, it's really important for Dominic that this party works. He's got a lot riding on it. And it's really important for us. As you say, Eliza, more work could come from this. Not just weddings and private parties. But why not his company's business functions too? We have to think big.'

Gemma giggled. 'Big? Mr Hunt is way too big for me anyway. He's so tall. And all those muscles. His face is handsome but kind of tough too, don't you think?'

'Shh,' hissed Eliza, putting her finger to her lips. 'He's coming.'

Andie screwed up her eyes for a moment. How mortifying if he'd caught them gossiping about him. She'd been just about to say he wasn't too big for her to handle.

Along with the other two, she looked up and straightened her shoulders as Dominic strode towards them. In his dark charcoal suit he looked every inch the billionaire businessman. And, yes, very big.

She caught her breath at how handsome he looked. At the

same time she caught his eye. And got the distinct impression that, of the three women in the room, she was the only one he really saw.

Did Andie get more and more beautiful every time he saw her? Dominic wondered. Or was it just the more he got to know her, the more he liked and admired her?

He had been impressed by her engaging and professional manner in the boardroom—the more so because he was aware she'd had such a short time to prepare her presentation. Her two business partners had been impressive too. It took a lot to win over his hard-nosed marketing people but, as a team, Party Queens had bowled them over.

The three women got up from their seats as he approached. Andie, tall and elegant in a deceptively simple caramel-coloured short dress—businesslike but with a snug fit that showed off her curves. Her sensational legs seemed to go on for ever to end in sky-high leopard-skin-print stilettos. He got it. She wanted to look businesslike but also let it be known who was the creative mind behind Party Queens. It worked.

Gemma—shorter, curvier, with auburn hair—and sophisticated, dark-haired Eliza were strikingly attractive too. They had a glint in their eyes and humour in their smiles that made him believe they could enjoy a party as well as plan them. But, in his eyes, Andie outshone them. Would any other woman ever be able to beat her? It was disturbing that a woman who he had known for such a short time could have made such an impression on him.

He addressed all three, while being hyper aware of Andie as he did so. Her hair pulled back in a loose knot that fell in soft tendrils around her face, her mouth slicked with coral gloss, those remarkable green eyes. 'As I'm sure you're aware,' he began, 'my marketing team is delighted at both the concept for the party and the way you plan to implement the concept to the timeline. They're confident the event will meet and exceed the target we've set for reputation management and positive media engagement.'

It sounded like jargon and he knew it. But how else could he translate the only real aim of the party: to make him look less the penny-pincher and more the philanthropist?

'We're very pleased to be working with such a professional team,' said Eliza, the business brains of the partnership. But all three were business savvy in their own way, he'd realised through the meeting.

'Thank you,' he said. He glanced at his watch. 'The meeting ran so late it's almost lunchtime. I'm extending an invitation to lunch for all of you,' he said. 'Not that restaurants around here, excellent as they are, could match the standard of your cooking, Gemma.'

'Thank you,' said Gemma, looking pleased. 'But I'm afraid I have an appointment elsewhere.'

'Me too, and I'm running late,' said Eliza. 'But we couldn't possibly let you lunch alone, Mr Hunt, could we, Andie?'

Andie flushed high on those elegant cheekbones. 'Of course not. I'd be delighted to join Dominic for lunch.'

Her chin tilted upwards and he imagined her friends might later be berated for landing her in this on her own. Not that he minded. The other women were delightful, but lunch one-on-one with Andie was his preferred option.

'There are a few details of the plan I need to finalise with Dominic anyway,' she said to her friends.

Dominic shook hands with Gemma and Eliza and they headed towards the elevators. He turned to Andie. 'Thank you for coming to lunch with me,' he said.

She smiled. 'Be warned, I'm starving. I was up at the crack of dawn finalising those mood boards for the presentation.'

'They were brilliant. There's only one thing I'd like to see changed. I didn't want to mention it in the meeting as it's my personal opinion and I didn't want to have to debate it.'

She frowned, puzzled rather than worried, he thought. 'Yes?'

He put his full authority behind his voice—he would not explain his reasons. Ever. 'The Christmas tree. The big one you have planned for next to the staircase. I don't want it.'

'Sure,' she said, obviously still puzzled. 'I thought it would be wonderful to have the tree where it's the first thing the guests see, but I totally understand if you don't want it there. We can put the Christmas tree elsewhere. The living room. Even in the area near where we'll be eating. Wherever you suggest.'

He hadn't expected this to be easy—he knew everyone would expect to see a decorated tree on Christmas Day. 'You misunderstood me. I mean I don't want a Christmas tree anywhere. No tree at all in my house.'

She paused. He could almost see her internal debate reflected in the slight crease between her eyebrows, the barely visible pursing of her lips. But then she obviously thought it was not worth the battle. 'Okay,' she said with a shrug of her slender shoulders. 'No tree.'

'Thank you,' he said, relieved he wasn't going to have to further assert his authority. At this time of year, Christmas trees were appearing all over the place. He avoided them when he could. But he would never have a tree in his home—a constant reminder of the pain and loss and guilt associated with the festive season.

They walked together to the elevator. When it arrived, there were two other people in it. They got out two floors below. Then Dominic was alone in the confined space of the elevator, aware of Andie's closeness, her warm scent. What was it? Sandalwood? Something exotic and sensual. He had the craziest impulse to hold her closer so he could nuzzle into the softness of her throat, the better to breathe it in.

He clenched his fists beside him and moved as far as he could away from her so his shoulder hit the wall of the elevator. That would be insanity. And probably not the best timing when he'd just quashed her Christmas tree display.

But she wouldn't be Andie if she didn't persevere. 'Not even miniature trees on the lunch table?' she asked.

'No trees,' he said.

She sighed. 'Okay, the client has spoken. No Christmas tree.'

The elevator came to the ground floor. He lightly placed his hand at the small of her back to steer her in the direction of the best exit for the restaurant. Bad idea. Touching Andie even in this casual manner just made him want to touch her more.

'But you're happy with the rest of the plan?' she said as they walked side by side towards the restaurant, dodging the busy Sydney lunchtime crush as they did.

'Very happy. Except you can totally discard the marketing director's suggestion I dress up as Santa Claus.'

She laughed. 'Did you notice I wrote it down but didn't take the suggestion any further?' Her eyes narrowed as she looked him up and down in mock inspection. 'Though it's actually a nice idea. If you change your mind—'

'No,' he said.

'That's what I thought,' she said, that delightful smile dancing around the corners of her mouth.

'You know it's been a stretch for me to agree to a Christmas party at all. You won't ever see me as Santa.'

'What if the marketing director himself could be convinced to play Santa Claus?' she said thoughtfully. 'He volunteered to help out on the day.'

'This whole party thing was Rob Cratchit's idea so that might be most appropriate. Take it as an order from his boss.'

'I'll send him an email and say it's your suggestion,' she said with a wicked grin. 'He's quite well padded and would make a wonderful Santa—no pillow down the front of his jacket required.'

'Don't mention that in the email or all hell will break loose,' he said.

'Don't worry; I can be subtle when I want to,' she said, that grin still dancing in her eyes as they neared the restaurant.

In Dominic's experience, some restaurants were sited well and had a good fit-out; others had excellent food. In this case, his favourite place to eat near the office had both—a spectacular site on the top of a heritage listed building right near the water and a superlative menu.

There had been no need to book—a table was always there for him when he wanted one, no matter how long the waiting list for bookings.

An attentive waiter settled Andie into a seat facing the view of Sydney Harbour. 'I've always wanted to eat at this restaurant,' she said, looking around her.

'Maybe we should have our meetings here in future?'

'Good idea,' she said. 'Though I'll have to do a detailed site inspection of your house very soon. We could fit in a meeting then, perhaps?'

'I might not be able to be there,' he said. 'I have a series of appointments in other states over the next two weeks. Any meetings with you might have to be via the Internet.'

Was that disappointment he saw cloud her eyes. 'That's a shame. I—'

'My assistant will help you with access and the security code,' he said. He wished he could cancel some of the meetings, but that was not possible. Perhaps it was for the best. The more time he spent with Andie, the more he wanted to break his rules and ask her on a date. But those rules were there for good reason.

'As you know, we have a tight timeline to work to,' she said. 'The more we get done early the better, to allow for the inevitable last-minute dramas.'

'I have every confidence in you that it will go to plan.'

'Me too,' she said with another of those endearing grins. 'I've organised so many Christmas room sets and table settings for magazine and advertising clients. You have to get creative to come up with something different each year. This is easier in a way.'

'But surely there must be a continuity?' he asked, curious even though Christmas was his least favourite topic of conversation.

'Some people don't want to go past traditional red and green and that's okay,' she said. 'I've done an entire room themed purple and the client was delighted. Silver and gold is always popular in Australia, when Christmas is likely to be sweltering—it seems to feel cooler somehow. But—'

The waiter came to take their orders. They'd been too busy talking to look at the menu. Quickly they discussed their favourites before they ordered: barramundi with prawns and asparagus for him; tandoori roasted ocean trout with cucumber salsa for her and an heirloom tomato salad to share. They each passed on wine and chose mineral water. 'Because it's a working day,' they both said at the exact time and laughed. *It felt like a date.* He could not let his thoughts stray that way. Because he liked the idea too much.

'You haven't explained the continuity of Christmas,' he said, bringing the conversation back to the party.

'It's nothing to do with the baubles and the tinsel and everything to do with the feeling,' she said with obvious enthusiasm. 'Anticipation, delight, joy. For some it's about religious observance, spirituality and new life; others about sharing and generosity. If you can get people feeling the emotion, then it doesn't really matter if the tree is decorated in pink and purple or red and green.'

How about misery and fear and pain? Those were his memories of Christmas. 'I see your point,' he said.

'I intend to make sure your party is richly imbued with that kind of Christmas spirit. Hannah told me some of the kids who will be coming would be unlikely to have a celebration meal or a present and certainly not both if it wasn't for your generosity.'

'I met with Hannah yesterday; she mentioned how important it will be for the families we're inviting. She seems to think the party will do a powerful lot of good. Your sister told me how special Christmas is in your family.' It was an effort for him to speak about Christmas in a normal tone of voice. But he seemed to be succeeding.

'Oh, yes,' said Andie. 'Heaven help anyone who might want to celebrate it with their in-laws or anywhere else but my parents' house.'

'Your mother's a marvellous cook.'

'True, but Christmas is well and truly my dad's day. My mother is allowed to do the baking and she does that months in advance. On the day, he cooks a traditional meal—turkey, ham, roast beef, the lot. He's got favourite recipes he's refined over the years and no one would dare suggest anything different.'

Did she realise how lucky she was? How envious he felt when he thought about how empty his life had been of the kind of family love she'd been gifted with. He'd used to think he could start his own family, his own traditions, but his ex-wife had disabused him of that particular dream. It involved trust and trust was not a thing that came easily to him. Not when it came to women. 'I can't imagine you would want to change a tradition.'

'If truth be told, we'd be furious if he wanted to change one little thing,' she said, her voice warm with affection for her father. *She knew.*

He could see where she got her confidence from—that rock-solid security of a loving, supportive family. But now he knew she'd been tempered by tragedy too. He wanted to know more about how she had dealt with the loss of her boyfriend. But not until it was appropriate to ask.

'What about you, Dominic—did you celebrate Christmas with your family?' she asked.

This never got easier—which was why he chose not to revisit it too often. 'My parents died when I was eleven,' he said.

'Oh, I'm so sorry,' she said with warm compassion in her eyes. 'What a tragedy.' She paused. 'You were so young, an only child…who looked after you?'

'We lived in England, in a village in Norfolk. My father was

English, my mother Australian. My mother's sister was staying with us at the time my parents died. She took me straight back with her to Australia.' It was difficult to keep his voice matter of fact, not to betray the pain the memories evoked, even after all this time.

'What? Just wrenched you away from your home?' She paused. 'I'm sorry. That wasn't my call to say that. You were lucky you had family. Did your aunt have children?'

'No, it was just the two of us,' he said and left it at that. There was so much more he could say about the toxic relationship with his aunt but that was part of his past he'd rather was left buried.

Wrenched. That was how it had been. Away from everything familiar. Away from his grandparents, whom he didn't see again until he had the wherewithal to get himself back to the UK as an adult. Away from the dog he'd adored. Desperately lonely and not allowed to grieve, thrust back down in Brisbane, in the intense heat, straight into the strategic battleground that was high school in a foreign country. To a woman who had no idea how to love a child, though she had tried in her own warped way.

'I'd prefer not to talk about it,' he said. 'I'm all grown up now and don't angst about the past.' Except when it was dark and lonely and he couldn't sleep and he wondered if he was fated to live alone without love.

'I understand,' she said. But how could she?

She paused to leave a silence he did not feel able to fill.

'Talking about my family,' she finally said, 'you're my mother's new number one favourite person.'

Touched by not only her words but her effort to draw him in some way into her family circle, he smiled. 'And why is that?'

'Seriously, she really liked you at dinner on Wednesday night. But then, when you had flowers delivered the next day, she was over the moon. Especially at the note that said she cooked the best lasagne you'd ever tasted.'

'I'm glad she liked them. And it was true about the lasagne.'

Home-made anything was rarely on the menu for him so he had appreciated it.

'How did you know pink was her favourite colour in flowers?'

'I noticed the flowers she'd planted in her garden.'

'But you only saw the garden so briefly.'

'I'm observant,' he said.

'But the icing on the cake was the voucher for dinner for two at their local bistro.'

'She mentioned she liked their food when we were talking,' he said.

'You're a thoughtful guy, aren't you?' she said, tilting her head to the side.

'Some don't think so,' he said, unable to keep the bitterness from his voice.

She lowered her voice to barely a whisper so he had to lean across the table to hear her, so close their heads were touching. Anyone who was watching would think they *were* on a date.

She placed her hand on his arm in a gesture of comfort which touched him. 'Don't worry. The party should change all that. I really liked Rob's idea that no media would be invited to the party. That journalists would have to volunteer to help on the day if they wanted to see what it was all about.'

'And no photographers allowed, to preserve our guests' privacy. I liked that too.'

'I really have a good feeling about it,' she said. She lifted her hand off his arm and he felt bereft of her touch.

He nodded. If it were up to him, if he didn't *have* to go ahead with the party, he'd cancel it at a moment's notice. Maybe there was a touch of Scrooge in him after all.

But he didn't want Andie to think that of him. Not for a moment.

He hadn't proved to be a good judge of women. His errors in judgement went right back to his aunt—he'd loved her when she was his fun auntie from Australia. She'd turned out to be a very different person. Then there'd been Melody—sweet, doomed Melody. At seventeen he'd been a man in body but a boy still in heart. He'd been gutted at her betrayal, too damn wet behind the ears to realise a teenage boy's love could never be enough for an addict. Then how could he have been sucked in by Tara? His ex-wife was a redhead like Melody, tiny and delicate. But her frail exterior hid an avaricious, dishonest heart and she had lied to him about something so fundamental to their marriage that he could never forgive her.

Now there was Andie. He didn't trust his feelings when he'd made such disastrous calls before. *'What you see is what you get,'* she'd said about her family.

Could he trust himself to judge that Andie was what she appeared to be?

He reined in his errant thoughts—he only needed to trust Andie to deliver him the party he needed to improve his public image. Anything personal was not going to happen.

CHAPTER SEVEN

'ANDIE, I NEED to see you.' Dominic's voice on her smartphone was harsh in its urgency. It was eight a.m. and Andie had not been expecting a call from him. He'd been away more than a week on business and she'd mainly communicated with him by text and email—and only then if it was something that needed his approval for the party. The last time she'd seen him was the Friday they'd had lunch together. The strictly business lunch that had somehow felt more like a date. But she couldn't let herself think like that.

'Sure,' she said. 'I just have to—'

'Now. Please. Where do you live?'

Startled at his tone, she gave him the address of the apartment in a converted warehouse in the inner western suburb of Newtown she shared with two old schoolfriends. Her friends had both already left for work. Andie had planned on a day finalising prop hire and purchase for Dominic's party before she started work for a tuxedo-and-tiara-themed twenty-first birthday party.

She quickly changed into skinny denim jeans and a simple loose-knit cream top that laced with leather ties at the neckline. Decided on her favourite leopard-print stilettos over flats. And make-up. And her favourite sandalwood and jasmine perfume.

What the heck—her heart was racing at the thought of seeing him. She didn't want to seem as though she were trying too hard—but then again she didn't want to be caught out in sweats.

When Dominic arrived she was shocked to see he didn't look *his* sartorial best. In fact he looked downright dishevelled. His black hair seemed as if he'd used his fingers for a comb and his dark stubble was one step away from a beard. He was wearing black jeans, a dark grey T-shirt and had a black leather jacket slung over his shoulders. Immediately he owned the high-ceilinged room, a space that overwhelmed men of lesser stature, with the casual athleticism of his stance, the power of his body with its air of tightly coiled energy.

'Are you alone?' he asked.

'Yes,' she said. *Yes!*

Her first thought was that he looked hotter than ever—so hot she had to catch her breath. This Dominic set her pulse racing even more than executive Dominic in his made-to-measure Italian suits.

Her second thought was that he seemed stressed—his mouth set in a grim line, his eyes red-rimmed and darkly shadowed. 'Are you okay?' she asked.

'I've come straight from the airport. I just flew in from Perth.' Perth was on the other side of Australia—a six-hour flight. 'I cut short my trip.'

'But are you okay?' She forced her voice to sound calm and measured, not wanting him to realise how she was reacting to his untamed good looks. Her heart thudded with awareness that they were alone in the apartment.

With the kind of friendly working relationship they had now established, it would be quite in order to greet him with a light kiss on his beard-roughened cheek. But she wouldn't dare. She might not be able to resist sliding her mouth across his cheek to his mouth and turning it into a very different kind of kiss. And that wouldn't do.

'I'm fine. I've just...been presented with...with a dilemma,' Dominic said.

'Coffee might help,' she said.

'Please.'

'Breakfast? I have—'

'Just coffee.'

But Andie knew that sometimes men who said they didn't want anything to eat needed food. And that their mood could improve immeasurably when they ate something. Not that she'd been in the habit of sharing breakfast with a man. Not since... She forced her mind back to the present and away from memories of breakfasts with Anthony on a sun-soaked veranda. Her memories of him were lit with sunshine and happiness.

Dominic dragged out a chair and slumped down at her kitchen table while she prepared him coffee. *Why was he here?* She turned to see him with his elbows on the tabletop, resting his head on his hands. Tired? Defeated? Something seemed to have put a massive dent in his usual self-assured confidence.

She slid a mug of coffee in front of him. 'I assumed black but here's frothed milk and sugar if you want.'

'Black is what I need,' he said. He put both hands around the mug and took it to his mouth.

Without a word, she put a thick chunk of fresh fruit bread, studded with figs and apricots, from her favourite baker in King Street in front of him. Then a dish of cream cheese and a knife. 'Food might help,' she said.

He put down his coffee, gave her a weary imitation of his usual glower and went to pick up the bread. 'Let me,' she said and spread it with cream cheese.

What was it about this man that made her want to comfort and care for him? He was a thirty-two-year-old billionaire, for heaven's sake. Tough, self-sufficient. Wealthier than she could even begin to imagine. And yet she sometimes detected an air of vulnerability about him that wrenched at her. A sense of something broken. But it was not up to her to try and fix him. He ate the fruit bread in two bites. 'More?' she asked.

He nodded. 'It's good,' he said.

Andie had to be honest with herself. She wanted to comfort him, yes. She enjoyed his company. But it was more than that. She couldn't deny that compelling physical attraction. He sat at her kitchen table, his leather jacket slung on the back of the chair. His tanned arms were sculpted with muscle, his T-shirt moulded ripped pecs and abs. With his rough-hewn face, he looked so utterly *male*.

Desire, so long unfamiliar, thrilled through her. She wanted to kiss him and feel those strong arms around her, his hands on her body. *She wanted more than kisses.* What was it about this not-my-type man who had aroused her interest from the moment she'd first met him?

When he'd eaten two more slices of fruit bread, he pushed his plate away and leaned back in his seat. His sigh was weary and heartfelt. 'Thank you,' he said. 'I didn't realise I was hungry.'

She slipped into the chair opposite him and nursed her own cooling cup of coffee to stop the impulse to reach over and take his hand. 'Are you able to tell me about your dilemma?' she asked, genuinely concerned.

He raked his hands through his hair. 'My ex-wife is causing trouble. Again.'

In her research into Dominic, Andie had seen photos of Tara Hunt—she still went by his name—a petite, pale-skinned red-head in designer clothes and an over-abundance of jewellery.

'I'm sorry,' she said, deciding on caution in her reaction. 'Do you want to tell me about it?' Was that why he wanted to see her? To cry on her shoulder about his ex-wife? Dominic didn't seem like a crying-on-shoulders kind of guy.

He went to drink more coffee, to find his mug was nearly empty. He drained the last drops. 'You make good coffee,' he said appreciatively.

'I worked as a barista when I was a student,' she said.

She and Anthony had both worked in hospitality, saving for vacation backpacker trips to Indonesia and Thailand. It seemed so long ago now, those days when she took it for granted they had a long, happy future stretched out ahead of them. They'd been saving for a trip to Eastern Europe when he'd died.

She took Dominic's mug from him, got up, refilled it, brought it back to the table and sat down again. He drank from it and put it down.

Dominic leaned across the table to bring him closer to her. 'Can I trust you, Andie?' he asked in that deep, resonant voice. His intense grey gaze met hers and held it.

'Of course,' she said without hesitation.

He sat back in his chair. 'I know you're friends with journalists, so I have to be sure what I might talk to you about today won't go any further.' The way he said it didn't sound offensive; in fact it made her feel privileged that he would consider her trustworthy. Not to mention curious about what he might reveal.

'I assure you, you can trust me,' she said.

'Thank you,' he said. 'Tara found out about my impending deal with Walter Burton and is doing her best to derail it.'

Andie frowned. 'How can she do that?'

'Before I married Tara, she worked for my company in the accounts department. She made it her business to find out everything she could about the way I ran things. I didn't know, but once I started dating her she used that knowledge to make trouble, hiding behind the shield of our relationship. None of my staff dared tell me.'

'Not good,' Andie said, wanting to express in no uncertain terms what she thought of his ex, yet not wanting to get into a bitching session about her.

'You're right about that,' he said. 'It's why I now never date employees.'

His gaze met hers again and held it for a long moment. Was there a message in there for her? If she wasn't a contractor, would he ask her out? If she hadn't promised her partners to stay away from him, would she suggest a date?

'That policy makes…sense,' she said. What about after Christmas, when she and Dominic would no longer be connected by business? Could they date then? A sudden yearning for that to happen surprised her with its intensity. *She wanted him.*

'It gets worse,' he continued. 'A former employee started his own business in competition with me—' Andie went to protest but Dominic put up his hand. 'It happens; that's legit,' he said. 'But what happened afterwards wasn't. After our marriage broke up, Tara used her knowledge of how my company worked to help him.'

Andie couldn't help her gasp of outrage. 'Did her…her betrayal work?'

'She gave him the information. That didn't mean he knew how to use it. But now I've just discovered she's working with him in a last-minute rival bid for the joint venture with Walter Burton.'

Andie shook her head in disbelief. 'Why?' Her research had shown her Tara Hunt had ended up with a massive divorce settlement from Dominic. Per day of their short marriage, she had walked away with an incredible number of dollars.

Dominic shrugged. 'Revenge. Spite. Who knows what else?'

'Surely Walter Burton won't be swayed by that kind of underhand behaviour?'

'Traditional values are important to Walter Burton. We know that. That's why we're holding the party to negate the popular opinion of me as a Scrooge.'

'So what does your ex-wife have to do with the deal?'

Dominic sighed, a great weary sigh that made Andie want to put comforting arms around him. She'd sensed from the get-go he was a private person. He obviously hated talking about this. Once more, she wondered why he had chosen to.

He drew those dark brows together in a scowl. 'Again she's

raked over the coals of our disastrous marriage and talked to her media buddies. Now she's claiming I was unfaithful—which is a big fat lie. According to her, I'm a womaniser, a player and a complete and utter bastard. She dragged out my old quote that I will never marry again and claims it's because I'm incapable of settling with one woman. It's on one of the big Internet gossip sites and will be all over the weekend newspapers.' He cursed under his breath.

Andie could see the shadow of old hurts on his face. He had once loved his ex enough to marry her. A betrayal like this must be painful, no matter how much time had elapsed. She had no such angst behind her. She knew Anthony had been loyal to her, as she had been to him. *First love.* Sometimes she wondered if they might have grown apart if he'd lived. Some of their friends who had dated as teenagers had split when they got older. But she dismissed those thoughts as disloyal to his memory.

Andie shook her head at Dominic's revelations about his ex—it got worse and worse. 'That's horrible—but can't you just ignore it?'

'I would ignore it, but she's made sure Walter Burton has seen all her spurious allegations set out as truth.'

Andie frowned. 'Surely your personal life is none of Mr Burton's business? Especially when it's not true.' She believed Dominic implicitly—why, she wasn't completely sure. Trust went both ways.

'He might think it's true. The *"bed-hopping billionaire"*,' the article calls me.' Dominic growled with wounded outrage. 'That might be enough for Burton to reconsider doing business with me.'

Andie had to put her hand over her mouth to hide her smile at the description.

But Dominic noticed and scowled. 'I know it sounds ludicrous, but to a moralistic family man like Walter Burton it makes me sound immoral and not the kind of guy he wants to do business with.'

'Why do you care so much about the deal with Mr Burton? If you have to pretend to be someone you're not, how can it be worth it?'

'You mean I should pretend *not* to be a bed-hopping billionaire?'

'You must admit the headline has a certain ring to it,' Andie said, losing her battle to keep a straight face.

That forced a reluctant grin from him. 'A tag like that might be very difficult to live down.'

'Is…is it true? Are you a bed-hopping guy?' She held her breath for his reply.

'No. Of course I've had girlfriends since my divorce. Serial monogamy, I think they call it. But nothing like what this scurrilous interview with my ex claims.'

Andie let out her breath on a sigh of relief. 'But do you actually need to pursue this deal if it's becoming so difficult? You're already very wealthy.'

Dominic's mouth set in a grim line. 'I'm not going to bore you with my personal history. But home life with my aunt was less than ideal. I finished high school and got out. I'd tried to run away before and she'd dragged me back. This time she let me go. I ended up homeless, living in a squat. At seventeen I saw inexplicably awful things a boy that age should never see. I never again want to be without money and have nowhere to live. That's all I intend to say about that.' He nodded to her. 'And I trust you not to repeat it.'

'Of course,' she said, rocked by his revelations, aching to know more. *Dominic Hunt was a street kid?* Not boring. There was so much more about his life than he was saying. She thought again about his scarred knuckles and broken nose. There had been nothing about his past in her online trawling. She hoped he might tell her more. It seemed he was far more complex than he appeared. Which only made him more attractive.

'My best friend and first business partner, Jake Marlow, is

also in with me on this,' he said. 'He wants it as much as I do, for his own reasons I'm not at liberty to share.'

'Okay,' she said slowly. 'So we're working on the party to negate the Scr…uh…the other reputation, to get Mr Burton on board. What do you intend to do about the bed-hopper one?'

'When Burton contacted me I told him that it was all scuttle-butt and I was engaged to be married.'

She couldn't help a gasp. 'You're engaged?' She felt suddenly stricken. 'Engaged to who?'

'I'm not engaged. I'm not even dating anyone.'

'Then why…?' she said.

He groaned. 'Panic. Fear. Survival. A gut reaction like I used to have back in that squat. When you woke up, terrified, in your cardboard box to find some older guy burrowing through your backpack and you told him you had nothing worth stealing even though there was five dollars folded tiny between your toes in your sock. If that money was stolen, you didn't eat.'

'So you lied to Mr Burton?'

'As I said, a panic reaction. But it gets worse.' Again he raked his fingers through his hair. 'Burton said he was flying in to Sydney in two weeks' time to meet with both me and the other guy. He wants to be introduced to my fiancée.'

Andie paused, stunned at what Dominic had done, appalled that he had lied. 'What will you do?'

Again he leaned towards her over the table. 'I want you to be my fiancée, Andie.'

CHAPTER EIGHT

DOMINIC WATCHED ANDIE'S reactions flit across her face—shock and indignation followed by disappointment. In him? He braced himself—certain she was going to say *no*.

'Are you serious?' she finally said, her hands flat down on the table in front of her.

'Very,' he said, gritting his teeth. He'd been an idiot to get himself into a mess like this. *Panic.* He shouldn't have given in to panic in that phone call with Walter Burton. He hadn't let panic or fear rule him for a long time.

Andie tilted her head to one side and frowned. 'You want me to *marry* you? We hardly know each other.'

Marriage? Who was talking about marriage? 'No. Just to *pretend*—' Whatever he said wasn't going to sound good. 'Pretend to be my fiancée. Until after the Christmas party.'

Andie shook her head in disbelief. 'To pretend to be engaged to you? To lie? No! I can't believe you asked me to…to even think of such a thing. I'm a party planner, not a…a…the type of person who would agree to that.'

She looked at him as though she'd never seen him before. And that maybe she didn't like what she saw. Dominic swallowed hard—he didn't like the feeling her expression gave him. She pushed herself up from the chair and walked away from the table, her body rigid with disapproval. He was very aware she wanted to distance herself from him. He didn't like that either. It had seemed so intimate, drinking coffee and eating breakfast at her table. And he *had* liked that.

He swivelled in his chair to face her. 'It was a stupid thing to do, I know that,' he said. He had spent the entire flight back from Perth regretting his impulsive action. 'But it's done.'

She turned around, glared at him. 'Then I suggest you undo it.'

'By admitting I lied?'

She shrugged. 'Tell Mr Burton your fiancée dumped you.'

'As if that would fly.'

'You think it's beyond belief that a woman would ever dump you?'

'I didn't say that.' Though it was true. Since it had ended with Melody, he had always been the one to end a relationship. 'It would seem too…sudden.'

'Just like the sudden engagement?'

'It wouldn't denote…stability.'

'You're right about that.' She crossed her arms in front of her chest—totally unaware that the action pushed up her breasts into an enticing cleavage in the V-necked top she wore. 'It's a crazy idea.'

'I'm not denying that,' he growled. He didn't need to have his mistake pointed out to him. 'But I'm asking you to help me out.'

'Why me? Find someone else. I'm sure there would be no shortage of candidates.'

'But it makes sense for my fiancée to be you.' He could be doggedly persistent when he wanted to be.

He unfolded himself from the too-small chair at the kitchen table. Most chairs were too small for him. He took a step towards her, only for her to take a step back from him. 'Andie. Please.'

Her hair had fallen across her face and she tossed it back. 'Why? We're just client and contractor.'

'Is that all it is between us?'

'Of course it is.' But she wouldn't meet his gaze and he felt triumphant. *So she felt it too.* That attraction that had flashed between them from the get-go.

'When I opened the door to the beautiful woman with the misbehaving skirt—' that got a grudging smile from her '—I thought it could be more than just a business arrangement. But you know now why I don't date anyone hired by the company.'

'And Party Queens has a policy of not mixing business with…with pleasure.' Her voice got huskier on the last words.

He looked her direct in the face, pinning her with his gaze. 'If it ever happened, it would be pleasure all the way, Andie, I think we both know that.' She hadn't quite cleared her face of a wisp of flyaway hair. He reached down and gently smoothed it back behind her ear.

She trembled under his touch. A blush travelled up her throat to stain her cheeks. 'I've never even thought about it, the…the *pleasure,* I mean,' she said.

She wouldn't blush like that if she hadn't. Or flutter her hands to the leather laces of her neckline. *Now who was lying?*

She took a deep breath and he tried to keep his gaze from the resulting further exposure of her cleavage. 'I don't want to be involved in this mad scheme in any way,' she said. 'Except to add your pretend fiancée—when you find one—to the Christmas party guest list.'

'I'm afraid you're already involved.'

She frowned. 'What do you mean?'

Dominic took the few steps necessary back to his chair and took out his smartphone from the inside pocket of his leather jacket. He scrolled through, then handed it to Andie.

She stared at the screen. 'But this is me. *Us.*'

The photo she was staring at was of him and her at a restaurant table. They were leaning towards each other, looking into each other's faces, Andie's hand on his arm.

'At the restaurant in Circular Quay, the day of the Friday meeting,' she said.

'Yes,' he said. The business lunch that had felt like a date. In this photo, it *looked* like a date.

She shook her head, bewildered. 'Who took it?'

'Some opportunistic person with a smartphone, I expect. Maybe a trouble-making friend of Tara's. Who knows?'

She looked back down at the screen, did some scrolling of her own. He waited for her to notice the words that accompanied the image on the gossip site.

Her eyes widened in horror. 'Did you see this?' She read out the heading. *'"Is This the Bed-Hopping Billionaire's New Conquest?"'* She swore under her breath—the first time he had heard her do so.

'I'm sorry. Of course I had no idea this was happening. But, in light of it, you can see why it makes sense that my fake fiancée should be you.'

She shook her head. 'No. It doesn't make any sense. That was a business lunch. Not the...the romantic rendezvous it appears to be in the picture.'

'You know that. I know that. But the way they've cropped the photo, that's exactly what it seems. Announce an engagement and suddenly the picture would make a whole lot of sense. Good sense.'

Her green eyes narrowed. 'This photo doesn't bother me. It will blow over. We're both single. Who even cares?' He'd been stunned to see the expression in his eyes as he'd looked into her face in the photo. It had looked as if he wanted to have her for dessert. Had she noticed? No wonder the gossip site had drawn a conclusion of romantic intrigue.

'If you're so indifferent, why not help me out?' he said. 'Be my fake fiancée, just until after Christmas.'

'Christmas is nearly a month away. Twenty-five days, to be precise. For twenty-five days I'd have to pretend to be your fiancée?'

'So you're considering it? Because we've already been "outed", so to speak, it wouldn't come out of the blue. It would be believable.'

'Huh! We've only known each other for two weeks. Who would believe it?'

'People get married on less acquaintance,' he said.

'Not people like me,' she said.

'You don't think anyone would believe you could be smitten by me in that time? I think I'm offended.'

'Of course not,' she said. 'I… I believe many women would be smitten by you. You're handsome, intelligent—'

'And personable, yes, you said. Though I bet you don't think I'm so personable right now.'

She glared at him, though there was a lilt to the corners of her mouth that made it seem like she might want to smile. 'You could be right about that.'

'Now to you—gorgeous, sexy, smart Andie Newman.' Her blush deepened as he sounded each adjective. 'People would certainly believe I could be instantly smitten with such a woman,' he said. 'In fact they'd think I was clever getting a ring on your finger so quickly.'

That flustered her. 'Th…thank you. I… I'm flattered. But it wouldn't seem authentic. We'd have to pretend so much. It would be such deception.'

With any other woman, he'd be waiting for her to ask: *What's in it for me?* Not Andie. He doubted the thought of a reward for her participation had even entered her head. He would have to entice her with an offer she couldn't refuse. And save the big gun to sway her from her final refusal.

'So you're going to say "yes"?'

She shook her head vehemently. 'No. I'm not. It wouldn't be right.'

'What's the harm? You'd be helping me out.'

She spun on her heel away from him and he faced her back view, her tensely hunched shoulders, for a long moment before she turned back to confront him. 'Can't you see it makes a mockery of...of a man and a woman committing to each other? To spending their lives together in a loving union? That's what getting engaged is all about. Not sealing a business deal.'

He closed his eyes at the emotion in her voice, the blurring of her words with choking pain. Under his breath he cursed fluently. Because, from any moral point of view, she was absolutely right.

'Were you engaged to...to Anthony?' he asked.

Her eyes when she lifted them to him glistened with the sheen of unshed tears. 'Not officially. But we had our future planned, even the names of our kids chosen. That's why I know promising to marry someone isn't something you do lightly. And not...not for a scam. Do you understand?'

Of course he did. He'd once been idealistic about love and marriage and sharing his life with that one special woman. But he couldn't admit it. Or that he'd become cynical that that kind of love would ever exist for him. Too much rode on this deal. Including his integrity.

'But this isn't really getting engaged,' he said. 'It's just...a limited agreement.'

Slowly she shook her head. 'I can't help you,' she said. 'Sorry.'

Dominic braced himself. He'd had to be ruthless at times to get where he'd got. To overcome the disadvantages of his youth. *To win.*

'What if by agreeing to be my fake fiancée you were helping someone else?' he said.

She frowned. 'Like who? Helping Walter Burton to make even more billions? I honestly can't say I like the sound of that guy, linking business to people's private lives. He sounds like a hypocrite, for one thing—you know, rich men and eyes of needles and all that. I'm not lying for him.'

'Not Walter Burton. I mean your nephew Timothy.' The little boy was his big gun.

'What do you mean, Timothy?'

Dominic fired his shot. 'Agree to be my fake fiancée and I will pay for all of Timothy's medical treatment—both immediate and ongoing. No limits. Hannah tells me there's a clinic in the United States that's at the forefront of research into treatment for his condition.'

Andie stared at him. 'You've spoken to Hannah? You've told Hannah about this? That you'll pay for Timothy if I agree to—'

He put up his hand. 'Not true.'

'But you—'

'I met with Hannah the day after the dinner with your family to talk about her helping me recruit the families for the party. At that meeting—out of interest—I asked her to tell me more about Timothy. She told me about the American treatment. I offered *then* to pay all the treatment—airfares and accommodation included.'

The colour rushed back into Andie's cheeks. 'That...that was extraordinarily generous of you. What did Hannah say?'

'She refused.'

'Of course she would. She hardly knows you. A Newman wouldn't accept charity. Although I might have tried to convince her.'

'Maybe you could convince her now. If Hannah thought I was going to be part of the family—her brother-in-law, in fact—she could hardly refuse to accept, could she? And isn't it the sooner the better for Timothy's treatment?'

Andie stared at Dominic for a very long moment, too shocked to speak. 'Th...that's coercion. Coercion of the most insidious kind,' she finally managed to choke out.

A whole lot more words she couldn't express also tumbled around in her brain. Ruthless. Conniving. Heartless. And yet... he'd offered to help Timothy well before the fake fiancée thing. *Not a Scrooge after all.* She'd thought she'd been getting to know him—but Dominic Hunt was more of a mystery to her than ever.

He drew his dark brows together. 'Coercion? I wouldn't go that far. But I did offer to help Timothy without any strings attached. Hannah refused. This way, she might accept. And your nephew will get the help he needs. I see it as a win-win scenario.'

Andie realised she was twisting the leather thronging that laced together the front of her top and stopped it. Nothing in her life had equipped her to make this kind of decision. 'You're really putting me on the spot here. Asking me to lie and be someone I'm not—'

'Someone you're not? How does that work? You'd still be Andie.'

She found it difficult to meet his direct, confronting gaze. Those observant grey eyes seemed to see more than she wanted him to. 'You're asking me to pretend to be…to pretend to be a woman in love. When…when I'm not.' She'd only ever been in love once—and she didn't want to trawl back in her memories to try and relive that feeling—love lost hurt way too much. She did have feelings for Dominic beyond the employer/contractor relationship—but they were more of the other 'l' word—lust rather than love.

His eyes seemed to darken. 'I suppose I am.'

'And you too,' she said. 'You would have to pretend to be in love with…with me. And it would have to look darn authentic to be convincing.'

This was why she was prevaricating. As soon as he'd mentioned Timothy, she knew she would have little choice but to agree. If it had been any other blackmailing billionaire she would probably have said "yes" straight away—living a lie for a month would be worth it for Timothy to get the treatment her family's combined resources couldn't afford.

But not *this* man. How could she blithely *pretend* to be in love with a man she wanted as much as she wanted him? It would be some kind of torture.

'I see,' he said. Had he seriously not thought this through?

'We would be playing with big emotions, here, Dominic. And other people would be affected too. My family thinks you hung the moon. They'd be delighted if we dated—a sudden engagement would both shock and worry them. At some stage I would have to introduce you to Anthony's parents—they would be happy for me and want to meet you.'

'I see where you're going,' he said, raking his hand through his hair once more in a gesture that was becoming familiar.

She narrowed her eyes. 'And yet…would it all be worth it for Hannah to accept your help for Timothy?' She put up her hand to stop him from replying. 'I'm thinking out loud here.'

'And helping me achieve something I really want.'

There must be something more behind his drive to get this American deal. She hoped she'd discover it one day, sooner rather than later. It might help her understand him.

'You've backed me into a corner here, Dominic, and I can't say I appreciate it. How can I say "no" to such an incredible opportunity for Timothy?'

'Does that mean your answer is "yes"?'

She tilted her chin upwards—determined not to capitulate too readily to something about which she still had serious doubts. 'That's an unusual way to put it, Dominic—rather like you've made me a genuine proposal.'

Dominic pulled a face but it didn't dull the glint of triumph in his eyes. He thought he'd won. But she was determined to get something out of this deal for herself too.

Andie had no doubt if she asked for recompense—money, gifts—he'd give it to her. Dominic was getting what he wanted. Timothy would be getting what he so desperately needed. But what about *her*?

She wasn't interested in jewellery or fancy shopping. What she wanted was *him*. She wanted to kiss him, she wanted to hold him and she very much wanted to make love with him. Not for fake—for real.

There was a very good chance this arrangement would end in tears—her tears. But if she agreed to a fake engagement with this man, who attracted her like no other, she wanted what a fiancée might be expected to have—*him*. She thought, with a little shiver of desire, about what he'd said: *pleasure all the way*. She would be fine with that.

'Would it help if I made it sound like a genuine proposal?' he said, obviously bemused.

That hurt. Because the way he spoke made it sound as if there was no way he would ever make a genuine proposal to her. Not that she wanted that—heck, she hardly knew the guy. But it put her on warning. *Let's be honest,* she thought. She wanted him in her bed. But she also wanted to make darn sure she didn't get hurt. This was just a business deal to him—nothing personal involved.

'Do it,' she said, pointing to the floor. 'The full down-on-bended-knee thing.'

'Seriously?' he said, dark brows raised.

'Yes,' she said imperiously.

He grinned. 'Okay.'

The tall, black denim-clad hunk obediently knelt down on one knee, took her left hand in both of his and looked up into her face. 'Andie, will you do me the honour of becoming my fake fiancée?' he intoned in that deep, so-sexy voice.

Looking down at his roughly handsome face, Andie didn't know whether to laugh or cry. 'Yes, I accept your proposal,' she said in a voice that wasn't quite steady.

Dominic squeezed her hand hard as relief flooded his face. He got up from bended knee and for a moment she thought he might kiss her.

'But there are conditions,' she said, pulling away and letting go of his hand.

CHAPTER NINE

ANDIE ALMOST LAUGHED out loud at Dominic's perplexed expression. He was most likely used to calling the shots—in both business and his relationships. 'Conditions?' he asked.

'Yes, conditions,' she said firmly. 'Come on over to the sofa and I'll run through the list with you. I need to sit down; these heels aren't good for pacing in.' The polished concrete floor was all about looks rather than comfort.

'Do I have any choice about these "conditions"?' he grumbled.

'I think you'll see the sense in them,' she said. This was not going to go all his way. There was danger in this game she'd been coerced into playing and she wanted to make sure she and her loved ones were not going to get hurt by it.

She led him over to the red leather modular sofa in the living area. The apartment in an old converted factory warehouse was owned by one of her roommates and had been furnished stylishly with Andie's help. She flopped down on the sofa, kicked off the leopard stilettos that landed in an animal print clash on the zebra-patterned floor rug, and patted the seat next to her.

As Dominic sat down, his muscular thighs brushed against hers and she caught her breath until he settled at a not-quite-touching distance from her, his arm resting on the back of the sofa behind her. She had to close her eyes momentarily to deal with the rush of awareness from his already familiar scent, the sheer maleness of him in such close proximity.

'I'm interested to hear what you say,' he said, angling his powerful body towards her. He must work out a lot to have a chest like that. She couldn't help but wonder what it would feel like to splay her hands against those hard muscles, to press her body against his.

But it appeared he was having no such sensual thoughts about *her.* She noticed he gave a surreptitious glance to his watch.

'Hey, no continually checking on the clock,' she said. 'You have to give time to an engagement. Especially a make-believe one, if we're to make it believable. Not to mention your fake fiancée just might feel a tad insulted.'

She made her voice light but she meant every word of it. She had agreed to play her role in this charade and was now committed to making it work.

'Fair enough,' he said with a lazy half-smile. 'Is that one of your conditions?'

'Not one on its own as such, but it will fit into the others.'

'Okay, hit me with the conditions.' He feinted a boxer's defence that made her smile.

'Condition Number One,' she said, holding up the index finger of her left hand. 'Hannah never knows the truth—not now, not ever—that our engagement is a sham,' she said. 'In fact, none of my family is *ever* to know the truth.'

'Good strategy,' said Dominic. 'In fact, I'd extend that. *No one* should ever know. Both business partners and friends.'

'Agreed,' she said. It would be difficult to go through with this without confiding in a friend but it had to be that way. *No one must know how deeply attracted she was to him.* She didn't want anyone's pity when she and Dominic went their separate ways.

'Otherwise, the fallout from people discovering they'd been deceived could be considerable,' he said. 'What's next?'

She held up her middle finger. 'Condition Number Two—a plausible story. We need to explain why we got engaged so quickly. So start thinking…'

'Couldn't we just have fallen for each other straight away?'

Andie was taken aback. She hadn't expected anything that romantic from Dominic Hunt. 'You mean like "love at first sight"?'

'Exactly.'

'Would that be believable?'

He shook his head in mock indignation. 'Again you continue to insult me…'

'I didn't mean…' She'd certainly felt *something* for him at first sight. Sitting next to him on this sofa, she was feeling it all over again. But it wasn't *love*—she knew only too well what it was like to love. To love and to lose the man she loved in such a cruel way. Truth be told, she wasn't sure she wanted to love again. It hurt too much to lose that love.

'I don't like the lying aspect of this any more than you do,' he said. He removed his arm from the back of the sofa so he could lean closer to her, both hands resting on his knees. 'Why not stick to the truth as much as possible? You came to organise my party. I was instantly smitten, wooed you and won you.'

'And I was a complete walkover,' she said dryly.

'So we change it—you made me work very hard to win you.'

'In two weeks—and you away for one of them?' she said. 'Good in principle. But we might have to fudge the timeline a little.'

'It can happen,' he said. 'Love at first sight, I mean. My parents…apparently they fell for each other on day one and were married within mere months of meeting. Or so my aunt told me.'

His eyes darkened and she remembered he'd only been eleven years old when left an orphan. If she'd lost her parents at that age, her world would have collapsed around her—as no doubt his had. But he was obviously trying to revive a happy memory of his parents.

'How lovely—a real-life romance. Did they meet in Australia or England?'

'London. They were both schoolteachers; my mother was living in England. She came to his school as a temporary mathematics teacher; he taught chemistry.'

Andie decided not to risk a feeble joke about their meeting being explosive. Not when the parents' love story had ended in tragedy. 'No wonder you're clever then, with such smart parents.'

'Yes,' he said, making the word sound like an end-of-story punctuation mark. She knew only too well what it was like not to want to pursue a conversation about a lost loved one.

'So we have a precedent for love at first sight in your family,' she said. 'I… I fell for Anthony straight away too. So for both of us an…an instant attraction—if not *love*—could be feasible.' Instant and ongoing for her—but he was not to know that.

That Dominic had talked about his parents surprised her. For her, thinking about Anthony—as always—brought a tug of pain to her heart but this time also a reminder of the insincerity of this venture with Dominic. She knew what real commitment should feel like. But for Timothy to get that vital treatment she was prepared to compromise on her principles.

'Love at first sight it is,' he said.

'*Attraction* at first sight,' she corrected him.

'Surely it would had to have led to love for us to get engaged,' he said.

'True,' she conceded. He tossed around concepts of love and commitment as if they were concepts with which to barter, not deep, abiding emotions between two people who cared enough about each other to pledge a lifetime together. *Till death us do part.* She could never think of that part of a marriage ceremony without breaking down. She shouldn't be thinking of it now.

'Next condition?' he said.

She skipped her ring finger, which she had trouble keeping upright, and went straight for her pinkie. 'Condition Number

Three: no dating other people—for the duration of the engagement, that is.'

'I'm on board with that one,' he said without hesitation.

'Me too,' she said. She hadn't even thought about any man but Dominic since the moment she'd met him, so that was not likely to be a hardship.

He sat here next to her in jeans and T-shirt like a regular thirty-two-year-old guy—not a secretive billionaire who had involved her in a scheme to deceive family and friends to help him make even more money. If he were just your everyday handsome hunk she would make her interest in him known. But her attraction went beyond his good looks and muscles to the complex man she sensed below his confident exterior. She had seen only intriguing hints of those hidden depths—she wanted to discover more.

Andie's thumb went up next. 'Resolution Number Four: I dump you, not the other way around. When this comes to an end, that is.'

'Agreed—and I'll be a gentleman about it. But I ask you not to sell your story. I don't want to wake up one morning to the headline *"My Six Weeks with Scrooge"*.'

He could actually *joke* about being a Scrooge—Dominic had come a long way.

'Of course,' she said. 'I promise not to say *"I Hopped Out of the Billionaire's Bed"* either. Seriously, I would never talk to the media. You can be reassured of that.'

'No tacky headlines, just a simple civilised break-up to be handled by you,' he said.

They both fell silent for a moment. Did he feel stricken by the same melancholy she did at the thought of the imagined break-up of a fake engagement? And she couldn't help thinking she'd like a chance to hop *into* his bed before she hopped *out* of it.

'On to Condition Number Five,' she said, holding up all five fingers as she could not make her ring finger stand on its own. 'We have to get to know each other. So we don't get caught out on stuff we would be expected to know about each other if we were truly…committing to a life together.'

How different this fake relationship would be to a real relationship—getting to know each other over shared experiences, shared laughter, shared tears, long lazy mornings in bed…

Dominic sank down further into the sofa, his broad shoulders hunched inward. 'Yup.' It was more a grunt than a word.

'You don't sound keen to converse?'

'What sort of things?' he said with obvious reluctance. Not for the first time, she had a sense of secrets deeply held.

'For one thing, I need to know more about your marriage and how it ended.' And more about his time on the streets. And about that broken nose and scarred knuckles. And why he had let people believe he was a Scrooge when he so obviously wasn't. Strictly speaking, she probably didn't *need* to know all that about him for a fake engagement. Fact was, she *wanted* to know it.

'I guess I can talk to you about my marriage,' he said, still not sounding convinced. 'But there are things about my life that I would rather remain private.'

What things? 'Just so long as I'm not made a fool of at some stage down the track by not knowing something a real fiancée would have known.'

'Fine,' he grunted in a response that didn't give her much confidence. She ached to know more about him. And yet there was that shadow she sensed. She wouldn't push for simple curiosity's sake.

'As far as I'm concerned, my life's pretty much an open book,' she said, in an effort to encourage him to open up about his life—or past, to be more specific. 'Just ask what you need to know about me and I'll do my best to answer honestly.'

Was any person's life truly an open book? Like anyone else, she had doubts and anxieties and dumb things she'd done that she'd regretted, but nothing lurked that she thought could hinder an engagement. No one would criticise her for finding love again after five years. In truth, she knew they would be glad for her. So would Anthony.

She remembered one day, lying together on the beach. *'I would die if I lost you,'* she'd said to Anthony.

'Don't say that,' he'd said. *'If anything happened to me, I'd want you to find another guy. But why are we talking like this? We're both going to live until we're a hundred.'*

'Why not schedule in a question-and-answer session?' Dominic said.

She pulled her thoughts back to the present. 'Good idea,' she said. 'Excellent idea, in fact.'

Dominic rolled his eyes in response.

'Oh,' she said. 'You weren't serious. I… I was.'

'No, you're right. I guess there's no room for spontaneity in a fake engagement.' It was a wonder he could get the words out when his tongue was so firmly in his cheek. 'A question-and-answer session it is. At a time to be determined.'

'Good idea,' she said, feeling disconcerted. Was all this just a game to him?

'Are there any more conditions to come?' he asked. 'You're all out of fingers on one hand, by the way.'

'There is one more very important condition to come—and may I remind you I do have ten fingers—but first I want to hear if there's anything you want to add.'

She actually had two more conditions, but the final condition she could not share with him: *that she could not fall for him.* She couldn't deal with the fallout in terms of pain if she were foolish enough to let down the guard on her heart.

Andie's beautiful green eyes had sparkled with good humour in spite of the awkward position he had put her into. *Coerced* her into. But now her eyes seemed to dim and Dominic wondered if she was being completely honest about being an 'open book'.

Ironically, he already knew more about Andie, the fake fiancée, than he'd known about Tara when he'd got engaged to her for real. His ex-wife had kept her true nature under wraps until well after she'd got the wedding band on her finger. *What you see is what you get.* He so wanted to believe that about Andie.

'My condition? You have to wear a ring,' he said. 'I want to get you an engagement ring straight away. Today. Once Tara sees that she'll know it's serious. And the press will too. Not to mention a symbol for when we meet with Walter Burton.'

She shrugged. 'Okay, you get me a ring.'

'You don't want to choose it yourself?' He was taken aback. Tara had been so avaricious about jewellery.

'No. I would find it…sad. Distressing. The day I choose my engagement ring is the day I get engaged for real. To me, the ring should be a symbol of a true commitment, not a…a prop for a charade. But I agree—I should wear one as a visible sign of commitment.'

'I'll organise it then,' he said. He had no idea why he should be disappointed at her lack of enthusiasm. She was absolutely right—the ring would be a prop. But it would also play a role in keeping it believable. 'What size ring do you wear?'

'I haven't a clue,' she said. She held up her right hand to show the collection of tiny fine silver rings on her slender fingers. Her nails were painted cream today. 'I bought these at a market and just tried them on until I found rings that fitted.' She slid off the ring from the third finger of her right hand. 'This should do the trick.' She handed it to him. It was still warm with her body heat and he held it on his palm for a moment before pocketing it.

'What style of engagement ring would you like?' he asked.

Again she shrugged. 'You choose. It's honestly not important to me.'

A hefty carat solitaire diamond would be appropriate—one that would give her a good resale value when she went to sell it after this was all over.

'Did you choose your ex-wife's engagement ring?' Andie asked.

He scowled at the reminder that he had once got engaged for real.

Andie pulled one of her endearing faces. 'Sorry. I guess that's a sensitive issue. I know we'll come to all that in our question-and-answer session. I'm just curious.'

'She chose it herself. All I had to do was pay for it.' That alone should have alerted him to what the marriage was all about—giving her access to his money and the lifestyle it bought.

'That wasn't very…romantic,' Andie said.

'There was nothing romantic about my marriage. Shall I tell you about it now and get all that out of the way?'

'If you feel comfortable with it,' she said.

'Comfortable is never a word I would relate to that time of my life,' he said. 'It was a series of mistakes.'

'If you're ready to tell me, I'm ready to listen.' He thought about how Andie had read his mood so accurately earlier this morning—giving him breakfast when he hadn't even been aware himself that he was hungry. She was thoughtful. And kind. Kindness wasn't an attribute he had much encountered in the women he had met.

'The first mistake I made with Tara was that she reminded me of someone else—a girl I'd met when I was living in the squat. Someone frail and sweet with similar colouring—someone I'd wanted to care for and look after.' It still hurt to think of Melody. Andie didn't need to know about her.

'And the second mistake?' Andie asked, seeming to understand he didn't want to speak further about Melody. She leaned forward as if she didn't want to miss a word.

'I believed her when she said she wanted children.'

'You wanted children?'

'As soon as possible. Tara said she did too.'

Andie frowned. 'But she didn't?'

Even now, bitterness rose in his throat. 'After we'd been married a year and nothing had happened, I suggested we see a doctor. Tara put it off and put it off. I thought it was because she didn't want to admit to failure. It was quite by accident that I discovered all the time I thought we'd been trying to conceive, she'd been on the contraceptive pill.'

Andie screwed up her face in an expression of disbelief and distaste. 'That's unbelievable.'

'When I confronted her, she laughed.' He relived the horror of discovering his ex-wife's treachery and the realisation she didn't have it in her to love. Not him. Certainly not a child. Fortunately, she hadn't been clever enough to understand the sub-clauses in the pre-nuptial agreement and divorce had been relatively straightforward.

'You had a lucky escape,' Andie said.

'That's why I never want to marry again. How could I ever trust another woman after that?'

'I understand you would feel that way,' she said. 'But not every woman would be like her. Me…my sisters, my friends. I don't know anyone who would behave with such dishonesty. Don't write off all women because of one.'

Trouble was, his wealth attracted women like Tara.

He was about to try and explain that to Andie when her phone started to sound out a bar of classical music.

She got up from the sofa and headed for the kitchen countertop to pick it up. 'Gemma,' she mouthed to him. 'I'd better take it.'

He nodded, grateful for the reprieve. Tara's treachery had got him into this fake engagement scenario with Andie, who was being such a good sport about the whole thing. He did not want to waste another word, or indeed thought, on his ex. Again, he thanked whatever providence had sent Andie into his life—Andie who was the opposite of Tara in every way.

He couldn't help but overhear Andie as she chatted to Gemma. 'Yes, yes, I saw it. We were having lunch after the meeting that Friday. Yes, it does look romantic. No, I didn't know anyone took a photo.'

Andie waved him over to her. 'Shall I tell her?' she mouthed.

He gave her the thumbs-up. 'Yes,' he mouthed back as he got up. There was no intention of keeping this 'engagement' secret. He walked over closer to Andie, who was standing there in bare feet, looking more beautiful in jeans than any other woman would look in a ball gown.

'Actually, Gemma, I…haven't been completely honest with you. I…uh…we…well, Dominic and I hit it off from the moment we first saw each other.'

Andie looked to Dominic and he nodded—she was doing well.

She listened to Gemma, then spoke again. 'Yes. We are… romantically involved. In fact…well…we're engaged.' She held the phone out from her ear and even Dominic could hear the excited squeals coming from Gemma.

When the squeals had subsided, Andie spoke again. 'Yes. It is sudden. I know that. But…well…you see I've learned that you have to grab your chance at happiness when you can. I… I've had it snatched away from me before.' She paused as she listened. 'Yes, that's it. I didn't want to wait. Neither did he. Gemma, I'd appreciate it if you didn't tell anyone just yet. Eliza? Well, okay, you can tell Eliza. I'd just like to tell my family first. What was that? Yes, I'll tell him.' She shut down her phone.

'So it's out,' he said.

'Yes,' she said. 'No denying it now.'

'What did Gemma ask you to tell me?'

She looked up at him. 'That she hoped you knew what a lucky guy you are to…to catch me.'

He looked down at her. 'I know very well how lucky I am. You're wonderful in every way and I appreciate what you're doing to help me.'

For a long moment he looked down into her face—still, serious, even sombre without her usual animated expression. Her eyes were full of something he couldn't put a name to. But not, he hoped, regret.

'Thank you, Andie.'

He stepped closer. For a long moment her gaze met his and held it. He saw wariness but he also saw the stirrings of what he could only read as invitation. To kiss his pretend fiancée would probably be a mistake. But it was a mistake he badly wanted to make.

He lifted his hand to her face, brushed first the smooth skin of her cheek and then the warm softness of her lips with the back of his knuckles. She stilled. Her lips parted under his touch and he could feel the tremor that ran through her body. He dropped his hand to her shoulder, then dipped his head and claimed her mouth in a firm gentle kiss. She murmured her surprise and pleasure as she kissed him back.

CHAPTER TEN

DOMINIC WAS KISSING her and it was more wonderful than Andie ever could have imagined. His firm, sensuous mouth was sure and certain on hers and she welcomed the intimate caress, the nudging of his tongue against the seam of her lips as she opened her mouth to his. His beard growth scratched her face but it was a pleasurable kind of pain. *The man knew how to kiss.*

But as he kissed her and she kissed him back she was shocked by the sudden explosion of chemistry between them that turned something gentle into something urgent and demanding. She wound her arms around his neck to bring him closer in a wild tangle of tongues and lips as she pressed herself against his hard muscular chest. He tasted of coffee and hot male and desire. Passion this instant, this insistent was a surprise.

But it was too soon.

She knew she wanted him. But she hadn't realised until now just how *much* she wanted him. And how careful she would have to be to guard her heart. Because these thrilling kisses told her that intimate contact with Dominic Hunt might just become an addiction she would find very difficult to live without. To him, this pretend engagement was a business ploy that might also develop into an entertaining game on the side. *She did not want to be a fake fiancée with benefits.*

When it came down to it, while she had dated over the last few years, her only serious relationship had been with a boy who had adored her, and whom she had loved with all her heart. Not a man like Dominic, who had sworn off marriage and viewed commitment so lightly he could pretend to be engaged. Her common sense urged her to stop but her body wanted more, more, more of him.

With a great effort she broke away from the kiss. Her heart was pounding in triple time, her breath coming in painful gasps. She took a deep steadying breath. And then another.

'That…that was a great start on Condition Number Six,' she managed to choke out.

Dominic towered over her; his breath came in ragged gasps. He looked so darkly sensual, her heart seemed to flip right over in her chest. 'What?' he demanded. 'Stopping when we'd just started?'

'No. I… I mean the actual kiss.'

He put his hand on her shoulder, lightly stroking her in a caress that ignited shivers of delight all through her.

'So tell me about your sixth condition,' he said, his deep voice with a broken edge to it as he struggled to control his breathing.

'Condition Number Six is that we…we have to look the part.'

He frowned. 'And that means…?'

'I mean we have to act like a genuine couple. To seem to other people as if we're…we're crazy about each other. Because it would have to be…something very powerful between us for us to get engaged so quickly. In…real life, I mean.'

She found it difficult to meet his eyes. 'I was going to say we needed to get physical. And we just did…get physical. So we…uh…know that there's chemistry between us. And that… that it works.'

He dropped his hand from her shoulder to tilt her chin upwards with his finger so she was forced to meet his gaze. 'There was never any doubt about that.'

His words thrummed through her body. That sexual attraction had been there for her the first time she'd met him. *Had he felt it too?*

'So the sixth condition is somewhat superfluous,' she said, her voice racing as she tried to ignore the hunger for him his kiss had ignited. 'I think we might be okay, there. You know, holding hands, arms around each other. Appropriate Public Displays of Affection.' It was an effort to force herself to sound matter of fact.

'This just got to be my favourite of all your conditions,' he said slowly, his eyes narrowing in a way she found incredibly sexy. 'Shall we practise some more?'

Her traitorous body wrestled down her hopelessly outmatched common sense. 'Why not?' she murmured, desperate to be in his arms again. He pulled her close and their body contact made her aware he wanted her as much as she wanted him. She sighed as she pressed her mouth to his.

Then her phone sang out its ringtone of a piano sonata.

'Leave it,' growled Dominic.

She ignored the musical tone until it stopped. But it had brought her back to reality. There was nothing she wanted more than to take Dominic by the hand and lead him up the stairs to her bedroom. She intended to have him before this contract between them came to an end.

But that intuition she usually trusted screamed at her that to make love with him on the first day of their fake engagement would be a mistake. It would change the dynamic of their relationship to something she did not feel confident of being able to handle.

No sooner had the ringtone stopped than it started again.

Andie untangled herself from Dominic's embrace and stepped right back from him, back from the seductive reach of his muscular arms.

'I… I have to take this,' she said.

She answered the phone but had to rest against the kitchen countertop to support knees that had gone shaky and weak.

Dominic leaned back against the wall opposite her and crossed his arms against his powerful chest. His muscles flexed as he did so and she had to force herself to concentrate on the phone call.

'Yes, Eliza, it's true. I know—it must have been a surprise to you. A party?' Andie looked up to Dominic and shook her head. He nodded. She spoke to Eliza. 'No. We don't want an engagement party. Yes, I know we're party queens and it's what we do.' She rolled her eyes at Dominic and, to her relief, he smiled. 'The Christmas party is more than enough to handle at the moment,' she said to Eliza.

We. She and Dominic were a couple now. A fake couple. It would take some getting used to. So would handling the physical attraction between them.

'The wedding?' Eliza's question about the timing of the wedding flustered her. 'We...we...uh...next year some time. Yes, I know next year is only next month. The wedding won't be next month, that's for sure.' *The* wedding—wouldn't a loved-up fiancée have said *our* wedding?

She finished the call to Eliza and realised her hands were clammy. 'This is not going to be easy,' she said to Dominic.

'I never thought it would be,' he said. Was there a double meaning there?

'I have no experience in this kind of deception. The first thing Eliza asked me was when are we getting married. She put me on the spot. I... I struggled to find an answer.'

He nodded slowly. 'I suggest we say we've decided on a long engagement. That we're committed but want to use the engagement time to get to know each other better.'

'That sounds good,' she said.

The deceptive words came so easily to him while she was so flustered she could scarcely think. She realised how hopelessly mismatched they were: he was more experienced, wealthier, from a completely different background. And so willing to lie.

And yet... That kiss had only confirmed how much she wanted him.

Her phone rang out again. 'Why do I get the feeling this phone will go all day long?' she said, a note of irritation underscoring her voice. She looked on the caller ID. 'It's my fashion editor friend, Karen. I knew Gemma wouldn't be able to stop at Eliza,' she told Dominic as she answered it.

The first part of the conversation was pretty much a repeat of the conversation she'd had with Gemma. But then Karen asked should she start scouting around for her wedding dress. Karen hunted down bargain-priced clothes for her; of course she'd want to help her with a wedding. 'My wedding dress? We… uh…haven't set a date for the wedding yet. Yes, I suppose it's never too early to think about the dress. Simple? Vintage inspired? Gorgeous shoes?' She laughed and hoped Karen didn't pick up on the shrill edge to her laughter. 'You know my taste only too well, Karen. A veil? A modest lace veil? Okay. Yes. I'll leave it to you. Thank you.'

'Your friends move fast,' Dominic said when she'd disconnected the call.

'They're so thrilled for me. After…after…well, you know. My past.' Her past of genuine love, unsullied by lies and deception.

'Of course,' he said.

She couldn't bring herself to say anything about the kisses they'd shared. It wasn't the kind of thing she found easy to talk about. Neither, it appeared, did he.

He glanced down at his watch. The action drew her attention to his hands. She noticed again how attractive they were, with long strong fingers. And thought how she would like to feel them on her body. Stroking. Caressing. Exploring. *She had to stop this.*

'I know I'm breaking the terms of one of your conditions,' he said. 'But I do have to get to the office. There are cancelled meetings in other states to reschedule and staff who need to talk to me.'

'And I've got to finalise the furniture hire for the Christmas party. With two hundred people for lunch, we need more tables and chairs. It's sobering, to have all those families in need on Christmas Day.'

'Hannah assures me it's the tip of a tragic iceberg,' said Dominic.

They both paused for a long moment before she spoke. 'I also have to work on a tiaras-and-tuxedos-themed twenty-first party. Ironic, isn't it, after what we've just been saying?' But organising parties was her job and brought not only employment to her and her partners but also the caterers, the waiting staff and everyone else involved.

'I didn't think twenty-first parties were important any more, with eighteen the legal age of adulthood,' Dominic said.

'They're still very popular. This lovely girl turning twenty-one still lives at home with her parents and has three more years of university still ahead of her to become a veterinarian. I have to organise tiaras for her dogs.'

'Wh...what?' he spluttered. 'Did you say you're putting a tiara on a *dog*?'

'Her dogs are very important to her; they'll be honoured guests at the party.'

He scowled. 'I like dogs but that's ridiculous.'

'We're getting more and more bookings for dog parties. A doggy birthday boy or girl invites their doggy friends. They're quite a thing. And getting as competitive as the kids' parties. Of course it's a learning curve for a party planner—considering doggy bathroom habits, for one thing.'

'That is the stupidest—'

Andie put up her hand. 'Don't be too quick to judge. The doggy parties are really about making the humans happy—I doubt the dogs could care less. Frivolity can be fun. Eliza and I have laid bets on how many boys will arrive wearing tiaras to the vet student's twenty-first.'

She had to smile at his bah-humbug expression.

'By the time I was twenty-one, I had established a career in real estate and had my first million in sight.'

That interested her. 'I'd love to know about—'

He cut her off. 'Let's save that for the question-and-answer session, shall we?'

'Which will start…?'

'This afternoon. Can you come to my place?'

'Sure. It doesn't hurt to visit the party site as many times as I can.'

'Only this time you'll be coming to collect your engagement ring.'

'Of…of course.' She had forgotten about that. In a way, she dreaded it. 'And to find out more about you, fake fiancé. We have to be really well briefed to face my family tomorrow evening.'

She and Anthony had joked that by the time they'd paid off their student loans all they'd be able to afford for an engagement ring would be a ring pull from a can of soft drink. The ring pull would have had so much more meaning than this cynical exercise.

She felt suddenly subdued at the thought of deceiving her family. Her friends were used to the ups and downs of dating. A few weeks down the track, they'd take a broken engagement in their stride. If those kisses were anything to go by, she might be more than a tad upset when her time with Dominic came to an end. She pummelled back down to somewhere deep inside her the shred of hope that perhaps something real could happen between them after the engagement charade was done.

'When will you tell your parents?' Dominic asked.

'Today. They'd be hurt beyond belief if they found out from someone else.'

'And you'll talk to Hannah about Timothy?'

'At the family dinner. We should speak to her and Paul together.'

'I hope she won't be too difficult to convince. I really want to help that little boy.'

'I know,' she said, thinking of how grateful her family would be to him. How glad she was she'd agreed to all this for her tiny nephew's sake. But what about Dominic's family? This shouldn't be all about hers. 'What about your aunt? Do we need to tell her?'

The shutters came slamming down. 'No. She's out of the picture.'

The way he said it let her know not to ask more. Not now anyway.

Dominic shrugged on his leather jacket in preparation to go. She stared, dumbstruck, feasting her eyes on him. *He was so hot.* She still felt awkward after their passionate kissing session. Should she reach up and kiss him on the cheek?

While she was making up her mind, he pulled her close for a brief, exciting kiss on her mouth. She doubted there could be any other type of kiss but exciting from Dominic. 'Happy to fulfil Condition Number Six at any time,' he said, very seriously.

She smiled, the tension between them immediately dissipated. But she wasn't ready to say goodbye just yet.

'Before you go…' She picked up her smartphone again. 'The first thing my friends who don't know you will want to see is a photo of my surprise new fiancé.'

He ran his hand over his unshaven chin. 'Like this? Can't it wait?'

'I like your face like that. It's hot. No need to shave on my behalf.' Without thinking, she put her fingers up to her cheek, where there was probably stubble rash. *His kiss had felt so good.*

'If you say so,' he said, looking pleased.

'Just lean against the door there,' she said. 'Look cool.'

He slouched against the door and sent her a smouldering look. The wave of want that crashed through her made her nearly drop the phone. 'Do I look *cool*?' he said in a self-mocking tone. 'I thought you liked *hot*?'

'You know exactly what I mean.' She was discovering a light-hearted side to Dominic she liked very much.

Their gazes met and they both burst into laughter. He looked even more gorgeous when he laughed, perfect teeth white in his tanned face, and she immediately captured a few more images of him. Who would recognise this good-humoured hunk in jeans and leather jacket as the billionaire Scrooge of legend?

'What about a selfie of us together?' she asked. 'In the interests of authenticity,' she hastily added.

Bad idea. She stood next to him, aware of every centimetre of body contact, and held her phone out in front of them. She felt more self-conscious than she could ever remember feeling. He pulled her in so their faces were close together. She smiled and clicked, and as she clicked again he kissed her on the cheek.

'That will be cute,' she said.

'Another?' he asked. This time he kissed her on the mouth. *Click. Click. Click.* And then she forgot to click.

After he had left, Andie spent more minutes than she should scrolling through the photos on her phone. *No one would know they were faking it.*

CHAPTER ELEVEN

DOMINIC NOW KNEW more about diamond engagement rings than even a guy who was genuinely engaged to be married needed to know. He'd thought he could just march into Sydney's most exclusive jewellery store and hand over an investment-sized price for a big chunk of diamond. Not so.

The sales guy—rather, *executive consultant*—who had greeted him and ushered him into a private room had taken the purchase very seriously. He'd hit Dominic with a barrage of questions. It was unfortunate that the lady was unable to be there because it was very important the ring would suit her personality. What were the lady's favourite colours? What style of clothes did she favour? Her colouring?

'Were you able to answer the questions?' Andie asked, her lips curving into her delightful smile.

She had just arrived at his house. After she'd taken some measurements in the old ballroom, he had taken her out to sit in the white Hollywood-style chairs by the pool. Again, she looked as if she belonged. She wore a natural-coloured linen dress with her hair piled up and a scarf twisted and tied right from the base of her neck to the top of her head. It could have looked drab and old-fashioned but, on her, with her vintage sunglasses and orange lipstick, it looked just right.

Last time she'd been there he'd been so caught up with her he hadn't thought to ask her would she like a drink. He didn't want a live-in housekeeper—he valued his privacy too much—but his daily housekeeper had been this morning and the refrigerator was well stocked. He'd carried a selection of cool drinks out to the poolside table between their two chairs.

'You're finding this story amusing, aren't you?' he said, picking up his iced tea.

She took off her sunglasses. 'Absolutely. I had no idea the rigmarole involved in buying an engagement ring.'

'Me neither. I thought I'd just march in, point out a diamond ring and pay for it.' This was a first for him.

'Me too,' said Andie. 'I thought that's what guys did when they bought a ring.'

'Oh, no. First of all, I'd done completely the wrong thing in not having you with me. He was too discreet to ask where you were, so I didn't have to come up with a creative story to explain your absence.'

'One less lie required anyway,' she said with a twist of her lovely mouth. 'Go on with the story—I'm fascinated.'

'Apparently, the done thing is to have a bespoke ring—like the business suits I have made to measure.'

'A bespoke ring? Who knew?' she said, her eyes dancing.

'Instead, I had to choose from their ready-to-wear couture pieces.'

'I had no idea such a thing existed,' she said with obvious delight. *Her smile.* It made him feel what he'd thought he'd never feel again, made him want what he'd thought he'd never want.

'You should have been there,' he said. 'You would have had fun.' He'd spent the entire time in the jewellery store wishing she'd been by his side. He could imagine her suppressing giggles as the consultant had run through his over-the-top sales pitch.

'Perhaps,' she said, but her eyes dimmed. 'You know my reasons for not wanting to get involved in the purchase. Anyway, what did you tell them about my—' she made quote marks in the air with her fingers '—"personal style"? That must have put you on the spot?'

'I told the consultant about your misbehaving skirt—only I didn't call it that, of course. I told him about your shoes that laced up your calves. I told him about your turquoise necklace and your outsized earrings. I told him about your leopard-print shoes and your white trousers.'

Andie's eyes widened. 'You remember all that about what I wear?'

'I did say I was observant,' he said.

Ask him to remember what Party Planners Numbers One to Three had been wearing for their interviews and he would scarcely recall it. But he remembered every detail about her since that errant breeze at his front door had blown Andie into his life.

At the jewellery store, once he'd relaxed into the conversation with the consultant, Dominic had also told him how Andie was smart and creative and a touch unconventional and had the most beautiful smile and a husky, engaging laugh. 'This is a lucky lady,' the guy had said. 'You must love her very much.'

That had thrown Dominic. 'Yes,' he'd muttered. *Love* could not enter into this. He did not want Andie to get hurt. And hurt wasn't on his personal agenda either. He didn't think he had it in him to love. To give love you had to be loved—and genuine love was not something that had been part of his life.

'So… I'm curious,' said Andie. What kind of ring did you—did I—end up with?'

'Not the classic solitaire I would have chosen. The guy said you'd find it boring.'

'Of course I wouldn't have found it boring,' she said not very convincingly.

'Why do I not believe you?' he said.

'Stop teasing me and show me the darn ring,' she said.

Dominic took out the small, leather, case from his inside suit jacket pocket. 'I hope you like it,' he said. *He wanted her to like it.* He didn't know why it was suddenly so important that she did.

He opened the case and held it out for Andie to see. Her eyes widened and she caught her breath. 'It…it's exquisite,' she said.

'Is it something you think you could wear?' he asked.

'Oh, yes,' she said. 'I love it.'

'It's called a halo set ring,' he said. 'The ring of little diamonds that surround the big central diamond is the halo. And the very narrow split band—again set with small diamonds—is apparently very fashionable.'

'That diamond is enormous,' she said, drawing back. 'I'd be nervous to wear it.'

'I got it well insured,' he said.

'Good,' she said. 'If I lost it, I'd be paying you back for the rest of my life and probably still be in debt.'

'The ring is yours, Andie.'

'I know, for the duration,' she said. 'I promise to look after it.' She crossed her heart.

'You misunderstand. The ring is yours to keep after…after all this has come to an end.'

She frowned and shook her head vehemently. 'No. That wasn't part of the deal. Timothy's treatment was the deal. I give this ring back to you when…when I dump you.'

'We'll see about that,' he said, not wanting to get into an argument with her. As far as he was concerned, this ring was *hers.* She could keep it or sell it or give it away—he never wanted it back. 'Now, shouldn't I be getting that diamond on your finger?'

He was surprised to find his hand wasn't steady as he took the ring out of its hinged case. It glittered and sparkled as the afternoon sunlight danced off the multi-cut facets of the diamonds. 'Hold out your hand,' he said.

'No', she said, again shaking her head. 'Give it to me and I'll put it on myself. This isn't a real engagement and I don't want to jinx myself. When I get engaged for real, my real fiancé will put my ring on my wedding finger.'

Again, Dominic felt disappointed. Against all reason. He wanted to put the ring on her finger. But he understood why he shouldn't. He felt a pang of regret that he most likely would never again be anyone's 'real fiancé'—and a pang of what he recognised as envy for the man who would win Andie's heart for real.

He put the ring back in its case. 'You do want to get married one day?'

He wasn't sure if she was still in love with the memory of her first boyfriend—and that no man would be able to live up to that frozen-in-time ideal. Melody had been his first love—but he certainly held no romanticised memories of her.

'Of course I do. I want to get married and have a family. I… I… It took me a long time to get over the loss of my dreams of a life with Anthony. I couldn't see myself with anyone but him. But that was five years ago. Now… I think I'm ready to move on.'

Dominic had to clear his throat to speak. 'Okay, I see your point. Better put on the ring yourself,' he said.

Tentatively, she lifted the ring from where it nestled in the velvet lining of its case. 'I'm terrified I'll drop it and it will fall into the pool.' She laughed nervously as she slid it on to the third finger of her left hand. 'There—it's on.' She held out her hand, fingers splayed to better display the ring. 'It's a perfect fit,' she said. 'You did well.'

'It looks good on you,' he said.

'That sales guy knew his stuff,' she said. 'I can't stop looking at it. It's the most beautiful ring I've ever seen.' She looked up at him. 'I still have my doubts about the wisdom of this charade. But I will enjoy wearing this magnificent piece of jewellery. Thank you for choosing something so perfect.'

'Thank you for helping me out with this crazy scheme,' he said. The scheme that had seemed crazy the moment he'd proposed it and which got crazier and crazier as it went along. But it was important he sealed that deal with Walter Burton. And was it such a bad thing to have to spend so much time with Andie?

Andie took a deep breath to try and clear her head of the conflicting emotions aroused by wearing the exquisite ring that sat so perfectly on her finger. *The ring pull would have been so much more valuable.* This enormous diamond with its many surrounding tiny diamonds symbolised not love and commitment but the you-scratch-my-back-and-I'll-scratch-yours deal between her and Dominic.

Still, she couldn't help wondering how he could have chosen a ring so absolutely *her*.

'I've been thinking about our getting-to-know-each-other session,' she said. 'Why don't we each ask the other three questions?'

'Short and to the point,' he said with obvious relief.

'Or longer, as needs might be. I want to be the best fake fiancée I can. No way do I want to be caught out on something important I should know about you. I didn't like the feeling this morning when I froze as Karen questioned me about our wedding plans.'

Dominic drank from his iced tea. To give himself time to think? Or plan evasive action? 'I see where you're going. Let's see if we can make it work.'

Andie settled back in the chair. She didn't know whether to be disappointed or relieved there was a small table between her and Dominic. She would not be averse to his thigh nudged against hers—at the same time, it would undoubtedly be distracting. 'Okay. I'll start. My Question Number One is: How did you get from street kid to billionaire?'

Dominic took his time to put his glass back down on the table. 'Before I reply, let's get one thing straight.' His gaze was direct. 'My answers are for you and you alone. What I tell you is to go no further.'

'Agreed,' she said, meeting his gaze full-on. 'Can we get another thing straight? You can trust me.'

'Just so long as we know where we stand.'

'I'm surprised you're not making me sign a contract.' She said the words half in jest but the expression that flashed across his face in response made her pause. She sat forward in her seat. 'You thought about a contract, didn't you?'

With Dominic back in his immaculate dark business suit, clean-shaven, hair perfectly groomed, she didn't feel as confident with him as she had this morning.

'I did think of a contract and quickly dismissed it,' he said. 'I do trust you, Andie.'

Surely he must be aware that she would not jeopardise Timothy's treatment in any way? 'I'm glad to hear that, Dominic, because this won't work if we don't trust each other—it goes both ways. Let's start. C'mon—answer my question.'

He still didn't answer. She waited, aware of the palm leaves above rustling in the same slight breeze that ruffled the aquamarine surface of the pool, the distant barking of a neighbour's dog.

'You know I hate this?' he said finally.

'I kind of get that,' she said. 'But I couldn't "marry" a man whose past remained a dark secret to me.'

Even after the question-and-answer session, she suspected big chunks of his past might remain a secret from her. Maybe from anyone.

He dragged in a deep breath as if to prepare himself for something unpleasant. 'As I have already mentioned, at age seventeen, I was homeless. I was living in an underground car park on the site of an abandoned shopping centre project in one of the roughest areas of Brisbane. The buildings had only got to the foundation stage. The car park was...well, you can imagine what an underground car park that had never been completed was like. It was a labyrinth of unfinished service areas and elevator shafts. No lights, pools of water whenever it rained, riddled with rats and cockroaches.'

'And human vermin too, I'll bet.' Andie shuddered. 'What a scary place for a teenager to be living—and dangerous.'

He had come from such a dark place. She could gush with sympathy and pity. But she knew instinctively that was not what he wanted to hear. Show how deeply moved she was at the thought of seventeen-year-old Dominic living such a perilous life and he would clam up. And she wanted to hear more.

Dominic's eyes assumed a dark, faraway look as though he was going back somewhere in his mind he had no desire to revisit. 'It was dangerous and smelly and seemed like hell. But it was also somewhere safer to sleep than on the actual streets. Darkness meant shadows you could hide in, and feel safe even if it was only an illusion of safety.'

She reached out and took the glass from his hand; he seemed unaware he was gripping it so tightly he might break it. 'Your home life must have been kind of hellish too for you to have preferred that over living with your aunt.'

'Hell? You could say that.' The grim set of his mouth let her know that no more would be forthcoming on that subject.

'Your life on the streets must have been…terrifying.'

'I toughened up pretty quick. One thing I had in my favour was I was big—the same height I am now and strong from playing football at school. It was a rough-around-the-edges kind of school, and I'd had my share of sorting out bullies there.' He raised his fists into a fighting position in a gesture she thought was unconscious.

So scratch the elite private school. She realised now that Dominic was a self-made man. And his story of triumph over adversity fascinated her. 'So you could defend yourself against thugs and…and predators.'

Her heart went out to him. At seventeen she'd had all the security of a loving family and comfortable home. But she knew first-hand from her foster sisters that not all young people were that fortunate. It seemed that the young Dominic had started off with loving parents and a secure life but had spiralled downwards from then on. What the heck was wrong with the aunt to have let that happen?

She reached over the table and trailed her fingers across his scarred knuckles. 'That's how you got these?' It was amazing the familiarity a fake engagement allowed.

'I got in a lot of fights,' he said.

'And this?' She traced the fine scar at the side of his mouth.

'Another fight,' he said.

She dropped her hands to her sides, again overwhelmed by that urge to comfort him. 'You were angry and frightened.'

He shifted uncomfortably in his seat. 'All that.'

'But then you ended up with this.' She waved her hand to encompass the immaculate art deco pool, the expensively landscaped gardens, the superb house. It was an oasis of beauty and luxury.

'My fighting brought me to the attention of the police. I was charged with assault,' he said bluntly.

She'd thought his tough exterior was for real—had sensed the undercurrents of suppressed rage.

'Believe me, the other guy deserved it,' he said with an expression of grim satisfaction. 'He was drug-dealing scum.'

'What happened? With the police, I mean.' He'd been seventeen—still a kid. All she'd been fighting at that age was schoolgirl drama.

'I got lucky. The first piece of luck was that I was under eighteen and not charged as an adult. The second piece of luck was I was referred to a government social worker—Jim, his name was. Poor man, having to deal with the sullen, unhappy kid I was then couldn't have been easy. Jim was truly one of the good guys—still is. He won my confidence and got me away from that squat, to the guidance of another social worker friend of his down the Queensland Gold Coast.'

'Sun, surf and sand,' she said. She knew it sounded flippant but Dominic would not want her to pity his young self.

'And a booming real estate market. The social worker down

there was a good guy too. He got me a job as a gofer in a real estate agency. I was paid a pittance but it was a start and I liked it there. To cut a long story short, I was soon promoted to the sales team. I discovered I was good at selling the lifestyle dream, not just the number of bedrooms and bathrooms. I became adept at gauging what was important to the client.'

'Because you were observant,' she said. And tough and resilient and utterly admirable.

'That's important. Especially when I realised the role the woman played in a residential sale. Win her over and you more than likely closed the sale.'

Andie could see how those good looks, along with intuition and charm and the toughness to back it up, could have accelerated him ahead. 'Fascinating. And incredible how you've kept all the details away from the public. Surely people must have tried to research you, would have wanted to know your story?'

'As a juvenile, my record is sealed. I've never spoken about it. It's a time of my life I want well behind me. Without Jim the social worker, I might have gone the other way.'

'You mean you could have ended up as a violent thug or a drug dealer? I don't believe that for a second.'

He shrugged those broad street-fighter shoulders. 'I appreciate your faith in me. But, like so many of my fellow runaways, I could so easily have ended up…broken.'

Andie struggled to find an answer to that. 'It…it's a testament to your strength of character that you didn't.'

'If you say,' he said. But he looked pleased. 'Once I'd made enough money to have my own place and a car—nowhere as good as your hatchback, I might add—I started university part-time. I got lucky again.'

'You passed with honours?' She hadn't seen a university degree anywhere in her research on him but there was no harm in asking.

'No. I soon realised I knew more about making money and how business operated than some of the teachers in my commerce degree. I dropped out after eighteen months. But in a statistics class I met Jake Marlow. He was a brilliant, misunderstood geek. Socially, I still considered myself an outcast. We became friends.'

'And business partners, you said.' He was four years older than she was, and yet had lived a lifetime more. And had overcome terrible odds to get where he had.

'He was playing with the concept of ground-breaking online business software tools but no bank would loan him the money to develop them. I was riding high on commissions. We set up a partnership. I put in the money he needed. I could smell my first million.'

'Let me guess—it was an amazing success?'

'That software is used by thousands of businesses around the world to manage their digital workflow. We made a lot of money very quickly. Jake is still developing successful new software.' His obvious pride in his friend warmed his words.

'And you're still business partners.'

He nodded. 'The success of our venture gave me the investment dollars I needed to also spin off into my own separate business developing undervalued homemaker centres. We call them bulky goods centres—furnishing, white goods, electricals.'

'I guess the Gold Coast got too small for you.' That part she'd been able to research.

'I moved to Sydney. You know the rest.'

In silence she drank her mineral water with lime, he finished his iced tea. He'd given her a lot to think about. Was that anger that had driven him resolved? Or could it still be bubbling under the surface, ready to erupt?

He angled himself to look more directly at her. 'Now it's your turn to answer my question, Andie,' he said. 'How did you get over the death of your…of Anthony?'

She hadn't been expecting that and it hit her hard. But he'd dug deep. She had to too. 'I… I don't know that I will ever be able to forget the shock of it. One minute he was there, the next minute gone. I… I was as good as a widow, before I'd had the chance to be a bride.'

Dominic nodded, as if he understood. Of course he'd lost his parents.

'We were staying the weekend at his parents' beach house at Whale Beach. Ant got up very early, left a note to say he'd gone surfing, kissed me—I was asleep but awake enough to know he was going out—and then he was gone. Of course I blamed myself for not going with him. Then I was angry he'd gone out by himself.'

'Understandably,' he said and she thought again how he seemed to see more than other people. She had no deep, dark secrets. But, if she did, she felt he'd burrow down to them without her even realising it.

'After Anthony died, I became terrified of the sea. I hated the waves—blamed them for taking him from me, which I know was all kinds of irrational. Then one day I went to the beach by myself and sat on the sand. I remember hugging my knees as I watched a teenage boy, tall and blond like Anthony, ride a wave all the way into the shore, saw the exultation on his face, the sheer joy he felt at being one with the wave.'

'If this is bringing back hurtful memories, you don't have to go any further.'

'I'm okay… When someone close dies, you look for a sign from them—I learned I wasn't alone in that when I had counselling. That boy on his board was like a message from Anthony. He died doing something he truly loved. I ran into the surf and felt somehow connected to him. It was a healing experience, a turning point in my recovery from grief.'

'That's a powerful story,' Dominic said.

'The point of it is, it's five years since he died and of course I've moved on. Anyone who might wonder if my past could affect our fake future can be assured of that. Anthony was part of my youth; we grew up together. In some ways I'm the person I am because of those happy years behind me. But I want happy years ahead of me too. I've dated. I just haven't met the right person.'

For the first time she wondered if she could feel more for Dominic than physical attraction. For a boy who had been through what he had and yet come through as the kind of man who offered to pay for a little boy's medical treatment? Who was more willing to open his house to disadvantaged people than celebrities? There was so much more to Dominic than she ever could have imagined—and the more she found out about him the more she liked about him.

And then there were those kisses she had not been able to stop thinking about—and yearning for more.

'I appreciate you telling me,' he said.

She poured herself another long, cool mineral water. Offered to pour one for Dominic, but he declined.

'On to my next question,' she said. 'It's about your family. Do you have family other than your aunt? My mother will certainly want to know because she's already writing the guest list for the wedding.'

'You told your mother about the engagement?'

'She couldn't be more delighted. In fact…well…she got quite tearful.' Andie had never felt more hypocritical than the moment she realised her mother was crying tears of joy for her.

'That's a relief,' he said.

'You could put it that way. I didn't realise quite how concerned they were about me being…lonely. Not that I am lonely, by the way—I have really good friends.' But it was not the same as having a special someone.

'I'm beginning to see that,' he said. 'I'm surprised we've been able to have this long a conversation without your phone going off.'

'That's because I switched it off,' she said. 'There'll probably be a million messages when I switch it back on.'

'So your mother didn't question our…haste?'

'No. And any guilt I felt about pulling the wool over her eyes

I forced firmly to the back of my mind. Timothy getting the treatment he needs is way more important to my family than me finding a man.' She looked at him. 'So now—the guest list, your family?'

'My aunt and my mother were the only family each other had. So there is no Australian family.'

'Your aunt has…has passed away?' There was something awkward here that she didn't feel comfortable probing. But they were—supposedly—planning to get married. It made sense for her to know something of his family.

'She's in the best of residential care, paid for by me. That's all I want to say about her.'

'Okay,' she said, shaken by the closed look on his face.

'I have family in the UK but no one close since my grandparents died.'

'So no guests from your side of the family for our imaginary wedding?'

'That's right. And I consider the subject closed. In fact, I've had a gutful of talking about this stuff.'

'Me too,' she said. Hearing about his difficult youth, remembering her early loss was making her feel down. 'I reckon we know enough about each other now to be able to field any questions that are thrown at us. After all, we're not pretending to have known each other for long.'

She got up from her chair, walked to the edge of the pool, knelt at the edge and swished her hand through the water. 'This is such a nice pool. Do you use it much?'

'Most days I swim,' he said, standing behind her. 'There's a gym at the back of the cabana too.'

She imagined him working out in his gym, then plunging into the pool, muscles pumped, spearing through the water in not many clothes, maybe in *no* clothes.

Stop it!

She got up, wishing she could dive in right now to cool herself down. 'Do you like my idea to hire some lifeguards so the guests can swim on Christmas Day?'

'It's a good one.'

'And you're okay with putting a new swimsuit and towel in each of the children's goody bags? Hannah pointed out that some of the kids might not have a swimsuit.'

'I meant to talk to you about that,' he said. Surely he wasn't going to query the cost of the kids' gifts? She would be intensely disappointed if he did. 'I want to buy each of the adults a new swimsuit too; they might not have one either,' he said. 'I don't want anyone feeling excluded for any reason we can avoid.'

She looked up at him. 'You're not really a Scrooge, are you?'

'No,' he said.

'I don't think people are going to be calling you that for much longer. Certainly not if I've got anything to do with it.'

'But not a word about my past.'

'That's understood,' she said, making a my-lips-are-sealed zipping motion over her mouth. 'Though I think you might find people would admire you for having overcome it.'

The alarm on her watch buzzed. 'I'm running late,' she said. 'I didn't realise we'd been talking for so long.'

'You have an appointment? I was going to suggest dinner.'

'No can do, I'm afraid.' Her first impulse was to cancel her plans, to jump at the opportunity to be with Dominic. But she would not put her life on hold for the fake engagement.

'I have a hot date with a group of girlfriends. It's our first Tuesday of the month movie club. We see a movie and then go to dinner. We're supposed to discuss the movie but we mainly catch up on the gossip.' She held out her hand, where the diamond flashed on the third finger of her left hand. 'I suspect this baby is going to be the main topic of conversation.'

She made to go but, before she could, Dominic had pulled her close for a kiss that left not a scrap of lipstick on her mouth and her hair falling out of its knot.

It was the kind of kiss she could get used to.

CHAPTER TWELVE

ANDIE SAT AT her desk in the Party Queens' headquarters. 'Headquarters' was rather a grand term for their premises. It comprised an industrial kitchen where Gemma could do her thing; a workroom used for making props; a storage area; and an area loosely termed an office, where she and her two partners squeezed in their desks.

To say they were frantically busy would be an understatement. The weeks leading up to Christmas and New Year were the busiest time of the year for established party planners. For a new company like Party Queens to be so busy was gratifying. But it was the months after the end of the long Aussie summer vacation they had to worry about for advance bookings. Business brain, Eliza, was very good at reminding them of that.

Andie's top priority was Dominic's Christmas party. Actually, it was no longer just his party. As his fiancée, she had officially become co-host. But that didn't mean she wasn't flat-out with other bookings, including a Christmas Eve party for the parents of their first eighteenth party girl. Andie wanted to pull out all the stops for the people who'd given Party Queens their very first job. And then there was the business of being Dominic's fake fiancée—almost a job on its own.

Andie had been 'engaged' to Dominic for ten days and so far

so good. She'd been amazed that no one had seriously queried the speed at which she had met, fallen in love with and agreed to marry a man she had known for less than a month.

The swooning sighs of 'love at first sight' and 'how romantic' from her girlfriends she understood, not so much the delight from her pragmatic father and the tears of joy from her mother. She hardly knew Dominic and yet they were prepared to believe she would commit her life to him?

Of course it was because her family and friends had been worried about her, wanted her to be happy, had been concerned she had grieved for Anthony for too long.

'Your dad and I are pleased for you, sweetheart, we really are,' her mother had said. 'We were worried you were so fearful about loving someone again in case you lost them, that you wouldn't let yourself fall in love again,' she'd continued. 'But Dominic is so strong, so right for you; I guess he just broke through those barriers you'd spent so long putting up. And I understand you didn't want to waste time when you knew what it was like to have a future snatched away from you.'

Really? She'd put up *barriers*? She'd just been trying to find someone worthy of stepping into Anthony's shoes. Now she'd found a man who had big boots of his own and would never walk in another man's shadow. *But he wasn't really hers.*

'You put us off the scent by telling us Dominic wasn't your type,' Gemma had said accusingly. Gemma, who was already showing her ideas for a fabulous wedding cake she planned to bake and decorate for her when the time came. Andie felt bad going through images of multi-tiered pastel creations with Gemma, knowing the cake was never going to happen.

Condition Number One, that she and Dominic didn't *ever* tell *anyone* about the deception, seemed now like a very good idea. To hear that their engagement had been a cold-blooded business arrangement was never going to go down well with all these people wishing them well.

At last Wednesday's family dinner, Dominic had been joyfully welcomed into the Newman family. 'I'm glad you saw sense about how hot he was,' her sister Bea had said, hugging her. 'And as for that amazing rock on your finger... Does Dominic have a brother? No? Well, can you find me someone just like him, please?'

But every bit of deception was all worth it for Timothy. After the family dinner, Andie and Dominic had drawn Hannah and Paul aside. Now that Dominic was to be part of the family—or so they thought—her sister and her husband didn't take much convincing to accept Dominic's offer of paying all Timothy's medical expenses.

Dominic's only condition was that they kept him posted on their tiny son's progress. 'Of course we will,' Hannah had said, 'but Andie will keep you updated and you'll see Timothy at family functions. You'll always be an important part of his life.' And the little boy had more chance of a better life, thanks to Dominic's generosity.

Later, Hannah had hugged her sister tight. 'You've got yourself a good man, Andie, a very, very good man.'

'I know,' said Andie, choked up and cringing inside. She was going to have to come up with an excellent reason to explain why she 'dumped' Dominic when his need for the fake engagement was over.

There had only been one awkward moment at the dinner. Her parents wanted to put an announcement of the engagement in the newspaper. 'Old-fashioned, I know, but it's the right thing to do,' her mother had said.

She'd then wanted to know what Dominic's middle name was for the announcement. Apparently full names were required, Andrea Jane Newman was engaged to Dominic *who*?

She had looked at Dominic, eyes widened by panic. She should have known that detail about the man she was supposedly going to marry.

Dominic had quickly stepped in. 'I've kept quiet about my

middle name because I don't like it very much,' he'd said. 'It's Hugo. Dominic Hugo Hunt.'

Of course everyone had greeted that announcement with cries of how much they loved the name Hugo. 'You could call your first son Hugo,' Bea had suggested.

That was when Andie had decided it was time to go home. She felt so low at deceiving everyone, she felt she could slink out of the house at ankle level. If it wasn't for Timothy, she would slide that outsize diamond off her finger and put an end to this whole deception.

Dominic had laughed the baby comment off—and made no further mention of it. He'd wanted a baby with his first wife—how did he feel about children now?

Her family was now expecting babies from her and Dominic. She had not anticipated having to handle that expectation. But of course, since then, the image of a dear little boy with black spiky hair and grey eyes kept popping into her mind. A little boy who would be fiercely loved and never have to face the hardships his father had endured.

She banished the bordering on insane thoughts to the area of her brain reserved for impossible dreams. Instead, she concentrated on confirming the delivery date of two hundred and ten—the ten for contingencies—small red-and-white-striped hand-knitted Christmas stockings for Dominic's party. They would sit in the centre of each place setting and contain all the cutlery required by that person for the meal.

She had decided on a simple red-and-white theme, aimed squarely at pleasing children as well as the inner child of the adults. Tables would be set up in the ballroom for a sit-down meal served from a buffet. She wanted it to be as magical and memorable as a Christmas lunch in the home of a billionaire should be—but without being intimidating.

Gemma had planned fabulous cakes, shaped and frosted like an outsize white candle and actually containing a tea light, to be the centrepiece of each table. Whimsical Santa-themed cupcakes would sit at each place with the name of the guest piped on the top. There would be glass bowls of candy canes and masses of Australian Christmas bush with its tiny red flowers as well as bowls of fat red cherries.

Andie would have loved to handle all the decorations herself but it was too big a job. She'd hired one of her favourite stylists to coordinate all the decorations. Jeremy was highly creative and she trusted his skills implicitly. And, importantly, he'd been happy to work on Christmas Day.

She'd been careful not to discuss anything too 'Christmassy' with Dominic, aware of his feelings about the festive season. He still hadn't shared with her just why he hated it so much; she wondered if he ever would. There was some deep pain there, going right back to his childhood, she suspected.

The alarm on her computer flashed a warning at her the same time the alarm on her watch buzzed. Not that she needed any prompts to alert her that she was seeing Dominic this evening.

He had been in meetings with Walter Burton all afternoon. Andie was to join them for dinner. At her suggestion, the meal was to be at Dominic's house. Andie felt that a man like Walter might prefer to experience home-style hospitality; he must be sick of hotels and restaurants. Not that Dominic's house was exactly the epitome of cosy, but it was elegant and beautiful and completely lacking in any brash, vulgar display of wealth.

A table set on the terrace at the front of the house facing the harbour. A chef to prepare the meal. A skilled waiter to serve them. All organised by Party Queens with a menu devised by Gemma. Eliza had, as a matter of course, checked with Walter's personal assistant as to the tycoon's personal dietary requirements.

Then there would be Andie, on her best fiancée behaviour. After all, Mr Burton's preference for doing business with a married man was the reason behind the fake engagement.

Not that she had any problem pretending to be an attentive fiancée. That part of the role came only too easily. Her heartbeat accelerated just at the thought of seeing Dominic this evening. He'd been away in different states on business and she'd only seen him a few times since the family dinner. She checked her watch again. There was plenty of time to get home to Newtown and then over to Vaucluse before the guest of honour arrived.

Dominic had been in Queensland on business and only flown back into Sydney last night. He'd met Walter Burton from a very early flight from the US this morning. After an afternoon of satisfactory meetings, Dominic had taken him back to his hotel. The American businessman would then make his own way to Vaucluse for the crucial dinner with Dominic and Andie.

As soon as he let himself in through the front door of the house Dominic sensed a difference. There was a subtle air of expectation, of warmth. The chef and his assistant were in the kitchen and, if enticing aromas had anything to do with it, dinner was under way. Arrangements of exotic orchids were discreetly arranged throughout the house. That was thanks to Andie.

It was all thanks to Andie. He would have felt uncomfortable hosting Walter Burton in his house if it weren't for her. He would have taken him to an upscale restaurant, which would have been nice but not the same. The older man had been very pleased at the thought of being invited to Dominic's home.

And now here she was, heading towards him from the terrace at the eastern end of the house where they would dine. He caught his breath at how beautiful she looked in a body-hugging cream top and matching long skirt that wrapped across the front and revealed, as she walked, tantalising glimpses of long slender legs and high heeled ankle-strap sandals. Her hair was up, but tousled strands fell around her face. Her only jewellery was her engagement ring. With her simple elegance, again she looked as if she belonged in this house.

'You're home,' she said in that husky voice, already so familiar.

Home. That was the difference in his house this evening. *Andie's presence made it a home.* And he had not felt he'd had a real home for a long time.

But Andie and her team were temporary hired help—she the lead actress in a play put on for the benefit of a visiting businessman. *This was all just for show.*

Because of Walter Burton, because there were strangers in the house, they had to play their roles—he the doting fiancé and she his betrothed.

Andie came close, smiling, raised her face for his kiss. Was that too for show? Or because she was genuinely glad to see him? At the touch of her lips, hunger for her instantly ignited. He closed his eyes as he breathed in her sweet, spicy scent, not wanting to let her go.

A waiter passed by on his way to the outdoor terrace, with a tray of wine glasses.

'I've missed you,' Andie murmured. For the waiter's benefit or for Dominic's? She sounded convincing but he couldn't be sure.

'Me too—missed you, I mean,' he said stiffly, self-consciously.

That was the trouble with this deception he had initiated. It was only too easy to get caught between a false intimacy and an intimacy that could possibly be real. Or could it? He broke away from her, stepped back.

'Is this another misbehaving skirt?' he asked.

He resisted the urge to run his hand over the curve of her hip. It would be an appropriate action for a fiancé but stepping over the boundaries of his agreement with Andie. Kisses were okay—their public displays of affection had to look authentic. Caresses of a more intimate nature, on the other hand, were *not* okay.

She laughed. 'No breeze tonight so we'll never know.' She lowered her voice. 'Is there anything else you need to brief me about before Mr Burton arrives? I've read through the background information you gave me. I think I'm up to speed on what a fiancée interested in her future husband's work would most likely know.'

'Good,' he said. 'I have every faith you won't let me down. If you're not sure of anything, just keep quiet and I'll cover for you. Not that I think I'll have to do that.'

'Fingers crossed I do you proud,' she said.

Walter Burton arrived punctually—Dominic would have been surprised if he hadn't. The more time he spent with his prospective joint venture partner, the more impressed he was by his acumen and professionalism. *He really wanted this deal.*

Andie greeted the older man with warmth and charm. Straight away he could see Walter was impressed.

She led him to the front terrace where the elegantly set round table—the right size for a friendly yet business orientated meal—had been placed against a backdrop of Sydney Harbour, sparkling blue in the light of the long summer evening. As they edged towards the longest day on December the twenty-second, it did not get dark until after nine p.m.

Christmas should be cold and dark and frosty. He pushed the painful thought away. Dwelling on the past was not appropriate here, not when an important deal hung in the balance.

Andie was immediately taken with Walter Burton. In his mid-sixties and of chunky build, his silver hair and close-trimmed silver beard gave him an avuncular appearance. His pale blue eyes actually sparkled and she had to keep reminding herself that he could not be as genial as he appeared and be such a successful tycoon.

But his attitude to philanthropy was the reason she was here, organising the party, pretending to be Dominic's betrothed. He espoused the view that making as much money as you could was a fine aim—so long as you remembered to share it with those who had less. 'It's a social responsibility,' he said.

Dominic had done nothing but agree with him. There was

not a trace of Scrooge in anything he said. Andie had begun to believe the tag was purely a media invention.

Walter—he insisted she drop the 'Mr Burton'—seemed genuinely keen to hear all the details of the Christmas party. He was particularly interested when she told him Dominic had actively sought to dampen press interest. That had, as intended, flamed media interest. They already had two journalists volunteer to help out on that day—quite an achievement considering most people wanted to spend it with their families or close friends.

Several times during the meal, Andie squeezed Dominic's hand under the table—as a private signal that she thought the evening was going well. His smile in return let her know he thought so too. The fiancée fraud appeared to be doing the trick.

The waiter had just cleared the main course when Walter sat back in his chair, relaxed, well fed and praising the excellent food. Andie felt she and Dominic could also finally relax from the knife-edge of tension required to impress the American without revealing the truth of their relationship.

So Walter's next conversational gambit seemed to come from out of the blue. 'Of course you understand the plight of your Christmas Day guests, Dominic, as you've come from Struggle Street yourself,' he said. 'Yet you do your utmost to hide it.'

Dominic seemed shocked into silence. Andie watched in alarm as he blanched under his tan and gripped the edge of the table so his knuckles showed white. 'I'm not sure what you mean,' he said at last.

Walter's shrewd eyes narrowed. 'You've covered your tracks well, but I have a policy of never doing business with someone I haven't fully researched. I know about young Nick Hunt and the trouble he got into.'

Dominic seemed to go even paler. 'You mean the assault charge? Even though it never went to court. Even though I was a juvenile and there should be no record of it. How did you—?'

'Never mind how I found out. But I also discovered how much Dominic Hunt has given back to the world in which he had to fight to survive.' Walter looked to Andie. 'I guess you don't know about this, my dear.'

'Dominic has told me about his past,' she said cautiously. She sat at the edge of her seat, feeling trapped by uncertainty, terrified of saying the wrong thing, not wanting to reveal her ignorance of anything important. 'I also know how very generous he is.'

'Generous to the point that he funds a centre to help troubled young people in Brisbane.' Andie couldn't help a gasp of surprise that revealed her total lack of knowledge. 'He hasn't told you about his Underground Help Centre?' Walter didn't wait for her to answer. 'It provides safe emergency accommodation, health care, counselling, rehab—all funded by your fiancé. Altogether a most admirable venture.'

Why had Dominic let everyone think he was a Scrooge?

'You've done your research well, Walter,' Dominic said. 'Yes, I haven't yet told Andie about the centre. I wanted to take her to Brisbane and show her the work we do there.'

'I'll look forward to that, darling,' she said, not having to fake her admiration for him.

Dominic addressed both her and Walter. 'When I started to make serious money, I bought the abandoned shopping centre site where I'd sought refuge as a troubled runaway and redeveloped it. But part of the site was always going to be for the Underground Help Centre that I founded. I recruited Jim, the social worker who had helped me, to head it up for me.'

Andie felt she would burst with pride in him. Pride and something even more heartfelt. He must hate having to reveal himself like this.

Walter leaned towards Dominic. 'You're a self-made man and I admire that,' he said. 'You're sharing the wealth you acquired by your own hard work and initiative and I admire that too. What I don't understand, Dominic, is why you keep all this such a big secret. There's nothing to be ashamed of in having pulled yourself up by your bootstraps.'

'I'm not ashamed of anything I've done,' Dominic said. 'But I didn't want my past to affect my future success. Especially, I didn't want it to rub off on my business partner, Jake Marlow.'

Andie felt as if she was floundering. Dominic had briefed her on business aspects she might be expected to know about tonight, but nothing about this. She could only do what she felt was right. Without hesitation, she reached out and took his hand so they stood united.

'People can be very judgemental,' she said to Walter. 'And the media seem to be particularly unfair to Dominic. I'm incredibly proud of him and support his reasons for wanting to keep what he does in Brisbane private. To talk about that terrible time is to relive it, over and over again. From what Dominic has told me, living it once would be more than enough for anyone.'

Dominic squeezed her hand back, hard, and his eyes were warm with gratitude. Gratitude and perhaps—just perhaps—something more? 'I can't stop the nightmares of being back there,' he said. 'But I can avoid talking about it and bringing those times back to life.'

Andie angled herself to face Walter full-on. She was finding it difficult to keep her voice steady. 'If people knew about the centre they'd find out about his living rough and the assault charge. People who don't know him might judge him unfairly. At the same time, I'd love more people to know how generous and kind he actually is and—' She'd probably said enough.

Walter chuckled. 'Another thing he's done right is his choice of fiancée.'

Dominic reached over to kiss her lightly on the lips. 'I concur, Walter,' he said. Was it part of the act or did he really mean it?

'Th...thank you,' stuttered Andie. She added Walter to the list of people who would be disappointed when she dumped Dominic.

'I'm afraid I can't say the same for your choice of first wife,' Walter said.

Dominic visibly tensed. 'What do you mean?'

'I met with her and your former employee this morning. He's an impressive guy, though not someone I feel I want to do business with. But your ex-wife made it clear she would do anything—and I stress *anything*—to seal the deal. She suggested that to me—happily married for more than forty years and who has never even looked at another woman.'

Dominic made a sound of utter disgust but nothing more. Andie thought more of him that he didn't say anything to disparage Tara, appalling though her behaviour had been. Dominic had more dignity.

'The upshot of this is, Dominic, that you are exactly the kind of guy I want to do business with. You and your delightful wife-to-be. You make a great team.'

Dominic reached over to take Andie's hand again. 'Thank you, Walter. Thank you from us both.'

Andie smiled with lips that were aching from all her false smiles and nodded her thanks. The fake engagement had done exactly what it was intended to. She should be jubilant for Dominic's sake. But that also meant there would soon be no need to carry on with it. And that made her feel miserable. *She wasn't doing a very good job of guarding her heart.*

When Andie said goodnight to Dominic, she clung to him for a moment longer than was necessary. Playing wife-to-be for the evening had made her start to wish a real relationship with Dominic could perhaps one day be on the cards.

Perhaps it was a good thing she wouldn't see Dominic again until Christmas Eve. He had to fly out to Minneapolis to finalise details with Walter, leaving her to handle the countdown to the Christmas party. And trying not to think too much about what had to happen after Christmas, when her 'engagement' would come to an end.

CHAPTER THIRTEEN

IT WAS MIDDAY on Christmas Eve and as Andie pushed open the door into Dominic's house she felt as if she was stepping into a nightmare. The staircase railings were decorated as elegantly as she'd hoped, with tiny lights and white silk cord. The wreath on the door was superb. But dominating the marble entrance hall was an enormous Christmas tree, beautifully decorated with baubles and ornaments and winking with tiny lights. She stared at it in shocked disbelief. *What the heck was that doing there?*

When she said it out loud she didn't say *heck* and she didn't say it quietly.

Her stylist Jeremy's assistant had been rearranging baubles on the lower branches of the tree. She jumped at Andie's outburst and a silver bauble smashed on to the marble floor. Calmly, very calmly, Andie asked the girl where Jeremy was. The girl scuttled out to get him.

Throughout all the Christmas party arrangements, through all the fake fiancée dramas, Andie had kept her cool. Now she was in serious danger of losing it. She had planned this party in meticulous detail. Of all the things that could go wrong, it would have to be this—Dominic would think she had deliberately defied his specific demand. And she didn't want him thinking badly of her.

Jeremy came into the room with a swathe of wide red ribbons draped over his outstretched arm. Andie recognised them as the ones to be looped and tied into extravagant bows on the back of the two hundred chairs in the ballroom.

She had to grit her teeth to stop herself from exploding. 'Why is there a Christmas tree in here?' Her heart was racing with such panic she had to put her hand on her chest to try and slow it.

'Because this entrance space cried out for one. How can you have a Christmas party without a tree?' Jeremy said. 'I thought you'd made a mistake and left it off the brief. Doesn't it look fabulous?'

'It does indeed look fabulous. Except the client specifically said *no tree*.' She could hear her voice rising and took a deep breath to calm herself.

How had she let this happen? Maybe she should have written *NO CHRISTMAS TREE* in bold capitals on every page of the briefing document. She'd arrived here very early this morning to let the decorating crew in and to receive final deliveries of the extra furniture. Jeremy had assured her that all was on track. And it was—except for this darn tree.

'But why?' asked Jeremy. 'It seems crazy not to have a tree.'

Crazy? Maybe. She had no idea why—because Dominic, for all his talk with Walter Burton over dinner that night that had seemed so genuine, still refused to let her in on the events in his past he held so tightly to himself. He'd drip-fed some of the details but she felt there was something major linked to Christmas he would not share. It made her feel excluded—put firmly in her place as no one important in his life. And she wanted to be important to him. She swallowed hard. *Had she really just admitted that to herself?*

'The client actually has a thing against Christmas trees,' she said. 'You might even call it a phobia. For heaven's sake, Jeremy, why didn't you call me before you put this up?' Her mouth was dry and her hands felt clammy at the thought of Dominic's reaction if he saw the tree.

'I'm sorry,' said Jeremy, crestfallen. 'You didn't specify not to include a tree in the decorations. I was just using my initiative.'

On other jobs she'd worked with Jeremy she'd told him to think for himself and not bother her with constant calls, so she couldn't be *too* cranky with him. Creative people could be tricky to manage—and Jeremy's work was superb. The tree was, in fact, perfect for the spot where he'd placed it.

She took a step back to fully appraise its impact. The tree looked spectacular, dressed in silver with highlights of red, in keeping with her overall colour scheme. She sighed her pleasure at its magnificence. This perfect tree would make a breathtaking first impression for the guests tomorrow. To the children it would seem to be the entrance to a magical world. It spoke of tradition, of hope, of generosity. Everything they were trying to achieve with this party. It would make Dominic look good.

The beautiful tree was beginning to work its magic on her. Surely it would on Dominic too? He'd come such a long way since that first day, when he'd been so vehemently anti everything Christmas. *Christmas was not Christmas without a tree.*

She took a series of deep, calming breaths. Dominic should at least have the chance to see the tree in place. To see how wonderful it looked there. Maybe the sight of this tree would go some way towards healing those hidden deep wounds he refused to acknowledge.

She turned to Jeremy, the decision firm in her mind. 'We'll leave it. You've done such a good job on the tree, it would be a real shame to have to take it down.'

'What about the client?'

'He's a client but he's also my fiancé.' The lie threatened to choke her but she was getting more adept at spinning falsehoods. 'Leave him to me. In the meantime, let me give you a hand with placing the final few ornaments on the lower branches,' she said. She was wearing work clothes—jeans, sneakers and a loose white shirt. She rolled up her sleeves and picked up an exquisite glass angel. Her hand wasn't quite steady—if only she was as confident as she had tried to appear.

Dominic was due back in to Sydney early this evening. *What if he hated the tree?* Surely he wouldn't. He seemed so happy with everything else she'd done for the party; surely he would fall in love with the tree.

But it would take a Christmas miracle for him to fall in love with *her*.

She longed for that miracle. Because she couldn't deny it to herself any longer—she had developed feelings for him.

Dominic had managed to get an earlier flight out of Minneapolis to connect with a non-stop flight to Sydney from Los Angeles. Nonetheless, it was a total flight of more than twenty hours. Despite the comfort of first class, he was tired and anxious to get away from the snow and ice of Minnesota and home to sunny Sydney. A bitterly cold Christmas wasn't quite as he'd remembered it to be.

Overriding everything else, he wanted to get home to Andie. He had thought about her non-stop the whole trip, wished she'd been with him. Next time, he'd promised Walter, he'd bring Andie with him.

As the car he'd taken from the airport pulled up in front of his house, his spirits lifted at the thought of seeing her. He hadn't been able to get through to her phone, so he'd called Party Queens. Eliza had told him she was actually at his house in Vaucluse, working on the decorations for the party.

On the spur of the moment, he'd decided not to let her know he'd got in early. It might be better to surprise her. He reckoned if she didn't know he was coming, she wouldn't have time to put on her fake fiancée front. Her first reaction to him would give him more of a clue of her real feelings towards him.

Because while he was away he had missed her so intensely, he'd been forced to face *his* real feelings towards *her*. He was falling in love with her. Not only was he falling in love with her; he realised he had never had feelings of such intensity about a woman.

Melody had been his first love—and sweet, damaged Melody had loved him back to the extent she was capable of love. But it hadn't been enough. That assault charge had happened because he had been protecting her. Protecting her from a guy assaulting her in an alley not far from the takeaway food shop where he'd worked in the kitchen in return for food and a few dollars cash in hand.

But the guy had been her dealer—and possibly her pimp. Melody had squealed at Dominic to leave the guy alone. She'd shrieked at him that she knew what she was doing; she didn't need protecting. Dominic had ignored her, had pulled the creep off her, smashed his fist into the guy's face. Then the dealer's mates had shown up and Dominic had copped a beating too. But, although younger than the low-lifes, he'd been bigger, stronger and inflicted more damage. The cops had taken him in, while the others had disappeared into the dark corners that were their natural habitat. And Melody had gone with them without a backward glance, leaving him with a shattered heart as well as a broken nose. He'd never seen her again.

Of course Melody hadn't been her real name. He'd been too naïve to realise that at the time. Later, when he'd set up the Underground Help Centre, he'd tried to find her but without any luck. He liked to think she was living a safe happy life somewhere but the reality was likely to be less cosy than that.

Then there'd been Tara—the next woman to have betrayed him. The least thought he gave to his ex-wife the better.

But Andie. Andie was different. He felt his heart, frosted over for so long, warm when he thought about her. *What you saw was what you got.* Not only smart and beautiful, but loyal and loving. He'd told her more about his past than he'd ever told anyone. He could be himself with her, not have to pretend, be Nick as well as Dominic. Be not the billionaire but the man. Their relationship could be real. *He could spend his life with Andie.*

And he wanted to tell her just that.

The scent of pine needles assaulted his senses even before he put his key in his front door. The sharp resin smell instantly revived memories of that Christmas Eve when he'd been eleven years old and the happy part of his childhood had come to its terrible end. Christmas trees were the thing he most hated about Christmas.

The smell made him nauseous, started a headache throbbing in his temples. Andie must be using pine in some of the decorations. It would have to go. He couldn't have it in the house.

He pushed the door silently open—only to recoil at what he saw.

There was a Christmas tree in his house. A whopping great Christmas tree, taking up half his entrance hallway and rising high above the banisters of the staircase.

What the hell? He had told Andie in no uncertain terms there was to be no Christmas tree—anywhere. He gritted his teeth and fisted his hands by his sides. *How could she be so insensitive?*

There was a team of people working on the tree and its myriad glitzy ornaments. Including Andie. He'd never thought she could be complicit in this defiance of his wishes. He felt let down. *Betrayed.*

She turned. Froze. Her eyes widened with shock and alarm when she saw him. A glass ornament slid from her hands and smashed on the floor but she scarcely seemed to notice.

'What part of "no Christmas tree" did you not get, Andie?'

She got up from her kneeling position and took a step towards him, put up her hands as if to ward off his anger. The people she was with scuttled out of the room, leaving them alone. But he bet they were eavesdropping somewhere nearby. The thought made him even more livid.

'Dominic, I'm sorry. I know you said no tree.'

'You're damn right I did.'

'It was a mistake. The tree was never meant to be here. There were some…some crossed lines. I wasn't expecting it either. But then I saw it and it's so beautiful and looks so right here. I thought you might…appreciate it, might see how right it is and want to keep it.'

He could feel the veins standing out on his neck, his hands clenched so tight they hurt. 'I don't see it as beautiful.'

Her face flushed. She would read that as an insult to her skills. He was beyond caring. 'Why? Why do you hate Christmas trees?' she said. 'Why this…this irrational dislike of Christmas?'

Irrational? He gritted his teeth. 'That's none of your concern.'

'But I want it to be. I thought I could help you. I—'

'You thought wrong.'

Now her hands were clenched and she was glaring at him. 'Why won't you share it with me—what makes you hurt so much at this time of year? Why do I have to guess? Why do I have to tiptoe around you?' Her voice rose with each question as it seemed her every frustration and doubt rushed to the surface.

Dominic was furious. How dared she put him through this… this humiliation?

'Don't forget your place,' he said coldly. 'I employ you.' With each word he made a stabbing motion with his finger to emphasise the words. 'Get rid of the tree. Now.'

He hated the stricken look on Andie's face, knowing he had put it there. But if she cared about him at all she never would have allowed that tree to enter his house. He could barely stand to look at her.

For a long moment she didn't say anything. 'Yes,' she said finally, her voice a dull echo of its usual husky charm. 'Yes, sir,' she added.

In a way he appreciated the defiance of the hissed 'sir'. But he was tired and jet-lagged and grumpy and burning with all the pain and loss he associated with Christmas—and Christmas trees in particular. Above all, he was disappointed in her that she thought so little of his wishes that she would defy him.

His house was festooned with festive paraphernalia. Everywhere he looked, it glittered and shone, mocking him. He'd been talked into this damn party against his wishes. *He hated Christmas.* He uttered a long string of curses worthy of Scrooge.

'I'm going upstairs. Make sure this tree is gone when I come back down. And all your people as well.' He glared in the general direction of the door through which her team had fled.

She met his glare, chin tilted upwards. 'It will take some time to dismantle the tree,' she said. 'But I assure you I will get rid of every last stray needle so you will never know it was there.' She sounded as though she spoke through gritted teeth. 'However, I will need all my crew to help me. We have to be here for at least a few more hours. We still have to finish filling the goody bags and setting the tables.' She glared at him. 'This is *your* party. And you know as well as I do that it must go on. To prove you're not the Scrooge people think you are.'

Some part of him wanted to cross the expanse of floor between them and hug her close. To tell her that of course he understood. That he found it almost impossible to talk about the damage of his childhood. To knuckle down and help her adorn his house for the party tomorrow. But the habits of Christmases past were hard to break.

So was the habit of closing himself off from love. Letting himself love Andie would only end in disappointment and pain, like it had with every other relationship. For her as well as himself. *It seemed he was incapable of love.*

'Text me when you're done,' he said.

He stomped up the stairs to his study. And the bottle of bourbon that waited there.

Andie felt humiliated, angry and upset. How dared Dominic speak to her like that? *'Don't forget your place.'* His harsh words had stabbed into her heart.

Jeremy poked his head around the door that connected through to the living room. She beckoned him to come in. She forced her voice to sound businesslike, refused to let even a hint of a tear burr her tone. 'I told you he wouldn't be happy with the tree.' Her effort at a joke fell very flat.

'Don't worry about it,' Jeremy said, putting a comforting hand on her shoulder. 'We'll get rid of this tree quick-smart. No matter your man is in a mood. The show has to go on. You've got two hundred people here for lunch tomorrow.'

'Thanks, Jeremy,' she said. 'Dominic has just got off a long flight. He's not himself.' But her excuses for him sounded lame even to her own ears.

Was that angry man glaring at her with his fists clenched at his sides the true Dominic? She'd known the anger was there bubbling below the surface, was beginning to understand the reasons for it. But she'd thought that anger that had driven him to violence was in his past. How could she possibly have thought she'd fallen in love with him? She didn't even know the man.

'What do you suggest we do with the tree?' Jeremy asked. 'There are no returns on cut trees.'

Andie's thoughts raced. 'We've got a Christmas Eve party happening elsewhere tonight. The clients have put up a scrappy old artificial tree that looks dreadful. We'll get this delivered to them with the compliments of Party Queens. Keep whatever ornaments you can use here; the rest we'll send with the tree. Let's call a courier truck now.'

Seething, she set to work dismantling the beautiful tree. As she did so, she felt as if she were dismantling all her hopes and dreams for love with Dominic. The diamond ring felt like a heavy burden on her finger, weighted by its duplicity and hypocrisy. While he'd stood there insulting her, she'd felt like taking the ring off and hurling it at him. If it had hit him and drawn blood she would have been glad. His words had been so harsh they felt like they'd drawn blood from her heart.

But of course she couldn't have thrown her ring at him while there were other people in the house. She would be professional right to the end. After all, wasn't she known for her skill at dealing with difficult people?

In spite of that, she'd had her fill of this particular difficult man. He'd got what he wanted from her in terms of his American deal. She'd got what her family needed for Timothy. Both sides of the bargain fulfilled. He'd been her employer, her fake fiancé—she'd liked to think they'd become friends of a sort. She'd wanted more—but that was obviously not to be. She'd stick it out for the Christmas lunch. Then she'd be out of here and out of his life.

The crew worked efficiently and well. When they were done and the tree was gone she waved them goodbye and wished them a Merry Christmas. But not before asking them to please not repeat what they might have heard today. Talk of Dominic's outburst could do serious damage to the rehabilitation of his Scrooge image.

By the time they had all gone it was early evening. She stood and massaged the small of her back where it ached. She would let Dominic know she was done and going home. But she had no intention of texting him as he'd asked. Not asked. *Demanded.* She had things to say that had to be said in person.

CHAPTER FOURTEEN

WITH A HEAVY HEART—wounded hearts *hurt*—Andie made her way up the stylishly decorated staircase, its tiny lights discreetly winking. She hadn't been up here before, as this part of the house was off-limits for the party. When she thought of it, she actually had no idea where Dominic could be.

The first two doors opened to two fashionably furnished empty bedrooms. The third bedroom was obviously his—a vast bed with immaculate stone-coloured linens, arched windows that opened to a sweeping view of the harbour. But he wasn't there.

Then she noticed a door ajar to what seemed like a study.

There was no response to her knock, so she pushed it open. The blinds were drawn. Dominic lay sprawled asleep on a large chesterfield sofa. The dull light of a tall, arching floor lamp pooled on him and seemed to put him in the spotlight.

His black lace-up business shoes lay haphazardly at the end of the sofa. He had taken off his jacket and removed his tie. The top buttons of his shirt were undone to reveal an expanse of bare, well-muscled chest her traitorous libido could not help but appreciate as it rose and fell in his sleep.

His right arm fell to the floor near a bottle of bourbon. Andie picked it up. The bottle was nearly full, with probably no more than a glassful gone. Not enough for him to be drunk—more likely collapsed into the sleep of utter exhaustion. She put the bottle on the desk.

There was a swivel-footed captain's chair near the sofa with a padded leather seat. She sat on the edge of it and watched Dominic as he slept. Darn it, but that wounded heart of hers beat faster as she feasted her eyes on his face, which had become so familiar. So...so—she nearly let herself think *so beloved.* But that couldn't be.

She swallowed hard at the lump that rose in her throat. Why on earth had she let herself fall for a man who was so difficult, so damaged, so completely opposite to the man who had made her so happy in the past?

Dominic's hair stood up in spikes. He obviously hadn't shaved since he'd left Minneapolis and his beard was in that stubble stage she found so incredibly sexy. She hadn't realised how long and thick his eyelashes were. His mouth was slightly parted. She longed to lean over and kiss it. She sighed. There would be no more kissing of this man.

He moaned in his sleep and she could see rapid eye movement behind his lids as if he were being tortured by bad dreams. She could not help but reach out to stroke his furrowed forehead. He returned to more restful sleep. Then his eyes flickered open. Suddenly he sat up, startling her. He looked around, disorientated, eyes glazed with sleep. He focused on her.

'Andie,' he breathed. 'You're here.' He gave a huge sigh, took her hand and kissed it. 'I didn't think I'd ever see you again.'

He didn't deserve to, she thought. But her resolve was weakening.

'Are you okay?' she said, trying to ignore the shivers of pleasure that ran up her arm from his kiss. He had been rude and hurtful to her.

'I've just had a horrible dream,' he said.

'What kind of dream?'

'A nightmare. I was in a cemetery and saw my own headstone.'

She shook her head. 'No, Dominic—I don't want to hear this.' The day of Anthony's funeral had been the worst day of her life. When she'd had to accept she'd never see him again. She couldn't bear to think of Dominic buried under a headstone.

But he continued in a dramatic tone she didn't think was appropriate for such a gruesome topic. 'It said: 'Here lies Dominic—they called him Scrooge'. And I think it was Christmas Day.'

Not so gruesome after all. She couldn't help a smile.

'You think my nightmare was funny?' he said, affronted.

'I'm sure it was scary at the time. But you'll never be called Scrooge again. Not after tomorrow. I… I'm sorry about what I said earlier. About your…your Scroogeness, I mean.'

He slammed the hand that wasn't holding hers against his forehead. 'The Christmas tree. I'm sorry, Andie. That was unforgivable. Pay your crew a bonus to make up for it, will you, and bill it to me.'

Did he think everything could be solved by throwing money at it?

'I'm also sorry about the tree, Dominic. It was an honest mistake. It's all gone now.'

Maybe she'd been in the wrong too, to imagine he might like the tree when he'd been so vehement about not having one in the house. But she hadn't been wrong about expecting better behaviour from him.

He shuddered. 'It was a shock. The smell of it. The sight of it. Brought back bad memories.'

She shifted in her seat but did not let go of his hand. 'Do you think it might be time to tell me why Christmas trees upset you so much? Because I didn't like seeing that anger. Especially not directed at me. How can I understand you when I don't know what I'm dealing with?'

He grimaced as if stabbed by an unpleasant memory. 'I suppose I have to tell you if I want you to ever talk to me again.'

'I'm talking to you now.'

She remembered what she'd said about recalling unpleasant memories being like reliving them. But this had to come out—one way or another. Better it was with words than fists.

'Christmas Eve is the anniversary of my parents' deaths.'

She squeezed his hand. 'Dominic, I'm so sorry.' That explained a lot. 'Why didn't you say so before?'

'I… I didn't want people feeling sorry for me,' he said gruffly.

'People wouldn't have… Yes, they would have felt sorry for you. But in a good way.' Could all this Scrooge business have been solved by him simply explaining that? 'Can you tell me about it now?'

'There…there's more. It was cold and frosty. My parents went out to pick up the Christmas tree. A deer crossed the road and they braked to avoid it. The road was icy and the car swerved out of control and crashed into a barrier. That's how they died. Getting the damn Christmas tree.'

She couldn't find the words to say anything other than she was sorry again.

'It was…it was my fault they died.'

Andie frowned. 'How could it be your fault? You were eleven years old.'

'My aunt told me repeatedly for the next six years it was my fault.'

'I think you'd better tell me some more about this aunt.'

'The thing is, it really *was* my fault. I'd begged my parents for a real tree. We had a plastic one. My best friend had a real one; I wanted a real one. If they hadn't gone out to get the tree I wanted they wouldn't have died.'

'You've been blaming yourself all these years? It was an accident. How any competent adult could let you blame yourself, I can't imagine.'

'Competent adult and my aunt aren't compatible terms,' he said, the bitterness underlying his words shocking her.

'I keep asking you about her; it's time you gave me some answers.' Though she was beginning to dread what she might hear.

'She used alcohol and prescription meds to mask her serious psychological problems. I know that now as an adult. As a kid, I lived with a bitter woman who swung between abuse and smothering affection.'

'And, as a kid, you put up with a lot in the hope of love,' Andie said softly, not sure if Dominic actually heard her. She could see the vulnerability in that strong-jawed handsome face, wondered how many people he had ever let be aware of it. She thought again of that little boy with the dark hair. Her vision of Dominic's son merged with that of the young, grieving, abused Dominic. And her heart went out to him.

The words spilled out of him now, words that expressed emotions dammed for years. 'She was particularly bad at Christmas because that's when she'd lost her sister—which was, in her eyes, my fault. When she got fed up with me, she locked me in a cupboard. The physical abuse stopped when I got bigger than her. The mental abuse went on until the day I ran away. Yet all that time she held down a job and presented a reasonable face to the world. I talked to a teacher at school and he didn't believe me. Told me to man up.'

'I honestly don't know what to say…' But she hated his aunt, even though she was aware she'd been a deeply troubled person. No child should be treated like that.

'Say nothing. I don't want to talk about it any more. I'm thirty-two years old. That was all a long time ago.'

'But, deep down, you're still hurting,' she whispered. 'Dominic, I'm so sorry you had to go through all that. And I admire you so much for what you became after such a difficult start.'

Words could only communicate so much. Again, she felt that urge to comfort him. This time, she acted on it. She leaned over to him and kissed him, tasted bourbon on his lips, welcomed the scrape of his stubble on her skin. Immediately, he took the kiss deeper.

The kiss went on and on, passion building, thrilling her. But it was more than sensual pleasure; it was a new sense of connection, of shared emotion as well as sensation.

He broke the kiss to pull her shirt up and over her head. His shirt was already half unbuttoned. It didn't take much to have it completely undone and to slide it off his broad shoulders and muscular arms. She caught her breath in awe at the male perfection of his body.

She wanted him. Dominic had got what he wanted from Walter. Timothy was booked for the treatment he needed. She had promised herself to go after what she wanted—him—and now was her time. It might never be more than this. She knew it and was prepared to take that risk. But she hoped for so much more.

She hadn't known him for long but she had the same kind of certainty—that it could be for ever—as she'd felt for Anthony. A certainty she'd thought she'd never feel again. *For ever love.* Had she been given a chance for that special connection again? She thought *yes*, but could she convince Dominic she could bring him the kind of happiness that had seemed to evade him—that he deserved?

He threw his head back and moaned his pleasure as she planted urgent kisses down the firm column of his throat, then back up to claim his mouth again. He tasted so good, felt so good.

He caught her hands. 'Andie, is this what you want? Because we have to stop it now if you don't,' he said, his voice husky with need.

'Don't you dare stop,' she murmured.

He smiled a slow, seductive smile that sent her heart rate rocketing. 'In that case…' He unfastened the catch on her jeans. 'Let's see if we can get these jeans to misbehave…'

* * *

Satisfied, replete, her body aching in the most pleasurable of ways, Andie drowsed in his arms as Dominic slept. But she couldn't let herself sleep.

If she'd been a different kind of person she would have stayed there. Perhaps convinced Dominic to shower with her when they woke. She would enjoy soaping down that powerful body. Heaven knew what kind of fun they could have with the powerful jets of water in his spacious double shower. Then they could retire to spend the rest of the evening in that enormous bed of his.

But Andie was not that person. There was the Christmas Eve party she had committed to this evening. As the party planner, she was obliged to call in to see all was well. She also had to check the big tree had made its way there safely—though the eighteen-year-old daughter had texted Andie to thank her, thrilled with the 'real tree'.

There was nothing like the smell of pine resin and the beauty of a natural tree. As eleven-year-old Dominic had known. Her heart went out to that little boy who lived in the damaged soul of the big male, sleeping naked next to her, his arm thrown possessively over her. She was also naked, except for her engagement ring, shining with false promise under the lamplight.

She had agreed to see her family tonight. Tomorrow, Christmas Day, would be the first Christmas lunch she had not spent with them. She was surprised her father had taken it so lightly. 'You have to stand by Dominic, love. That party is not just a job for you now. You're his future wife.'

If only.

Reluctantly, she slid away from Dominic, then quietly got dressed. She would see him in the morning. Tomorrow was Christmas Day, a holiday she loved and he hated. Now she could see why. She ached to turn things around for him—if he would let her.

She looked at his face, more relaxed than she had seen it, and smiled a smile that was bittersweet. They had made love and it had been magnificent. But nothing had changed between them. Tomorrow she was facing the biggest party of her career so far. She would be by the side of the man she had fallen in love with, not knowing for how much longer he would be a part of her life.

When the truth was, she wanted Dominic for Christmas. Not just his body—his heart as well.

Somehow, tomorrow she would have to confess to Dominic the truth of how she felt about him. That she wanted to try a relationship for real. She hoped he felt the same. If so, this would be the best Christmas she had ever had. If not… Well, she couldn't bear to think about *if not.*

CHAPTER FIFTEEN

DOMINIC AWOKE ON Christmas morning as he was accustomed to waking on December the twenty-fifth—alone. It was very early, pale sunlight filtering through the blinds. He reached out his hand to the sofa beside him in the vain hope that Andie might still be there, only to find the leather on that side disappointingly cool to the touch. He closed his eyes again and breathed in the scent of her that lingered in the room, on his skin. Then was overtaken by an anguished rush of longing for her that made him double over with gut-wrenching pain.

He remembered her leaving his side, her quiet footsteps around the room, the rustling as she slid on her clothes. Then her leaning towards him, murmuring that she had to go. She had duties, obligations. He'd pulled her back close to him, tried to convince her with his hands, with his mouth why she should stay. But she'd murmured her regret, kissed him with a quick fierce passion, told him he had jet lag to get over. Then she'd gone.

All he'd wanted to say to her still remained unsaid.

Of course she'd gone to the other people in her life who needed her and loved her. The only commitment she'd made to him was based on the falsehoods he'd engendered and coerced her into. She'd played her role to perfection. So well he was uncertain what might be fact and what might be fiction. But surely making love to him with such passion and tenderness had not been play-acting?

He noticed the bourbon bottle on the desk, lid on, barely touched. This would be the first Christmas he could remember that he hadn't tried to obliterate. The first Christmas that he woke to the knowledge that while Andie might not be here now, she soon would be. And that his perfect, empty house would be filled with people. People who had known hardship like he had and whom he was in the position to help by making their Christmas Day memorable.

Not for the first time, he thought of the possibility of opening a branch of the Underground Help Centre here in Sydney, where it was so obviously needed. Profits from the joint venture with Walter could help fund it. He had much to learn from Walter—he could see it was going to end up a friendship as well as a business partnership.

For the first Christmas in a long time he had something to look forward to—and it was all thanks to Andie.

He hauled himself off the sofa and stretched out the cricks in his back. The sofa was not the best place to sleep—though it had proved perfectly fine for energetic lovemaking. He paused, overwhelmed by memories of the night before. *Andie.* Hunger for her threatened to overwhelm him again—and not just for her beautiful, generous body. He prayed to whatever power that had brought her to him to let him keep her in his life. He hoped she would forgive the way he'd behaved—understand why. And know that it would never happen again.

He headed down the stairs and stood in the entrance hall. Not a trace of the tree remained, thank heaven. He breathed in. And none of that awful smell. Andie had been well meaning but misguided about the tree—now she understood.

The ballroom was all set up, with tables and chairs adorned in various combinations of red and white. A large buffet table area stretched along the wall closest to the kitchen. He'd approved the menu with Gemma and knew within hours it would be groaning with a lavish festive feast. The dishes had been chosen with the diverse backgrounds of the guests in mind—some were refugees experiencing their first Christmas in Australia.

He still couldn't have tolerated a tree in the house but he had to admit to a stirring of interest in the celebrations—more interest than he'd had in Christmas since he'd been a child. Andie was clever—children would love all this and adults should also respond to the nostalgia and hope it evoked. Hadn't she said Christmas was about evoking emotion?

Thanks to the tragedy on Christmas Eve all those years ago, thanks to the way his aunt had treated him in the years that followed, the emotions the season had evoked for him had been unhappy in the extreme. Was there a chance now for him to forge new, happy memories with a kind, loving woman who seemed to understand his struggles?

Andie had said he could trust her, but after his display of anger over the Christmas tree last night would she let herself trust *him*?

There was a large Santa Claus figurine in the corner with rows of canvas, sunshine-themed goody bags stacked around it. Of course it should have been a tree—but the Santa worked okay too as a compromise. The sturdy bags could double as beach bags, the ever-practical Andie had pointed out to him. She had thought of everything. There were gifts there for the volunteers too.

The house seemed to hum with a quiet anticipation and he could feel his spirits rise. Christmas Day with Andie in his house must surely be a step up on the ones he'd been forced to endure up until now.

He swung open the doors and headed to his gym for a workout.

An hour later Andie arrived with the chef and his crew. Dominic had long given her a pass code to get in and out of fortress Vaucluse.

She was wearing working gear of shorts, T-shirt and sneakers. Later she would change into her beautiful new red lace dress and gorgeous shoes—strappy and red with tassels—in time to greet their guests. She took her dress on its hanger and her bag into the downstairs bathroom. As she did, she noticed the doors to the garden were open and someone was in the pool. She went out to investigate.

Of course it was Dominic, his powerful body spearing through the water. No wonder he had such well-developed muscles with vigorous swimming like this. She watched, mesmerised at his rhythmic strokes, the force of his arms and powerful kick propelling him with athletic grace.

She didn't say anything but maybe her shadow cast on the water alerted him to her presence. Maybe he caught sight of her when he turned his head to breathe. He swam to the edge of the pool and effortlessly pulled himself out of the water, muscles rippling. He wasn't even out of breath.

She almost swooned at the sight of him—could a man be more handsome? Memories of the ecstasy they had given each other the night before flashed through her, tightening her nipples and flooding her body with desire.

His wet hair was slick to his head, the morning sunlight refracted off droplets of water that clung to his powerfully developed shoulders and cut chest, his veins stood out on his biceps, pumped from exertion. And then there were the classic six-pack, the long, strong legs. He didn't have a lot of body hair for such a dark man, but what there was seemed to flag his outrageous masculinity.

She wanted him more than ever. Not just for a night. For many nights. Maybe every night for the rest of her life. There was so much she wanted to say to him but, for all the connection and closeness and *certainty* she had felt last night, she didn't know how to say it.

Her engagement ring glinted on her left hand. The deal with Walter was done. Dominic's Scrooge reputation was likely to be squashed after the party today. How much longer would this ring stay on her finger? What, if anything, would be her role in Dominic's life? She wanted to say something about last night, bring up the subject of the future, but she just couldn't. 'Happy Christmas,' she said instead, forcing every bit of enthusiasm she could muster into her voice.

He grabbed a towel from the back of the chair and slung it around his shoulders, towelling off the excess water. 'H… Happy Christmas to you too,' he said, his voice rusty in the way of someone unused to uttering those particular words. She wondered how long since he had actually wished anyone the Season's greetings.

He looked down into her face and she realised by the expression in his eyes that he might be as uncertain as she was. Hope flared in her heart. 'Dominic, I—'

'Andie, I—'

They both spoke at the same time. They laughed. Tried again.

'About last night,' he said.

'Yes?' she said.

'I wanted to—'

But she didn't hear what he had to say, didn't get a chance to answer because at that moment the chef called from the doors that opened from the ballroom that Gemma and Eliza were there and needed to be buzzed in.

Dominic groaned his frustration at the terminated conversation. Andie echoed his groan.

'Later,' she said as she turned away, knowing that it would be highly unlikely for them to get another private moment together for the next few hours.

Dominic found the amount of noise two hundred people could generate—especially when so many of them were children—quite astounding. He stood on the edge of the party, still at the meet-and-greet stage, with appetisers and drinks being passed around by waiters dressed as Christmas elves.

Santa Claus, otherwise known as Rob Cratchit, his Director of Marketing, sidled up next to him. 'It's going even better than I expected,' he said through his fake white beard. 'See that woman over there wiping tomato sauce off the little boy's shirt? She's a journalist, volunteering for the day, and one of your most strident Scrooge critics. She actually called you a multi-million-dollar miser. But I think she's already convinced that today is not some kind of cynical publicity stunt.'

'Good,' said Dominic. Strange that the original aim of this party—to curry favour with Walter Burton—seemed to have become lost. Now it was all about giving people who had it tough a heart-warming experience and a good meal. And enjoying it with Andie by his side.

'Good on you for dressing up as Santa Claus,' he said to Rob. Andie had been right—Rob made the perfect Santa and he had the outgoing personality to carry it off.

'Actually, *you're* the Santa Claus. I talked to one nice lady, a single mum, who said her kids would not have got Christmas lunch or a Christmas present this year, unless a charity had helped out. She said this was so much better than charity. You should mingle—a lot of people want to thank you.'

'I'm not the mingling type,' Dominic said. 'I don't need to be thanked. I just signed the cheques. It should be Andie they're thanking; this was all her idea.'

'She's brilliant,' said Rob. 'Smart of you to snap her up so quickly. You're a lucky man.'

'Yes,' said Dominic, not encouraging further conversation. He'd never been happy discussing his personal life with anyone. The thought that—unless he said something to her—this might be the last day he had with Andie in his life was enough to sink him into a decidedly unfestive gloom.

He hadn't been able to keep his eyes off Andie as she flitted around the room, looking her most beautiful in a very stylish dress of form-fitting lace in a dusky shade of Christmas red. It was modest but hugged every curve and showed off her long, gorgeous legs. He tried not to think of how it had felt to have those legs wrapped around him last night…

'Well, mustn't linger,' said Rob. 'I have to be off and do the *ho-ho-ho* thing.'

As Rob made his way back into the throng, Andie rang a bell for attention and asked everyone to move towards the entrance hall. 'Some of the children and their parents are singing carols for us today.' She'd told Dominic a few of the adults were involved in street choirs and had been happy to run through the carols with the kids.

There was a collective gasp from the 'audience' as they saw the children lined up on the stairs, starting from the tiniest to the teenagers with the adults behind. Again Andie had been right—the stairs made the most amazing showcase for a choir. Each of the choir members wore a plain red T-shirt with the word *'choir'* printed in white lower-case letters. It was perfect, gave them an identity without being ostentatious.

Andie met his gaze from across the room and she smiled. He gave her a discreet thumbs-up. Professional pride? Or something more personal?

The choir started off with the Australian Christmas carol 'Six White Boomers' where Santa's reindeer were replaced by big white kangaroos for the Australian toy delivery. It was a good icebreaker, and had everyone laughing and clapping and singing along with the chorus.

As Dominic watched, he was surprised to see Andie playing guitar up on the balcony with two other guitarists. She was singing too, in a lovely warm soprano. He remembered that photo of her playing guitar in the hallway of her parents' home and realised how much there was he still didn't know about her—and how much he wanted to know.

When the choir switched to classics like 'Silent Night' and 'Away in a Manger', Dominic found himself transported back to the happy last Christmas when his parents were alive and they'd gone carol singing in their village. *How could he have forgotten?*

The music and the pure young voices resonated and seemed to unlock a well of feeling he'd suppressed—unable perhaps to deal with the pain of it during those years of abuse by his aunt. He'd thought himself incapable of love—because he had been without love. But he *had* been loved back then, by his parents and his grandparents—loved deeply and unconditionally.

He'd yearned for that love again but had never found it. His aunt had done her best to destroy him emotionally but the love that had nurtured him as a young child must have protected him. The realisation struck him—he had loved women incapable of loving him back, and all this time had thought the fault was his when those relationships had failed.

Andie's voice soared above the rest of the choir. Andie, who he sensed had a vast reserve of love locked away since she'd lost her boyfriend. He wanted that love for himself and he wanted to give her the love she needed. How could he tell her that?

He tried to join in with the words of the carol but his throat closed over. He pretended to cough. Before he made an idiot of himself by breaking down, he pushed his way politely through the crowd and made his way out to the cabana, the only place where he could be alone and gather his thoughts.

But he wasn't alone for long. Andie, her eyes warm with concern, was soon with him. 'Dominic, are you okay?' she said, her hand on his arm. 'I know how you feel about Christmas and I was worried—'

'I'm absolutely fine—better than I've been for a long time,' he said.

He picked up her left hand. 'Take off your ring and give it to me, please.'

Andie froze. She stared at him for a long moment, trying to conceal the pain from the shaft of hurt that had stabbed her heart. So it had come to this so soon. Her use was over. Fake fiancée no longer required. Party planner no longer required. Friend, lover, confidante and whatever else she'd been to him no longer required. *She was surplus to requirements.*

Dominic had proved himself to be generous and thoughtful way beyond her initial expectations of Scrooge. But she must not forget the cold, hard fact—people who got to be billionaires in their twenties must have a ruthless streak. And he'd reneged on his offer that she could keep the ring—not that she'd had any intention of doing so. To say she was disappointed would be the world's biggest understatement.

She felt as though all the energy and joy was flowing out of her to leave just a husk. The colour drained from her face—she must look like a ghost.

With trembling fingers, she slid off the magnificent ring and gave it back to him, pressing it firmly into the palm of his hand. Her finger felt immediately empty, her hand unbalanced.

'It's yours,' she said and turned on her heel, trying not to stagger. She would not cry. She would not say anything snarky to him. She would just walk out of here with dignity. *This was her worst Christmas Day ever.*

'Wait! Andie! Where are you going?'

She turned back to see Dominic with a look of bewilderment on his handsome, tough face. 'You're not going to leave me here with your ring?'

Now it was her turn to feel bewildered. '*My* ring? Then why—?' she managed to choke out.

He took her hand again and held it in a tight grip. 'I'm not doing a good job of this, am I?'

He drew her closer, cleared his throat. 'Andie, I… I love you, and I'm attempting to ask you to marry me. I'm hoping you'll say "yes", so I can put your ring back on your wedding finger where it belongs, as your *real* fiancé, as a *real* engagement ring. Just like you told me you wanted.'

She was stunned speechless. The colour rushed back into her face.

'Well?' he prompted. 'Andrea Jane Newman, will you do me the honour of becoming my wife?'

Finally she found her words. Although she only needed the one. 'Yes,' she said. 'I say "yes".'

With no further ado, he slid the beautiful ring back into its rightful place. To her happy eyes it seemed to flash even more brilliantly.

'Dominic, I love you too. I think maybe it *was* love at first sight the day I met you. I never really had to lie about that.'

She wound her arms around his neck and kissed him. They kissed for a long time. Until they were interrupted by a loud knock on the door of the pool house. Gemma.

'Hey, you two, I don't know what's going on in there and I don't particularly want to know, but we're about to serve lunch and your presence is required.'

'Oh, yes, of course—we're coming straight away,' Andie called, flustered.

Dominic held her by the arm. 'Not so fast. There's something else I want to ask you. What would you like for Christmas?'

His question threw her. She had to think very hard. But then it came to her. 'All I want for Christmas is for us to get married as soon as possible. I… I don't want to wait. You…you know why.'

Anthony would have wanted this for her—to grab her second chance of happiness. She knew that as certainly as if he'd been there to give her his blessing.

'That suits me fine,' Dominic said. 'The sooner you're my wife the better.'

'Of course it takes a while to organise a wedding. Next month. The month after. I don't want anything too fussy anyway, just simple and private.'

'We'll have to talk to the Party Queens,' he said.

She laughed. 'Great idea. I have a feeling we'll be the best people for the job.'

She could hardly believe this was true, but the look in his

eyes told her she could believe it. She wound her arms around his neck again. 'Dominic Hugo Hunt, you've just made this the very best Christmas of my life.'

He heaved a great sigh and she could see it was as if the weight of all those miserable Christmases he'd endured in the past had been thrown off. 'Me too,' he said. 'And all because of you, my wonderful wife-to-be.'

CHAPTER SIXTEEN

ANDIE FOUND HERSELF singing 'Rudolph the Red-Nosed Reindeer' as she drove to Dominic's house five days later. She couldn't remember when she'd last sung in the car—and certainly not such a cheesy carol as 'Rudolph'. No, wait. 'Six White Boomers' was even cheesier. But the choir had been so wonderful at Dominic's Christmas party she'd felt it had become the heart of the very successful party. The carols had stayed in her head.

It had only been significant to her, but it was the first time she'd played her guitar and sung in public since Anthony had died. She'd healed in every way from the trauma of his loss, although she would never forget him. Her future was with Dominic. How could she ever have thought he was not her type?

She didn't think Dominic would be burdened with the Scrooge label for too much longer. One of his most relentless critics had served as a volunteer at the party—and had completely changed her tune. Andie had committed to heart the journalist's article in one of the major newspapers.

Dominic Hunt appears more Santa Claus than Scrooge, having hosted a lavish Christmas party, not for celebri-

ties and wealthy silvertails but for ordinary folk down on their luck. A publicity stunt? No way.

She suspected Dominic's other private philanthropic work would eventually be discovered—probably by the digging of this same journalist. But, with the support of her love and the encouragement of Walter Burton, she thought he was in a better place to handle the revelations of his past if and when they came to light.

Dominic had invited her for a special dinner at his house this evening, though they'd had dinner together every evening since Christmas—and breakfast. She hadn't been here for the last few days; rather, he'd stayed at her place. She didn't want to move in with him until they were married.

But he'd said they had to do something special this evening as they wouldn't be able to spend New Year's Eve together—December the thirty-first would be the Party Queens' busiest night yet.

She was looking forward to dinner together, just the two of them. It was a warm evening and she wore a simple aqua dress that was both cool and elegant. Even though they were now engaged for real, they were still getting to know each other—there was a new discovery each time they got the chance to truly talk.

As she climbed the stairs to his house, she heard the sounds of a classical string quartet playing through the sound system he had piped through the house. Dominic had good taste in music, thank heaven. But when she pushed open the door, she was astounded to see a live quartet playing in the same space where the ill-fated Christmas tree had stood. She smiled her delight. It took some getting used to the extravagant gestures of a billionaire.

Dominic was there to greet her, looking darkly handsome in a tuxedo. She looked down at her simple dress in dismay. 'I didn't realise it was such an occasion or I would have worn something dressier,' she said.

Dominic smiled. 'You look absolutely beautiful. Anyway, if all goes well, you'll be changing into something quite different.'

She tilted her head to the side. 'This is all very intriguing,' she said. 'I'm not quite sure where you're going with it.'

'First of all, I want to say that everything can be cancelled if you don't want to go ahead with it. No pressure.'

For the first time she saw Dominic look like he must have looked as a little boy. He seethed with suppressed excitement and the agony of holding on to a secret he was desperate to share.

'Do tell,' she said, tucking her arm through the crook of his elbow, loving him more in that moment than she had ever loved him.

A big grin split his face. 'I'm going to put my hands over your eyes and lead you into the ballroom.'

'Okay,' she said, bemused. Then she guessed it. The family had been determined to give her an engagement party. Now that she and Dominic actually were genuinely engaged she would happily go along with it. She would act suitably surprised. And be very happy. Getting engaged to this wonderful man was worth celebrating.

She could tell she was at the entrance to the ballroom. 'You can open your eyes now,' said Dominic, removing his hands.

There was a huge cry of 'Surprise!' Andie was astounded to see the happy, smiling faces of all her family and friends as well as a bunch of people she didn't recognise but who were also smiling.

What was more, the ballroom had been transformed. It was exquisitely decorated in shades of white with hints of pale blue. Round tables were set up, dressed with white ruffled cloths and the backs of the chairs looped with antique lace and white roses. It was as if she'd walked into a dream. She blinked. But it was all still there when she opened her eyes.

Dominic held her close. 'We—your family, your friends, me—have organised a surprise wedding for you.'

Andie had to put her hand to her heart to stop it from pounding out of her chest. 'A wedding!'

She looked further through the open glass doors to see a bridal arch draped with filmy white fabric and white flowers set up among the rows of blue agapanthus blooming in the garden. Again she blinked. Again it was still there when she opened her eyes.

'Your wedding,' said Dominic. '*Our* wedding. You asked to be married as soon as possible. I organised it. With some help from the Party Queens. Actually, a *lot* of help from the Party Queens. Jake Marlow and some other friends of mine are also here.'

'It…it's unbelievable.'

'Only if it's what you want, Andie,' Dominic said, turning to her so just she could hear. 'If it's too much, if you'd rather organise your own wedding in your own time, this can just turn into a celebration of our engagement.'

'No! I want it. It's perfect.' She turned to the expectant people who seemed to have all held their breath in anticipation of her response and gone silent. 'Thank you. I say I do—well, I'm *soon* going to say I do!'

There was an eruption of cheers and happy relieved laughter. 'Here comes the bride,' called out one of her brothers.

Andie felt a swell of joy and happy disbelief. It was usually her organising all the surprise parties. To have Dominic do this for her—well, she felt as if she was falling in love with him all over again.

But the party planner in her couldn't resist checking on the details. 'The rings?' she asked Dominic. He patted his breast pocket. 'Both ready-to-wear couture pieces,' he said.

'And this is all legal?'

'Strictly speaking, you need a month's notice of intent to be married—and we filled out our form less than a month ago. But I got a magistrate to approve a shorter notice period. It's legal all right.'

Her eyes smarted with tears of joy. This was really happening. She was getting married today to the man she adored and in front of the people she loved most in the world.

Her fashion editor friend, Karen, dashed out from the guests and took her by the arm. 'Hey! No tears. I've got my favourite hair and make-up artist on hand and we don't want red eyes and blotchy cheeks. Let's get your make-up done. She's already done your bridesmaids.'

'My bridesmaids?'

'Your sisters, Hannah and Bea, Gemma, Eliza and your little niece, Caitlin. The little nephews are ring-bearers.'

'You guys have thought of everything.'

Turning around to survey the room again, she noticed a fabulous four-tiered wedding cake, covered in creamy frosting and blue sugar forget-me-nots. It was exactly the cake she'd talked about with Gemma. She'd bet it was chocolate cake on the bottom layers and vanilla on the top—Gemma knew she disliked the heavy fruitcake of traditional wedding cakes.

'Wait until you see your wedding dresses,' said Karen.

'Dresses?'

'I've got you a choice of three. You'll love them all but there's one I think you'll choose. It's heavy ivory lace over silk, vintage inspired, covered at the front but swooping to the back.'

'And a veil? I always wanted to wear a veil on my wedding day.' This all felt surreal.

'I've got the most beautiful wisp of silk tulle edged with antique lace. You attach it at the back of a simple halo band twisted with lace and trimmed with pearls. A touch vintage, a touch boho—very Andie. Oh, and your mother's pearl necklace for your "something borrowed".'

'It sounds divine.' She hugged Karen and thanked her. 'I think you know my taste better than I do myself.'

It *was* divine. The dress, the veil, the silk-covered shoes that tied with ribbons around her ankles, the posy of white old-fashioned roses tied with mingled white and blue ribbon. The bridesmaids in their pale blue vintage style dresses with white rosebuds twisted through their hair. The little boys in adorable mini white tuxedos.

As she walked down the magnificent staircase on her father's arm, Andie didn't need the guests' *oohs* and *aahs* to know she looked her best and the bridal party was breathtaking. She felt surrounded by the people she cared for most—and who cared for her. She wouldn't wish anything to be different.

Dominic was waiting for her at the wedding arch, flanked by his best man, Jake Marlow—tall, broad-shouldered, blond and not at all the geek she'd imagined him to be—with her brothers and Rob Cratchit as groomsmen.

She knew she had to walk a stately, graceful bride's walk towards her husband-to-be. But she had to resist the temptation to pick up her skirts and run to him and the start of their new life as husband and wife.

Dominic knew the bridesmaids looked lovely and the little attendants adorable. But he only had eyes for Andie as she walked towards him, her love for him shining from her eyes.

As she neared where he waited for her with the celebrant, a stray breeze picked up the fine layers of her gown's skirts and whirled them up and over her knees. She laughed and made no attempt to pin them down.

As her skirts settled back into place, their glances met and her lips curved in an intimate exchange of a private joke that had meaning only for two. It was just one of many private connections he knew they would share, bonding and strengthening their life as partners in the years of happy marriage that stretched out ahead of them.

Finally she reached him and looked up to him with her dazzling smile. He enfolded her hand in his as he waited with her by his side to give his wholehearted assent to the celebrant's question. 'Do you, Dominic Hugo Hunt, take this woman, Andrea Jane Newman, to be your lawful wedded wife?'

CHAPTER SEVENTEEN

Christmas Day the following year.

ANDIE STOOD WITHIN the protective curve of her husband's arm as she admired the fabulous Christmas tree that stood in the entrance of their Vaucluse home. It soared almost to the ceiling and was covered in exquisite ornaments that were set to be the start of their family collection, to be brought out year after year. Brightly wrapped gifts were piled around its base.

Christmas lunch was again being held here today, but this time it was a party for just Andie's family and a few other waifs and strays who appreciated being invited to share their family's celebration.

The big Scrooge-busting party had been such a success that Dominic had committed to holding it every year. But not here this time. This year he'd hired a bigger house with a bigger pool and invited more people. He'd be calling in to greet his guests later in the day.

Andie hadn't had to do a thing for either party. She'd had her input—how could a Party Queen not? But for this private party the decorating, table settings and gift-wrapping had all been done by Dominic and her family.

After much cajoling, Andie had convinced her father to

transfer his centre of cooking operations to Dominic's gourmet kitchen—just for this year. Although Dad had grumbled and complained about being away from familiar territory, Andie knew he was secretly delighted at the top-of-the-range equipment in the kitchen. The aromas that were wafting to her from the kitchen certainly smelled like the familiar traditional family favourites her father cooked each year. She couldn't imagine they would taste any less delicious than they would cooked in her parents' kitchen.

It was people who made the joy of Christmas and all the people she cherished the most were here to celebrate with her.

And one more.

The reason for all the disruption lay cradled in her arms. Hugo Andrew Hunt had been born in the early hours of Christmas Eve.

The birth had been straightforward and he was a healthy, strong baby. Andie had insisted on leaving the hospital today to be home for Christmas. Dominic had driven her and Hugo home so slowly and carefully they'd had a line of impatient cars honking their horns behind them by the time they'd got back to Vaucluse. He was over the moon about becoming a father. This was going to be one very loved little boy.

'Weren't you clever, to have our son born on Christmas Eve?' he said.

'I'm good at planning, but not *that* good,' she said. 'He came when he was ready. Maybe…maybe your parents sent him.' She turned her head so she could look up into Dominic's eyes. 'Now Christmas Eve will be a cause for celebration, not mourning, for you.'

'Yes,' he said. 'It will—because of you.'

Andie looked down at the perfect little face of her slumbering son and felt again the rush of fierce love for this precious being she'd felt when the midwife had first laid him on her tummy. He had his father's black hair but it was too soon to tell what colour his eyes would be.

Her husband, he-who-would-never-be-called-Scrooge-again, gently traced the line of little Hugo's cheek with his finger. 'Do you remember how I said last year was the very best Christmas of my life? Scratch that. This one is even better.'

'And they will get better and better,' she promised, turning her head for his kiss.

As they kissed, she heard footsteps on the marble floor and then an excited cry from her sister Bea. 'They're home! Andie, Dominic and baby Hugo are home!'

* * * * *

Crown Prince's Chosen Bride

Dear Reader,

Australia seems a long way away from royalty and castles and centuries of European tradition, doesn't it? In fact, Sydney might be the last place you'd think of for a prince and a commoner to meet and fall in love. Truth is, Frederik, Crown Prince of Denmark, met lovely Aussie, Mary Donaldson, on a night out with friends in Sydney. One day Mary, Crown Princess of Denmark, will be queen...

So I felt it was quite believable in *Crown Prince's Chosen Bride* for gorgeous Tristan, Crown Prince of Montavia, to be incognito on vacation in Sydney when he meets party planner and chef Gemma Harper (whom we first met as one of the Party Queens in *Gift-Wrapped in Her Wedding Dress*).

Tristan is enchanted by her, and Gemma, despite all resolve, falls for him. But everything is stacked against these two—protocol, custom and Gemma's own fears. It seems the meeting between prince and party planner can only lead to heartbreak...

I'm very taken with the idea that it just takes love to turn an ordinary life into a fairy tale. Gemma and Tristan have to navigate some twists and turns in their journey to their fairy-tale life together. I hope you enjoy taking that journey with them!

Warm regards,

Kandy Shepherd

To Cathleen Ross, in gratitude for your friendship!

CHAPTER ONE

USING AN OLD-FASHIONED wooden spoon and her favourite vintage-style ceramic bowl, Gemma Harper beat the batter for the cake she was baking to mark the end of her six months' self-imposed exile from dating.

Fittingly, the cake was a mixture of sweet and sour—a rich white chocolate mud cake, flavoured with the sharp contrast of lemon and lime. For Gemma, the six months had been sweet with the absence of relationship angst and tempered by sour moments of loneliness. But she'd come out of it stronger, wiser, determined to break the cycle of choosing the wrong type of man. *The heartbreaking type.*

From now on things would be different, she reminded herself as she gave the batter a particularly vigorous stir. She would not let a handsome face and a set of broad shoulders blind her to character flaws that spelled ultimate doom to happiness. She would curb the impulsiveness that had seen her diving headlong into relationships because she thought she was in love with someone she, in fact, did not really know.

And she was going to be much, *much* tougher. Less forgiving. No more giving 'one last chance' and then another to a cheating, lying heartbreaker, unworthy of her, whose false promises she'd believed.

She was twenty-eight and she wanted to get married and have kids before too many more years sped by.

'No more Ms Bad Judge of Men,' she said out loud.

It was okay to talk to herself. She was alone in the large industrial kitchen at the converted warehouse in inner-city Alexandria, the Sydney suburb that was headquarters to her successful party planning business. Party Queens belonged to her and to her two business partners, Andie Newman and Eliza Dunne. The food was Gemma's domain, Andie was the creative genius and Eliza the business brain.

After several years working as a chef and then as a food editor on magazines, in Party Queens Gemma had found her dream job. Going into partnership with Andie and Eliza was the best decision she'd ever made. And throwing herself headlong into work had been the best thing she could have done to keep her mind off men. She would do anything to keep this business thriving.

Gemma poured the batter into a high, round pan and carefully placed it into a slow oven, where it would cook for one and a half hours. Then she would cover it with coconut frosting and garnish it with fine curls of candied lemon and lime peel. Not only would the cake be a treat for her and her partners to share this afternoon, in celebration of the end of her man-free six months, it was also a trial run for a client's wedding cake.

Carefully, she settled the cake in the centre of the oven and gently closed the oven door.

She turned back to face the island countertop, to find she was no longer alone. A tall, broad-shouldered man stood just inside the door. She gasped, and her hand—encased in a hot-pink oven mitt—went to her heart.

'Who are you and how the heck did you get in here?' she asked, her voice high with sudden panic.

Even through her shock she registered that the intruder was very handsome, with a lean face and light brown hair. *Just her type.* No. *No longer her type*—not after six months of talking herself out of that kind of very good-looking man. Especially if he was a burglar—or worse.

She snatched up a wooden spoon in self-defence. Drips of cake batter slid down her arm, but she scarcely noticed.

The man put up his hands as if to ward off her spoon. 'Tristan Marco. I have a meeting this morning with Eliza Dunne. She called to tell me she was caught in traffic and gave me the pass code for the door.'

The stranger seemed about her age and spoke with a posh English accent laced with a trace of something else. Something she couldn't quite place. French? German? He didn't look Australian. Something about his biscuit-coloured linen trousers, fine cream cotton shirt and stylish shoes seemed sartorially European.

'You can put down your weapon,' he said, amusement rippling through his voice.

Gemma blushed as she lowered the wooden spoon. What good would a spoon have been against a man taller than six foot? She took a deep breath in an attempt to get her heart rate back to somewhere near normal. 'You gave me quite a shock, walking in on me like that. Why didn't you press the buzzer?'

He walked further into the room so he stood opposite the island counter that separated them. This close she noticed vivid blue eyes framed by dark brows, smooth olive skin, perfect teeth.

'I'm sorry to have frightened you,' he said in that intriguing accent and with an expressive shrug of his broad shoulders. 'Ms Dunne did not tell me anyone else would be here.'

Gemma took off her oven mitts, used one to surreptitiously wipe the batter dribbles from her arm and placed them on the countertop.

'I wasn't frightened. It's just that I'm on my own here and—' *now wasn't* that *a dumb thing to say to a stranger?* '—Eliza will be here very soon.'

'Yes, she said she would not be long,' he said. His smile was both charming and reassuring. 'I'm looking forward to meeting her. We have only spoken on the phone.'

He was gorgeous. Gemma refused to let the dangerous little fluttering of awareness take hold. She had just spent six months talking herself out of any kind of instant attraction. She was not going to make those old mistakes again.

'Can I help you in the meantime?' Gemma asked. 'I'm Gemma Harper—one of Eliza's business partners.'

To be polite, she moved around the countertop to be nearer to him. Realising she was still in her white chef's apron, she went to untie it, then stopped. Might that look as if she was *undressing* in front of this stranger?

She gave herself a mental shake. *Of course it wouldn't.* Had six months without a date made her start thinking like an adolescent? Still, there was no real need to take the apron off.

She offered him her hand in a businesslike gesture that she hoped negated the pink oven mitts and the wielding of the wooden spoon. He took it in his own firm, warm grip for just the right amount of time.

'So you are also a Party Queen?' he asked. The hint of a smile lifted the corners of his mouth.

'Yes, I'm the food director,' she said, wishing not for the first time that they had chosen a more staid name for the business. It had all started as a bit of a lark, but now, eighteen months after they had launched, they were one of the most popular and successful party planning businesses in Sydney. And still being teased about being Party Queens.

'Did you…did you want to see Eliza about booking a party?' she asked cautiously. To her knowledge, the steadfastly single Eliza wasn't dating anyone. But his visit to their headquarters might be personal. Lucky Eliza, if that was the case.

'Yes, I've been planning a reception with her.'

'A reception? You mean a wedding reception?'

The good ones were always taken. She banished the flickering disappointment the thought aroused. This guy was a stranger and a client. His marital status should be of no concern to her. Yet she had to admit there was something about him she found very attractive beyond the obvious appeal of his good looks. Perhaps because he seemed somehow…different.

'No. Not a wedding.' His face seemed to darken. 'When I get married, it will not be *me* arranging the festivities.'

Of course it wouldn't. In her experience it was always the bride. It sometimes took the grooms a while to realise that.

'So, if not a wedding reception, what kind of reception?'

'Perhaps "reception" is not the right word. My English…' He shrugged again.

She did like broad shoulders on a man.

'Your English sounds perfect to me,' she said, her curiosity aroused. 'Do you mean a business reception?'

'Yes and no. I have been speaking to Eliza about holding a party for me to meet Australians connected by business to my family. It is to be held on Friday evening.'

It clicked. 'Of course!' she exclaimed. 'The cocktail party at the Parkview Hotel on Friday night.' It was now Monday, and everything was on track for the upscale event.

'That is correct,' he said.

'I manage the food aspect of our business. We're using the hotel's excellent catering team. I've worked with them on devising the menu. I think you'll be very happy with the food.'

'It all looked in order to me,' he said. 'I believe I am in capable hands.'

Everything fell into place. Tristan Marco was their mystery client. Mysterious because his event had been organised from a distance, by phone and email, in a hurry, and by someone for whom Eliza had been unable to check credit details. The client had solved that problem by paying the entire quoted price upfront. A very substantial price for a no-expenses-spared party at a high-end venue. She, Eliza and Andie had spent quite some time speculating on what the client would be like.

'You are in the best possible hands with our company,' she reassured him.

He looked at her intently, his blue eyes narrowed. 'Did I speak with you?' he said. 'I am sure I would have remembered your voice.'

She certainly would have remembered *his*.

Gemma shook her head. 'Eliza is our business director. She does most of our client liaison. You are not what we—' She clapped her hand to her mouth. *Put a zip on it, Gemma.*

'Not what you what?' he asked with a quizzical expression.

'Not…not what we expected,' she said. Her voice trailed away, and she looked down in the direction of his well-polished Italian shoes.

'What *did* you expect?'

She sighed and met his gaze full on. There was no getting out of this. She really needed to curb her tendency to blurt things out without thinking. That was why she worked with the food and Eliza and Andie with the clients.

'Well, we expected someone older. Someone not so tall. Someone heavier. Someone perhaps even…bald. With a twirling black moustache. Maybe…maybe someone like Hercule Poirot. You know…the detective in the Agatha Christie movies?'

Someone not so devastatingly handsome.

Thank heaven, he laughed. 'So are you disappointed in what you see?' He stood, arms outspread, as if welcoming her inspection.

Gemma felt suddenly breathless at the intensity of his gaze, at her compulsion to take up his unspoken offer to admire his tall, obviously well-muscled body, his lean, handsome face with those incredibly blue eyes, the full sensual mouth with the top lip slightly narrower then the lower, the way his short brown hair kicked up at the front in a cowlick.

'Not at all,' she said, scarcely able to choke out the words. *Disappointed was* not *the word that sprang to mind.*

'I am glad to hear that,' he said very seriously, his gaze not leaving hers. 'You did not know me, but I knew *exactly* what to expect from Party Queens.'

'You...you did?' she stuttered.

'Party Queens was recommended to me by my friend Jake Marlowe. He told me that each of the three partners was beautiful, talented and very smart.'

'He...he did?' she said, her vocabulary seeming to have escaped her.

Billionaire Jake Marlowe was the business partner of Andie's husband, Dominic. He'd been best man at their wedding two Christmases ago. Who knew he'd taken such an interest in them?

'On the basis of my meeting with you, I can see Jake did not mislead me,' Tristan said.

His formal way of speaking and his charming smile made the compliment sound sincere when it might have sounded sleazy. *Had he even made a slight bow as he spoke?*

She willed herself not to blush again but without success. 'Thank you,' was all she could manage to say.

'Jake spoke very highly of your business,' Tristan said. 'He told me there was no better party-planning company in Sydney.'

'That was kind of him. It's always gratifying to get such good feedback.'

'I did not even talk with another company,' Tristan said with that charming smile.

'Wow! I mean...that's wonderful. I...we're flattered. We won't let you down, I promise you. The hotel is a perfect venue. It overlooks Hyde Park, it's high end, elegant and it prides itself on its exemplary service. I don't think I've ever seen so much marble and glamour in one place.'

She knew she was speaking too fast, but she couldn't seem to help it.

'Yes. The first thing I did was inspect it when I arrived in Sydney. You chose well.' He paused. 'I myself would prefer something more informal, but protocol dictates the event must be formal.'

'The protocol of your family business?' she asked, not quite sure she'd got it right.

He nodded. 'That is correct. It must be upheld even when I am in another country.'

'You're a visitor to Australia?' Another piece of the puzzle fell into place. The phone calls had all come from Queensland, the state to the north of New South Wales. Where Jake Marlowe lived, she now realised.

'Yes,' he said.

She still couldn't place the accent, and it annoyed her. Gemma had studied French, German and Italian—not that she'd had much chance to practise them—and thought she had a good ear.

'What kind of business does your family run?' she asked.

That was another thing the Party Queens had wondered about as they'd discussed their mystery client. *He was still a mystery.*

Tristan was still too bemused by the vision of this cute redhead wearing bright pink oven mitts and wielding a wooden spoon as a weapon to think straight. He had to consider his reply and try not to be distracted by the smear of flour down her right cheek that seemed to point to her beautiful full mouth. While he'd been speaking with her, he'd had to fight the urge to lean across and gently wipe it off.

Should he tell her the truth? Or give the same evasive replies he'd given to others during his incognito trip to Sydney? He'd been here four days, and no one had recognised him…

Visiting Australia had been on his list to do before he turned thirty and had to return home to step up his involvement in 'the business'. He'd spent some time in Queensland with Jake. But for the past few days in Sydney, he had enjoyed his anonymity, relished being just Tristan. No expectations. No explanations. Just a guy nearing thirty, being himself, being independent, having fun. It was a novelty for him to be an everyday guy. Even when he'd been at university in England, the other students had soon sussed him out.

He would have to tell Party Queens the truth about himself and the nature of his reception sooner or later, though. *Let it be later.*

Gemma Harper was lovely—really lovely—with her deep auburn hair, heart-shaped face and the shapely curves that the professional-looking white apron did nothing to disguise. He wanted to enjoy talking with her still cloaked in the anonymity of being just plain Tristan. When she found out his true identity, her attitude would change. It always did.

'Finance. Trade. That kind of thing,' he replied.

'I see,' she said.

He could tell by the slight downturn of her mouth that although she'd made the right polite response, she found his family business dull. More the domain of the portly, bald gentleman she'd imagined him to be. Who could blame her? But he didn't want this delightful woman to find *him* dull.

He looked at the evidence of her cooking on the countertop, smelled something delicious wafting from the oven.

'And chocolate,' he added. 'The world's best chocolate.'

Now her beautiful brown eyes lit up with interest. *He'd played the right card.*

'Chocolate? You're talking about my favourite food group. So you're from Switzerland?'

He shook his head.

'Belgium? France?' she tried.

'Close,' he said. 'My country is Montovia. A small principality that is not far from those countries.'

She paused, her head tilted to one side. 'You're talking about Montovian chocolate?'

'You know it?' he asked, surprised. His country was known more for its financial services and as a tax haven than for its chocolate and cheese—undoubtedly excellent as they were.

She smiled, revealing delightful dimples in each cheek. He caught his breath. *This Party Queen really was a beauty.*

'Of course I do,' she said. 'Montovian chocolate is sublime. Not easy to get here, but I discovered it when I visited Europe. Nibbled on it, that is. I was a backpacker, and it's too expensive to have much more than a nibble. It's… Well, it's the gold standard of chocolate.'

'I would say the platinum standard,' he said, pleased at her reaction.

'Gold. Platinum. It's just marvellous stuff,' she said. 'Are you a *chocolatier*?'

'No,' he said. 'I am more on the…executive side of the business.' That wasn't stretching the truth too far.

'Is that why you're here in Sydney? The reason for your party? Promoting Montovian chocolate?'

'Among other things,' he said. He didn't want to dig himself in too deep with deception.

She nodded. 'Confidential stuff you can't really talk about?'

'That's right,' he said. He didn't actually like to lie. Evade—*yes*. Lie—*no*.

'Don't worry—you'd be surprised at what secrets we have to keep in the party business,' she said. 'We have to be discreet.'

She put her index finger to her lips. He noticed she didn't wear any rings on either hand.

'But the main reason I am in Sydney is for a vacation,' he said, with 100 per cent truthfulness.

'Really? Who would want a vacation from Montovian chocolate? I don't think I'd ever leave home if I lived in Montovia,' she said with another big smile. 'I'm joking, of course,' she hastened to add. 'No matter how much you love your job, a break is always good.'

'Sydney is a marvellous place for a vacation. I am enjoying it here very much,' he said.

And enjoying it even more since he'd met her. Sydney was a city full of beautiful women, but there was something about

Gemma Harper that had instantly appealed to him. Her open, friendly manner, the laughter in her eyes, those dimples, the way she'd tried so unsuccessfully to look ferocious as she'd waved that wooden spoon. She was too pretty to ever look scary. Yet according to his friend Jake, all three of the partners were formidably smart businesswomen. Gemma interested him.

'March is the best time here,' she said. 'It's the start of autumn down-under. Still hot, but not too hot. The sea is warm and perfect for swimming. The school holidays are over. The restaurants are not crowded. I hope you're enjoying our lovely city.' She laughed. 'I sound like I'm spouting a travel brochure, don't I? But, seriously, you're lucky to be here at this time of year.'

The harbourside city was everything Tristan had hoped it would be. But he realised now there was one thing missing from his full enjoyment of Sydney—female company. The life he'd chosen—correction, the life he had had chosen *for* him—meant he often felt lonely.

'You are the lucky one—to live in such a beautiful city on such a magnificent harbour,' he said.

'True. Sydney *is* great, and I love living here,' she said. 'But I'm sure Montovia must be, too. When I think of your chocolate, I picture snow-capped mountains and lakes. Am I right?'

'Yes,' he said. He wanted to tell her more about his home but feared he might trip himself up with an untruth. His experience of life in Montovia was very different from what a tourist might find.

'That was a lucky guess, then,' she said. 'I must confess I don't know anything about your country except for the chocolate.'

'Not many people outside of Europe do, I've discovered,' he said with a shrug.

And that suited him fine in terms of a laid-back vacation. Here in Sydney, half a world away from home, he hadn't been recognised. He liked it that way.

'But perhaps our chocolate will put us on the map down-under.'

'Perhaps after your trip here it will. I think…'

She paused midsentence, frowned. He could almost see the cogs turning.

'The menu for your reception… We'll need to change the desserts to showcase Montovian chocolate. There's still time. I'll get on to it straight away.' She slapped her hand to her mouth. 'Sorry. I jumped the gun there. I meant if you approve, of course.'

'Of course I approve. It's a very good idea. I should have thought of it myself.' Only devising menus was quite out of the range of his experience.

'Excellent. Let me come up with some fabulous chocolate desserts, and I'll pass them by you for approval.'

He was about to tell her not to bother with the approval process when he stopped himself. *He wanted to see her again.* 'Please do that,' he said.

'Eliza shouldn't be too much longer—the traffic can't be that bad. Can I take you into our waiting area? It's not big, but it's more comfortable than standing around here,' she said.

'I am comfortable here,' he said, not liking the idea of her being in a different room from him. 'I like your kitchen.' All stainless steel and large industrial appliances, it still somehow seemed imbued with her warmth and welcome.

Her eyes widened. They were an unusual shade of brown—the colour of cinnamon—and lit up when she smiled.

'Me, too,' she said. 'I have a cake in the oven, and I want to keep an eye on it.'

He inhaled the citrus-scented air. 'It smells very good.'

She glanced at her watch. 'It's a new recipe I'm trying, but I think it will be delicious. I don't know how long you're planning to meet with Eliza for, but the cake won't be ready for another hour or so. Then it has to cool, and then I—'

'I think our meeting will be brief. I have some more sight-seeing to do—I've booked a jet boat on the harbour. Perhaps another time I could sample your cake?' He would make certain there would be another time.

'I can see that a cake wouldn't have the same appeal as a jet boat,' she said, with a smile that showed him she did not take offence. 'What else have you seen of Sydney so far?' she asked.

'The usual tourist spots,' he said. 'I've been to the Opera House, Bondi Beach, climbed the Sydney Harbour Bridge.'

'They're all essential. Though I've never found the courage to do the bridge climb. But there's also a Sydney tourists don't get to see. I recommend—'

'Would you show me the Sydney the tourists don't see? I would very much like your company.'

The lovely food director's eyes widened. She hesitated. 'I… I wonder if—'

He was waiting for her reply, when a slender, dark-haired young woman swept into the room. Tristan silently cursed under his breath in his own language at the interruption. She immediately held out her hand to him.

'You must be Mr Marco? I'm so sorry to have kept you waiting—the traffic was a nightmare. I'm Eliza Dunne.'

For a moment he made no acknowledgment of the newcomer's greeting—and then he remembered. He was using Marco as a surname when it was in fact his second given name. He didn't actually have a surname, as such. Not when he was always known simply as Tristan, Crown Prince of Montovia.

CHAPTER TWO

GEMMA CLOSED HER eyes in sheer relief at Eliza's well-timed entrance. *What a lucky escape.* Despite all her resolve not to act on impulse when it came to men, she'd been just about to agree to show Tristan around Sydney.

And that would have been a big mistake.

First, Party Queens had a rule of staff not dating clients. The fact that Andie had broken the rule in spectacular fashion by falling in love with and marrying their billionaire client Dominic Hunt was beside the point. She, Gemma, did not intend to make any exceptions. The business was too important to her for her to make messy mistakes.

But it wasn't just about the company rules. If she'd said yes to Tristan she could have told herself she was simply being hospitable to a foreign visitor—but she would have been lying. And lying to herself about men was a bad habit she was trying to break. She found Tristan way too appealing to pretend that being hospitable was all it would be.

'Thank you for taking care of Mr Marco for me, Gemma,' Eliza said. 'The traffic was crazy—insane.'

'Gemma has looked after me very well,' Tristan said, again with that faint hint of a bow in her direction.

Her heart stepped up a beat at the awareness that shimmered through her.

'She hasn't plied you with cake or muffins or cookies?' asked Eliza with a teasing smile.

'The cake isn't baked yet,' Gemma said. 'But I have cookies and—'

'Perhaps another cake, another time,' Tristan said with a shrug of those broad shoulders, that charming smile. 'And I could give you chocolate in return.'

The shrug. The accent. Those blue, blue eyes. *The Montovian chocolate.*

Yes! her body urged her to shout.

No! urged her common sense.

'Perhaps...' she echoed, the word dwindling away irresolutely.

Thankfully, Eliza diverted Tristan's attention from her as she engaged him in a discussion about final guest numbers for his party.

Gemma was grateful for some breathing space. Some deep breathing to let her get to grips with the pulse-raising presence of this gorgeous man.

'I'll let you guys chat while I check on my cake,' she said as she went back around the countertop.

She slipped into the pink oven mitts and carefully opened the oven door. As she turned the pan around, she inhaled the sweet-sharp aroma of the cake. Over the years she had learned to gauge the progress of her baking by smell. Its scent told her this cake had a way to go. This kind of solid mud cake needed slow, even cooking.

That was what she'd be looking for in a man in future. A slow burn. Not instant flames. No exhilarating infatuation. No hopping into bed too soon. Rather a long, slow getting to know each other before any kind of commitment—physical or otherwise—was made. The old-fashioned word *courtship* sprang to mind.

She'd managed six months on her own. She was in no rush

for the next man. There was no urgency. Next time she wanted to get it right.

Still, no matter what she told herself, Gemma was super-aware of Tristan's presence in her kitchen. And, even though he seemed engrossed in his conversation with Eliza, the tension in the way he held himself let her know that he was aware of her, too. The knowledge was a secret pleasure she hugged to herself. It was reassuring that she could still attract a hot guy. Even if there was no way she should do anything about it.

She scraped clean her mixing bowl and spoon and put them in the dishwasher while keeping an ear on Tristan and Eliza's conversation about the party on Friday and an eye on Tristan himself. On those broad shoulders tapering to narrow hips, on the long legs she imagined would be lean and hard with muscle.

Catching her eye, he smiled. Her first instinct was to blush, then smile back. For a long moment their gazes held before she reluctantly dragged hers away and went back to the tricky task of finely slicing strips of candied lemon peel.

Okay, she wasn't in dating exile any more. There was no law to say she couldn't flirt just a little. But she had spent six months fine-tuning her antennae to detect potential heartbreak. And there was something about this handsome Montovian that had those antennae waving wildly with a message of caution. They detected a mystery behind his formal way of speaking and courteous good manners. It wasn't what he'd said but what he *hadn't* said.

Then there was the fact Tristan was only here for a few days. To be a good-looking tourist's vacation fling was *not* what she needed in order to launch herself back into the dating pool. She had to be totally on guard, so she wouldn't fall for the first gorgeous guy who strolled into her life.

She'd learned such painful lessons from her relationship with Alistair. It had been love at first sight for both of them—or so she'd thought. Followed by an emotional rollercoaster that had lasted for eighteen months. Too blinded by desire, love—whatever that turbulent mix of emotions had been—she'd only seen the Alistair she'd wanted to see. She had missed all the cues that would have alerted her he wasn't what he'd sworn he was.

She'd heard the rumours before she'd started to date him. But he'd assured her that he'd kicked his cocaine habit—*and* his reputation as a player. When time after time he'd lapsed, she'd always forgiven him, given him the one more chance he'd begged for. And then another. After all, she'd loved him and he'd loved her—hadn't he?

Then had come the final hurt and humiliation of finding him in the bathroom at a party with a so-called 'mutual friend'. Doing *her* as well as the drugs. Gemma doubted she'd ever be able to scour that image from her eyes.

After that there'd been no more chances, no more Alistair. She'd spent the last six months trying to sort out why she always seemed to fall for the wrong type of man. Her dating history was littered with misfires—though none as heart-wrenchingly painful as Alistair's betrayal.

On her first day back in the dating world she wasn't going to backtrack. Tristan was still a mystery man. He had perhaps not been completely honest about himself and was on vacation from a faraway country. How many more strikes against him could there be?

But, oh, he was handsome.

Eliza had suggested that Tristan follow her into her office. But he turned towards Gemma. 'I would like to speak to Gemma again first, please,' he said, with unmistakable authority.

Eliza sent Gemma a narrow-eyed, speculative glance. 'Sure,' she said to Tristan. 'My office is just around the corner. I'll wait for you there.'

Gemma could hear the sound of her own heart beating in the sudden silence of the room as Eliza left. Her mouth went dry as Tristan came closer to face her over the countertop.

His gaze was very direct. 'So, Gemma, you did not get a chance to answer me—will you show me your home town?'

It took every bit of resolve for her not to run around to the other side of the countertop and babble, *Of course. How about we start right now?*

Instead she wiped her suddenly clammy hands down the sides of her apron. Took a deep breath to steady her voice. 'I'm sorry, Tristan. But I… I can't.'

He looked taken aback. She got the distinct impression he wasn't used to anyone saying *no* to him.

He frowned. 'You are sure?'

'It wouldn't be…appropriate,' she said.

'Because I am a client?' he asked, his gaze direct on hers.

She shifted from foot to foot, clad in the chef's clogs she wore in the kitchen. 'That's right,' she said. 'I'm sorry, but it's company policy.'

Just for a moment, did disappointment cloud those blue eyes? 'That is a shame. As I said, I would very much enjoy your company.'

'I…well, I would enjoy yours, too. But…uh…rules are rules.'

Such rules *could* be broken—as Andie had proved. But Gemma was determined to stick to her resolve, even if it was already tinged with regret.

His mouth twisted. 'I know all about rules that have to be followed whether one likes it or not,' he said with an edge to his voice. 'I don't like it, but I understand.'

What did he mean by that? Gemma wasn't sure if he was referring to the Party Queens rules or a different set of rules that might apply to him. She sensed there might be a lot she didn't understand about him. And now would never get a chance to.

'Thank you,' she said. 'I'll email the amended dessert menu to you.'

'Dessert menu?'

'Using Montovian chocolate for your party,' she prompted.

'Of course,' he said. 'I will look forward to it. I am sorry I will not be seeing more of Sydney with you.'

'I... I'm sorry, too.' But she would not toss away all that hard work she'd done on her insecurities.

'Now I must let you get back to work while I speak with Eliza,' he said, in what sounded very much like dismissal.

Gemma refused to admire his back view as he left the kitchen. *She liked a nice butt on a man.* For better or for worse, that ship had sailed. And she felt good about her decision. She really did.

But she was on edge as she prepared the coconut frosting by melting white chocolate and beating it with coconut cream. She kept glancing up, in case Tristan came back into the room. Was so distracted she grated the edge of her finger as well as the fine slivers of lemon and lime peel that would give the frosting its bite. But a half-hour later, when his meeting with Eliza concluded, he only briefly acknowledged her as he passed by the doorway to her kitchen.

She gripped her hands so tightly her fingernails cut into her hands. The sudden feeling of loss was totally irrational. She would *not* run after him to say she'd changed her mind.

An hour later, as Gemma was finishing her work on the cake, Eliza popped her head around the door.

'Cake ready?' she asked. 'The smell of it has been driving me crazy.'

'Nearly ready. I've been playing with the candied peel on top and tidying up the frosting,' Gemma said. 'Come and have a look. I think it will be perfect for the Sanderson wedding.'

'Magnificent,' Eliza said. She sneaked a quick taste of the leftover frosting from the bowl. 'Mmm...coconut. Nice touch. You really are a genius when it comes to food.'

Gemma knew her mouth had turned downwards. 'Just not such a genius when it comes to guys.'

Eliza patted her on the shoulder. 'Come on—you've done so well with your sabbatical. Aren't we going to celebrate your freedom to date—I mean to date *wisely*—with this cake?'

Both Gemma and Andie had been totally supportive during her man break. Had proved themselves again and again to be good friends as well as business partners.

Gemma nodded. 'I know…' she said, unable to stop the catch in her voice. It was the right thing to have turned down Tristan's invitation, but that didn't stop a lingering sense of regret, of wondering *what might have been*.

'What's brought on this fit of the gloomies?' Eliza asked. 'Oh, wait—don't tell me. The handsome mystery man—Tristan Marco. He's just your type, isn't he? As soon as I saw him, I thought—'

Gemma put up her hand to stop her. 'In looks, yes, I can't deny that. He's really hot.' She forced a smile. 'Our guesses about him were *so* far off the mark, weren't they?'

'He's about as far away from short, bald and middle-aged as he could be,' Eliza agreed. 'I had to stop myself staring at him for fear he'd think I was incredibly bad mannered.'

'You can imagine how shocked I was when he told me *he* was our client for the Friday night party. But I don't think he told me everything. There's still a lot of the mystery man about him.'

'What do you mean, *still* too much mystery? What did you talk about here in your kitchen?'

Gemma filled Eliza in on her conversation with Tristan, leaving out his invitation for her to show him around Sydney. Eliza would only remind her that dating clients was a no-no. And, besides, she didn't want to talk about it—she'd made her decision.

Eliza nodded. 'He told me much the same thing—although he was quite evasive about the final list of guests. But what the heck? It's his party, and he can invite anyone he wants to it as long as he sticks with the number we quoted on. We're ahead financially, so it's all good to me.'

'That reminds me,' Gemma said. 'I have to amend the desserts for Friday to include Montovian chocolate. And he needs to approve them.'

'You can discuss the menu change with him on Wednesday.'

Gemma stopped, the blunt palette knife she'd used to apply the frosting still in her hand. 'Wednesday? Why Wednesday?'

'Tristan is on vacation in Sydney. He's asked me to book a private yacht cruise around the harbour on Wednesday. And to organise an elegant, romantic lunch for two to be taken on board.'

A romantic lunch for two?

Gemma let go of the palette knife so it landed with a clatter on the stainless steel benchtop, using the distraction to gather her thoughts. So she'd been right to distrust mystery man Tristan. He'd asked her to show him around Sydney. And at the same time he was making plans for a romantic tryst with another woman on a luxury yacht.

Thank heaven she'd said *no.*

Or had she misread him? Had his interest only been in her knowledge of local hotspots? After a six-month sabbatical, maybe her dating skills were so rusty she'd mistaken his meaning.

Still, she couldn't help feeling annoyed. Not so much at Tristan but at herself, for having let down her guard even if only momentarily. If she'd glimpsed that look of interest in *his* eyes, he would have seen it in *hers*.

'Which boat did you book?' she asked Eliza.

The cooking facilities on the charter yachts available in Sydney Harbour ranged from a basic galley to a full-sized luxury kitchen.

'Because it will be midweek, I managed to get the *Argus* on short notice.'

'Wow! Well done. He should love that.'

'He did. I showed him a choice of boats online, but the *Argus* was the winner hands down.'

'His date should be really impressed,' Gemma said, fighting off an urge to sound snarky.

'I think that was the idea—the lucky lady.'

The *Argus* was a replica of a sixty-foot vintage wooden motor yacht from the nineteen-twenties and the ultimate in luxury. Its hourly hire rate was a mind-boggling amount of dollars. To book it for just two people was a total extravagance. Party Queens had organised a corporate client's event for thirty people on the boat at the start of summer. It was classy, high-tech and had a fully equipped kitchen. Tristan must *really* want to impress his date.

'So I'm guessing if lunch is on the *Argus* we won't be on a tight budget.'

'He told me to "spend what it takes",' said Eliza with a delighted smile. The more dollars for Party Queens, the happier Eliza was.

Gemma gritted her teeth and forced herself to think of Tristan purely as a client, not as an attractive man who'd caught her eye. It would be better if she still thought of him as bald with a pot belly. 'It's short notice, but of course we can do it. Any restrictions on the menu?'

Planning party menus could involve dealing with an overwhelming array of food allergies and intolerances.

'None that he mentioned,' said Eliza.

'That makes things easier.' Gemma thought out loud. 'An elegant on-board lunch for two… I'm thinking seafood—fresh and light. A meal we can prep ahead and our chef can finish off on board. We'll book the waiter today.'

'"Romantic" is the keyword, remember? And he wants the best French champagne—which, of course, I'll organise.' Eliza had an interest in wine as well as in spreadsheets.

'I wonder who his guest is?' Gemma said, hoping she wouldn't betray her personal interest to Eliza.

'Again, he didn't say,' Eliza said.

Gemma couldn't help a stab of envy towards Tristan's date, for whom he was making such an effort to be *romantic*. But he was a client. And she was a professional. If he wanted romantic, she'd give him romantic. In spades.

'But tell me—why will *I* be meeting with Tristan on Wednesday?'

'He wants you to be on board for the duration—to make sure everything is perfect. His words, not mine.'

'What? A lunch for two with a chef and a waiter doesn't need a supervisor, as well. You know how carefully we vet the people who work for us. They can be trusted to deliver the Party Queens' promise.'

Eliza put up her hands in a placatory gesture. 'Relax. I know that. I know the yacht comes with skipper and crew. But Tristan asked for you to be on board, too. He wants you to make sure everything goes well.'

'No!' Gemma said and realised her protest sounded over-the-top. 'I… I mean there's no need for me to be there at all. I'll go over everything with the chef and the waiter to make sure the presentation and service is faultless.'

Eliza shook her head. 'Not good enough. Tristan Marco has specifically requested your presence on board.'

Gemma knew the bottom line was always important to Eliza. She'd made sure their business was a success financially. With a sinking heart Gemma realised there would be no getting out of this. And Eliza was only too quick to confirm that.

'You know how lucrative his party on Friday is for us, Gemma. Tristan is an important client. You really have to do this. Whether you like it or not.'

CHAPTER THREE

ON WEDNESDAY MORNING Gemma made her way along the harbourside walk on the northern shore of Sydney Harbour. Milson's Point and the Art Deco North Sydney Swimming Pool were behind her as she headed towards the wharf at Lavender Bay, where she was to join the *Argus*. As she walked she realised why she felt so out of sorts—she was jealous of Tristan's unknown date. And put out that he had replaced her so quickly.

It wasn't that she was jealous of the other woman's cruise on a magnificent yacht on beautiful Sydney Harbour. Or the superb meal she would be served, thanks to the skill of the Party Queens team. No. What Gemma envied her most for was the pleasure of Tristan's company.

Gemma seethed with a most unprofessional indignation at the thought of having to dance attendance on the couple's romantic rendezvous. There was no justification for her feelings—Tristan had asked to spend time with her and she had turned him down. In fact, her feelings were more than a touch irrational. But still she didn't like the idea of seeing Tristan with another woman.

She did not want to do this.

Why had he insisted on her presence on board? This was a romantic lunch for *two*, for heaven's sake. There was only so much for her to do for a simple three-course meal. She would have too much time to observe Tristan being charming to his date. *And, oh, how charming the man could be.*

If she was forced to watch him kiss that other woman, she might just have to jump off board and brave the sharks and jellyfish to swim to shore.

Suck it up, Gemma, you turned him down.

She forced herself to remember that she was the director of her own company, looking after an important client. To convince herself that there were worse things to do than twiddle her thumbs in the lap of luxury on one of the most beautiful harbours in the world on a perfect sunny day. And to remind herself to paste a convincing smile on her face as she did everything in her power to make her client's day a success.

As she rounded the boardwalk past Luna Park fun fair, she picked up her pace when she noticed the *Argus* had already docked at Lavender Bay. The charter company called it a 'gentleman's cruiser', and the wooden boat's vintage lines made it stand out on a harbour dotted with slick, modern watercraft. She didn't know much about boats, but she liked this one—it looked fabulous, and it had a very well-fitted-out kitchen that was a dream to work in.

The Lavender Bay wharf was on the western side of the Sydney Harbour Bridge, virtually in its shadow, with a view right through to the gleaming white sails of the Opera House on the eastern side. The water was unbelievably blue to match the blue sky. The air was tangy with salt. How could she stay down on a day like this? *She would make the most of it.*

Gemma got her smile ready as she reached the historic old dock. She expected that a crew member would greet her and help her on board. But her heart missed a beat when she saw it was Tristan who stood there. Tristan…in white linen trousers and a white shirt open at the neck to reveal a glimpse of muscular chest, sleeves rolled back to show strong, sinewy forearms. Tristan looking tanned and unbelievably handsome, those blue eyes putting the sky to shame. Her heart seemed almost literally to leap into her throat.

She had never been more attracted to a man.

'Let me help you,' he said in his deep, accented voice as he extended a hand to help her across the gangplank.

She looked at his hand for a long moment, not sure what her reaction would be at actually touching him. But she knew she would need help to get across because she felt suddenly shaky and weak at the knees. She swallowed hard against a painful swell of regret.

What an idiot she'd been to say no *to him.*

Gemma looked as lovely as he remembered, Tristan thought as he held out his hand to her. Even lovelier—which he hadn't thought possible. Her auburn hair fell to her shoulders, glinting copper and gold in the sunlight. Her narrow deep blue cut-off pants and blue-and-white-striped top accentuated her curves in a subtle way he appreciated. But her smile was tentative, and she had hesitated before taking his hand and accepting his help to come on board.

'Gemma, it is so good to see you,' he said while his heart beat a tattoo of exultation that she had come—and he sent out a prayer that she would forgive him for insisting in such an autocratic manner on her presence.

She had her rules—he had his. His rules decreed that spending time with a girl like Gemma could lead nowhere. But he hadn't been able to stop thinking about her. So her rules had had to be bent.

'The Party Queens motto is No Job Too Big or Too Small,' Gemma said as she stepped on board. 'This...this is a very small job.'

He realised he was holding her hand for longer than would be considered polite. That her eyes were flickering away from the intensity of his gaze. But he didn't want to let go of her hand.

'Small…but important.' Incredibly important to him as the clock ticked relentlessly away on his last days of freedom.

She abruptly released her hand from his. Her lush mouth tightened. 'Is it? Then I hope you'll be happy with the menu.'

'Your chef and waiter are already in the kitchen,' he said. 'You have created a superb lunch for us.'

'And your guest for lunch? Is she—?'

At that moment a crew member approached to tell him they were ready to cast off from the dock and start their cruise around the harbour.

Tristan thanked him and turned to Gemma. 'I'm very much looking forward to this,' he said. *To getting to know her.*

'You couldn't have a better day for exploring the harbour,' she said with a wave of her hand that encompassed the impossibly blue waters, the boats trailing frothy white wakes behind them, the blue sky unmarred by clouds.

'The weather is perfect,' he said. 'Did Party Queens organise that for me, too?'

It was a feeble attempt at humour and he knew it. Gemma seemed to know it, too.

But her delightful dimples flirted in her cheeks as she replied, 'We may have cast a good weather spell or two.'

He raised his eyebrows. 'So you have supernatural powers? The Party Queens continue to surprise me.'

'I'd be careful who you're calling a witch,' she said with a deepening of the dimples. 'Andie and Eliza might not like it.'

A witch? She had bewitched him, all right. He had never felt such an instant attraction to a woman. Especially one so deeply unsuitable.

'And you?' In his country's mythology the most powerful witches had red hair and green eyes. This bewitching Australian had eyes the colour of cinnamon—warm and enticing. 'Are *you* a witch, Gemma Harper?' he asked slowly.

She met his gaze directly as they stood facing each other on the deck, the dock now behind them. 'I like to think I'm a witch in the kitchen—or it could be that I just have a highly developed intuition for food. But if you want to think I conjured up these blue skies, go right ahead. All part of the service.'

'So there is no limit to your talents?' he said.

'You're darn right about that,' she said with an upward tilt of her chin.

For a long moment their eyes met. Her heart-shaped face, so new to him, seemed already familiar—possibly because she had not been out of his thoughts since the moment they'd met. He ached to lift his hand and trace the freckles scattered across the bridge of her nose with his finger, then explore the contours of her mouth, her top lip with its perfect, plump bow. *He ached to kiss her.*

But there could be no kissing. Not with this girl, who had captured his interest within seconds of meeting her. Not when there were rules and strictures guiding the way he spent his life. When there were new levels of responsibility he had to step up to when he returned home. He was on a deadline—everything would change when he turned thirty, in three months' time. These next few days in Sydney were the last during which he could call his time his own.

His life had been very different before the accident that had killed his brother. Before the *spare* had suddenly become the *heir*. His carefree and some might even say hedonistic life as the second son had been abruptly curtailed.

There had been unsuitable girlfriends—forbidden to him now. He had taken risks on the racing-car circuit and on horseback, had scaled the mountains that towered over Montovia. Now everything he did came under scrutiny. The Crown took priority over everything. Duty had always governed part of his life. Now it was to be his all.

But he had demanded to be allowed to take this vacation—insisted on this last freedom before he had to buckle under to duty. To responsibility. For the love of his country.

His fascination with Gemma Harper was nowhere on the approved official agenda…

'I'm trying to imagine what other feats of magic you can perform,' he said, attempting to come to terms with the potent spell she had cast on him. The allure of her lush mouth. The warmth of her eyes. The inexplicable longing for her that had led him to planning this day.

He should not be thinking this way about a commoner.

She bit her lip, took a step back from him. 'My magic trick is to make sure your lunch date goes smoothly. But I don't need a fairy's wand for that.' Her dimples disappeared. 'I want everything to be to your satisfaction. Are you happy with the *Argus*?'

Her voice was suddenly stilted, as if she had extracted the laughter and levity from it. *Back to business* was the message. And she was right. A business arrangement. That was all there should be between them.

'It's a very handsome boat,' he said. He was used to millionaire's toys. Took this level of luxury for granted. But that didn't stop him appreciating it. And he couldn't put a price on the spectacular view. 'I'm very happy with it for this purpose.'

'Good. The *Argus* is my favourite of any of the boats we've worked on,' she said. 'I love its wonderful Art Deco style. It's from another era of graciousness.'

'Would you like me to show you around?' he said.

If she said yes, he would make only a cursory inspection of the luxury bedrooms, the grand stateroom. He did not want her to get the wrong idea. Or to torture himself with thoughts of what could never be.

She shook her head. 'No need. I'm familiar with the layout,' she said. 'We held a corporate party here earlier in the spring. I'd like to catch up with my staff now.'

'Your waiter has already set up for lunch on the deck.'

'I'd like to see how it looks,' she said.

She had a large tan leather bag slung over her shoulder. 'Let me take your bag for you,' he said.

'Thank you, but I'm fine,' she said, clutching on to the strap.

'I insist,' he said. The habits of courtliness and chivalry towards women had been bred into him.

She shrugged. 'Okay.' Reluctantly, she handed it to him.

The weight of her bag surprised him, and he pretended to stagger on the deck. 'What have you got in here? An arsenal of wooden spoons?'

Her eyes widened, and she laughed. 'Of course not.'

'So I don't need to seek out my armour?'

It was tempting to tell her about the suits of medieval armour in the castle he called home. As a boy he'd thought everyone had genuine armour to play with—it hadn't been until he was older that he'd become aware of his uniquely privileged existence. Privileged and restricted.

But he couldn't reveal his identity to her yet. He wanted another day of just being plain Tristan. Just a guy getting to know a girl.

'Of course you don't need armour. Besides, I wasn't actually going to *hit* you with that wooden spoon, you know.'

'You had me worried back in that kitchen,' he teased. He was getting used to speaking English again, relaxing into the flow of words.

'I don't believe that for a second,' she said. 'You're so much bigger than me, and—'

'And what?'

'I… I trusted that you wouldn't hurt me.'

He had to clear his throat. 'I would never hurt you,' he said. And yet he wasn't being honest with her. Inadvertently, he *could* hurt her. But it would not be by intent. *This was just one day.*

'So what's really in the bag?' he asked.

'It's only bits and pieces of my favourite kitchen equipment—just in case I might need them.'

'Just in case the chef can't do his job?' he asked.

'You *did* want me here to supervise,' she said, her laughter gone as he reminded her of why she thought she was on board.

'And supervise I need to. Please. I have to see where we will be serving lunch.'

There was a formal dining area inside the cabin, but Tristan was glad Party Queens had chosen to serve lunch at an informal area with the best view at the fore of the boat. Under shelter from the sun and protected from the breeze. The very professional waiter had already set an elegant table with linen mats, large white plates and gleaming silver.

Gemma nodded in approval when she saw it. Then straightened a piece of cutlery into perfect alignment with another without seeming to be aware she was doing it.

'Our staff have done their usual good job,' she said. 'We'll drop anchor at Store Beach at lunchtime. That will be very *romantic*.'

She stressed the final word with a tight twist of her lips that surprised him.

'I don't know where Store Beach is, but I'm looking forward to seeing it,' he said.

'It's near Manly, which is a beachside suburb—the start of our wonderful northern beaches. Store Beach is a secluded beach accessible only from the water. I'm sure you and your…uh…*date* will like it.' She glanced at her watch. 'In the meantime, it's only ten o'clock. We can set up for morning tea or coffee now, if you'd like?'

'Coffee would be good,' he said. Sydney had surprised him in many ways—not least of which was with its excellent European-style coffee.

Gemma gave the table setting another tweak and then stepped away from it. 'All that's now lacking is your guest. Are we picking her up from another wharf, or is she already on board?'

'She's already on board,' he said.

'Oh…' she said. 'Is she—?' She turned to look towards the passageway that led to the living area and bedrooms.

'She's not down there,' he said.

'Then where—?'

He sought the correct words. 'She…she's right here,' he said.

'I don't see anyone.' She frowned. 'I don't get it.'

He cleared his throat. '*You* are my guest for lunch, Gemma.'

She stilled. For a long moment she didn't say anything. Tristan shifted from foot to foot. He couldn't tell if she was pleased or annoyed.

'Me?' she said finally, in a voice laced with disbelief.

'You said there was a rule about you not spending time outside of work with clients. So I arranged to have time with you while you were officially at work.'

Her shoulders were held hunched and high. 'You…you tricked me. I don't like being tricked.'

'You could call it that—and I apologise for the deception. But there didn't seem to be another way. I had to see you again, Gemma.'

She took a deep intake of breath. 'Why didn't you just ask me?'

'Would you have said "yes"?'

She bowed her head. 'Perhaps not.'

'I will ask you now. Will you be my guest for lunch on board the *Argus*?'

She looked down at the deck.

He reached out his hand and tilted her chin upwards so she faced him. 'Please?'

He could see the emotions dancing across her face. Astonishment. A hint of anger. And could that be relief?

Her shoulders relaxed, and her dimples made a brief appearance in the smoothness of her cheeks. 'I guess as you have me trapped on board I have no choice but to say "yes".'

'Trapped? I don't wish you to feel trapped…' He didn't want to seem arrogant and domineering—job descriptions that came with the role of crown prince. His brother had fulfilled them impeccably. They sat uncomfortably with Tristan. 'Gemma, if this is unacceptable to you, I'll ask the captain to turn back to Lavender Bay. You can get off. Is that what you want?'

She shook her head. 'No. That's not what I want. I… I want to be here with you. In fact, I can't tell you how happy I am there's no other woman. I might have been tempted to throw her overboard.'

Her peal of laughter that followed was delightful, and it made him smile in response.

'Surely you wouldn't do that?'

She looked up at him, her eyes dancing with new confidence. 'You might be surprised at what I'm capable of,' she murmured. 'You don't know me at all, Tristan.'

'I hope to remedy that today,' he said.

Already he knew that this single day he'd permitted himself to share with her would not be enough. He had to anchor his feet to the deck so he didn't swing her into his arms. He must truly be bewitched. Because he couldn't remember when he'd last felt such anticipation at the thought of spending time with a woman.

'Welcome aboard, Gemma,' he said—and had to stop himself from sweeping into a courtly bow.

CHAPTER FOUR

GEMMA COULDN'T STOP SMILING—in relief, anticipation and a slowly bubbling excitement. After all that angst, *she* was Tristan's chosen date for the romantic lunch. *She* was the one he'd gone to so much effort and expense to impress. The thought made her heart skitter with wonder and more than a touch of awe.

She'd joked about casting spells, but *something* had happened back there in her kitchen—some kind of connection between her and Tristan that was quite out of the ordinary. It seemed he had felt it, too. She ignored the warning of the insistent twitching of her antennae. This magical feeling was *not* just warm and fuzzy lust born from Tristan's incredible physical appeal and the fact that she was coming out of a six-month man drought.

Oh, on a sensual level she wanted him, all right—her knees were still shaky just from the touch of his hand gripping hers as he'd helped her across the gangplank. But she didn't want Tristan just as a gorgeous male body to satisfy physical hunger. *It was something so much deeper than that.* Which was all kinds of crazy when he was only going to be around for a short time. And was still as much of a mystery to her as he had been the day they'd met.

For her, this was something more than just physical attraction. But what about him? Was this just a prelude to seduction? Was he a handsome guy with all the right words—spoken in the most charming of accents—looking for a no-strings holiday fling?

She tried to think of all those 'right' reasons for staying away from Tristan but couldn't remember one of them. By tricking her into this lunch with him, he had taken the decision out of her hands. But there was no need to get carried away. This was no big deal. *It was only lunch.* It would be up to her to say *no* if this was a net cast to snare her into a one-night stand.

She reached up and kissed him lightly on the cheek in an effort to make it casual. 'Thank you.'

She was rewarded by the relief in his smile. 'It is absolutely my pleasure,' he said.

'Does Eliza know?' she asked. *Had her friend been in on this deception?*

Tristan shook his head. 'I didn't tell her why I wanted you on board. I sense she's quite protective of you. I didn't want anything to prevent you from coming today.'

Of course Eliza was protective of her. Andie, too. Her friends had been there to pick up the pieces after the Alistair fallout. Eliza had seemed impressed with Tristan, though—impressed with him as a client...maybe not so impressed with him as a candidate for Gemma's first foray back into the dating world. He was still in many ways their Mr Mystery. *But she could find out more about him today.*

'I did protest that I wasn't really needed,' she said, still secretly delighted at the way things had turned out. 'Not when there are a chef and a waiter and a crew on the boat.'

'I'm sure the bonus I added to the Party Queens fee guaranteed your presence on board. She's a shrewd businesswoman, your partner.'

'Yes, she is,' Gemma agreed. No wonder Eliza hadn't objected to Gemma's time being so wastefully spent. How glad she was now that Eliza had insisted she go. But she felt as though the tables had been turned on her, and she wasn't quite sure where she stood.

She looked up at Tristan. Her heart flipped over at how handsome he was, with the sea breeze ruffling his hair, his eyes such a vivid blue against his tan. He looked totally at home on this multi-million-dollar boat, seemingly not impressed by the luxury that surrounded them. She wondered what kind of world he came from. One where money was not in short supply, she guessed.

'I… I'm so pleased about this…this turn of events,' she said. 'Thrilled, in fact. But how do we manage it? I… I feel a bit like Cinderella. One minute I'm in the kitchen, the next minute I'm at the ball.'

He seemed amused by her flight of fancy, and he smiled. What was it about his smile that appealed so much? His perfect teeth? The warmth in his eyes? The way his face creased into lines of good humour?

'I guess you could see it like that…' he said.

'And if I'm Cinderella… I guess *you're* the prince.'

His smile froze, and tension suddenly edged his voice. 'What…what do you mean?'

Gemma felt a sudden chill that was not a sea breeze. It perplexed her. 'Cinderella… The ball… The prince… The pumpkin transformed into a carriage… You know…' she said, gesturing with her hands. 'Don't you have the story of Cinderella in your country?'

'Uh…of course,' he said with an obvious relief that puzzled her. 'Those old fairytales originally came from Europe.'

So she'd unwittingly said the wrong thing? Maybe he thought she had expectations of something more than a day on the harbour. Of getting her claws into him. She really was out of practice. At dating. At flirting. Simply talking with a man who attracted her.

'I meant… Well, I meant that Cinderella meets the prince and you…well, you're as handsome as any fairytale prince and… Never mind.'

She glanced down at her white sneakers, tied with jaunty blue laces. Maybe this wasn't the time to be making a joke about a glass slipper.

Tristan nodded thoughtfully. 'Of course. And I found Cinderella in her kitchen…'

She felt uncomfortable about carrying this any further. He seemed to be making too much effort to join in the story. His English was excellent, but maybe he'd missed the nuances of the analogy. Maybe he had trouble with her Australian accent.

'Yes. And talking of kitchens, I need to talk to the chef and—' She made to turn back towards the door that led inside the cabin.

Tristan reached out and put his hand on her arm to stop her.

'You don't need to do anything but enjoy yourself,' he said, his tone now anything but uncertain. 'I've spoken to your staff. They know that you are my honoured guest.'

He dropped his hand from her arm so she could turn back to face him. 'You said that? You called me your "honoured guest"?' There was something about his formal way of speaking that really appealed to her. His words made her want to preen with pleasure.

'I did—and they seemed pleased,' he said.

Party Queens had a policy of only hiring staff they personally liked. The freelance chef on board today was a guy she'd worked with in her restaurant days. But it was the Australian way to be irreverent… She suspected she might be teased about this sudden switch from staff to guest. Especially having lunch in the company of such an exceptionally good-looking man.

'They were pleased I'm out of their hair?' she asked.

'Pleased for *you*. They obviously hold their boss in high regard.'

'That's nice,' she said, nodding.

Hospitality could be a tense business at times, what with deadlines and temperamental clients and badly behaving guests. It was good to have it affirmed that the staff respected her.

'What about lunch?' she said, indicating the direction of the kitchen. 'The—?'

Tristan waved her objections away. 'Relax, Gemma.' A smile hovered at the corners of his mouth. As if he were only too aware of how difficult she found it to give up control of her job. 'I'm the host. You are my guest. Forget about what's going on in the kitchen. Just enjoy being the guest—not the party planner.'

'This might take some getting used to,' she said with a rueful smile. 'But thank you, yes.'

'Good,' he said.

'I'm not sure of one thing,' she said. 'Do you still want me as your tour guide? If that's the case, I need to be pointing out some sights to you.'

She turned from him, took a few steps to the railing and looked out, the breeze lifting her hair from her face.

'On the right—oh, hang on…don't we say "starboard" on a boat? To *starboard* are the Finger Wharves at Walsh Bay. The configuration is like a hand—you know, with each wharf a finger. The wharves are home to the Sydney Theatre Company. It's a real experience to go to the theatre there and—'

'Stop!'

She turned, to see Tristan with his hand held up in a halt sign. His hands were attractive, large with long elegant fingers. Yes, nice hands were an asset on a man, too. She wondered how they would feel—

She could not go there.

Gemma knew she'd been chattering on too much about the wharves. Gabbling, in fact. But she suddenly felt…*nervous* in Tristan's presence. And chatter had always been her way of distancing herself from an awkward situation.

She spluttered to a halt. 'You don't want to know about the

wharves? Okay, on the left-hand side—I mean the *port* side—is Luna Park and…'

Tristan lowered his hand. Moved closer to her. So close they were just kissing distance apart. She tried not to look at his mouth. That full lower lip…the upper lip slightly narrower. *A sensual mouth was another definite asset in a man.* So was his ability to kiss.

She flushed and put her hand to her forehead. Why was she letting her thoughts run riot on what Tristan would be like to kiss? She took a step back, only to feel the railing press into her back. It was a little scary that she was thinking this way about a man she barely knew.

'There's no need for you to act like a tour guide,' he said. 'The first day I got here I took a guided tour of the harbour.'

'But you asked me to show you the insider's Sydney. The Wharf Theatre is a favourite place of mine and—'

'That was just a ploy,' he said.

Gemma caught her breath. 'A ploy?'

'I had to see you again. I thought there was more chance of you agreeing to show me around than if I straight out asked you to dinner.'

'Oh,' she said, momentarily lost for words. 'Or…or lunch on the harbour?'

Her heart started to thud so hard she thought surely he must hear it—even over the faint thrumming of the boat's motor, the sound of people calling out to each other on the cruiser that was passing them, the squawk of the seagulls wheeling over the harbour wall, where a fisherman had gutted his catch.

'That is correct,' Tristan said.

'So…so you had to find another way?' To think that all the time she'd spent thinking about *him*, he'd been thinking about *her*.

For the first time Gemma detected a crack in Tristan's self-assured confidence. His hands were thrust deep into the pockets of his white trousers. 'I… I had to see if you were as…as wonderful as I remembered,' he said, and his accent was more pronounced.

She loved the way he rolled his r*'s.* Without that accent, without the underlying note of sincerity, his words might have sounded sleazy. But they didn't. They sent a shiver of awareness and anticipation up her spine.

'And…and are you disappointed?'

She wished now that she'd worn something less utilitarian than a T-shirt—even though it was a very smart, fitted T-shirt, with elbow-length sleeves—and sneakers. They were work clothes. Not 'lunching with a hot guy' clothes. Still, if she'd had to dress with the thought of impressing Tristan, she might still be back at her apartment, with the contents of her wardrobe scattered all over the bed.

'Not at all,' he said.

He didn't need to say the words. The appreciation in his eyes said it all. Her hand went to her heart to steady its out-of-control thud.

'Me neither. I mean, I'm not disappointed in *you.*' *Aargh, could she sound any dumber?* 'I thought you were pretty wonderful, too. I… I regretted that I knocked back your request for me to show you around. But…but I had my reasons.'

His dark eyebrows rose. 'Reasons? Not just the company rules?'

'Those, too. When we first started the business, we initiated a "no dating the clients" rule. It made sense.'

'Yet I believe your business partner Andie married a client, so that rule cannot be set in concrete.'

'How did you know that?' She answered her own question, 'Of course—Jake Marlowe.' The best friend of the groom. 'You're right. But Andie was the exception.' Up until now there had been no client who had made *Gemma* want to bend the rules.

'And the other reasons?'

'Personal. I… I came out of a bad relationship more…more than a little wounded.'

'I'm sorry to hear that.' His eyes searched her face. 'And now?'

She took a deep breath. Finally she had that heartbeat under control. 'I've got myself sorted,' she said, not wanting to give any further explanation.

'You don't wear a ring. I assumed you were single.' He paused. '*Are* you single?'

Gemma was a bit taken aback by the directness of his question. 'Very single,' she said. Did that sound too enthusiastic? As if she were making certain he knew she was available?

Gemma curled her hands into fists. She had to stop second guessing everything she said. Tristan had thought she was wonderful in her apron, all flushed from the heat of the oven and without a scrap of make-up. She had to be herself. Not try and please a man by somehow attempting to be what he wanted her to be. She'd learned that from her mother—and it was difficult to unlearn.

Her birth father had died before she was born and her mother, Aileen, had brought Gemma up on her own until she was six. Then her mother had met Dennis.

He had never wanted children but had grudgingly accepted Gemma as part of a package deal when he'd married Aileen. Her mother had trained Gemma to be grateful to her stepfather for having taken her on. To keep him happy by always being a sweet little girl, by forgiving his moody behaviour, his lack of real affection.

Gemma had become not necessarily a *people* pleaser but a man pleaser. She believed that was why she'd put up with Alistair's bad behaviour for so long. It was a habit she was determined to break.

She decided to take charge of the conversation. 'What about you, Tristan? Are you single, too?'

He nodded. 'Yes.'

'Have you ever been married?'

'No,' he said. 'I… I haven't met the right woman. And you?'

'Same. I haven't met the right man.' Boy, had she met some wrong ones. But those days were past. *No more heartbreakers.*

The swell from a passing ferry made her rock unsteadily on her feet as she swayed with the sudden motion of the boat.

Tristan caught her elbow to steady her. 'You okay?' he said.

The action brought him close to her. So close she could feel the strength in his body, smell the fresh scent of him that hinted at sage and woodlands and the mountain country he came from. There was something so *different* about him—almost a sense of *other*. It intrigued her, excited her.

'F-fine, thank you,' she stuttered.

His grip, though momentary, had been firm and warm on her arm, and her reaction to the contact disconcerted her. She found herself trembling a little. Those warning antennae waved so wildly she felt light-headed. She shouldn't be feeling this intense attraction to someone she knew so little about. *It was against her every resolve.*

She took another steadying breath, as deep as she could without looking too obvious. The *Argus* had left the Harbour Bridge behind. 'We're on home territory for me now,' she said, in a determinedly conversational tone. 'Come over to this side and I'll show you.'

'You live around here?' he said as he followed her.

'See over there?' She waved to encompass the park that stretched to the water under the massive supports for the bridge overhead, the double row of small shops, the terraced houses, the multi-million-dollar apartments that sat at the edge of the water. 'You can just see the red-tiled roof of my humble apartment block.'

Tristan walked over to the railing, leaned his elbows on the top, looked straight ahead. Gemma stood beside him, very aware that their shoulders were almost nudging.

'Sydney does not disappoint me,' he said finally.

'I'm glad to hear that,' she said. 'What made you come here on your vacation?'

He shrugged. 'Australia is a place I always wanted to see. So far from Europe. Like the last frontier.'

Again, Gemma sensed he was leaving out more than he was saying. Her self-protection antennae were waving furiously. She had finetuned them in those six months of sabbatical, so determined not to fall into old traps, make old mistakes. Would he share more with her by the end of the day?

'I think you need to travel west of Sydney to see actual last-frontier territory,' she said. 'No kangaroos hopping around the place here.'

'I would like to see kangaroos that aren't in a zoo,' he said. He turned to face her. 'Living in Sydney must be like living in a resort,' he said.

Gemma tried to see the city she'd lived in all her life through his eyes. It wasn't that she took the beauty of the harbour for granted—it was just that she saw it every day. 'I hadn't thought about it like that but, yes, I see what you mean,' she said. Although she'd worked too hard ever to think she was enjoying a resort lifestyle.

'Do you like living here?' he said.

'Of course,' she said. 'Though I haven't actually lived anywhere else to compare. Sometimes I think I'd like to try a new life in another country. If Party Queens hadn't been such a success, I might have looked for a job as a chef in France. But in the meantime Sydney suits me.'

'I envy you in some ways,' he said. 'Your freedom. The lack of stifling tradition.'

She wondered at the note of yearning in his voice.

'There's a lot more to Sydney than these areas, of course,' she said. 'The Blue Mountains are worth seeing.' She stopped herself from offering to show them to him. He didn't want a tour guide. She didn't want to get too involved. *This was just lunch.*

'I would like to see more, but I go back home on Monday afternoon. With the party on Friday, there is not much time.'

'That's a shame,' she said, keeping her voice light and neutral. She knew this—*Tristan*—was only for today…an interlude. But she already had the feeling that a day, a week, a month wouldn't ever be enough time with him.

'I have responsibilities I must return to.' His tone of voice indicated that he might not be 100 per cent happy about that.

'With your family's corporation? Maybe you could consider opening an Australian branch of the business here,' she said.

He looked ahead of him, and she realised he was purposely not meeting her eyes. 'I'm afraid that is not possible—delightful as the thought might be.'

He turned away from the railing and went over to where he had put down her bag. Again, he pretended it was too heavy to carry, though she could see that with his muscles it must be effortless for him.

'Let's stash your bag somewhere safe and see about that coffee.'

'You don't want to see more sights?'

He paused, her bag held by his side. 'Haven't I made it clear, Gemma? Forgive my English if I haven't. I've seen a lot of sights in the time I've been in Australia. In the days I have left the only sight I want to see more of is *you*.'

CHAPTER FIVE

TRISTAN SAT OPPOSITE Gemma at a round table inside the cabin. After his second cup of coffee—strong and black—he leaned back in his chair and sighed his satisfaction.

'Excellent coffee, thank you,' he said. Of all the good coffee he'd enjoyed in Australia, he rated this the highest.

Gemma looked pleased. 'We're very fussy about coffee at Party Queens—single origin, fair trade, the best.'

'It shows,' Tristan said.

He liked Party Queens' meticulous attention to detail. It was one of the reasons he felt confident that his reception on Friday would be everything he wanted it to be—although for reasons of security he hadn't shared with them the real nature of the gathering.

'Not true,' Tristan muttered under his breath in his own language. He could have told Eliza by now. The reason he was holding back on the full facts was that he wanted to delay telling Gemma the truth about himself for as long as possible. Things would not be the same once his anonymity was gone.

'I'm glad you like the coffee. How about the food?' she asked.

Her forehead was pleated with the trace of a frown, and he realised she was anxious about his opinion.

'Excellent,' he pronounced. Truth be told, he'd scarcely noticed it. Who would be interested in food when he could feast his eyes on the beautiful woman in front of him?

To please her, he gave his full attention to the superbly arranged fruit platter that included some of the ripe mangoes he had come to enjoy in Queensland. There was also a selection of bite-sized cookies—both savoury, with cheese, and sweet, studded with nuts—arranged on the bottom tier of a silver stand. On the top tier were small square cakes covered in dark chocolate and an extravagant coating of shredded coconut.

'It all looks very good,' he said.

'I know there's more food than we can possibly eat, but we knew nothing about your lunch date and her tastes in food,' Gemma said.

'In that case I hope you chose food *you* liked,' he said.

'As a matter of fact, I did,' she said, with a delightful display of dimples.

'What is this cake with the coconut?' he asked.

'You haven't seen a lamington before?'

He shook his head.

'If Australia had a national cake it would be the lamington,' she said. 'They say it was created in honour of Lord Lamington, a nineteenth-century governor.'

'So this cake has illustrious beginnings?'

'You could call it a grand start for a humble little cake. In this case they are perhaps more illustrious, as I made them using the finest Montovian chocolate.'

'A Montovian embellishment of an Australian tradition?'

'I suspect our traditions are mere babies compared to yours,' she said with another flash of dimples. 'Would you like to try one?'

Tristan bit into a lamington. 'Delicious.'

Truth be told, he preferred lighter food. He had to sit through so many official dinners, with course after rich course, that he ate healthily when he had the choice. The mangoes were more to his taste. But he would not hurt her feelings by telling her so.

Gemma looked longingly at the rest of the cakes. 'I have the world's sweetest tooth—which is a problem in this job. I have to restrict myself to just little tastes of what we cook, or I'd be the size of a house.'

'You're in very good shape,' he said.

She had a fabulous body. Slim, yet with alluring curves. He found it almost impossible to keep his eyes from straying to it. He would have liked to say more about how attractive he found her, but it would not be appropriate. *Not yet...perhaps not ever.*

She flushed high on her cheekbones. 'Thank you. I wasn't fishing for a compliment.'

'I know that,' he said.

The mere fact that she was so unassuming about her beauty made him want to shower her with compliments. To praise the cuteness of her freckles, her sensational curves. To admit to the way he found himself wanting to make her smile just to see her dimples.

There was so much he found pleasing about her. But he was not in a position to express his interest. Gemma wasn't a vacation-fling kind of girl—he'd realised that the moment he met her. And that was all he could ever offer her.

It was getting more difficult by the minute to keep that at the top of his mind.

'I'll try just half a lamington and then some fruit,' she said.

She sliced one into halves with a knife and slowly nibbled on one half with an expression of bliss, her eyes half closed. As she licked a stray shred of coconut from her lovely bow-shaped top lip, she tilted back her head and gave a little moan of pleasure.

Tristan shifted in his seat, gripped the edge of the table so hard it hurt. It was impossible for his thoughts not to stray to speculation about her appetite for other pleasures, to how she would react to his mouth on hers, his touch…

There was still a small strand of coconut at the corner of her mouth. He ached to lean across the table, taste the chocolate on her lips, lick away that stray piece of coconut.

She looked at him through eyes still half narrowed with sensual appreciation. 'The Montovian chocolate makes that the best lamington I've ever tasted.'

She should *always* have chocolate from Montovia.

Tristan cleared his throat. He had to keep their conversation going to distract himself. In his hedonistic past he had been immune to the seduction techniques of worldly, sophisticated temptresses, who knew exactly what they were doing as they tried to snare a prince. Yet the unconscious provocation of this lovely girl eating a piece of cake was making him fall apart.

'I believe you're a trained chef?' he said. 'Tell me how that happened.'

'How I became a chef? Do you really need to know that?'

'I know very little about you. I need to know everything.'

'Oh,' she said, delightfully disconcerted, the flush deepening on her creamy skin. 'If that's what you want...'

'It is what I want,' he said, unable to keep the huskiness from his voice. There was so much more he wanted from her, but it was impossible for him to admit to the desire she was arousing in him.

'Okay,' she said. 'I was always interested in food. My mother wasn't really into cooking and was delighted to let me take over the kitchen whenever I wanted.' She helped herself to some grapes, snipping them from the bunch with a tiny pair of silver scissors.

'So you decided to make a career of it?' It wouldn't be an easy life, he imagined. Hard physical work, as well as particular skills required and—

He completely lost his train of thought. Instead he watched, spellbound, as Gemma popped the fat, purple grapes one by one into her luscious mouth.

Inwardly, he groaned. *This was almost unbearable.*

'Actually, I was all set to be a nutritionist,' she said, seemingly unaware of the torment she was putting him through by the simple act of eating some fruit. 'I started a degree at the

University of Newcastle, which is north of Sydney. I stayed up there during the vacations and—'

'Why was that? I went to university in England but came home for at least part of every vacation.'

He'd loved the freedom of living in another country, but home had always been a draw card for him—the security and continuity of the castle, the knowledge of his place in the hierarchy of his country. His parents, who were father and mother to him before they were king and queen.

Gemma pulled a face—which, far from contorting her features, made her look cute. *Had she cast a spell on him?*

'Your home might have been more…welcoming than mine,' she said.

A shadow darkened her warm brown eyes at what was obviously an unpleasant memory. It made him sad for her. His memories of childhood and adolescence were happy. Life at the castle as the 'spare' had been fun—he had had a freedom never granted to his brother. A freedom sorely lost to him now—except for this trip. There had always been some tension between his father and mother, but it had been kept distanced from him. It hadn't been until he'd grown up that he'd discovered the cause of that tension—and why both his parents were so unhappy.

'You were not welcome in your own home?' he asked.

'My mother was always welcoming. My stepfather less so.'

'Was he…abusive?' Tristan tensed, and his hands tightened into fists at the thought of anyone hurting her.

She shook her head. The sunshine slanting in through the windows picked up amber highlights and copper glints in her hair as it fell around her face. He wanted to reach out and stroke it, see if it felt as fiery as it looked.

'Nothing like that,' she said. 'And he wasn't unkind—just indifferent. He didn't want children, but he fell in love with my mother when I was a little kid and I came as part of the package deal.'

'A "package deal"? That seems a harsh way to describe a child.'

Again he felt a surge of protectiveness for her. It was a feeling new to him—this desire to enfold her in safety and shield her from any harm the world might hurl at her. A girl he had known for only a matter of days…

Her shrug of one slender shoulder was obviously an effort to appear nonchalant about an old hurt, but it was not completely successful. 'He couldn't have one without the other. Apparently he wanted my mother badly—she's very beautiful.'

'As is her daughter.' He searched her face. It was disconcerting, the way she seemed to grow lovelier by the minute.

'Thank you.' She flushed again. 'My mother always told me I had to be grateful to my stepfather for looking after us. *Huh.* Even when I was little I looked after myself. But I did my best to please him—to make my mother happy.' She wrinkled her neat, straight nose. 'Why am I telling you all this? I'm sure you must find it boring.'

'You could never be boring, Gemma,' he said. 'I know that about you already.'

It was true. Whether or not she'd cast some kind of witch's spell over him, he found everything about her fascinating. He wanted nothing more than to find out all about her. Just for today, the rest of his life was on hold. It was just him and Gemma, alone in the curious intimacy of a boat in the middle of Sydney Harbour. Like a regular, everyday date of the kind that would not be possible for him once he was back home.

'Are you sure you want to hear more of my ordinary little story?' she asked, her head tilted to one side.

'Nothing could interest me more.'

She could read out loud the list of ingredients from one of her recipes and he'd hang on every word, watching the expressions flit across her face, her dimples peeking in and out. Although so far there didn't appear to be a lot to smile about in her story.

The good-looking dark-haired waiter came to clear their coffee cups and plates. Gemma looked up and smiled at him as she asked him to leave the fruit. Tristan felt a surge of jealousy—until he realised the waiter was more likely to be interested in *him* rather than *her*. Gemma thanked him and praised the chef.

After the waiter had left, she leaned across the table to Tristan. Her voice was lowered to barely above a whisper. 'It feels weird, having people I know serve me,' she said. 'My instinct is to jump up and help. I'm used to being on the other side of the kitchen door.'

Tristan had been used to people serving him since he was a baby. An army of staff catered to the royal family's every need. He'd long ago got used to the presence of servants in the room—so much that they'd become almost invisible. When he went back he would have a hand-picked private staff of his own to help him assume his new responsibilities as crown prince.

The downside was that there was very little privacy. Since his brother had died every aspect of his life had been under constant, intense scrutiny.

Gemma returned to her story. 'Inevitably, when I was a teenager I clashed with my stepfather. It made my mother unhappy. I was glad to leave home for uni—and I never went back except for fleeting visits.'

'And your father?'

'You mean my birth father?'

'Yes.'

'He died before I was born.' Her voice betrayed no emotion. It was as if she were speaking about a stranger.

'That was a tragedy.'

'For my mother, yes. She was a ski instructor in the French resort of Val d'Isère, taking a gap year. My father was English—also a ski instructor. They fell madly in love, she got pregnant, they got married and soon after he got killed in an avalanche.'

'I'm sorry—that's a terrible story.'

Skiing was one of the risky sports he loved, along with mountaineering and skydiving. The castle staff was doing everything it could to wean him off those adrenaline-pumping pastimes. He knew he had to acquiesce. The continuity of the royal family was paramount. His country had lost one heir to an accident and could not afford to lose him, too.

But he railed against being cosseted. Hated having his independence and choice taken away from him. Sometimes the price of becoming king in future seemed unbearably high. But duty overruled everything. Tragedy had forced fate's hand. He accepted his inheritance and everything that went with it—no matter the cost to him. *He was now the crown prince.*

Gemma made a dismissive gesture with her hands. 'I didn't know my father, so of course I never missed him. But he was the love of my mother's life. She was devastated. Then his posh parents arrived at the resort, looked down their noses at my mother, questioned the legality of my parents' marriage—it *was* totally legit, by the way—and paid her to forget she was ever married and to never make a claim on them. They even tried to bar her from the funeral back in England.' Her voice rose with indignation.

'You sound angry,' he said. But what her father's parents had done was something *his* parents had done when he and his brother were younger. They would have paid any amount of money to rid the family of an unsuitable woman. Someone who might reflect badly on the throne. A commoner. *Someone like Gemma.*

His parents' actions had slammed home the fact that marriage for a Montovian prince had nothing to do with love or passion. It was about tradition and duty and strategic alliance. When he had discovered the deep hypocrisy of his parents' relationship, his cynicism about the institution of marriage—or at least how it existed in Montovia—had been born.

That cynicism had only been reinforced by his brother's marriage to the daughter of a duke. The castle had trumpeted it as a 'love match'. Indeed, Carl had been grateful to have found such a pretty, vivacious bride as Sylvie. Only after the splendid wedding in the cathedral had she revealed her true self—venal and avaricious and greedy for the wealth and status that came with being a Montovian princess. She'd cared more for extravagant jewellery than she had for his brother.

Consequently, Tristan had avoided marriage and any attempts to get him to the altar.

He schooled his face to appear neutral, not to give Gemma any indication of what he was thinking. Her flushed face made it very clear that she would *not* be sympathetic to those kind of regal machinations.

'You're darn right. I get angry on behalf of my poor mother—young and grieving,' she said. 'She wanted to throw the money in their faces, but she was carrying me. She swallowed her pride and took the money—for my sake. I was born in London, then she brought me home to Sydney. She said her biggest revenge for their treatment of her was that they never knew they had a grandchild.'

Tristan frowned. He was part of a royal family with a lineage that stretched back hundreds of years. Blood meant everything. 'How did you feel about that?'

Gemma toyed with the remainder of the grapes. He noticed her hands were nicked with little scars and her nails were cut short and unpolished. There were risks in everything—even cooking.

'Of course, I've always felt curious about my English family,' she said. 'I look nothing like my mother or her side of the family. When I was having disagreements with my stepfather, I'd dream of running away to find my other family. I know who they are. But out of loyalty to my mother I've never made any attempt to contact my Clifford relatives.'

'So your name is really Gemma Clifford?'

She shook her head. 'My stepfather adopted me. Legally I bear his name. And that's okay. For all his faults, he gave me a home and supported me.'

'Until you went to university in Newcastle?'

'Whatever his other faults, he's not mean. He kept on paying me an allowance. But I wanted to be independent—free of him and of having to pretend to be someone I was not simply to please him. I talked my way into a part-time kitchen hand's job at the best restaurant in the area. As luck would have it, the head chef was an incredibly talented young guy. He became a culinary superstar in Europe in the years that followed. Somehow he saw talent in me and offered me an apprenticeship as a chef. I didn't hesitate to ditch my degree and accept—much to my parents' horror. But it was what I really wanted to do.'

'Have you ever regretted it?'

'Not for a minute.'

'It seems a big jump from chef to co-owning Party Queens,' Tristan said.

Gemma offered the remaining grapes to him. When he refused, she popped some more into her mouth. He waited for her to finish them.

'It's a roundabout story. When my boss left for grander culinary pastures, his replacement wasn't so encouraging of me. I left the Newcastle restaurant and went back to Sydney.'

'To work in restaurants?'

'Yes—some very good ones. But it's still a very male-dominated industry. Most of the top chefs are men. Females like me only too often get relegated to being pastry chefs and are passed over for promotion. I got sick of the bullying in the kitchen. The sexist behaviour. I got the opportunity to work on a glossy women's magazine as an assistant to the food editor and grabbed it. In time I became a food editor myself, and my career took off.'

'That still doesn't explain Party Queens,' he said. 'Seems to me there's a gap there.' He'd trained as a lawyer. He was used to seeing what was missing from an argument, what lay beneath a story.

She leaned across the table and rested on her elbows. 'Are

you interviewing me?' Her words were playful, but her eyes were serious.

'Of course not. I'm just interested. You're very successful. I want to know how you got there.'

'I've worked hard—be in no doubt about that. But luck plays a part in it, too.'

'It always does,' he said.

Lucky he had walked in on her in her kitchen. Lucky he'd been born into a royal family. And yet there were days when he resented that lucky accident of birth. Like right here, right now, spending time with this woman, knowing that he could not take this attraction, which to his intense gratification appeared to be mutual, *anywhere*. Because duty to his country required sacrificing his own desires.

'There's bad luck too, of course,' Gemma went on. 'Andie was lifestyle editor on the magazine—she'd trained as an interior designer. Eliza was on the publishing side. We became friends. Then the magazine closed without warning and we were all suddenly without a job.'

'That must have been a blow,' he said. He had never actually worked for an employer, apart from his time as a conscript in the Montovian military. His 'job prospects'—short of an exceedingly unlikely revolution—were assured for life.

Again, Gemma shrugged one slender shoulder. 'It happens in publishing. We rolled with it.'

'I can see that,' he said. He realised how resilient she was. And independent. She got more appealing by the minute.

'People asked us to organise parties for them while we were looking for other jobs—between us we had all the skills. The party bookings grew, and we began to see we had a viable business. That's how Party Queens was born. We never dreamed it would become as successful as it has.'

'I'm impressed. With you and with your business. With all this.' He indicated the *Argus*, the harbour, the meal.

'We aim to please,' she said with that bewitching smile.

He could imagine only too well how she might please him and he her.

But he was not here in Sydney to make impossible promises to a girl next door like Gemma. Nor did he want to seduce her with lies just for momentary physical thrills.

Or to put his own heart at any kind of risk.

This could be for only one day.

CHAPTER SIX

GEMMA COULDN'T REMEMBER when she'd last felt so at ease with a man. So utterly comfortable in his presence. Had she *ever* before felt like this?

But she didn't want to question the *why* of it. Just to enjoy his company while she had the chance.

After she'd polished off all the grapes, she and Tristan had moved back out onto the deck. He hadn't eaten much—no more cake and just some mango. She'd got the impression he was very disciplined in his eating habits—and probably everything else. But getting to know Tristan was still very much a guessing game.

The *Argus* had left the inner harbour behind and set course north for Manly and their lunchtime destination of Store Beach. The sun had moved around since they'd gone inside for coffee, and the crew had moved two vintage steamer-style wooden deckchairs into the shade, positioned to take advantage of the view.

She adjusted the cushions, which were printed with anchor motifs, and settled down into one of them. Tristan was to her right, with a small table between them. But as soon as she'd sat down, she moved to get up again.

'My hat,' she explained. 'I need to get it from my bag. Even though we're in the shade, I could get burned.'

Immediately, Tristan was on his feet. 'Let me get it for you,' he said, ushering her to sit back down.

'There's no need. Please… I can do it,' she protested.

'I insist,' he said in a tone that brooked no further resistance.

Gemma went to protest again, then realised that would sound ungracious. *She wasn't used to being cared for by a man.* 'Thank you,' she conceded. 'It's right at the top of the bag.'

'Next to the rolling pins?' he said.

'But no wooden spoons,' she said with a smile.

Not only would Alistair not have dreamed of fetching her hat for her, he would have demanded she get him a beer while she was up. *Good manners were very appealing in a man.*

Tristan held himself with a mix of upright bearing and athletic grace as he headed back into the cabin. Gemma lay back and watched him through her sunglasses. His back view was every bit as pleasing as his front. Broad shoulders tapered to a wide back and then narrow hips. *There could be no doubt that a good butt was also an asset in a man.*

He looked effortlessly classy in the white linen trousers and the loose white shirt. They were so perfectly cut she wondered if they'd been tailored to fit him. Could you get men's casual clothes made to measure? She knew you could have suits bespoke. Anything was possible if you had enough money, she supposed.

He returned with her hat—a favourite white panama. She reached out to take it from him, but he came to the side of her chair and bent down to put it on her head. His face was very close. She could almost imagine he was bending down to kiss her. If he did, she wouldn't stop him. No…she might even kiss him first. She was thankful her sunglasses masked her eyes, so her expression didn't give her away.

'Nice hat,' he said as he placed it on her head. As he tugged it into place, his hands strayed lightly over her hair, her ears, her throat—just the merest touch, but it was enough to set her trembling.

She forced her voice to sound steady—not to betray how excitingly unnerving she found his nearness. 'I've had this hat for years, and I would be greatly distressed if I lost it.'

Again she caught his scent. She remembered how years ago in high school she'd dated a perfectly nice boy who'd had everything going for him, but she hadn't liked the way he'd smelled. Not that he'd been unclean or unwashed—it was just his natural scent that had turned her off. But Tristan's fresh scent sent her nerve endings into a flurry of awareness.

Was there *anything* about Tristan she didn't find appealing?

His underlying mystery, that sense of him holding back still had her guard up—but perhaps that mystery was part of his appeal. And it was in her power to find out what made Tristan tick. *Just ask him, Gemma.*

There were many points of interest she could draw his attention to on their way to Manly. But she would not waste time on further guidebook lectures. *The only sight I want to see more of is you,* he'd said.

Did he have any idea of how good those words made her feel?

Her self-esteem had taken a terrible battering from Alistair. Six months had not been enough to fix it fully. Just hours in Tristan's company had her feeling better about herself than she had for a long time. The insistent twitching of her antennae told her that his charming words might be calculated to disarm and seduce. But her deeper instincts sensed sincerity—though for what purpose she was still at a loss.

Enjoy the moment, she told herself, *because that's all you've got with him.*

After Tristan had settled into his deckchair, she turned to him, slipped off her sunglasses. 'Your interview technique is so good you know quite a lot about me. Now it's my turn to discover Tristan.'

He gestured with his hands to indicate emptiness. 'There is not much I can tell you,' he said.

Did he mean that literally?

For all the instant intimacy of the situation, she still sensed those secrets. Her antennae waved gently, to remind her to be wary of men who were not what they seemed.

'Ask me questions—I will see if I can answer them,' he said.

As in, he would see if he was *able* to answer her questions? Or *allowed* to answer them? Or he just plain didn't *want* to answer them?

She chose her first question with care. 'What language do you speak in Montovia?' she asked. 'French? German? I think I can detect both in your accent.'

'We speak Montovian—our own language,' he said. 'We are a small country and it is influenced by the other European countries that surround us.'

'Say something to me in Montovian,' she said. 'I'm interested in languages.'

'I've been told it is not an attractive language, so I am warning you,' he said. 'Even to my ears it sounds quite harsh.'

He turned to her and spoke a few sentences as he gazed into her eyes. She tried to ignore the way his proximity made her heart race.

'I didn't understand a word of that, but your language is not unattractive.' And neither was his voice—deep, masculine, arresting. 'What did you actually say to me?'

'You really want to know?'

'Yes.'

'I said that the beauty of this magnificent harbour could not compare to the beauty of the woman sitting beside me.'

Spoken by anyone else, the words might have sounded corny, over the top. But spoken with Tristan's accent they were swoon worthy.

'Oh,' she said, again lost for words. She felt herself blush—

that was the problem with being a creamy-skinned redhead… there was no hiding her reactions. 'Seriously?'

He smiled. 'You'll never know, will you? Unless you learn Montovian—and no one outside of my country learns Montovian.'

'Why not?'

'Because it is only spoken in Montovia. I also speak German, French, Italian and Spanish,' he said.

'I'm seriously impressed,' she said. 'I studied French and Italian at school. Then German at night school before I went to Europe on a backpackers' bus tour. But I never use those languages here, and I fear I've lost what skills I had.'

'You'd pick them up again in the right environment. I was out of the habit of speaking English, but I'm getting better at it every day.' His eyes narrowed in that intense way he had of looking at her, as if he were seeking answers—to what, she didn't know. 'Especially talking to you, Gemma'.

'You've inspired me to study some more so that—'

Only just in time she caught herself from saying, *So that next time I'll surprise you by speaking fluent French.* She was surprised at the sharp twist of pain at the reminder that there would be no next time for her and Tristan.

She finished her sentence, hoping he hadn't noticed the pause. 'So that my skills don't just dwindle away. Did you learn English at school?'

'Yes. I also had a tutor. My parents felt it was essential we spoke good English.'

'"We"? You have brothers and sisters?'

Tristan stared out to sea. 'I have a younger sister. I… I had an older brother. He…he died when his helicopter came down in the mountains a year ago.'

Gemma wasn't sure what to say that wouldn't be a cliché. 'I… I'm so sorry to hear that,' was the best she could manage.

His jaw tightened. 'It was…terrible. His wife and their little boy were with him. My family will never get over it.'

Gemma was too shocked to speak. She went to reach out and put her hand on his arm but decided against it, not sure how welcome her touch would be in this moment of remembered tragedy.

'I carry the loss of my brother with me in my heart. There is not a day that I do not think of him.'

'I'm so sorry,' she said again. She wished she could give him comfort. But they were still essentially strangers.

He took a deep breath. 'But enough of sadness,' he said. He turned to her. 'I don't want to talk about tragic things, Gemma.'

There was a bleakness in his eyes, and his face seemed shadowed. She was an only child. She couldn't imagine how it would feel to lose a sibling—*and* his sibling's family. 'No,' she agreed.

How lucky she'd been in her life not to have suffered tragedy. The loss of her birth father hadn't really touched her, though she suspected her mother still secretly grieved. Gemma *had* had her share of heartbreak, though. She had genuinely loved Alistair, and the way their relationship had ended had scarred her—perhaps irredeemably. It would be difficult to trust again.

A silence fell between them that Gemma didn't know quite how to fill. 'Tell me more about Montovia,' she said eventually. 'Are there magnificent old buildings? Do you have lots of winter sports? Do you have a national costume?'

'Yes to all of that. Montovia is very beautiful and traditional. It has many medieval buildings. There is also a modern administrative capital, where the banks and financial services are situated.'

'And the chocolate?'

'The so-important chocolate? It is made in a charming old factory building near the lake, which is a tourist attraction in its own right.'

I'd love to go there some day.

Her words hung unspoken in the air between them. Never could she utter them. He was a tourist—just passing through before he went back to his own life. And she was a woman guarding her heart against falling for someone impossible.

'That sounds delightful,' she said.

'There is a wonderful chocolate shop and tea room near my home. I used to love to go there when I was a child. So…so did my brother and sister.'

Gemma wondered about his sister, but didn't want to ask. 'Where do you live?' she said instead.

He took another deep breath. It seemed to Gemma that he needed to steady himself against unhappy thoughts. His brother must be entwined in Tristan's every childhood memory.

'I live in the old capital of Montovia—which is also called Montovia.'

'That could get confusing, couldn't it?'

'Everyone knows it. The town of Montovia grew up around the medieval castle and the cathedral and sits on the edge of a lake.'

Gemma sat forward in her chair. 'A castle? You live near a *castle*?'

'But of course. Montovia is ruled by a hereditary monarchy.'

'You mean a king and a queen?'

'Yes.'

'I wasn't expecting that. I assumed Montovia would be a republic—a democracy.'

'It is… We have a hereditary monarchy, but also a representative democracy with an elected parliament—and a legal system, of course.'

'So the king and queen are figureheads?'

He shook his head. 'They are rulers, with the power to dissolve parliament. Although that has never happened.'

'Castles and kings and queens—it sounds like something out of a fairytale.' She was too polite to say it sounded feudalistic. Not when he sounded so passionate, defending a way of life that didn't seem of this century.

'On the contrary, it is very real. Our country is prosperous.

Montovians are very patriotic. Each of our subjects—I…uh… I mean the people…would fight to the death to protect their way of life. We have compulsory military service to ensure we are ready in case they should ever have to.'

'You mean conscription?'

'Yes. For all males aged eighteen. Women can volunteer, and many do.'

She shuddered. 'I don't think I would want to do that.'

'They would probably welcome someone like you as a cook.'

He smiled. Was he teasing her?

'But I'd still have to do the military training. I've seen what soldiers have to do—running with big packs on their back, obstacle courses, weapons…' Her voice dwindled away at the sheer horror of even contemplating it.

'Sign up even as a cook and you'd have to do the training. And no wooden spoons as weapons.'

'You'll never let me forget that, will you?'

'Never,' he said, his smile widening into a grin.

Until he went on his way and never gave this girl in Sydney another thought.

Why were they even talking about this? She was unlikely to visit Montovia, let alone sign up for its military.

'Did you serve?' she asked.

'Of course. My time in the army was one of the best times of my life.'

Oh, yes. She could imagine him in uniform. With his broad shoulders and athletic build. That must be where his bearing came from. Tristan in uniform would be even hotter than Tristan in casual clothes. Or Tristan without any—

Don't go there, Gemma.

But her curiosity about Montovia was piqued. When she went home this evening, she would look up the country and its customs on the internet.

'Did you actually have to go to battle?' she asked.

'I spent time with the peacekeeping forces in eastern Europe.

My brother went to Africa. It was good for us to see outside our own protected world.'

'You know, I wasn't really aware that such kingdoms as Montovia still existed.'

'Our royal family has ruled for centuries,' he said—rather stiffly, she thought. 'The people love the royal family of Montovia.'

'Do *you*?' she asked. 'You're not harbouring any secret republican leanings?'

His eyebrows rose, and he looked affronted. 'Never. I am utterly loyal to the king and queen. My country would not be Montovia without the royal family and our customs and traditions.'

Gemma was silent for a long moment. 'It's all so outside of my experience. As a child I led an everyday suburban existence in a middle-class suburb of Sydney. You grew up in a town with a medieval castle ruled by a king and queen. What…what different lives we must lead.'

He steepled his fingers together. 'Yes. Very different.'

Tristan was glad of the interruption when the waiter brought out a tray with the cool drinks they had ordered. *He had to be more careful.* He'd been on tenterhooks while chatting with Gemma for fear that he would inadvertently reveal the truth about himself and his family. There had been a few minor slip-ups, but nothing that couldn't be excused as a mistake with his English.

He drank iced tea as Gemma sipped on diet cola. It was too early for anything stronger.

The longer he maintained this deception, the harder it would become to confess to it. But did that really matter? After the party on Friday night he wouldn't need to be in any further contact with Party Queens. Or with Gemma.

He could leave the reveal until she found out for herself—when he appeared at his party wearing his ceremonial sash and medals. No doubt she would be shocked, would maybe despise him for lying to her. Her opinion should not matter—he would never see her again after the party.

But her opinion of him did matter. *It mattered very much.*

Just now there had been an opportunity for him to explain his role in the royal family of Montovia—but he had not been able to bring himself to take it. He was still hanging on fiercely to the novelty of being just Tristan in Gemma's eyes.

'I haven't finished my interrogation yet,' she said, a playful smile lifting the corners of her mouth.

He liked it that she was unaware of his wealth and status. It must be obvious to her that he was rich. But she seemed more interested in *him* than in what he had. It was refreshing.

'You said you went to university in England?' she asked.

'To Cambridge—to study European law.'

Her finely arched auburn brows rose. 'You're a lawyer?'

'I don't actually practise as a lawyer. I have always worked for…for my family's business. A knowledge of European law is necessary.'

For trade. For treaties. For the delicate negotiations required by a small country that relied in some measure on the goodwill of surrounding countries—but never took that goodwill for granted.

'Is it your father's business?'

'Yes. And it was my grandparents' before that.' Back and back and back, in an unbroken chain of Montovia's hereditary monarchy. It had been set to continue in his brother's hands—not his.

Tristan knew he could not avoid talking about his brother, much as it still hurt. There'd been an extravagance of public mourning for his brother's death—and the death of his little son, whose birth had placed a second male between Tristan and the throne. But with all the concern about his unexpected succession to the position of crown prince, Tristan hadn't really been able to mourn the loss of Carl, his brother and best friend. Not Carl the crown prince. And his sweet little nephew.

This trip away had been part of that grieving process. Being with Gemma was helping.

'My brother played a senior role in the…the business. I now have to step up to take his role.'

'And you're not one hundred per cent happy about that, are you?'

'I never anticipated I would have to do it. The job is not my choice.'

Not only had he loved his brother, he had also admired the way Carl had handled the role of crown prince. Tristan had never resented not being the heir. He had never been sure if he had an unquestioning allegiance to the old ways in order not to challenge the archaic rules that restricted the royal family's existence even in the twenty-first century. One onerous rule in particular…

'Will it bring more responsibility?' Gemma asked. 'Will you be more involved in the chocolate side of things?'

For a moment he wasn't sure what she meant. Then he remembered how he had deliberately implied that chocolate was part of his family's business.

'More the finance and managerial side,' he said. And everything else it took to rule the country.

'I'm sure you will rise to the challenge and do a wonderful job,' she said.

He frowned. 'Why do you say that, Gemma, when we scarcely know each other?'

Her eyes widened. 'Even in this short time I'm convinced of your integrity,' she said. 'I believe you will want to honour your brother's memory by doing the best job you can.'

His integrity. Short of downright lying, he had been nothing but evasive about who he was from the moment they'd met. How would she react when she found out the truth?

The longer he left it, the worse it would be.

He turned to face her. 'Gemma, I—'

Gemma suddenly got up from her deckchair, clutching her

hat to her head against a sudden gust of wind. 'We're passing across the Heads.'

'The Heads?'

'It's the entrance from the ocean to Sydney Harbour, guarded by two big headlands—North Head and South Head. But, being exposed to the Pacific Ocean, the sea can get rough here, so prepare for a rocky ride ahead.'

CHAPTER SEVEN

TRISTAN HAD PLANNED with military precision in order to make this day with Gemma happen. But one important detail had escaped his plan.

He cursed his inattention with a blast of favourite curse words. Both relatively sheltered when they'd been conscripted to the military, he and his brother had expanded their vocabulary of new and interesting words with great glee. He had never lost the skill.

Gemma was standing beside him at the bow of the *Argus*. 'Do I detect some choice swearing in Montovian?' she asked with a teasing smile.

'Yes,' he said, still furious with himself.

'Can you translate for me?'

'No,' he said.

'Or tell me what it was all about?'

Exasperated, he waved his hand to encompass the view. 'Look at this place—Store Beach…even more perfect than you said it would be.'

'And there's a problem with that?'

The *Argus* had dropped anchor some one hundred metres from shore. The beach was more what he would call a bay, with a sheltered, curving stretch of golden sand. Eucalypt trees and other indigenous plants grew right down to where the sand started. The water rippled through shades of azure to wash up on the beach in a lacy white froth. The air was tangy with salt and the sharp scent of the eucalypts. It took no stretch of the imagination to feel as if they were on a remote island somewhere far away.

'Not a problem with the beach,' he said. 'It's difficult to believe such a pristine spot could be so close to a major city.'

'That's why we chose Store Beach for your lunch date,' she said. 'And, being midweek, we've got it all to ourselves. So what's the problem?'

'It's hot, the water looks awesome, I want to swim. But I didn't think to bring a swimsuit—or order one for you.'

Her eyebrows rose. 'For me? *Order* a swimsuit for me?'

'Of course. You would not have known to bring one as you thought you would be working. There is a concierge at my hotel—I should have asked her to purchase a choice of swimsuits for you.'

Gemma's brows drew together in a frown. 'Are you serious?'

'But of course.'

'You are, aren't you?' Her voice was underscored with incredulity.

'Is there something wrong with that?'

'Nothing *wrong*, I guess. But it's not the kind of thing an Australian guy would do, that's for sure. None that *I* know, anyway.'

Tristan realised he might sound arrogant, but went ahead anyway. 'It is the kind of thing I would do, and I am annoyed that I did not do so.'

She tilted her head to one side, observing him as if he were an object of curiosity. 'How would you have known my size?'

'I have observed your figure.' He couldn't help but cast an appreciative eye over the curves of her breasts and hips, her trim waist. 'I would have made a very good estimate.'

Immediately, he suspected he might have said the wrong thing. Again he muttered a Montovian curse. Under stress—and the way she was looking at him *was* making him stressed—he found his English wasn't turning out quite the way he wanted it to.

Thankfully, after a stunned silence on her part, Gemma erupted into a peal of delightful laughter. 'Okay… I'm flattered you've made such a close observation of my figure.'

'It's not that I… I didn't mean—'

Her voice was warm with laughter. 'I think I know what you mean.'

'I did not say something…inappropriate?'

'You kinda did—but let's put it down to culture clash.'

'You do not think me…bad mannered? Rude?'

Crass. That was the word he was seeking. It was at the tip of his tongue. He had a master's degree in law from a leading English university. Why were his English language skills deserting him?

It was *her.*

Gemma.

Since the moment she'd come at him with her wooden spoon and pink oven mitts she'd had him—what was the word?—*discombobulated.* He was proud he had found the correct, very difficult English word, but why didn't he feel confident about pronouncing it correctly? The way she made him feel had him disconcerted, disorientated, behaving in ways he knew he should not.

But the way she was smiling up at him, with her dimples and humour in her brown eyes, made him feel something else altogether. *Something that was forbidden for him to feel for a commoner.*

She stretched up on her toes to kiss him lightly on the cheek, as she had done when she'd boarded the boat. This time her lips lingered longer, and she was so close he inhaled her heady scent of vanilla and lemon and a hint of chocolate, felt the warmth of her body. He put his hand to his cheek, where he had felt the soft tenderness of her lips, and held it there for a moment too long.

'I don't think you're at all rude,' she said. 'I think you're charming and funny and generous…and I… I…'

For a long moment her gaze held his, and the flush high on her cheekbones deepened. Tristan held his breath, on tenterhooks over what she might say next. But she took a step back, took a deep, steadying breath—which made her breasts rise enticingly under her snug-fitting top—and said something altogether different from what he'd hoped she might say.

'And I can solve your swimsuit problem for you,' she said.

'You can?'

'First the problem of a swimsuit for me. That impossibly big bag of mine also contains a swimsuit and towel. The North Sydney Olympic Pool is on the way from Lavender Bay wharf to my apartment in Kirribilli. I intended to swim there on my way home—as I often do.'

'That's excellent—so you at least can dive in and swim.'

'So can you.'

'But I—'

'I understand if you don't want to go in salt water in your smart white trousers. Or…or in your underwear.'

Her voice had faltered when she'd mentioned his underwear. A sudden image of her in *her* underwear flashed through his mind—lovely Gemma, swimming in lacy sheer bra and panties, her auburn hair streaming behind her in the water…

He had to clear his throat to speak. 'So what do you suggest?'

'In a closet in the stateroom is a selection of brand-new swimwear for both men and women. Choose a swimsuit and the cost of it will be added to the boat hire invoice.'

'Perfect,' he said. 'You get everything right, don't you, Party Queen Gemma?'

Her expression dimmed. 'Perhaps not everything. But I'll claim this one.'

'Shall we go swimming?' he asked. 'I saw a swimming platform aft on the boat.' His skin prickled with heat. He should have worn shorts and a T-shirt instead of trying to impress

Gemma in his bespoke Italian sportswear. 'I can't wait to get into that water.'

'Me, too. I can't think of anything I would rather do on a beautiful day like this.'

Tristan could think of a number of things he'd like to do with *her* on a beautiful day like this. All of which involved them wearing very few clothes—if any at all.

Gemma changed quickly and went back out onto the deck, near the swimming platform at the back. Tristan had gone into the stateroom to choose a swimsuit and change. She felt inexplicably shy as she waited for him. Although she swam often, she never felt 100 per cent comfortable in a swimsuit. The occupational hazard of a career filled with tempting food made her always think she needed to lose a few pounds to look her best in Lycra.

Her swimsuit was a modest navy racer-back one-piece, with contrast panels of aqua and white down the sides. More practical than glamorous. Not, in fact, the slightest bit seductive. Which was probably as well…

The door from the stateroom opened and Tristan headed towards her. Tristan had confessed to 'observing' her body. She smiled at the thought of his flustered yet flattering words. She straightened her shoulders and sucked in her tummy. And then immediately sucked in a breath as well at the sight of him. He'd looked good in his clothes, but without them—well, *nearly* without them—he was breathtaking in his masculinity.

Wearing stylish swim shorts in a tiny dark-blue-and-purple check and nothing else, he strode towards her with athletic grace and a complete lack of self-consciousness. *He was gorgeous.* Those broad shoulders, the defined muscles of his chest and arms, the classic six-pack belly and long, leanly muscled legs were in perfect proportion. He didn't have much body hair—just a dusting in the right places, set off against smooth golden skin.

He smiled his appreciation of *her* in a swimsuit. His smile and those vivid blue eyes, his handsome, handsome face and the warmth of his expression directed at her, all made her knees so wobbly she had to hold on to the deck railing for support. Her antennae didn't just wave frantically—they set off tiny, shrill alarms.

She realised she was holding her breath, and it came out as a gasp she had to disguise as a cough.

'Are you okay?' Tristan asked.

'F-fine,' she said as soon as she was able to recover her voice. As fine as a red-blooded woman *could* be when faced with a vision of such masculine perfection and trying to pretend she wasn't affected.

The crew had left a stack of red-and-white-striped beach towels in a basket on the deck. Tristan picked one up and handed it to her. 'Your swimsuit is very smart,' he said.

The open admiration in his eyes when he looked at her made her decide she had no cause for concern about what he thought of her shape.

She had to clear her throat. 'So…so is yours.'

Tristan picked up a towel for himself and slung it around his neck. As he did so, Gemma noticed something that marred all that physical perfection—a long, reddish scar that stretched along the top of his shoulder.

Tristan must have noticed the line of her gaze. 'You have observed my battle wound?'

She frowned. 'I thought you said you didn't go to war?'

'I mean my battle wound from the polo field. I came off one of my ponies and smashed my collarbone.'

She wanted to lean over and stroke it but didn't. 'Ouch. That must have hurt.'

'Yes. It did,' he said with understatement.

She didn't know if it was Tristan's way or just the way he spoke English. She wondered how different he might be if she were able to converse with him in fluent Montovian.

'I have a titanium plate and eight pins in it.'

'And your pony?' Gemma wasn't much of a horseback rider, but she knew that what was called a polo 'pony' was actually a very expensive and highly trained thoroughbred horse. Polo was a sport for the very wealthy.

'He was not hurt, thank heaven—he is my favourite pony. We have won many chukkas together.'

'Can you still play polo?'

'I hope to be able to play in the Montovian team this summer.'

She could imagine Tristan in the very tight white breeches and high black boots of a polo player, fearlessly ducking and weaving in perfect unison with a magnificent horse.

'You play polo for your country?'

'I have that honour, yes,' he said.

Again she got that feeling of *otherness*. Not only did he and she come from different countries and cultures, it seemed Tristan came from a different side of the tracks, as well. The posh, extremely wealthy side. Her stepfather was hardly poor, but he was not wealthy in the way she suspected Tristan was wealthy. Dennis was an orthodontist, with several lucrative practices. She could thank him for her perfectly aligned teeth and comfortable middle-class upbringing.

As a single mother, I could never have given you this life, her mother had used to say, reinforcing her instructions for Gemma always to be grateful and acquiescent. *Why couldn't you have married someone who didn't always make me feel in the way?* Gemma had wanted to shout back. But she had loved her mother too much to rebel.

Running a string of polo ponies, hiring a luxury yacht on Sydney Harbour for just two people, the upcoming no-expenses-spared function on Friday night all seemed to speak of a very healthy income. If she thought about it, Tristan had actually *bought* her company on the boat today—and it had been a very expensive purchase.

But she didn't care about any of that.

She liked Tristan—*really* liked him—and he was far and

away the most attractive man she had ever met. It was a waste of time to worry when she just wanted to enjoy his company.

She reached into her outsize bag for her high-protection sunscreen. 'You go in the water. I still have to put on some sun protection,' she said to Tristan.

'I'll wait for you,' he said.

Aware of Tristan's intense gaze, she felt self-conscious smoothing cream over her arms and legs, then twisting and turning to get to the spot on her back she could never quite reach. 'Australia is probably not the best climate for me,' she said. 'I burn, I blister, I freckle...'

'I think your pale skin is lovely,' he said. 'Don't try to tan it.'

'Thank you,' she said. It wasn't a compliment she heard often in a country obsessed with tanning.

'Let me help,' said Tristan. He grabbed the tube of sunscreen before she could protest. 'Turn around.'

She tensed as she heard him fling the towel from around his neck, squeeze cream from the tube. Then relaxed as she felt his hands on her back, slowly massaging in the cream with strong, sure fingers, smoothing it across her shoulders and down her arms in firm, sweeping motions.

The sensation of his hands on her body was utter bliss—she felt as if she was melting under his touch. When his hands slid down her back, they traced the sides of her breasts, and her nipples tightened. His breath fanned her hair, warm and intimate. She closed her eyes and gave herself over to sensation. *To Tristan.*

Her breathing quickened as her body responded to him, and from behind her she heard his breath grow ragged. He rested his hands on her waist. She twisted around, her skin slick with cream, and found herself in the circle of his arms.

For a long, silent moment she looked up into his face—already familiar, dangerously appealing. She knew he would see in her eyes the same mix of yearning and desire and wariness she saw in his: the same longing for something she knew was unwise. She swayed towards him as he lowered his head and splayed her hands against his bare, hard chest, his warm skin. She sighed as his lips touched hers in the lightest of caresses, pressed her mouth against his as she returned his kiss.

He murmured against her mouth. 'Gemma, I—'

Then another voice intruded. 'Gemma, I need to get your opinion on the plating of the yellow-tail kingfish *carpaccio*. Do you want— Oh. *Sorry*. I didn't realise I was interrupting—'

Gemma broke away from Tristan's kiss. Glared over his shoulder to her chef, who had his hands up in surrender as he backed away.

'No need. I'll sort the *carpaccio* out for myself.'

But he had a big grin plastered on his face, and she knew the team at Party Queens would find out very soon that Gemma had been caught kissing the client. She muttered a curse in English—one she was sure Tristan would understand. *She wanted to keep Tristan to herself.*

Tristan's arms remained firmly around her, and she didn't really want to leave them. But when he pulled her towards him again, she resisted. 'It's as well our chef came along,' she said. 'We shouldn't really be starting something we can't continue, should we?'

Tristan cleared his throat, but his voice was husky when he replied. 'You are right—we should not. But that does not stop me wanting to kiss you.'

She took a step back. 'Me neither. I mean I want to kiss *you*, too. But…but you're only here a few days and I—'

I'm in danger of falling for you, even though I hardly know you and I have to protect myself from the kind of pain that could derail me.

'I understand. It would be best for both of us.' He sounded as if he spoke through gritted teeth.

Disappointment flooded through her but also relief that he hadn't pressed for more. After the world of promise in that brief, tender kiss, she might have been tempted to ignore those frantically waving antennae and throw away every self-protective measure and resolve she had made in that lonely six months.

'Yes,' was all she could murmur from a suddenly choked throat.

'What I really need is to get into that cold water,' he said.

'You mean…like a cold shower?'

'Yes,' he said, more grimly than she had heard him speak before.

'Me, too,' she said.

He held out his hand. 'Are you coming with me?'

CHAPTER EIGHT

AS TRISTAN SWAM alongside Gemma, seeing her pale limbs and the auburn hair floating around her shoulders reminded him of the Montovian myths of water nymphs. Legend had it that these other-world temptresses in human form inhabited the furthest reaches of the vast lakes of Montovia. They were young, exquisite and shunned human contact.

If a man were to come across such a nymph, he would instantly become besotted, bewitched, obsessed by her. His beautiful nymph would entice him to make love to her until he was too exhausted to swim and he'd drown—still in her embrace—in the deepest, coldest waters. The rare man who survived and found his way home would go mad with grief and spend the rest of his life hunting the shores of the lakes in a desperate effort to find his nymph again.

Montovians were a deeply superstitious people—even the most well educated and sophisticated of them. Tristan shrugged off those ancient myths, but in a small part of his soul they lived on despite his efforts to deny them.

Gemma swam ahead of him with effortless, graceful strokes, ducking beneath the water, turning and twisting her body around. How did he describe how she seemed in the water? *Joy-*

ous. That was the word. She was quite literally in her element, playing in the water like some…well, like a nymph enchantress.

She turned back to face him, her hair slicked back off her face, revealing her fine bone structure, the scattering of freckles across the bridge of her nose. She trod water until he caught up with her.

'Isn't the water wonderful?' she said. 'I would have hated you if I'd had to stay in the kitchen while you cavorted in the sea with that other woman—uh, that other woman who didn't actually exist.'

'You would have "hated" me?' he asked.

'Of course not. I… I… You…'

Again he got the sense that she had struggled with the urge to say something significant—and then changed her mind.

'I'm very thankful to you for making this day happen. It… it's perfect.'

'I also am grateful that you are here with me,' he replied. 'It is a day I will not forget.'

How could he forget Gemma? He would bookmark this time with her in his mind to revisit it in the lonely, difficult days he would face on his return to Montovia.

A great lump of frustration and regret seemed to choke him as he railed against the fate that had led him to this woman when duty dictated he was not able to follow up on the feelings she aroused in him. When he'd been second in line to the throne, he had protested against the age-old rules governing marriage in Montovia. Now he was crown prince, that avenue had been closed to him.

Not for the first time he wished his brother had not gone up in his helicopter that day.

'Do you want to swim to shore?' she asked. 'C'mon—I'll race you.'

She took off in an elegant but powerful freestyle stroke. Tristan was fit and strong, but he had to make an effort to keep up with her.

They reached the beach with her a few strokes ahead. He followed her as they waded through the shallows to the sand, unable to keep his eyes off her. Her sporty swimsuit showed she meant business when she swam. At the same time it clung to every curve and showcased the smooth expanse of her back, her shapely behind, her slender strong legs.

Gemma Harper was a woman who got even more attractive the better he knew her. *And he wanted her.*

She stopped for him to catch up. Her eyes narrowed. 'I hope you didn't let me win on purpose in some chivalrous gesture?'

'No. You are a fast swimmer. It was a fair race.'

He was very competitive in the sports he played. Being bested by a woman was something new, and he respected her skill. But how could a Montovian, raised in a country where the snow-fed lakes were cold even in midsummer, compete with someone who'd grown up in a beachside city like Sydney?

'I used to race at school—but that was a long time ago. Now I swim for fun and exercise. And relaxation.' She looked at him as if she knew very well that he was not used to being beaten. 'You'd probably beat me at skiing.'

'I'm sure you'd challenge me,' he said. 'Weren't both your parents ski instructors?'

'Yes, but I've only ever skied in Australia and New Zealand. Skiing in Europe is on my wish list—if I ever get enough time away from Party Queens to get there, that is.'

Tristan uttered something non-committal in reply instead of the invitation he wished he could make. There was nothing he would like better than to take her skiing with him. Show her the family chalet, share his favourite runs on his favourite mountains, help her unwind après-ski in front of a seductively warm log fire… But next winter, and the chance of sharing it with Gemma, seemed far, far away.

The sand was warm underfoot as he walked along the beach with her, close enough for their shoulders to nudge against each other occasionally. Her skin was cool and smooth against his and he found it difficult to concentrate on anything but her, difficult to clear his mind of how much he wanted her—and could not have her.

He forced himself to look around him. She'd brought him to an idyllic spot. The vegetation that grew up to the sand was full of birdlife. He saw flashes of multi-coloured parrots as they flew through the trees, heard birdsong he couldn't identify.

'How could you say Sydney is not like living in a resort when a place like this is on your doorstep?' he asked.

'I guess you *would* feel like you were on vacation if you lived around here,' she said. She waved her hand at the southern end of the beach. 'Manly, which seems more like a town than a suburb, is just around the bay. You can hire a two-man kayak there and paddle around to here with a picnic. It would be fun to do that sometime.'

But not with him. He would be far away in Montovia, doing his duty, honouring his family and his country. No longer master of his own life. 'That would be fun,' he echoed. He could not bear the thought of her kayaking to this beach with another man.

She sat down on the sand, hugging her knees to her chest. He sat down next to her, his legs stretched out ahead. The sun was warm on his back, but a slight breeze kept him cool.

'Did you wonder why this beach is called Store Beach?' she asked.

'Not really. But I think you are going to tell me.'

'How did you get to know me so quickly?' she asked, her head tilted to one side in the manner he already found endearing.

'Just observant, I guess,' he said. *And because he was so attracted to her.* He wanted to know every little thing about her.

'There must be a tour guide inside me, fighting to get out,' she joked.

'Set her free to tell me all about the beach,' he said. This sea nymph had bewitched him so thoroughly that sitting on a beach listening to the sound of her voice seemed like heaven.

'If you insist,' she said with a sideways smile. 'Behind us, up top, is an isolation hospital known as the Quarantine Station. Stores for the station were landed here. For the early settlers from Europe it was an arduous trip of many months by sailing ship. By the time some of them got here, they had come down with contagious illnesses like smallpox. They were kept here—away from the rest of Sydney. Some got better…many died.'

Tristan shuddered. 'That's a gruesome topic for a sunny day.'

'The Quarantine Station closed after one hundred and fifty years. They hold ghost tours there at night. I went on one—it was really spooky.'

Her story reminded Tristan of what a very long way away from home he was. Even a straightforward flight was twenty-two hours. Any kind of relationship would be difficult to maintain from this distance—even if it were permitted.

'If I had time I would like to go on the ghost tour, but I fear that will not be possible,' he said.

Had he been here as tourist Tristan Marco, executive of a nebulous company that might or might not produce chocolate, he would have added, *Next time I'll do the ghost tour with you.* But he could not in all fairness talk about 'next time' or 'tomorrow.' Not with a woman to whom he couldn't offer any kind of relationship beyond a no-strings fling because she had not been born into the 'right' type of family.

'We should be heading back to the boat for lunch,' she said. 'I'm looking forward to being a guest for the awesome menu I planned. Swimming always makes me hungry.'

He stood up and offered her his hand to help her. She hesitated, then took it and he pulled her to her feet. She stood very close to him. Tristan took a step to bring her even closer. Her hair was still damp from the sea and fell in tendrils around her face. He smoothed a wayward strand from her cheek and tucked it around her ear. He heard her quick intake of breath at his touch before she went very still.

She looked up at him without saying a word. Laughter danced in her eyes and lifted the corners of her lovely mouth. He kept his hand on her shoulder, and she swayed towards him in what he took as an invitation. There was nothing he wanted more than to kiss her. He could not resist a second longer.

He kissed her—first on her adorable dimples, one after the other, as he had longed to do from the get go. Then on her mouth—her exquisitely sensual mouth that felt as wonderful as it looked, warm and welcoming under his. With a little murmur that sent excitement shooting through him, she parted her lips. He deepened the kiss. She tasted of chocolate and salt and her own sweet taste. Her skin was cool and silky against his, her curves pressed enticingly against his body.

All the time he was kissing her Tristan, knew he was doing so under false pretences. He was not used to deception, had always prided himself on his honesty. He wanted more—wanted more than kisses—from this beautiful woman he held in his arms. But he could not deceive her any longer about who he really was—and what the truth meant to them.

Tristan was kissing her—seriously kissing her—and it was even more wonderful than Gemma had anticipated. She had wanted him, wanted *this*, from the time she had first seen him in her kitchen. Her heart thudded in double-quick time, and pleasure thrummed through her body.

But she was shocked at how quickly the kiss turned from something tender into something so passionate that it ignited in her an urgent hunger to be closer to him. Close, closer…as close as she could be.

She had never felt this wondrous sense of connection and certainty. That time was somehow standing still. That she was meant to be here with him. That this was the start of something life-changing.

They explored with lips and tongues. Her thoughts, dazed with desire, started to race in a direction she had not let them until now. *Could* there be a tomorrow for her and Tristan? Why had she thought it so impossible? He wasn't flying back to the moon, after all. Long distance could work. Differences could be overcome.

Stray thoughts flew around her brain, barely coherent, in between the waves of pleasure pulsing through her body.

Tristan gently bit her bottom lip. She let out a little sound of pleasure that was almost a whimper.

He broke away from the kiss, chest heaving as he gasped for breath. She realised he was as shocked as she was at the passion that had erupted between them. Shocked and…and shaken.

Gemma wound her arms around his neck, not wanting him to stop but glad they were on a public beach so that there would be no temptation to sink down on the sand together and go further than kisses. She gave her frantic antennae their marching orders. This. To be with him. It was all she wanted.

'Tristan…' she breathed. 'I feel like I'm in some wonderful dream. I… I don't want this day to end.'

Then she froze as she saw the dismay in his eyes, felt the tension in his body, heard his low groan. She unwound her arms from around his neck, crossed them in front of her chest. She bit her lip to stop her mouth from trembling. Had she totally misread the situation?

'You might not think that when you hear what I have to say to you.' The hoarse words rushed out as if they'd been dammed up inside him and he could not hold on to them any longer.

She couldn't find the words to reply.

'Gemma. We have to talk.'

Did any conversation *ever* go well when it started like that? Why did those four words, grouped together in that way, sound so ominous?

'I'm listening,' she said.

'I have not been completely honest with you.'

Gemma's heart sank to the level of the sand beneath her bare feet. Here it came. He was married. He had a girlfriend back home. Or good old *I'm not looking for commitment.*

Those antennae were now flopped over her forehead, weary

and defeated from trying to save her from her own self-defeating behaviour.

She braced herself in readiness.

A pulse throbbed under the smooth olive skin at his temple. 'My family business I told you about…?'

'Yes?' she said, puzzled at the direction he was taking.

'It isn't so much a *business* as such…'

Her stomach clenched. The wealth. The mystery. Her sense that he was being evasive. 'You mean it's a…a criminal enterprise? Like the mafia or—?'

He looked so shocked she would have laughed at his expression if she'd had the slightest inclination to laugh. Or even to smile.

'No. Not that. You've got it completely wrong.'

She swallowed against a suddenly dry throat. 'Are you… are you a spy? From your country's intelligence service? If so, I don't know what you're doing with me. I don't know anything. I—'

The shock on his face told her she'd got that wrong, too.

'No, Gemma, nothing like that.'

He paused, as if gathering the strength to speak, and then his words came out in a rush.

'My family is the royal family of Montovia. My parents are the king and queen.'

CHAPTER NINE

GEMMA FELT AS if all the breath had been knocked out of her by a blow to the chest. She stared at him in total disbelief. 'You're kidding me, right?'

'I'm afraid I am not. King Gerard and Queen Truda of Montovia are my parents.'

'And…and you?'

'I am the crown prince—heir to the throne.'

Gemma felt suddenly light-headed and had to take in a few short, shallow breaths to steady herself. Strangely, she didn't doubt him. Those blue eyes burned with sincerity and a desperate appeal for her to believe him.

'A…a prince? A real-life prince? You?'

That little hint of a bow she'd thought she'd detected previously now manifested itself in a full-on bow to her. A formal bow—from a prince who wore swim shorts and had bare feet covered in sand.

'And…and your family business is—?'

'Ruling the country…as we have done for centuries.'

It fitted. Beyond all belief, it fitted. All the little discrepancies in what he'd said fell into place.

'So…what is a prince doing with a party planner?' Hurt

shafted her that she'd been so willingly made a fool of. 'Slumming it?'

Despite all her resolutions, she'd slid back into her old ways. Back at the dating starting gates, she'd bolted straight for the same mistake. She'd fallen for a good-looking man who had lied to her from the beginning about who he was. Lied big-time.

She backed away from him on the sand. Stared at him as if he were a total stranger, her hands balled by her sides. Her disappointment made her want to lash out at him in the most primitive way. But she would not be so uncivilised.

Her voice was cold with suppressed fury, and when she spoke it was as if her words had frozen into shards of ice to stab and wound him. 'You've lied to me from the get go. About who you are—what you are. You lied to get me onto the boat. I don't like liars.'

And she didn't want to hear any more lies.

Frantically, she looked around her. Impenetrable bushland behind her. A long ocean swim to Manly in front of her. And she in a swimsuit and bare feet.

Tristan put out a hand. 'Gemma. I—'

She raised both hands to ward him off. 'Don't touch me,' she spat.

Tristan's face contorted with an emotion she couldn't at first identify. Anger? Anger at *her*?

No—anger at himself.

'Don't say that, Gemma. I… I liked you so much. You did not know who I was. I wanted to get to know you as Tristan, not as Crown Prince Tristan. It was perhaps wrong of me.'

'Isn't honesty one of the customs of your country? Or are princes exempt from telling the truth?'

His jaw clenched. 'Of course not. I'm furious at myself for not telling you the truth earlier. I am truly sorry. But I had to see you again—and I saw no way around it. If you had known the truth, would you have relaxed around me?'

She crossed her arms firmly against her chest. But the sincerity of his words was trickling through her hostility, slowly dripping on the fire of her anger.

'Perhaps not,' said. She would have been freaking out, uncertain of how to behave in front of royalty. As she was now.

'Please. Forgive me. Believe the sincerity of my motives.'

The appeal in his blue eyes seemed genuine. *Or was she kidding herself?* How she wanted to believe him.

'So…no more lies? You promise every word you say to me from now on will be the truth?'

'Yes,' he said.

'Is there any truth in what you've told me about you? About your country? You really *are* a prince?'

'I am Tristan, Crown Prince of Montovia.'

'Prince Tristan…' She slowly breathed out the words, scarcely able to comprehend the truth of it. *Of all the impossible men, she'd had to go and fall for a prince.*

'And everything else you told me?'

'All true.'

'Your brother?'

The pain in his eyes let her know that what he'd told her about his brother's death was only too true.

'Carl was crown prince, heir to the throne, and he trained for it from the day he was born. I was the second in line.'

'The heir and the spare?' she said.

'As the "spare," I had a lot more freedom to live life the way I wanted to. I rebelled against the rules that governed the way we perform our royal duties. Then everything changed.'

'Because of the accident? You said it's your brother's job you are stepping up to in the "family business," didn't you? The job of becoming the next king?'

'That is correct.'

Gemma put her hands to her temples to try and contain the explosion of thoughts. 'This is surreal. I'm talking to a *prince*, here. A guy who's one day going to be king of a country and have absolute power over the lives of millions people.'

'Not so many millions—we are a small country.'

She put down her hands so she could face him. 'But still... You're a prince. One day you'll be a king.'

'When you put it like that, it sounds surreal to me, too. To be the king was always my brother's role.'

Her thoughts still reeled. 'You don't just live *near* the castle, do you?'

'The castle has been home to the royal family for many hundreds of years.'

'And you probably *own* the town of Montovia—and the chocolate shop with the tea room where you went as a little boy?'

'Yes,' he said. 'It has always been so.'

'What about the chocolate?'

'Every business in Montovia is, strictly speaking, our business. But businesses are, of course, owned by individuals. They pay taxes for the privilege. The chocolate has been made by the same family for many years.'

'Was your little nephew a prince, too?'

'He...little Rudolph...*was* a prince. As son of the crown prince, he was next in line to the throne. He was only two when he died with his mother and father.'

'Truly...truly a tragedy for your family.'

'For our country, too. My brother would have been a fine ruler.'

She shook her head, maintained her distance from him. 'It's a lot to take in. How were you allowed to come to Australia on your own if you're the heir? After what happened to your brother?'

'I insisted that I be allowed this time on my own before I take up my new duties. Duties that will, once I return, consume my life.'

'You're a very important person,' she said slowly.

'In Montovia, yes.'

'I would have thought you would be surrounded by bodyguards.'

Tristan looked out to sea and pointed to where a small white cruiser was anchored. 'You might not have noticed, but the *Argus* was discreetly followed by that boat. My two Montovian bodyguards are on it. My parents insisted on me being under their surveillance twenty-four hours a day while I was in a foreign country.'

'You mean there are two guys there who watch you all the time? Did they see us kissing?' She felt nauseous at the thought of being observed for the entire time—both on the boat and on the beach.

'Most likely. I am so used to eyes being on me I do not think about it.'

'You didn't think you could have trusted me with the truth?'

'I did not know you,' he said simply. 'Now I do.'

Their lives were unimaginably different. Not just their country and their culture. He was *royalty*, for heaven's sake.

'I don't have to call you your royal highness, do I?' She couldn't help the edge to her voice.

'To you I am always Tristan.'

'And my curtsying skills aren't up to scratch.'

Pain tightened his face. 'This is why I went incognito. You are already treating me differently now you know I am a prince. Next thing you'll be backing away from me when you leave the room.'

'Technically we're on a beach, but I get your drift. I'm meant to back away from you across the sand?'

'Not now. But when—' he crossed himself rapidly '—when, God forbid, my father passes and I become king, then—'

'I'd have to walk backwards from your presence.'

'Yes. Only in public, of course.'

'This is…this is kind of incomprehensible.' It was all so unbelievable, and yet she found herself believing it. And no matter how she tried, she could not switch off her attraction to him.

A shadow crossed over his face. 'I know,' he said. 'And… and it gets worse.'

'How can it get worse than having to back away out of the presence of a guy my own age? A guy I've made friends with? Sort of friends—considering I don't generally make pals of people who lie to me.'

'Only "friends", Gemma?' he said, his brows lifted above saddened eyes. 'I think we both know it could be so much more than that.'

Tristan stepped forward to close the gap between them. This time she didn't back away. He traced her face lightly with his fingers, across her cheekbones, down her nose, around her lips. She had the disconcerting feeling he was storing up the sight of her face to remember her.

'Yes,' she admitted. 'I… I think I knew that from the get go.'

It was difficult to speak because of the little shivers of pleasure coursing through her at his touch.

'I did also,' he said. 'I have never felt this way. It was…*instant* for me. That was why I had to see you again—no matter what I had to do to have you with me.'

'I told you I could cast spells,' she said with a shaky smile. 'Seriously, I felt it too. Which is why I resisted you. Whether you're a prince or just a regular guy, I don't trust the "instant" thing.'

'The *coup de foudre*? I did not believe it could happen either—certainly not to me.'

She frowned. 'I'm not sure what you mean?'

'The bolt of lightning. The instant attraction out of nowhere. I have had girlfriends, of course, but never before have I felt this…this intensity so quickly.'

She *had* felt it before—which was why she distrusted it. Why did it feel so different this time?

It was him. *Tristan.* He was quite unlike anyone she had ever met.

She braced her feet in the sand. 'So how does it get worse?'

'First I must apologise, Gemma, for luring you onto the boat.'

'Apologise? There's no need for that. I'm having a wonderful day…enjoying being with you. We could do it again tomorrow—I have vacation days due to me. Or I could take you to see kangaroos…maybe even a koala.'

'You would want that?'

'We could try and make this work.' She tried to tone down the desperation in her voice, but she felt he was slipping away from her. 'We live on different sides of the world—not different planets. Though I'm not so sure about how to handle the prince thing. That's assuming you want to date me?' She laughed—a nervous, shaky laugh that came out as more of a squeak. 'I feel more like Cinderella than ever…'

Her voice trailed away as she read the bleak expression in his eyes. This was not going well.

'Gemma, you are so special to me already. Of course I would like to date you—if it were possible. But before you plan to spend more time with me you need to hear this first,' he said. 'To know why I had no right to trick you. You said you would never hate me, but—'

'So tell me,' she said. 'Rip the sticking plaster off in one go.'

'I am not free to choose my own wife. The heir to the throne of Montovia must marry a woman of noble blood. It is forbidden for him to marry a commoner.'

His words hit her like blows. 'A…a "commoner"? I'm not so sure I like being called a commoner. And we're not talking marriage—we hardly know each other.'

'Gemma, if the way I feel about you was allowed to develop, it would get serious. *Very* serious.'

He spoke with such conviction she could not help but find his words thrilling. The dangerous, impossible kind of thrilling.

'I… I see,' she said. Until now she hadn't thought beyond today. 'I believe it would get serious for me, too.' *If she allowed herself to get involved.*

'But it could not lead to marriage for us. Marriage for a crown prince is not about love. It is about tradition. My brother's death changed everything. Brought with it an urgency to prepare me for the duties that face me. As crown prince I am expected to marry. I must announce my engagement on my thirtieth birthday. A suitable wife has been chosen for me.'

'An arranged marriage? Surely not in this day and age?'

'There is no compulsion for me to marry her. She has been deemed "suitable" if I cannot find an aristocratic wife on my own. And my time is running out.'

Pain seared through her at the thought of him with another woman. But one day together, a few kisses, gave her no claim on him.

'When do you turn thirty?'

'On the eighteenth of June.'

She forced her voice to sound even, impartial. 'Three months. Will you go through with it? Marry a stranger?'

'Gemma, I have been brought up believing that my first duty is to my country—above my own desires. As second in line to the throne I might have tried to defy it. I even told my family I would not marry if I could not choose my own bride. But as crown prince, stepping into the shoes of my revered brother, who married the daughter of a duke when he was twenty-six and had a son by the time he was twenty-eight, I have no choice but to marry.'

'But not…never…to someone like me…' Her voice trailed away as the full impact of what he was saying hit her. She looked down to where she scuffed the sand with her bare toes. She had humiliated herself by suggesting a long-distance relationship.

Tristan placed a gentle finger under her chin so she had to look up at him. 'I am sorry, Gemma. That is the way it has always been in Montovia. Much as I would wish it otherwise.' His mouth twisted bitterly. 'Until I met you I was prepared to accept my fate with grace. Now it will be that much harder.'

'Aren't princess brides a bit short on the ground these days?'

'To be from an aristocratic family is all that is required—

she does not need to be actual royalty. In the past it was about political alliances and dowries...'

Nausea brewed deep in the pit of her stomach. Why hadn't he told her this before he'd kissed her? Before she'd let herself start to spin dreams? Dreams as fragile as her finest meringue and as easily smashed.

Sincere as he appeared now, Tristan had deceived her. She would never have allowed herself to let down her guard if she'd known all this.

Like Alistair, he had presented himself as a person different from what he really was. And she, despite all best intentions, had let down her guard and exposed her heart. Tristan had started something he knew he could not continue with. That had been dishonest and unfair.

She could not let him know how much he had hurt her. Had to carry away from this some remaining shreds of dignity. For all his apologies, for all his blue blood, he was no better than any other man who had lied to her.

'I'm sorry, too, Tristan,' she said. 'I... I also felt the *coupe de foudre*. But it was just...physical.' She shrugged in a show of nonchalance. 'We've done nothing to regret. Just...just a few kisses.'

What were a few kisses to a prince? He probably had gorgeous women by the hundred, lining up in the hope of a kiss from him.

'Those kisses meant something to me, Gemma,' he said, his mouth a tight line.

She could not deny his mouth possessing hers had felt both tender and exciting. But... 'The fact is, we've spent not even a day in each other's company. I'm sure we'll both get over it and just remember a...a lovely time on the harbour.'

The breeze that had teased the drying tendrils of her hair had dropped, and the sun beat down hot on her bare shoulders. Yet she started to shiver.

'We should be getting back to the boat,' she said.

She turned and splashed into the water before he could see the tears of disappointment and loss that threatened. She swam her hardest to get to the boat first, not knowing or caring if Tristan was behind her.

Tristan stood on the shore and watched Gemma swim away from him in a froth of white water, her pale arms slicing through the water, her vigorous kicks making very clear her intention to get as far away from him as quickly as possible.

He picked up a piece of driftwood and threw it into the bush with such force that a flock of parrots soared out of a tree, their raucous cries admonishing him for his lack of control. He cursed loud and long. *He had lost Gemma.*

She was halfway to the boat already. He wished he could cast a wide net into the sea and bring her back to him, but he doubted she wanted more of his deceitful company.

In Montovian mythology, when a cunning hunter tried to capture a water nymph and keep her for himself, he'd drag back his net to find it contained not the beautiful woman he coveted but a huge, angry catfish, with rows of razor-sharp teeth, that would set upon him.

The water nymphs held all the cards.

An hour later Gemma had showered and dressed and was sitting opposite Tristan at the stylishly laid table on the sheltered deck of the *Argus*. She pushed the poached lobster salad around her plate with her fork. Usually she felt ravenous after a swim, but her appetite had completely deserted her.

Tristan was just going through the motions of eating, too. His eyes had dulled to a flat shade of blue, and there were lines of strain around his mouth she hadn't noticed before. All the easy camaraderie between them had disintegrated into stilted politeness.

Yet she couldn't bring herself to be angry with him. He seemed as miserable as she was. Even through the depths of her shock and disappointment she knew he had only deceived her because he'd liked her and wanted her to like him for himself. Neither of them had expected the intensity of feeling that had resulted.

She still found it difficult to get her head around his real identity. For heaven's sake, she was having lunch with a *prince.* A prince from a kingdom still run on medieval rules. He was royalty—she was a commoner. *Deemed not worthy of him.* Gemma had grown up in an egalitarian society. The inequality of it grated. She did not believe herself to be *less.*

She made another attempt to eat, but felt self-conscious as she raised her fork to her mouth. Did Tristan's bodyguards have a long-distance lens trained on her?

She slid her plate away from her, pushed her chair back and got up from the table.

'I'm sorry, Tristan, I can't do this.'

With his impeccable manners, he immediately got up, too. 'You don't like the food?' he said. But his eyes told her he knew exactly what she meant.

'You. Me. What could have been. What can never be. Remember what I said about the sticking plaster?'

'You don't want to prolong the pain,' he said slowly.

Of course he understood. In spite of their differences in status and language and upbringing, he already *got* her.

This was heartbreaking. He was a real-life Prince Charming who wanted her but couldn't have her—not in any honourable way. And she, as Cinderella, had to return to her place in the kitchen.

'I'm going to ask the skipper to take me to the wharf at Manly and drop me off.'

'How will you get home?'

'Bus. Ferry. Taxi. Please don't worry about me. I'm very good at looking after myself.'

She turned away from him and carried with her the stricken expression on his face to haunt her dreams.

CHAPTER TEN

GEMMA STRUGGLED TO hear what Andie was saying to her over the rise and fall of chatter, the clink of glasses, the odd burst of laughter—the soundtrack to another successful Party Queens function. The Friday night cocktail party at the swish Parkview Hotel was in full swing—the reception being held to mark the official visit of Tristan, crown prince of Montovia, to Sydney.

Gemma had explained to her business partners what had happened on the *Argus* and had excluded herself from any further dealings with him. Tristan had finalised the guest list with Eliza on Thursday.

Tristan's guests included business leaders with connections to the Montovian finance industry, the importers and top retailers of the principality's fine chocolate and cheese, senior politicians—both state and federal—even the governor of the state.

If she didn't have to be here to ensure that the food service went as it should for such an important function, she wouldn't have attended.

Her antennae twitched. Okay, so she was lying to herself. How could she resist the chance to see him again? On a strictly 'look, don't touch' basis. Because no matter how often she told herself that she'd had a lucky escape to get out after only a day, before she got emotionally attached, she hadn't been able to stop thinking about him.

Not that it had been an issue. Tristan was being the ideal host and was much in demand from his guests. He hadn't come anywhere near her, either, since the initial formal briefing between Party Queens and its client. She shouldn't have felt hurt, but she did—a deep, private ache to see that after all that angst on the *Argus* it seemed he'd been able to put her behind him so easily.

The secret of his identity was now well and truly out. There was nothing the media loved more than the idea of a handsome young European prince visiting Australia. Especially when he was reported to be 'one of the world's most eligible bachelors.' She knew there were photographers swarming outside the hotel to catch the money shot of Prince Charming.

'What did you say, Andie?' she asked her friend again.

Tall, blonde Andie leaned closer. 'I said you're being very brave. Eliza and I are both proud of you. It must be difficult for you, seeing him like this.'

'Yeah. It is. I'm determined to stay away from him. After all it was only one day—it meant nothing.' One day that had quite possibly been one of the happiest days of her life—until that conversation on Store Beach. 'No big deal, really—unless I make it a big deal.'

'He lied to you. Just remember that,' said Andie.

'But he—' It was on the tip of her tongue to defend Tristan by saying he hadn't out-and-out lied, just skirted around the truth. But it was the same thing. Lying by omission. And she wasn't going to fall back into bad old ways by making excuses for a man who had misled her.

But she couldn't help being aware of Tristan. Just knowing he was here had her on edge. He was on the other side of the room, talking to two older men. He looked every inch the prince in an immaculately tailored tuxedo worn with a blue, gold-edged sash across his chest. Heaven knew what the rows of medals pinned to his shoulder signified—but there were a lot of them. He was the handsome prince from all the fairytales she had loved when she was a kid.

Never had that sense of *other* been stronger.

'Don't worry,' said Andie. 'Eliza and I are going to make darn sure you're never alone with him.'

'Good,' said Gemma, though her craven heart *longed* to be alone with him.

'You didn't do all that work on yourself over six months to throw it away on an impossible crush. What would Dr B think?'

The good thing about having worked on a women's magazine was that the staff had had access to the magazine's agony aunt. Still did. 'Dr B' was a practising clinical psychologist and—pushed along by her friends—Gemma had trooped along to her rooms for a series of consultations. In return for a staff discount, she hadn't minded seeing her heavily disguised questions appearing on the agony aunt's advice page in her new magazine.

Dear Dr B,
I keep falling for love rats who turn out to be not what they said they were—yet I put up with their bad behaviour. How can I break this pattern?

It was Dr B who had helped Gemma identify how her unbalanced relationship with her stepfather had given her an excessive need for approval from men. It was Dr B who had showed her how to develop her own instincts, trust her antennae. And given her coping strategies for when it all got too hard.

'I can deal with this,' she said to Andie. 'You just watch me.'

'While you watch Tristan?'

Gemma started guiltily. 'Is it that obvious? He's just so *gorgeous*, Andie.'

'That he is,' said Andie. 'But he's not for you. If you start to weaken, just think of all that stuff you dug up on the internet about Montovia's Playboy Prince.'

'How could I forget it?'

Gemma sighed. She'd been shocked to the core at discovering his reputation. Yet couldn't reconcile it with the Tristan she knew.

Was she just kidding herself?

She must not slide back into bad old habits. People had warned her about Alistair, but she'd wanted to believe his denials about drugs and other women. Until she'd been proved wrong in the most shockingly painful way.

Andie glanced at her watch. 'I need to call Dominic and check on Hugo,' she said. 'He had a sniffle today and I want to make sure he's okay.'

'As if he *wouldn't* be okay in the care of the world's most doting dad,' Gemma said.

Andie and Dominic's son, Hugo, was fifteen months old now, and the cutest, most endearing little boy. Andie often brought him into the Party Queens office, and Gemma doted on him. One day she wanted a child of her own. She was twenty-eight. That was yet another reason not to waste time on men who were Mr Impossible—or Crown Prince Impossible.

'Where's Eliza?' Andie asked. 'I don't want to leave you by yourself in case that predatory prince swoops on you.'

'No need for name-calling,' said Gemma, though Andie's choice of words made her smile. 'Eliza is over there, talking with the best man at your wedding, Jake Marlowe. He's a good friend of Tristan's.'

'So I believe… Dominic is pleased Jake's in town.'

'From the look of it, I don't know that Eliza would welcome the interruption. She seems to be getting on *very* well with Jake. You go and make your phone call. I'm quite okay here without a minder, I assure you. I'm a big girl.'

Gemma shooed Andie off. She needed to check with the hotel liaison representative about the service at the bar. She thought they could do with another barman on board. For this kind of exclusive party no guest should be left waiting for a drink.

But before she could do so a bodyguard of a different kind

materialised by her shoulder. She recognised him immediately as one of the men who had been discreetly shadowing Tristan. She shuddered at the thought that he'd been spying on her and Tristan as they'd kissed on the beach.

'Miss Harper, His Royal Highness the Crown Prince Tristan would like a word with you in the meeting room annexe through that door.' He spoke English, with a coarser version of Tristan's accent.

She looked around. Tristan was nowhere to be seen. From the tone of this burly guy's voice, she didn't dare refuse the request.

Neither did she want to.

Tristan paced the length of the small breakout room and paced back again. Where was Gemma? Would she refuse to see him?

He had noticed her as soon as he'd got to the hotel. Among a crowd of glittering guests she had stood out in the elegant simplicity of a deep blue fitted dress that emphasised her curves and her creamy skin. Her hair was pulled up and away from her face to tumble to her shoulders at the back. She was lovelier than ever.

He had to see her.

He was taking a risk, stepping away from the party like this. His idyllic period of anonymity was over. He was the crown prince once more, with all the unwanted attention that warranted.

The local press seemed particularly voracious. And who knew if one of his invited guests might be feeding some website or other with gossipy Prince Charming titbits? That was one of the nicknames the media had given him. They would particularly be looking out for any shot of him with a woman. They would then speculate about her and make her life hell. That girl could not be Gemma. She did not deserve that.

And then she was there, just footsteps away from him. Her high heels brought her closer to his level. The guard left discreetly, closing the door behind him and leaving Tristan alone with her. Could lightning strike twice in the same place? For he felt again that *coup de foudre*—that instant sensation that this was *his woman*.

His heart gave a physical leap at the expression on her face—pure, unmitigated joy at seeing him. For a moment he thought—hoped—she might fling herself into his arms. Where he would gladly welcome her.

Then the shutters came down, and her expression became one of polite, professional interest.

'You wanted to see me? Is it about the canapés? Or the—?'

'I wanted to see you. Alone. Without all the circus around us. I miss you, Gemma. I haven't been able to stop thinking about you.'

Her face softened. 'There isn't a moment since I left the *Argus* that I haven't thought about *you*.'

Those words, uttered in her sweet, melodious voice, were music to his ears.

He took a step towards her, but she put up her hand in a halt sign.

'But nothing has changed, has it? I'm a commoner and you're a prince. Worse, the Playboy Prince, so it appears.'

Her face crumpled, and he saw what an effort it was for her to maintain her composure.

'I… I didn't think you were like that…the way the press portrayed you.'

The Playboy Prince—how he hated that label. Would he ever escape the reputation earned in those few years of rebellion?

'So you've dug up the dirt on me from the internet?' he said gruffly.

She would only have had to type *Playboy Prince* into a search engine and his name would come up with multiple entries.

'Is it true? All the girlfriends? The parties? The racing cars and speedboats?'

There was a catch in her voice that tore at him.

He gritted his teeth. 'Some of it, yes. But don't believe all you read. My prowess with women is greatly exaggerated.'

'You're never photographed twice with the same woman on your arm—princesses, heiresses, movie stars. All beautiful. All glamorous.'

'And none special.'

No one like Gemma.

'Is that true? I… I don't know what to believe.' Her dress was tied with a bow at the waistline, and she was pleating the fabric of its tail without seeming to realise she was doing so.

'I got a lot of attention as a prince. Opportunities for fun were offered, and I took them. There were not the restraints on me that there were on my brother.'

'If I'd been willing, would I have been just another conquest to you? A Sydney fling?'

'No. Never. You are special to me, Gemma.'

'That sounds like something the Playboy Prince might say. As another ploy.'

There was a cynical twist to her mouth he didn't like.

'Not to you, Gemma. Do not underestimate me.'

She was not convinced.

He cursed under his breath. He wanted her to think well of him. Not as some spoiled, privileged young royal. Which he had shown all the signs of being for some time.

'There was a reason for the way I behaved then,' he said. 'I was mad about an English girl I'd met at university. She was my first serious girlfriend. But my parents made it clear they did not approve.'

'Because she was a commoner?'

'Yes. If she'd been from a noble family they would have welcomed her. She was attractive, intelligent, talented. My parents—and the crown advisers—were worried that it might get serious. They couldn't allow that to happen. They spoke to her family. No doubt money changed hands. She transferred to a different university. I was angry and upset. She refused to talk to me. I realised then what it meant to have my choice of life partner restricted by ancient decrees.'

'So you rebelled?'

'Not straight away. I still believed in the greater good of the throne. Then I discovered the truth behind my parents' marriage. The hypocrisy. It was an arranged marriage—my father is older than my mother. He has a long-time mistress. My mother discreetly takes lovers.' He remembered how gutted he'd felt at the discovery.

'What a shock that must have been.'

'These days they live separate lives except for state occasions. And yet they were determined to force me along the same unhappy path—for no reason I could see. I was young and hot-headed. I vowed if I couldn't marry the girl I wanted then I wouldn't marry at all.'

She sagged with obvious relief. 'That's understandable.'

'So you believe me?'

Slowly, she nodded. 'In my heart I didn't want to believe the person I was reading about was the person I had found so different, so...*wonderful*.'

'I was unhappy then. I was totally disillusioned. I looked at the marriages in my family. All were shams. Even my brother's marriage was as cynical an arrangement as any other Montovian royal marriage.'

'And now?'

She looked up at him with those warm brown eyes. Up close he saw they had golden flecks in them.

'It is all about duty. Duty before personal desire. All the heroes in our culture put duty first. They sacrifice love to go to war or to make a strategic marriage. That now is my role. Happiness does not come into the equation for me.'

'What would make you happy, Tristan?'

'Right now? To be alone with my beautiful Party Queen. To be allowed to explore what...what we feel for each other. Like an everyday guy and his girl. That would make me happy.' He shrugged. 'But it cannot be.'

There was no such thing as happiness in marriage for Montovian royalty.

This sea nymph had totally bewitched him. He had not been able to stop thinking about her. Coming up with one scheme after another that would let him have her in his life and explore if she might be the one who would finally make him want to marry—and discarding each as utterly impossible.

'I… I would like that, too,' she said. 'To be with you, I mean.'

He took both her hands in his and pulled her to him. She sighed—he could not tell if it was in relief or surrender—and relaxed against him. He put his arms around her and held her close. She laid her head on his shoulder, and he dropped a kiss on her sweetly scented hair.

Then he released her and stepped back. 'We cannot risk being compromised if someone comes in,' he explained. 'The last thing we want is press speculation.'

'I… I didn't realise that your life was under such scrutiny,' she said.

'That is why I wanted to be incognito. We could not have had that day together otherwise. I do not regret keeping the truth from you, Gemma. I do not regret that day. Although I am sorry if I hurt you.'

She had abandoned the obsessive pleating of the bow on her dress. But her hands fluttered nervously. Looking into her face, he now understood what it meant to say that someone had her heart in her eyes.

She felt it, too. That inexplicable compulsion, that connection. His feelings for Gemma might be the most genuine emotions he had ever experienced. Not *love* at first sight. He didn't believe that could happen so quickly. But something powerful and intense. Something so much more than physical attraction.

'We…we could have another day…together,' she said cautiously, as if she were testing his reaction.

'What do you mean?'

'We could have *two* days. I'm offering you that chance. You don't leave until Monday morning. All day Saturday and Sunday stretch out before us.'

She was tempting him almost beyond endurance. 'You would want us to spend the weekend together knowing it could never be more than that? Not because I don't *want* it to be more, but because it would never be allowed?'

'Yes. I do want that. I… I ache to be with you. I don't want to spend a lifetime regretting that I didn't take a chance to be with you. I keep trying to talk sense to myself—tell myself that I hardly know you; that you're leaving. But at some deep, elemental level I feel I *do* know you.' She shook her head. 'I'm not explaining this very well, am I?'

'I understand you very well—for it is how I also feel. But I do not want to hurt you, Gemma.'

'And I certainly don't want to get hurt,' she said. 'Or hurt *you*, for that matter. But I don't want to be riddled with regret.'

'Remember in three months' time I must announce my engagement to a suitable bride. I cannot even offer to take you as my mistress—that would insult both you and the woman who will become my wife. I will not cheat on her. I will *not* have a marriage like that of my parents.'

'I understand that. Understand and admire you for your honesty and…and moral stance. I'm offering you this time with me, Tristan, with no strings attached. No expectations. Just you and me together. As we will never be allowed to be again.'

He was silent for a moment too long. Common sense, royal protocol—all said he should say no. If the press found out it would be a disaster for her, uncomfortable for him. The Playboy Prince label would be revived. While such a reputation could be laughed off, even admired, for the second or third in line to the throne, it was deeply inappropriate for the crown prince and future king.

Gemma looked up at him. She couldn't mask the longing in

her eyes—an emotion Tristan knew must be reflected in his own. Her lovely, lush mouth trembled.

'I should go,' she said in a low, broken voice. 'People will notice we've left the room. There might be talk that the prince is too friendly with the party planner. It…it could get awkward.'

She went to turn away from him.

Everything in Tristan that spoke of duty and denial and loyalty to his country urged him to let her walk away.

But something even stronger urged him not to lose his one chance to be with this woman with whom he felt such a powerful connection. If he didn't say something to stop her, he knew he would never see her again.

He couldn't bear to let her go—no matter the consequences.

Tristan held out his hand to her.

'Stay with me, Gemma,' he said. 'I accept your invitation to spend this time together.'

CHAPTER ELEVEN

NEXT MORNING, in the grey light of dawn, Tristan turned to Gemma, who was at the wheel of her car. 'Where exactly are you taking me?'

'We're heading west to my grandmother's house in the Megalong Valley in the Blue Mountains. She died a few years ago, and she left her cottage to me and my two cousins. We use it as a weekender and for vacations.'

'Is it private?'

'Utterly private. Just what we want.'

He and Gemma had plotted his escape from the hotel in a furtive whispered conversation the previous night, before they had each left the annexe room separately to mingle with his guests. There had been no further contact with each other until this morning.

While it was still dark, she had driven to his hotel in the city and parked her car a distance away. He had evaded his bodyguards and, with his face covered by a hoodie, had met her without incident. They had both laughed in exhilaration as she'd gunned the engine and then floored the accelerator in a squeal of tyres.

'The valley is secluded and rural—less than two hundred people live there,' Gemma said. 'You might as well be ten hours away from Sydney as two. The cottage itself is on forty acres of garden, pasture and untamed bushland. We can be as secluded as we want to be.'

She glanced quickly at him, and he thrilled at the promise in her eyes. This was a relaxed Gemma, who had pulled down all the barriers she'd put up against him. She was warm, giving—and his without reservation for thirty-six hours.

'Just you and me,' he said, his voice husky.

'Yes,' she said, her voice laced with promise. 'Do you think there's any chance your goons—sorry, your bodyguards—could find us?'

'I was careful. I left my laptop in my suite and I've switched off my smartphone so it can't be tracked. But I did leave a note to tell them I had gone of my own free will on a final vacation and would be back late Sunday night. The last thing we want them to think is that I've been kidnapped and start a search.'

'Is kidnapping an issue for you?' Her grip visibly tightened on the steering wheel.

'It is an issue for anyone with wealth. The royal children are always very well guarded.'

'I'm not putting you at risk, am I? I… I couldn't bear it if I—'

'Here, the risk is minimal. Please do not concern yourself with that. We are more at risk from the media. But I checked that no one was lurking about at my hotel.'

'Can you imagine the headlines if they did find us? *Playboy Prince in Secluded Love Nest with Sydney Party Planner*.'

Tristan rather liked the concept of a love nest. 'They would most likely call you a *sexy* party planner.'

Gemma made a snort of disgust, then laughed. 'I'll own sexy. Or how about: *Playboy Prince Makes Aussie Conquest*? They'll want to get the local angle in, I'm sure.'

'You could also be *Mystery Redhead*?' he suggested.

He found he could joke about the headlines the press might make about his life—there had been enough of them in the past. Now he was crown prince he did not want to feature in any more. He appreciated the effort Gemma was making to preserve their privacy.

They made up more outrageous headlines as Gemma drove along the freeway until Sydney was behind them.

'Are you going to unleash your inner tour guide and tell me about the Blue Mountains?' Tristan asked as the road started to climb.

'How did you know I was waiting for my cue?' she said.

'Please, go ahead and tell me all I need to know—plus *more* than I need to know,' he said.

'Now that I've been invited…' she said, with a delightful peal of laughter.

Tristan longed to show her Montovia some day—and pushed aside the melancholy thought that that was never likely to happen. He had thirty-six hours with her stretching ahead of him—bonus hours he had not thought possible. He would focus his thoughts on how he could make them special for her.

'They're called the Blue Mountains because they seem to have a blue haze over them from a distance, caused by the eucalypt oil from the trees,' she said.

'I didn't know that,' he said.

'Don't think of them as mountains like Montovian mountains. Australia is really old, geologically, and the mountains would have been underwater for millions of years. They're quite flat on top but very rugged. There are some charming small towns up there, and it's quite a tourist destination.'

It wasn't that he found what she was saying boring. On the contrary, visiting Australia had long been on his 'to do' list. But Tristan found himself getting drowsy.

For the last three nights he had slept badly, kept awake by thoughts of Gemma and how much he wanted her to be part of his life. Now she was next to him and they were together. Not for long enough, but it was more than he could have dreamed of. For the moment he was content. To drift off to the sound of her voice was a particular kind of joy…

When he awoke, Gemma was skilfully negotiating her car down a series of hairpin bends on a narrow road where the Australian bush grew right to the sides.

'You've woken just in time for our descent into the valley,' she said. 'Hold on—it's quite a twisty ride.'

The road wound through verdant rainforest and huge towering indigenous trees before emerging onto the valley floor. Tristan caught his breath in awe at the sight of a wall of rugged sandstone mountains, tinged red with the morning sun.

'It's magnificent, isn't it?' she said. 'You should see it after heavy rain, when there are waterfalls cascading down.'

The landscape alternated harshness with lush pastures dotted with black and white cattle. There was only the occasional farmhouse.

'Do you wonder why I'm driving so slowly?' Gemma asked.

'Because it's a narrow road?' he ventured.

'Because—ah, here they are. Look!'

A group of kangaroos bounded parallel to the road. Tristan wished he had a camera. His smartphone was switched off, and he didn't dare risk switching it back on.

'You have to be careful in the mornings and evenings not to hit them as they cross the road.' She braked gently. 'Like that—right in front of the car.'

One after the other the kangaroos jumped over a low spot in the fence and crossed the road. Halfway across, the largest one stopped and looked at him.

'He is as curious about me as I am about him,' Tristan whispered, not wanting to scare the creature. 'I really feel like I am in Australia now.'

'I promised you kangaroos in the wild, and I've delivered,' Gemma said with justifiable triumph.

While he could promise her nothing.

As Gemma showed Tristan around the three-bedroom, one-bathroom cottage, she wondered what he really thought of it.

He was, after all, used to living in a castle. The royal castle of Montovia was splendid—as befitted the prosperous principality.

Her internet research had showed her a medieval masterpiece clinging to the side of a mountain and overlooking a huge lake ringed by more snow-topped mountains. Her research had not shown her the private rooms where the family lived, but even if they were only half as extravagant as the public spaces Tristan had grown up in, they would be of almost unimaginable splendour.

And then there was a summer palace, at the other end of the lake. And royal apartments in Paris and Florence.

No doubt wherever he lived, he was waited on hand and foot by servants.

But she would not be intimidated. She was proud of her grandma's house—she and her cousins would probably always call it that, even though it was now their names on the deed of ownership.

She loved how it had been built all those years ago by her grandfather's family, to make the most of the gun-barrel views of the escarpment. To a prince it must seem very humble. But Gemma would never apologise for it.

Tristan stood on the wide deck her grandfather had added to the original cottage. It looked east, to the wall of the escarpment lit by the morning sun, and it was utterly private. No one could see them either from the neighbouring property or from the road.

Tristan put his arm around her to draw her close, and she snuggled in next to him. No more pretence that what they felt was mere friendship. She'd known when she'd invited him to spend his final weekend with her what it would lead to—and it was what she wanted.

Tristan looked at the view for a long time before he spoke. 'It's awe-inspiring to see this ancient landscape all around. And to be able to retreat to this charming house.'

She should have known that Tristan would not look down his princely nose at her beloved cottage.

'I've always loved it here. My grandmother knew what the situation was with my stepfather and made sure I was always welcome whenever I wanted. Sometimes I felt it was more a home than my house in Sydney.'

He turned to look back through the French doors and into the house, with its polished wooden floors and simple furnishings in shades of white.

'Was it like this when your grandmother had it? I think not.'

'Good guess. I loved my grandma, but not so much her taste in decorating. When I inherited with my cousins Jane and John—they're twins—I asked Andie to show us what to do with it to bring it into the twenty-first century. Not only did she suggest stripping it back to the essentials and painting everything we could white, but she used the house as a makeover feature for the magazine. We got lots of free help in return for having the house photographed. We put in a new kitchen and remodelled the bathroom, and now it's just how we want it.'

'The canny Party Queens wave their magic wands again?'

'You could put it like that.'

He pulled her into his arms. 'You're an amazing woman, Gemma Harper. One of many talents.'

'Thank you, Your Highness. And to think we're only just getting to know each other… I have many hidden talents you have yet to discover.'

'I've been keeping *my* talents hidden, too,' he said. 'But for no longer.'

He traced the outline of her mouth with his finger, the light pressure tantalising in its unexpected sensuality. Her mouth swelled under his touch, and she ached for him to kiss her there. Instead he pressed kisses along the line of her jaw and down to the sensitive hollows of her throat. She closed her eyes, the better to appreciate the sensation. How could something so simple ignite such pleasure?

She tilted back her head for more, but he teased her by planting feather-light kisses on her eyelids, one by one, and then her nose.

'Kiss me properly,' she begged, pressing her aching mouth to his.

He laughed deep in his throat, then deepened the kiss into something harder and infinitely more demanding. She wound her arms around his neck to pull him closer, craving more. Her antennae thrummed softly—not in warning but in approval. She wanted him. She needed him. He was hers. Not forever, she knew that. But for *now.*

This was the first time she had walked into a less-than-ideal relationship with her eyes wide open. It was her choice. With Tristan she had not been coerced or tricked. She just hoped that when the time came she would be able to summon the inner strength to let him go without damage to her heart and soul—and not spend a lifetime in futile longing for him.

But she would not think of that now. Her mind was better occupied with the pleasure of Tristan's mouth, his tongue, his hands skimming her breasts, her hips.

He broke away from the kiss so he could undo the buttons of her shirt. She trembled with pleasure when his fingers touched bare skin. He knew exactly what he was doing, and she thrilled to it.

'I haven't shown you around outside,' she said breathlessly. 'There are horses. I know you like horses. More kangaroos maybe…'

Oh! He'd pulled her shirt open with his teeth. Desire, fierce and insistent, throbbed through her. She slid his T-shirt over his head, gasped her appreciation of his hard, muscular chest.

He tilted her head back to meet his blue eyes, now dark with passion. 'How many times do I have to tell you? The only sight I'm interested in is you. *All of you.*'

CHAPTER TWELVE

THE SUNLIGHT STREAMING through the bedroom window told Gemma she had slept for several hours and that it must be heading towards noon. She reached out her hand to find the bed empty beside her, the sheets cooling.

But his lingering scent on the pillow—on *her*—was proof Tristan had been there with her. So were the delicious aches in her muscles, her body boneless with satisfaction. She stretched out her naked limbs, luxuriating in the memories of their lovemaking. Was it the fact he was a prince or simply because he was the most wonderful man she had ever met that made Tristan such an awesome lover?

She wouldn't question it. Tristan was Tristan, and she had never been gladder that she'd made the impulsive decision to take what she could of him—despite the pain she knew lay ahead when they would have to say goodbye.

Better thirty-six hours with this man than a lifetime with someone less perfect for her.

Her tummy rumbled to let her know the hour for breakfast was long past and that she'd had very little to eat the night before.

The aroma of freshly brewed coffee wafted to her nostrils, and she could hear noises coming from the kitchen. She sat up immediately—now fully awake. Tristan must be starving, too. How could she have slept and neglected him? *How could she have wasted precious time with him by sleeping?*

She leapt out of bed and burrowed in the top drawer of the chest of drawers, pulled out a silk wrap patterned with splashes of pink and orange and slipped it on. She'd given the wrap to her grandmother on her last birthday and kept it in memory of her.

She rushed out to the kitchen to find Tristan standing in front of the open fridge, wearing just a pair of blue boxer shorts. Her heart skipped a beat at the sight. Could a man be more perfectly formed?

He saw her and smiled a slow smile. The smile was just for her, and memories of their passionate, tender lovemaking came rushing back. The smile told her his memories of her were as happy. They were so good together. He was a generous lover, anticipating her needs, taking her to heights of pleasure she had not dreamed existed. She in turn revelled in pleasing him.

All this she could see in his smile. He opened his arms, and she went straight to them, sighing with pleasure as he pulled her close and slid his hands under the wrap. His chest was warm and hard, and she thrilled at the power of his body. He hadn't shaved, and the overnight growth of his beard was pleasantly rough against her cheek.

For a long moment they stood there, wrapped in each other's arms. She rested her head against his shoulder, felt the steady thud of his heartbeat, breathed in the male scent of him—already so familiar—and knew there was nowhere else she would rather be.

'You should have woken me,' she murmured.

'You looked so peaceful I did not have the heart,' he said. 'After all, you drove all the way here. And I only woke half an hour ago.'

'I… I don't want to waste time sleeping when I could be with you.'

'Which is why I was going to wake you with coffee.'

'A good plan,' she said.

'Hold still,' he said as he wiped under her eye with his finger.

'Panda eyes?' She hadn't removed her mascara the night before in the excitement of planning their escape.

'Just a smear of black,' he said. 'It's good now.'

She found it a curiously intimate gesture—something perhaps only long-time couples did. It was difficult to believe she had only met him on Monday. And would be losing him by the next Monday.

'You've been busy, by the look of it,' she said.

The table was set for a meal. She noticed he had set the forks and spoons face down, as she'd seen in France. The coffee machine hissed steam, and there were coffee mugs on the countertop.

'I hope you don't mind.'

'Of course not. The kitchen is designed for people to help themselves. No one stands on ceremony up here. It's not just me and my cousins who visit. We let friends use it, too.'

'I went outside and picked fresh peaches. The tree is covered in them.'

'You picked tomatoes, too, I see.'

Her grandmother's vegetable garden had been her pride and joy, and Gemma was determined to keep it going.

'Are you hungry?'

'Yes!'

'We could have breakfast, or we could have lunch. Whatever you choose.'

'Maybe brunch? You're going to *cook*?'

'Don't look so surprised.'

'I didn't imagine a prince could cook—or would even know his way around a kitchen.'

'You forget—this prince spent time in the army, where his title did not earn him any privileges. I also studied at university in England, where I shared a kitchen with other students.

I chose not to have my own apartment. I wanted to enjoy the student experience like anyone else.'

'What about doing the dishes?' she teased.

'But of course,' he replied in all seriousness. 'Although I cannot say I enjoy that task.'

She pressed a quick kiss to his mouth—his beautiful, sensual mouth which she had now thoroughly explored. He tasted of fresh, ripe peach. 'Relax. The rule in this kitchen is that whoever cooks doesn't have to do the dishes.'

'That is a good rule,' he said in his formal way.

She could not resist another kiss, and then squealed when he held her close and turned it into something deeper, bending her back over his arm in dramatic exaggeration. She laughed as he swooped her back upright.

He seemed so blessedly normal. And yet last night he had worn the ceremonial sash and insignia indicating his exalted place in a hereditary monarchy that stretched back hundreds of years. He'd hobnobbed with the highest strata of Sydney society with aplomb. It was mind-blowing.

'The fridge and pantry are well stocked,' she said. 'It's a long way up the mountain if we run out of something.'

'I have already examined them. Would you like scrambled eggs and bacon with tomatoes? And whole-wheat toast?'

'That sounds like a great idea. It makes a pleasant change for someone to cook for me.'

'You deserve to be cherished,' he said with a possessive arm still around her. 'If only—'

'No "if onlys",' she said with a sudden hitch to her voice. 'We'll go crazy if we go there.'

To be cherished by him was an impossible dream…

She was speared by a sudden shaft of jealousy over his arranged bride. Did that well-born woman have any idea how fortunate she was? Or *was* she so fortunate? To be married to a man in a loveless marriage for political expediency might not make for a happy life. As it appeared had been the case for Tristan's parents.

'So—what to do after brunch?' she asked. 'There are horses on the property that we're permitted to ride. Of course they're not of the same calibre as your polo ponies, but—'

'I do not care what we do, so long as I am with you.'

'Perhaps we could save the horses for tomorrow?' she said. 'Why don't we walk down to the river and I'll show you some of my favourite places? We can swim, if you'd like.'

'I didn't pack my swim shorts.'

'There's no need for swimsuits,' she said. 'The river is on our property, and it's completely private.'

A slow smile spread across his face, and her body tingled in response. Swimming at the river this afternoon might be quite the most exciting it had ever been. She decided to pack a picnic to take with them, so they could stay there for as long as they wanted.

Gemma woke during the night to find Tristan standing by the bedroom window. The only light came from a full moon that sat above the enormous eucalypts that bounded the garden. It seemed every star in the universe twinkled in the dark canopy of the sky.

He was naked, and his body, silvered by the moonlight, looked like a masterpiece carved in marble by a sculptor expert in the depiction of the perfect male form.

Gemma slid out of bed. She was naked, too, and she slid her arms around him from behind, resting her cheek on his back. He might look like silvered marble but he felt warm, and firm, and very much a real man.

'You okay?' she murmured.

He enfolded her hands with his where they rested on his chest.

'I am imagining a different life,' he said, his voice low and husky. 'A life where I am a lawyer, or a businessman working in Sydney. I live in a water-front apartment in Manly with my beautiful party-planner wife.'

She couldn't help an exclamation and was glad he couldn't see her face.

'You know her, of course,' he said, squeezing her hand. 'She and I live a resort life, and she swims every day in the sea. We cross the harbour by ferry to get to work, and I dream of the day I can have my own yacht. On some weekends we come up here, just the two of us, and ride horses together and plan for the day that we…that we—' His voice broke.

He turned to face her. In the dim light of the moon his face was in shadow, but she could see the anguish that contorted his face.

'Gemma, I want it so much.' His voice was hoarse and ragged.

'It…it sounds like a wonderful life,' she said, her own voice less than steady. 'But it's a fantasy. As much a fantasy as that party planner living with you as a princess in a fairytale castle. We…we will only get hurt if we let ourselves imagine it could actually happen.'

'There is… I could abdicate my role as crown prince.'

For a long moment Gemma was too shocked to say anything. 'You say that, but you know you could never step down from your future on the throne. Duty. Honour. Responsibility to the country you love. They're ingrained in you. You couldn't live with that decision. Besides, I wouldn't let you.'

'Sometimes that responsibility feels like a burden. I was not born to it, like my brother.'

'But you *will* rise to it.'

He cradled her face in his hands, looked deep into her eyes, traced the corner of her mouth with his thumb. 'Gemma, you must know how I feel about you—that I am falling in lo—'

'No.' She put her hand over his mouth to stop him. 'Don't go there,' she said. 'You can't say the *L* word until you can follow it with a proposal. And we know that's not going to happen. Not for us. Not for a prince and a party planner. I… I feel it, too. But I couldn't bear it if we put words to it. It would make our parting so much more painful than…than it's already going to be.'

She reached up and pulled his head down to hers, kissed him with all the passion and feeling she could bring to the kiss. Felt her tears rolling down her cheeks.

'This. This is all we can have.'

Tristan held Gemma close as she slept, her head nestled in his shoulder. He breathed in her sweet scent. Already he felt that even blindfolded he would recognise her by her scent.

His physical connection with this special woman was like nothing he had ever experienced. Their bodies were in sync, as though they had made love for a lifetime. He couldn't label what they shared as *sex*—this was truly making *love*.

Being together all day, cooking companionably—even doing the dishes—had brought a sense of intimacy that was new to him. Was this what a *real* marriage could be like? As opposed to the rigid, hypocritical structure of a royal marriage?

What he felt with Gemma was a heady mix of physical pleasure and simple joy in her company. Was that how marriage should be?

There was no role model for a happy marriage in his family. His parents with their separate lives… His brother's loveless union… And from what he remembered of his grandparents, his grandmother had spent more time on the committees of her charitable organisations than she had with his grandfather. Except, of course, when duty called.

Duty. Why did he have to give up his chance of love for *duty*?

Because he didn't have a choice.

He had never felt for another woman what he felt for Gemma. Doubted he ever would. She was right—for self-protection neither of them could put a label on what they felt for each other—but he knew what it was.

She gave a throaty little murmur as she snuggled closer. He dropped a kiss on her bare shoulder.

The full impact of what he would miss out on, what he had to give up for duty, hit him with the impact of a sledgehammer.

Feeling as he did for Gemma, how could he even contemplate becoming betrothed to another woman in three months' time? He could taste the bitterness in his mouth. Another loveless, miserable royal marriage for Montovia.

He stayed awake for hours, his thoughts on an endless loop that always seemed to end with the Montovian concept of honour—sacrificing love for duty—before he eventually slept.

When Tristan awoke it was to find Gemma dropping little kisses over his face and murmuring that breakfast was ready. He had other ideas, and consequently it was midmorning before they got out of bed.

They rode the horses back down to the river. He was pleased at how competent Gemma was in the saddle. Despite their differences in social status, they had a lot in common, liked doing the same things, felt comfortable with each other. *If only...*

He felt a desperate urgency as their remaining time together ticked on—a need to landmark each moment. Their last swim. Their last meal together. The last time they'd share those humble domestic duties.

He was used to being brave, to denying his feelings, but he found this to be a kind of torture.

Gemma had *not* been trained in self-denial. But she was brave up until they'd made love for the last time.

'I can't bear knowing we will never be together like this again,' she said, her voice breaking. 'Knowing that I will never actually see you again, except in the pages of a magazine or on a screen.'

She crumpled into sobs, and there was no consoling her. How could he comfort her when he felt as if his heart was being wrenched out of him and pummelled into oblivion?

Tristan tilted her chin up so he could gaze deep into her eyes, reddened from where she'd tried to scrub away her tears. Her lovely mouth trembled. It was a particular agony to know he was the cause of her pain.

He smoothed her hair, bedraggled and damp with tears, from her face. 'Gemma, I am sorry. I should not have pursued you when I knew this could be the only end for us.'

She cleared her voice of tears. Traced his face with her fingers in a gesture he knew with gut-wrenching certainty was a farewell.

'No. Never say that,' she said. 'I don't regret one moment I've spent with you. I wish it could be different for us. But we went into this with our eyes open. And now…and now I know what it *should* be like between a man and a woman. I had no idea, you see, that it could be like this.'

'Neither did I,' he choked out. Nor what an intolerable burden duty to his beloved country could become.

'So no beating ourselves up,' she said.

But for all her brave words he had to take the wheel of her car and drive back to Sydney. She was too distressed to be safe.

Only too quickly he pulled up the car near his hotel and killed the engine. The unbearable moment of final farewell was upon them.

He gave her the smartphone he had bought to use in Australia so they could easily stay in touch. 'Keep it charged,' he said.

'I won't use it, you know,' she said, not meeting his eyes. 'We have to make a clean break. I'll go crazy otherwise.'

'If that's what you want,' he said, scarcely able to choke out the words with their stabbing finality. But he stuffed the phone into her bag anyway.

'It's the only way,' she said, her voice muffled as she hid her face against his shoulder. 'But…but I'll never forget you and… and I hope you have a good life.'

All the anger and ambivalence he felt towards his role as heir to the throne threatened to overwhelm him. 'Gemma, I want you to know how much I—'

She pushed him away. 'Just go now, Tristan. Please.'

He wanted to be able to say there could be more for them, but he knew he could not. Instead he pulled the hoodie up over his face, got out of the car and walked back to his life as crown prince without looking back.

CHAPTER THIRTEEN

Ten weeks later

GEMMA SAT ON the bed in a guest room at the grand gated Georgian house belonging to her newly discovered English grandparents. She was a long way from home, here in the countryside near Dorchester, in the county of Dorset in the south-west of England.

In her less-than-steady hand she held the smartphone Tristan had insisted on leaving with her on the last day she'd seen him. It was only afterwards that she'd realised why. If she needed to get in touch with him she doubted the castle staff would put through a call to the crown prince from some unknown Australian girl.

The phone had been charging for the last hour.

She had never used it—rather had kept to her resolve never to contact him. That had not been easy in the sad black weeks that had followed the moment when he had stumbled from her car and had not looked back. But she had congratulated herself on how well she had come through the heartbreak of having her prince in her life for such a short time before she'd had to let him go.

The only time she had broken down was when she had

flicked through a gossip magazine to be suddenly confronted by an article about the crown prince of Montovia's upcoming birthday celebrations. It had included photos of Tristan taken at the Sydney reception, looking impossibly handsome. A wave of longing for him had hit her with such intensity she'd doubled over with the pain of it.

Would contacting him now mean tearing the scab off a wound better left to heal?

When she thought about her time with him in Sydney—she refused to think of it as a fling—it had begun to take on the qualities of a fondly remembered dream. After this length of time she might reasonably have expected to start dating again. Only she hadn't.

'Don't go thinking of him as your once-in-a-lifetime love,' Andie had warned.

'I never said he was,' Gemma had retorted. 'Just that he *could* have been if things had been different.'

Now, might she have been given another chance with Tristan?

Gemma put down the phone, then picked it up again. Stared at it as if it might give her the answer. Should she or shouldn't she call him?

She longed to tell Tristan about her meeting with the Cliffords. But would he be interested in what she had to say? Would he want to talk to her after all this time? *Would he even remember her?*

She risked humiliation, that was for sure. By now he might be engaged to some princess or a duchess—that girl in Sydney a distant memory.

But might she always regret it if she didn't share with Tristan the unexpected revelation that had come from her decision to seek out her birth father's family?

Just do it, Gemma.

With trembling fingers she switched on the phone and the screen lit up. So the service was still connected. It was meant to be. She *would* call.

But then she was astounded to find a series of recent missed calls and texts of escalating urgency flashing up on the screen. All from Tristan. All asking her to contact him as soon as possible.

Why?

It made it easy to hit Call rather than have to take the actual step of punching out his number.

He answered almost straightaway. Her heart jolted so hard at the sound of his voice she lost *her* voice. She tried to say hi, but only a strangled gasp came out.

'Gemma? Is that you?'

'Yes,' she finally managed to squeak out.

'Where *are* you?' he demanded, as if it had been hours rather than months since they'd last spoken. 'I've called the Party Queens office. I've called both Andie and Eliza, who will not tell me where you are. Are you at the cottage? Are you okay?'

Gemma closed her eyes, the better to relish the sound of his voice, his accent. 'I'm in Dorset.'

She wondered where he was—in some palatial room in his medieval castle? It was difficult to get her head around the thought.

There was a muffled exclamation in Montovian. 'Dorset, England?'

She nodded. Realised that of course he couldn't see her. 'Yes.'

'So close. And I didn't know. What are you doing there?'

'Staying with my grandparents.'

'They…they are not alive. I don't understand…'

She could almost see his frown in his words.

'My birth father's parents.'

'The Clifford family?'

He'd remembered the name. 'Yes.'

What else did he remember? She hadn't forgotten a moment of their time together. Sometimes she revisited it in dreams. Dreams from which she awoke to an overwhelming sense of loss and yearning for a man she'd believed she would never see again—or hear.

'The people who paid your mother off? But they are not known to you...'

She realised she was gripping the phone so tensely her fingers hurt. 'They are now. I came to find them. After all your talk of your birthright and heritage, I wanted to know about mine. I told my mother I could no longer deny my need to know just because my stepfather felt threatened that she'd been married before.'

Her time with Tristan had made her want to take charge of her life and what was important to her.

'Those people—did they welcome you?'

'It seems I look very much like my father,' she said. In fact her grandmother had nearly fainted when Gemma had introduced herself.

'They were kind?'

The concern in his voice made her think Tristan still felt something for her.

'Very kind. It's a long story. One I'd like to share with you, Tristan.' She held her breath, waiting for his answer.

'I would like to hear it. And there is something important I have to tell you.'

'Is that why you were calling me?'

'Yes. I wanted to fly to Australia to see you.'

'You were going to fly all that way? But it's only two weeks until your birthday party.'

'I want to see you. Can you to come to Montovia?'

For a long moment she was too shocked to reply. 'Well, yes, I would like to see Montovia,' she finally choked out. *Tristan.* She just wanted to see Tristan. Here, there, Australia—she didn't care where. 'When?'

'Tomorrow.'

Excitement or trepidation? Which did she feel more? 'I'll look up flights.'

'I will send a private jet,' he said, without hesitation.

Of course he would.

'And a limousine to pick you up from where you are in Dorset.'

'There's no need. I have a rental car… I can drive—'

'I will send the car.'

When she'd flown to England from Australia she'd had no intention of contacting Tristan. Certainly not of visiting Montovia. The meeting with her grandparents had changed everything.

It wasn't until after she had disconnected the phone that she realised she hadn't asked Tristan what was so important that he'd left all those messages.

The next day the limousine arrived exactly on time and took her to Bristol airport. She was whisked through security and then onto the tarmac.

It wasn't until she began to climb the steps to board the plane that she started to feel nervous. *What the heck was she doing here?*

She'd been determined to take charge of her own life after so many years of acquiescing to men, but then with one word from Tristan—actually, two words: *private* and *jet*—she'd rolled over and gone passive again.

Then he was there, and thoughts of anything else were crowded out of her mind.

Tristan.

He stood at the top of the steps, towering over her. Tall, broad-shouldered, wearing an immaculately tailored business suit in deepest charcoal with a narrow grey tie. His hair was cut much shorter—almost military in style. When she'd last seen him he hadn't shaved for two days and had been wearing blue jeans and a T-shirt. The time before that he'd been wearing nothing at all.

He looked the same, but not the same.

And it was the *not the same* that had her feet seemingly stuck to the steps and her mouth unable to form words of greeting.

He was every bit as handsome as she remembered. But this Tristan appeared older, more serious. A man of wealth and stratospheric status—greeting her on board a private jet that was to fly her to his castle. While she was still very much just Gemma from Sydney.

Gemma looked the same as Tristan had remembered—her hair copper bright, her heart-shaped face pretty, her lovely body discreetly shown off in deep pink trousers and a white jacket. As he watched her, he thought his heart would burst with an explosion of emotion.

He had never lost faith that he would see her again. That faith had paid off now, after all those dark hours between the moment he had said goodbye to her in Sydney and this moment, when he would say hello to her again. Hours during which he had honoured her request not to contact her. Hours when he had worked with all the driven frenzy of the Montovian fisherman searching for his water nymph to find a way they could be together.

But Gemma stood frozen, as though she were uncertain whether to step up or back down. There wasn't a dimple in sight.

Was it fear of flying? Or fear of *him*?

He hadn't said he'd be on the jet to meet her—he'd had to reschedule two meetings with his father and the inner circle of court advisers to make the flight. He hadn't wanted to make a promise he might not have been able to keep. Perhaps she was too shocked at his presence to speak.

He cursed under his breath. Why hadn't he thought to radio through to the chauffeur?

Because he'd been too damn excited at the thought of seeing her so soon to follow through on detail.

Now he wanted to bound down those steps, sweep her into his arms and carry her on board. The dazed look in her cinnamon-coloured eyes made him decide to be more circumspect. What had he expected? That she would fall back into his arms when, for all she knew, the situation hadn't changed between them and he still could not offer her anything more than a tryst?

Tristan urged himself to be patient. He took a step down to her, his arms outstretched in welcome. 'Gemma. I can't believe you're in Europe.'

For a long moment she looked up at him, searching his face. He smiled, unable to hide his joy and relief at seeing her again.

At last her lovely mouth tilted upwards and those longed-for dimples flirted once more in her cheeks. Finally she closed the remaining steps between them.

'Tristan. I can't believe it's you. I… I thought I would never see you again. Your smile…it's still the same.'

That puzzled him. Of course his smile was still the same. Probably a lot warmer and wider than any smile on his face since he'd last seen her. But all he could think about was Gemma. Back in his arms where she belonged.

He held her close for a long moment measured by the beating of her heart against him. He breathed in her essence, her scent heart-rendingly familiar.

Gratitude that everything had worked out surged through him. He didn't know how she had come to be just an hour's flight away from him, but he didn't question it. The need to kiss her was too strong—questions and answers could come later.

He dipped his head to claim her mouth. She kissed him back, at first uncertainly and then with enthusiasm.

'Tristan…' she murmured in that throaty, familiar way.

At last. Now everything was going to be as he wanted it.

CHAPTER FOURTEEN

GEMMA HAD ONLY ever seen the inside of a private jet in movies. Was this a taste of the luxury in which Tristan lived? If so, she guessed it was her first look at his life in Montovia. The armchair-like reclining seats, the sofas, the bathrooms… All slick and sleek, in leather, crystal and finest wool upholstery. The royal Montovian coat of arms—an eagle holding a sword in its beak—was embroidered on the fabrics and etched into crystal glasses. No wonder Tristan had not been overly impressed with the *Argus*—it must have seemed everyday to him.

Once they were in the air the attendant, in a uniform that also bore the royal coat of arms, served a light lunch, but Gemma was too tightly wound to eat. Tristan didn't eat much either. She wanted to tell him her news but didn't know how to introduce the topic. They sat in adjoining seats—close, but not intimate. She wasn't yet ready for intimate.

She was grateful when he asked outright. 'So, tell me about your meeting with your new grandparents.'

'They're not new—I mean they've been there all the time, but they didn't know I existed, of course.'

'They honestly had never checked up on your mother over the years?'

The words spilled out of her. 'Their shock at meeting me

appeared genuine. The dimples did it, I think; my grandmother has them too. Eliza had joked that the Cliffords would probably want a DNA test, but they scarcely looked at my birth certificate. They loved their son very much. I think they see me as some kind of unexpected gift. And I… Well, I like them a lot.'

'It must have been exciting for you to finally find out about your father,' he said. 'Did it fill a gap for you?'

'A gap I didn't really know was there,' she said. 'You know I had only ever seen one photo of my father? The Cliffordses' house is full of them. He was very handsome. Apparently, he was somewhat of an endearing bad boy, who dropped out of Oxford and was living as a ski bum when he met my mother. His parents were hoping he'd get it out of his system and come back to the fold, but then he…he died. The revelation that he was married came as a huge shock to them.'

'What about the way they treated your mother?'

'I'm not making any excuses for them. I still think it was despicable. But apparently there's some serious money in the family, and there had been gold-diggers after him before. I told them my mother had no idea about any of that. She was clueless about English class distinctions.'

'For your sake, I am glad it's worked out for you…'

Gemma could sense the unspoken question at the end of his sentence. 'But you want to know why I decided to share my adventure with you.'

'Yes,' he said. 'I know you turned on the smartphone I left you because you decided to get in touch with me. I can only suppose it was because of your meeting with your new family.'

'You're right. But before I tell you I want to ask you something.' She felt her cheeks flush warm. 'It's your birthday in two weeks' time. I… I saw in a magazine that you have a big party planned. Are you…are you engaged to be married? To the girl your parents chose for you? Or anyone else?'

'No,' he said, without hesitation.

She could not help her audible sigh of relief.

Tristan met her gaze. 'What about you? Is there another man in your life?'

'There has been no one since…since you.'

'Good,' he said fiercely, his relief also apparent.

Seeing Tristan again told her why she had felt no interest in dating other men. Their attraction was as strong, as compelling, as overwhelming as it had ever been.

'Before I tell you what happened at my grandparents' house, let me say I come to you with no expectations,' she said. 'I realise when it comes down to it we…well, we've only known each other a week, but—'

Tristan made a sound of impatience that definitely involved Montovian cursing. 'A *week*? I feel I have known you a lifetime, Gemma. I know all I need to know about you.'

He planted a swift kiss on her mouth—enough to thrill her and leave her wanting more. She would have liked to turn to him, pull his head back to hers—but not before she'd had her say.

'You might want to know this, as well,' she said. 'You're speaking to a person who is, in the words of her newly discovered grandmother, "very well bred".'

Tristan frowned. 'I'm not sure what you mean.'

It had taken her a while to get her head around what she'd learned. Now she felt confident of reciting the story, but still her words came out in a rush. As if she still didn't quite believe it.

'It seems that on my grandmother's side I am eighth cousin to Prince William, the Duke of Cambridge, through a common distant ancestor, King George II, and also connected by blood to the Danish royal family. One of the connections was "on the wrong side of the blanket", but apparently that doesn't matter as far as genealogy is concerned.'

'But…but this is astonishing.'

She couldn't blame Tristan for his shocked expression; she was sure her grandparents had seen the same look on her face.

'I thought so, too,' she said. 'In fact I couldn't believe it could possibly be true. But they showed me the family tree—to which I am now going to be added, on the short little branch that used to end with my father.'

Tristan shook his head in disbelief. 'After all I have done—'

'What do you mean? What have you done?'

'It is not important,' he said with a slight shake of his head. 'Not now.'

The way he'd said that had made it sound as though it *was* important. She would have to ask him about it at another time. Right now she was more concerned at the impact of her own news.

'I… I wanted to ask you if that connection is strong enough for… Well, strong enough to make things between us not so impossible as when I was just a commoner. Not that I'm not a commoner still, really. But as far as bloodlines are concerned—that's what my grandmother calls them—I… I have more of a pedigree than I could ever have imagined.'

He nodded thoughtfully. 'Forgive me, Gemma. This is a lot to take in.'

A chill ran up her spine. Was she too late? 'I'd hoped it might make a difference to…to us. That is if there *is* an "us".'

His dark brows rose, as if she had said something ridiculous. 'As far as I am concerned there was an "us" from the moment you tried to attack me with that wooden spoon.'

She smiled at the reminder. 'You are never, ever going to let me forget that, are you?'

'Not for the rest of our lives,' he said.

She could see it took an effort for him to keep his voice steady.

'Gemma, I've been utterly miserable without you.'

It was still there between them—she could see it in his eyes, hoped he saw it in hers. The attraction that was so much more than physical. If it no longer had to be denied because of the discovery of her heritage, where might it go from here?

Like champagne bubbles bubbling to the top of a glass, excitement fizzed through her.

'Me...me too. Though I've tried very hard to deny it. Kept congratulating myself on how well I'd got over you. I had no hope, you see. I didn't know—none of us did—that the requisite noble blood was flowing in my veins.'

'Stay with me in Montovia, Gemma. Be my guest of honour at the party. Let me woo you as a prince *can* woo the eighth cousin of a prince of this country.'

Again that word *surreal* flashed through her mind. Perhaps this was all meant to be. Maybe she and Tristan were part of some greater plan. Who knew? And Party Queens could manage without her. She hadn't taken a break since the business had started.

'Yes, Tristan,' she said. 'Show me Montovia. I couldn't think of anything better than spending the next few weeks with you.'

She hugged his intention to 'woo' her—what a delightfully old-fashioned word—to herself like something very precious. Then she wound her arms around his neck and kissed him.

By the time the jet started its descent into Montovia, and the private airfield that served the castle, she and Tristan were more than ready to go further than kisses. She felt they were right back where they'd left off in her grandmother's cottage. He might be a prince, but more than that he was the man she wanted—wanted more than ever.

And they had two weeks together.

She couldn't remember when she'd felt happier.

Gemma caught her breath in admiration as, on Tristan's command to the pilot, the jet swooped low over the town of old Montovia. In the soft light of late afternoon it looked almost too beautiful to be real.

The medieval castle, with its elaborate towers and turrets, clung to the side of a forest-covered mountain with the ancient town nestled below. The town itself was set on the shore of a lake that stretched as far as she could see, to end in the reflections of another snow-capped mountain range. A medieval cathedral dominated the town with its height and grandeur.

'You can see from here how strategically they built the castle, with the mountains behind, the lake in front, the steep winding road, the town walls,' said Tristan, from where he sat beside her. 'The mountains form a natural barricade and fortification—it would be an exceptional army that could scale them. Especially considering there's snow and ice on the passes most months of the year.'

He kept his hand on her shoulder as he showed her what to look for out of the window. Gemma loved the way he seemed to want to reassure himself she was there, with a touch, a quick kiss, a smile. It was like some kind of wonderful dream that she was here with him after those months of misery. And all because she'd followed up on her curiosity about her father.

'It's good to see you taking your turn as tour guide,' she said. 'There's so much I want to know.'

'Happy to oblige,' he said with his charming smile. 'I love Montovia, and I want you to love it, too.'

For just two weeks? She didn't dare let herself think there could be more…

She reached out to smooth his cowlick back into place—that unruly piece of hair that refused to stay put. It was a small imperfection. He was still beautiful in the way of a virile man.

That inner excitement continued to bubble. Not because of castles and lakes and mountains. But because of Tristan. *She loved him.* No longer did she need to deny it—to herself or anyone else. She loved him—and there was no longer any roadblock on a possible future together.

'The castle was originally a fortress, built in the eleventh century on the ruins of a Roman *castellum*,' he said. 'It was added to over the centuries to become what it is now. The south extension was built not as a fortress but to showcase the wealth and power of the royal family.'

Gemma laughed. 'You know, I didn't see all that strategy stuff at all. I only saw how beautiful the setting is, how picturesque the town, with those charming old houses built around the square. Even from here I can see all the flower boxes and hanging baskets. Do you realise how enchanting cobbled streets are to Australian eyes? And it looks like there's a market being held in the town square today.'

'The farmers from the surrounding cantons bring in their goods, and there's other household stuff for sale, too—wooden carvings, metalwork, pottery. We have a beautiful Christmas market in December.'

'I can't wait to see more of the countryside. And to walk around the town. Am I allowed to? Are you? What about your bodyguards?'

'We are as safe as we will ever be in our own town. We come and go freely. Here the royal family are loved, and strangers are rare except for tourists.'

'Do you mean strangers are not welcome?' A tiny pinprick was threatening to leak the happiness from her bubble.

'Are you asking will you be welcome?'

'I might be wondering about it,' she said, quaking a little. 'What will you tell your family about me?'

'They know all about the beautiful girl I met in Sydney. They know I flew to England to get her today. You will be their guest.'

That surprised her. Why would he have told anyone about his interlude with an unsuitable commoner? And wouldn't she be staying with *him*, not his family?

'Will I be seen as an interloper?'

'You are with me—that automatically makes you not a stranger.'

She noticed a new arrogance to Tristan. He was crown prince

of this country. Was he really still the Tristan she had fallen for in Sydney? Or someone else altogether?

'I'm glad to hear that,' she said. She paused. 'There's another thing. A girly thing. I'm worried about my clothes. When I left Sydney I didn't pack for a castle. I've only got two day dresses with me. And nothing in the slightest bit formal. I wasn't expecting to travel.' She looked down at what she was wearing. 'Already this white jacket is looking less than its best. What will your parents think of me?'

Being taken home to meet a boyfriend's parents was traumatic at best. When they were a king and queen, the expectation level went off the scale.

'You are beautiful, Gemma. My mother and father are looking forward to meeting you. They will not even notice your clothes. You look fine in what you are wearing.'

Hmm. *They lived in a castle.* She very much doubted casual clothes would be the order of the day. In Dorset she'd felt totally underdressed even in her newly found grandparents' elegant house. At least she'd managed to pop into Dorchester and buy a dress, simply cut in navy linen.

'I have so many questions. When will I meet your parents? Will…will we be allowed to stay together? Do I—?'

'First, you are invited to dinner tonight, to meet my parents and my sister. Second, you will stay in one of the castle's guest apartments.'

Again there was that imperious tone.

'By myself?'

Her alarm must have shown on her face.

'Don't worry, it is not far from mine.'

'Your apartment?'

'We each have our independent quarters. I am still in the apartment I was given when I turned eighteen. The crown prince's much grander apartment will be mine when its refurbishment is complete. I wanted my new home to be completely different. I could not live there with sad memories of when the rooms were Carl's.'

'Of course…' Her words trailed away.

She shouldn't be surprised that she and Tristan wouldn't be allowed to share a room. Another pinprick pierced that lovely bubble. She hadn't anticipated being left on her own. And she very much feared she would be totally out of her depth.

CHAPTER FIFTEEN

TRISTAN WANTED TO have Gemma to himself for a little longer before he had to introduce her to his family. He also wanted to warn his parents and his sister not to say anything about the work he'd done on what he had privately termed 'Project Water Nymph' in the months since he'd been parted from Gemma.

He sensed in her a reticence he had not expected—he'd been surprised when she'd reminded him she'd only known him for a week. There was no such reticence on his part—he had no doubt that he wanted her in his life. But instinct now told him she might feel pressured if she knew of the efforts he'd gone to in order to instigate change.

Not that he regretted the time he'd spent on the project—it had all been to the good in more ways than one. But news of her noble connections had removed some of that pressure. So long as no one inadvertently said something to her. He wanted her to have more time here before he told her what he'd been doing while she'd been tracking down her English connections.

'Let me show you my favourite part of the castle before I take you to your rooms,' he said. 'It is very old and very simple—not like the rooms where we spend most of our time. I find it peaceful. It is where I go to think.'

'I'd love that,' she said, with what seemed like genuine interest.

'This part of the castle is open to the public in the summer, but not until next month,' he said. 'We will have it to ourselves today.'

He thought she would appreciate the most ancient part of the castle, and he was not disappointed. She exclaimed her amazement at all his favourite places as he led her along the external pathways and stone corridors that hugged the walls of the castle, high above the town.

'This is the remains of the most heavily barricaded fortress,' he explained. 'See the slits in the walls through which arrows were fired? Those arched lookouts came much later.'

Gemma leaned her elbows on the sill of the lookout. 'What a magnificent view across the lake to the mountains! It sounds clichéd, but everywhere I look in your country I see a postcard.'

With her hair burnished by the late-afternoon sun, and framed by the medieval arch, Gemma herself looked like a beautiful picture. To have her here in his home was something he'd thought he'd never see. He wanted to keep her here more than he'd ever wanted anything. This image of Gemma on her first day in Montovia would remain in his mind forever.

He slipped his arms around her from behind. She leaned back against his chest. For a long time they looked at the view in a companionable silence. He was the first to break it. 'To me this has the same kind of natural grandeur as the view from the deck of your grandmother's cottage,' he said.

'You're right,' she said. 'Very different, but awe-inspiring in the same way.'

'I wish we could stay here much longer, but I need to take you to your rooms now so that you can have some time to freshen up before dinner.'

And so that he'd have time to prepare his family for his change in strategy.

* * *

If this was a guest apartment, Gemma could only imagine what the royal family's apartments were like. It comprised a suite of elegantly decorated rooms in what she thought was an antique French style. Andie would know exactly how to describe it.

Gemma swallowed hard against a sudden lump in her throat. Andie and Party Queens and Sydney and her everyday life seemed far, far away. She was here purely for Tristan. Without his reassuring presence she felt totally lost and more than a tad terrified. What if she made a fool of herself? It might reflect badly on Tristan, and she *so* didn't want to let him down. She might have been born with noble blood in her veins, but she had been raised as just an ordinary girl in the suburbs.

She remembered the times in Sydney when she had thought about Tristan being *other*. Here, in this grand castle, surrounded by all the trappings of his life, she might as well be on a different planet for all she related to it. Here, *she* was *other*.

A maid had been sent to help her unpack her one pitifully small suitcase. She started to speak to her in Montovian, but at Gemma's lack of response switched to English. The more Gemma heard Montovian spoken, the less comprehensible it seemed. How could she let herself daydream about a future with Tristan in a country where she couldn't even speak the language?

She stood awkwardly by while the maid shook out her hastily packed clothes and woefully minimal toiletries and packed them away in the armoire. Knowing how to deal with servants was totally outside of her experience.

The maid asked Gemma what she wanted to wear to dinner, and when Gemma pointed out the high-street navy dress, she took it away to steam the creases out. By the time Gemma had showered in the superb marble bathroom—thankfully full of luxurious bath products—her dress was back in the bedroom, looking 100 per cent better than it had.

Did you tip the maids? She would have to ask Tristan.

There was so much she needed to ask him, but she didn't want to appear so ignorant he might regret inviting her here.

Her antennae gave a feeble wave, to remind her that Tristan had fallen for her the way she was. He wouldn't expect her to be any different. She would suppress her tremors of terror, watch and learn and ask questions when necessary.

She dressed in the navy sheath dress and the one pair of high-heeled shoes she'd brought with her, a neutral bronze. The outfit had looked fine in an English village, but here it looked drab—the bed was better dressed than she was, with its elegant quilted toile bedcover.

Then she remembered the exquisite pearl necklace her new grandmother had insisted on giving her from her personal jewellery collection. The strand was long, the pearls large and lustrous. It lifted the dress 100 per cent.

As she applied more make-up than she usually would Gemma felt her spirits rise. Darn it, she had royal blood of her own—even if much diluted. She would *not* let herself be intimidated. Despite their own personal problems, the king and queen had raised a wonderful person like Tristan. How could they *not* be nice people?

When Tristan, dressed in a different immaculate dark business suit, came to escort her to dinner, he told her she looked perfect and she more than half believed him.

Feeling more secure with Tristan by her side, Gemma tried not to gawk at the splendour of the family's dining room, with its ornate ceilings and gold trimmings, its finely veined white marble and the crystal chandeliers that hung over the endless dining table. Or at the antique silk-upholstered furniture and priceless china and silver. And these were the private rooms—not the staterooms.

Tristan had grown up with all this as his birthright.

How would she ever fit in? Even though he hadn't actually come out and said it, she knew she was on trial here. Now there was no legal impediment to them having a future together, it was up to her to prove she *could* fit in.

Tristan's parents were seated in an adjoining sitting room in large upholstered chairs—not thrones, thank heaven. His blonde mother, the queen, was attractive and ageless—Gemma suspected some expert work on her face—and was exquisitely groomed. She wore a couture dress and jacket, and outsize diamonds flashed at her ears, throat and wrists. His father had dark greying hair and a moustache, a severe face and was wearing an immaculately tailored dark suit.

Tristan had said they dressed informally for dinner.

Thank heaven she'd changed out of the cotton trousers and the jacket grubby at the cuffs.

Ordinary parents would have risen to greet them. Royal parents obviously did not. Why hadn't Tristan briefed her on what was expected of her? What might be second nature to him was frighteningly alien to her.

Prompted perhaps by some collective memory shared with her noble ancestors, Gemma swept into a deep curtsy and murmured, 'Your Majesties.'

It was the curtsy with which she'd started and ended every ballet class for years when she'd been a kid. She didn't know if it was a suitable curtsy for royalty, but it seemed to do the trick. Tristan beamed, and his mother and father smiled. Gemma almost toppled over in her relief.

'Thank you, my dear,' said his mother as she rose from her chair. 'Welcome.' She had Tristan's blue eyes, faded to a less vivid shade.

The father seemed much less forbidding when he smiled. 'You've come a long way to reach us. Montovia makes you welcome.'

Tristan took her hand in a subtle declaration that they were a couple, but Gemma doubted his parents needed it. She suspected his mother's shrewd gaze missed nothing.

When Tristan's sister joined them—petite, dark-haired Natalia—Gemma sensed she might have a potential friend at the castle.

'Tristan mentioned you might need to buy some new clothes?' Natalia said. 'I'd love to take you shopping. And of course you'll need something formal for Tristan's party next week.'

Royals no doubt needed to excel at small talk, and any awkwardness was soon dispelled as they sat down at the table. If she hadn't already been in love with Tristan, Gemma would have fallen in love with him all over again as he effortlessly included her in every conversation.

He seemed pleased when she managed a coherent exchange in French with his mother and another in German with his father.

'I needed to fill all my spare time after you left Sydney so I wouldn't mope,' she whispered to him. 'I found some intensive language classes.'

'What do you think about learning Montovian?' he asked.

'I shall have to, won't I?' she said. 'But who will teach me?'

There was a delicious undercurrent running between her and Tristan. She knew why she was here in his country—to see if she would like living in Montovia. But it was a formality, really. If she wanted to be with him, here she would have to stay. Nothing had been declared between them, so there was still that thrilling element of anticipation—that the best was yet to come.

'*I* will teach you, of course,' he said, bringing his head very close to hers so their conversation remained private.

'It seems like a very difficult language. I might need a lot of attention.'

'If attention is what you need, attention is what you shall get,' he said in an undertone. 'Just let me know where I need to focus.'

'I think you might already know where I need attention,' she said.

'Lessons should start tonight, then,' he said, and his eyes narrowed in the way she found incredibly sensuous.

'I *do* like lessons from you,' she murmured. 'All sorts of lessons.'

'I shall come to your room tonight, so we can start straight away,' he said.

She sat up straighter in her antique brocade dining chair. 'Really?'

'You didn't think I was going to let you stay all by yourself in this great rattling castle?'

'I did wonder,' she said.

'I have yearned to be alone with you for close on three months. Protocol might put us in different rooms. That doesn't mean we have to stay there.'

The soup course was served. But Gemma felt so taut with anticipation at the thought of being alone—completely alone—with Tristan she lost her appetite and just pushed the soup around in her bowl.

It was the first of four courses; each course was delicious, if a tad uninspired and on the stodgy side. Gemma wondered who directed the cook, and wondered, if she were to end up staying in Montovia, if she might be able to improve the standard of the menus without treading on any toes.

The thought took her to a sudden realisation—one she had not had time to consider. She knew the only way she would be staying in Montovia was if she and Tristan committed to something permanent.

Finding out the truth about her father's family had precipitated their reunion with such breakneck speed, putting their relationship on a different footing, that she hadn't had time to think about the implications.

If she and Tristan… If she stayed in Montovia she would have to give up Party Queens. In fact she supposed she would have to give up any concept of having her own life. Though there was actually no reason why she couldn't be involved with the business remotely.

She had spent much of the last year working to be herself—not the version of herself that others expected her to be. Without her work, without her friends, without identification with her own nationality, would she be able to cope?

Would being with Tristan be enough?

She needed to talk to Tristan about that.

CHAPTER SIXTEEN

BUT SHE DIDN'T actually have much time alone with Tristan. The next day his parents insisted on taking them to lunch at their mountain chalet, more than an hour and a half's drive away from the castle. The honour was so great there was no way she could suggest she would rather be alone with Tristan.

The chalet was comparatively humble. More like a very large, rustic farmhouse, with gingerbread wood carving and window boxes planted with red geraniums. A hearty meal was served to them by staff dressed in traditional costume—full dirndl skirts for the women and leather shorts and embroidered braces for the men.

'Is this the real Montovia?' she asked Tristan. 'Because if it is, I find it delightful.'

'It is the traditional Montovia,' he said. 'The farmers here still bring their cattle up to these higher pastures in the summer. In winter it is snowed in. People still spend the entire winter in the mountains. Of course, this is a skiing area, and the roads are cleared.'

Would she spend a winter skiing here? Perhaps all her winters?

That evening was taken up with his cousin and his girlfriend joining them for the family dinner. They were very pleasant, but Gemma was surprised at how stilted they were with her. At one point the girlfriend—a doctor about her own age—started to say how grateful she was to Gemma, but her boyfriend cut her off before she could finish the sentence.

Natalia, too, talked about her brother's hard work in changing some rule or another, before being silenced by a glare from Tristan.

And although they all spoke perfect English, in deference to her, there were occasional bursts of rapid Montovian that left Gemma with the distinct impression that she was being left out of something important. It wasn't a feeling she liked.

She tackled Tristan about it when he came to her room that night.

'Tristan, is there something going on I should know about?'

'What do you mean?' he said, but not before a flash of panic tightened his face.

'I mean, Mr Marco, you made a promise not to lie to me.'

'No one is lying. I mean… *I* am not lying.'

'"No one"?' She couldn't keep the hurt and betrayal from her voice.

'I promise you this is not bad, Gemma.'

'Better tell me, then,' she said, leading him over to the elegant chaise longue, all gilt-edged and spindly legged, but surprisingly comfortable.

Tristan sank down next to her. He should have known his family would let the secret slip. No way did he want Gemma to feel excluded—not when the project had been all about including her.

'Have I told you about the myth of the Montovian water nymph?' he asked.

'No, but it sounds intriguing.'

Tristan filled her in on the myth. He told her how he saw her as *his* sea nymph, with her pale limbs and floating hair enticing him in the water of Sydney Harbour.

'When I got back to Montovia, I was like the fisherman who

escaped his nymph's deadly embrace but went mad without her and spent his remaining years searching the lake for her.'

Gemma took his hand. 'I was flailing around by myself, too, equally as miserable.'

He dropped a kiss on her sweet mouth. 'This fisherman did not give up easily. I searched the castle archives through royal decrees and declarations to find the origin of the rule that kept us apart. Along the way I found my purpose.'

'I'm not sure what you mean.' she said.

'Remember, I've been rebelling against this rule since my Playboy Prince days? But I began to realise I'd gone about it the wrong way—perhaps a hangover from being the "spare". I'd been waiting for *someone else* to change the rules.'

He gave an unconsciously arrogant toss of his head.

'So I decided *I* was the crown prince. *I* was the lawyer. *I* was the person who was going to bring the royal family of Montovia kicking and screaming into the twenty-first century. All motivated by the fact I wanted the right to choose my own bride, no matter her status or birth.'

'So this was about *me*?'

'Yes. Other royal families allow marriage to commoners. Why not ours?'

'Be careful who you're calling a commoner,' she said. 'Now I know why I disliked the term so much. My noble blood was protesting.'

Tristan laughed. He loved her gift of lightening up a situation. It would stand her in good stead, living in a society like Montovia's.

'I practically lived in the archives—burrowing down through centuries of documents. My research eventually found that the rule could be changed by royal decree,' he said. 'In other words, it was in the power of the king—my father—to implement a change.'

'You must have been angry he hadn't already done so.'

'I was at first. Then I realised my father genuinely believed he was bound by law. Fact is, he has suffered from its restrictions more than anyone. He has loved his mistress since they were teenagers. She would have been his first choice of bride.'

Gemma slowly shook her head. 'That's so sad. Sad for your father, sad for his mistress and tragic for your mother.'

'It is all that. Until recently I hadn't realised my father's relationship with his mistress stretched back that far. They genuinely love each other. Which made me all the more determined to change the ruling—not just for my sake but for future generations of our family.'

'How did you go about it?'

'I recruited some allies. My sister Natalia who—at the age of twenty-six—has already refused offers of marriage from six eligible, castle-approved suitors.'

'"Suitors". That's such an old-fashioned word,' she mused.

'There is nothing modern about life in the royal castle of Montovia, I can assure you. But things are changing.'

'And you like being that agent of change?'

'I believe my brother would have preserved the old ways. I want to be a different kind of king for my country.'

'That's what you meant by finding your purpose.' She put her hand gently on his cheek, her eyes warm with approval. 'I'm proud of you.'

'Thank you,' he said. 'You met my next recruit tonight—my cousin, who is in love with that lovely doctor he met during their time in the military. Then my mother came on board. She suggested we recruit my father's mistress. It is too late for them, but they want to see change.'

'Your father must have felt outnumbered.'

'Eventually he agreed to give us a fair hearing. We presented a united front. Put forward a considered argument. And we won. The king agreed to issue a new decree.'

'And you did all that—'

'So I could be with my sea nymph.'

For a long, still moment he searched her face, delighted in her slow smile.

'A lesser man might have given up,' she said.

'A lesser man wouldn't have had you to win. If I hadn't met you and been shown a glimpse of what life could be like, I would have given in to what tradition demanded.'

'Instead you came to terms with the role you were forced to step up to, and now Montovia will get a better ruler when the time comes.'

'All that.'

'I wish I'd known what you were doing,' she said.

'To get our hopes up and for them to come to nothing would have been a form of torture. I called you as soon as I got the verdict from the king.'

She frowned. 'What about your arranged bride? Where did she fit into this?'

'I discovered she did not want our marriage any more than I did. She was being pressured by her ambitious father. He was given sufficient reparation that he will not cause trouble.'

'So why didn't you tell me all this when I told you about my grandparents?'

'I did not want you to feel pressured by what I had done. My feelings for you have been serious from the start. I realised you'd need time to get used to the idea.'

She reached up and put her hand on his face. 'Isn't it already serious between us?'

He took her hand and pressed a kiss into her palm. 'I mean committed. It would be a very different life for you in Montovia. You will have to be sure it is what you want.'

'Yes,' she said slowly.

Tristan felt like the fisherman with his net. He wanted to secure Gemma to live with him in his country. But he knew, like the water nymph, she had to make that decision to swim to shore by herself.

CHAPTER SEVENTEEN

ON FRIDAY MORNING Tristan's sister, Natalia, took Gemma shopping to St Pierre, the city that was the modern financial and administrative capital of Montovia.

Gemma would rather have gone with Tristan, but he had asked Natalia to take her, telling them to charge anything she wanted to the royal family's account. No matter the cost.

St Pierre was an intriguing mix of medieval and modern, but Gemma didn't get a chance to look around.

'You can see the city another time,' Natalia said. 'Montovians dress more formally than you're probably used to. The royal family even more so. You need a whole new wardrobe. Montovians expect a princess to look the part.'

'*You* certainly do,' said Gemma admiringly.

Natalia dressed superbly. Gemma hoped she would be able to help her choose what she needed to fit in and do the right thing by Tristan. She suspected the white jacket might never get an airing again.

Natalia looked at her a little oddly. 'I wasn't talking about me. I was talking about you, when you become crown princess.'

Gemma was too stunned to speak for a moment. 'Me? Crown princess?'

'When you and Tristan marry you will become crown princess. Hadn't you given that a thought?'

Natalia spoke as though it were a done deed that Gemma and Tristan would marry.

'It might sound incredibly stupid of me, but no.'

In the space of just a few days she'd been whisked away by private jet and landed in a life she'd never known existed outside the pages of glossy magazines. She hadn't thought any further than being with the man she loved.

Natalia continued. 'You will become Gemma, crown princess of Montovia—the second highest ranking woman in the land after the queen—and you will have all the privileges and obligations that come with that title.'

Gemma's mouth went suddenly dry and her heart started thudding out of control. How could she, a girl from suburban Sydney, become a princess? She found the thought terrifying.

'It's all happened so incredibly quickly,' she said to Natalia. 'All I've focused on is Tristan—him stepping up to the role of crown prince and making it his own. I… I never thought about what it meant for me.'

Panic seemed to grasp her stomach and squeeze it hard. She took some deep breaths to try and steady herself but felt the blood draining from her face.

Natalia had the same shrewd blue eyes as her mother, the queen. 'Come on, let's get you a coffee before we start shopping. But you need to talk about this to Tristan.'

'Yes…' Gemma said, still dazed by the thought. *They had not talked nearly enough.*

Natalie regarded her from the other side of the table in the cafe she had steered Gemma to. She pushed across a plate of knotted sugar cookies. 'Eat one of these.'

Gemma felt a little better after eating the cookie. It seemed it was a traditional Montovian treat. She must get the recipe…

'The most important thing we've got to get sorted is a show-stopping formal gown for next Saturday night,' said Natalie.

'Tristan's birthday is a real milestone for him. My brother has changed the way royal marriages have worked for centuries so you two can be together. All eyes will be on you. We've got to have you looking the part.'

Again, terror gripped Gemma. But Natalia put a comforting hand on her arm.

'There are many who are thankful to you for being a catalyst for change. Me included.'

'That's reassuring,' said Gemma. Although it wasn't. Not really. What about those who *didn't* welcome change—and blamed her for it?

'The more you look like a princess, the more you'll be treated like one,' said Natalia.

Natalia took her into the kind of boutiques where price tags didn't exist. The clothes she chose for Gemma—from big-name designers, formal, sophisticated—emphasised the impression that she was hurtling headfirst into a life she'd never anticipated and was totally unprepared for.

She had to talk to Tristan.

But by the time she got back to the castle, sat through another formal dinner with his family—this time feeling more confident, in a deceptively simple black lace dress and her pearls—she was utterly exhausted.

She tried to force her eyes to stay open and wait for Tristan, but she fell fast asleep in the vast antique-style bed before he arrived.

During the night she became aware of him sleeping beside her, with a possessive arm around her waist, but when she woke in the morning he was gone. And she felt groggy and disorientated from a horrible dream.

In it, she had been clad only in the gauzy French bra and panties Natalia had helped her buy. Faceless soldiers had been dragging her towards a huge, grotesquely carved throne while she shouted that she wasn't dressed yet.

CHAPTER EIGHTEEN

BEING CROWN PRINCE brought with it duties Tristan could not escape. He hated leaving Gemma alone for the morning, but the series of business meetings with his father and the Crown's most senior advisers could not be avoided.

Gemma had still been asleep when he'd left her room. He'd watched her as she'd slept, an arm flung over her head to where her bright hair spilled over the pillow. Her lovely mouth had twitched and her eyelids fluttered, and he'd smiled and wondered what she was dreaming about. He'd felt an overwhelming rush of wonder and gratitude that she was there with him.

Like that fisherman, desperately hunting for his water nymph, the dream of being reunited with Gemma was what had kept him going through those months in the gloomy castle archives. He saw the discovery of her noble blood as confirmation by the fates that making her his bride was meant to be.

He'd gently kissed her and reluctantly left the room.

All throughout the first meeting he'd worried about her being on her own but had felt happier after he'd been able to talk to her on the phone. She'd reassured him that she was dying to explore the old town and had asked him for directions to his childhood favourite chocolate shop and tea room. He'd arranged for his driver to take her down and back. They'd confirmed that she'd meet him back at the castle for lunch.

But now it was lunchtime, and she wasn't in the rose garden, where he'd arranged to meet her. She wasn't answering her phone. His driver confirmed that he had brought her back to the castle. Had she gone back to her room for a nap?

He knocked on the door to her guest apartment. No answer. He pushed it open, fully expecting to find her stretched out on the bed. If so, he would revise his plans so that he could join her on the bed and *then* go out to lunch.

But the bed was empty, the apartment still and quiet. There was a lingering trace of her perfume, but no Gemma. *Where was she?*

A wave of guilt washed over him because he didn't know. He shouldn't have left her on her own. He'd grown up in the labyrinth of the castle. But Gemma was totally unfamiliar with it. She might actually have got lost. Be wandering somewhere, terrified. He regretted now that he'd teased her, telling her that some of the rooms were reputed to be haunted.

As he was planning where to start looking for her, a maid came into the room with a pile of fresh towels in her arms. She dipped a curtsy. Asked if he was looking for his Australian guest. She had just seen Miss Harper in the kitchen garden…

Tristan found Gemma standing facing the view of the lake, the well-tended gardens that supplied fruit and vegetables for the castle behind her. Her shoulders were bowed and she presented a picture of defeat and misery.

What the heck was wrong?

'Gemma?' he called. 'Are you okay?'

As he reached her she turned to face him. He gasped. All colour had drained from her face, so that her freckles stood out in stark contrast, her eyes were red rimmed and even her hair seemed to have lost its sheen. She was dressed elegantly, in linen trousers and a silk top, but somehow the look was dishevelled.

He reached out to her but she stepped back and he let his arms fall by his sides. 'What's happened?'

'I… I can't do this, Tristan.' Her voice was thick and broken.

'Can't do what? I don't know what you mean.'

She waved to encompass the castle and its extensive grounds. 'This. The castle. The life. It's so different. It's so *other*.' She paused. 'That's why I came here.' She indicated the vegetable garden, with its orderly plantings. 'Here it is familiar; here I feel at home. I… I pulled a few weeds from those carrots. I hope you don't mind?'

He wasn't exactly sure what she meant by 'other', but her misery at feeling as if she didn't fit in emanated from her, loud and clear.

'I'm sorry, Gemma. I didn't know you were feeling like this. I shouldn't have left you on your own.'

Her chin tilted upwards. 'I don't need a nursemaid, Tristan. I can look after myself.'

'You're in a foreign country, and you need a guide. Like you were *my* guide when I was in your home country.'

She took a deep, shuddering breath. 'I need so much more than a guide to be able to fit in here,' she said. 'I… I was so glad to be here with you—so excited that we could be together when we thought we never could.'

Was so glad?

'Me, too. Nothing has made me happier,' he said.

'But I didn't think about what it would mean to be a *princess*. A princess worthy of you. I'm a Party Queen—not a real queen in waiting. You need more than…than me…for Montovia.'

'Let me be the judge of that,' he said. 'What's brought this on, Gemma? Has someone scared you?'

Who could feel so threatened by the change of order they might have tried to drive her away? When he found who it was, heads would roll.

Gemma sniffed. 'It started with Natalia, she—'

His sister? He was surprised that she would cause trouble. 'I thought you liked her, that she was helping you?'

'I do. She was. But—'

He listened as she recounted what had happened the day before in St Pierre.

'I felt so…ignorant,' Gemma concluded. 'It hadn't even entered my head that I would be crown princess. And I have no idea of what might be expected of me.'

Mentally, Tristan slammed his hand against the side of his head. Why look for someone to blame when it was himself he should be blaming? He had not prepared her for what was ahead. Because she'd made such a good impression on his family, he had made assumptions he shouldn't have. Once she had swept into that magnificent curtsy, once he had seen the respect with which she interacted with his parents, he'd been guilty of assuming she would be okay.

His gut twisted painfully when he thought about how unhappy she was. And she hadn't felt able to talk to him. The man who loved her.

Tristan spoke through gritted teeth. 'My fault. I should have prepared you. Made it very clear to everyone that—'

'That I'm wearing my princess learner plates?' she said with another sniffle.

He was an intelligent, well-educated man who'd thought he knew this woman. Yet he'd had no idea of what she'd gone through since he'd dumped her into his world and expected her to be able to negotiate it without a map of any kind.

'What else?'

'The maid. I asked her to help me with a few phrases in Montovian, so I could surprise you. She told me her language was so difficult no outsider could ever learn to speak it. Then she rattled off a string of words that of course I didn't understand and had no chance of repeating. I felt… I felt helpless and inadequate. If I can't learn the language, how can I possibly be taken seriously?'

'She loses her job today,' he said, with all the autocracy a crown prince could muster.

Gemma shook her head. 'Don't do that. She was well-meaning. She was the wrong person to ask for help. I should have asked—'

'*Me*. Why didn't you?'

'I… I didn't want to bother you,' she whispered. 'You have so much on your plate with your new role. I… I'm used to being independent.' She looked down at her feet, in their smart new Italian walking shoes.

'I'm sorry, Gemma. I've let you down. I can't tell you how gutted I am that you are so unhappy.'

She looked up at him, but her eyes were guarded. 'I was okay until Natalia mentioned something this morning about when I become queen. She was only talking about the kind of jewellery I'd need, but I freaked. Becoming crown princess is scary enough. But *queen*!'

Now Tristan gritted his teeth. He'd let duty rule him again—to his own personal cost. Those meetings this morning should have been postponed. He might have lost Gemma. Might still lose her if he didn't look after her better. And that would be unendurable.

'Anything else to tell me?'

She twisted the edge of her top between her fingers. 'The old man in the chocolate shop. He—'

'He said something inappropriate?' He found it hard to reconcile that with his memories of the kindly man.

'On the contrary. He told me what a dear little boy you were, and how he was looking forward to treating *our* children when we brought them in for chocolate.'

'And that was a problem?' Tristan was puzzled at the way Gemma had taken offence at those genial words.

'Don't you see? *Children*. We've never talked about children. We haven't talked about our future at all. I feel totally unprepared for all this. All I know is that we want to be together. But is it enough?'

He did not hesitate. 'Yes. I have no doubt of that.'

She paused for so long dread crept its way into his heart.

'I… I'm not sure it is. You can do better than me. And I fear that if I try to be someone I'm not—like I spent so much of my life doing—I will lose myself and no longer be the person you fell in love with. You've grown up in this royal life. It's all so shockingly different for me—and more than a little scary. I don't want to make your life a misery because I'm unhappy. Do you understand that?'

'I will do anything in my power to make you happy.' His voice was gruff.

'I've been thinking maybe your ancestors had it right. When your new spouse comes from the same background and understands your way of life, surely that must be an advantage?'

'No,' he said stiffly. 'Any advantage is outweighed by the massive *dis*advantage of a lack of love in such a marriage.'

'I'm not so sure,' she said. 'Tristan, I need time to think this through.'

Tristan balled his hands into fists. He was not going to beg. She knew how he felt—how certain he had always been about her. But perhaps he had been wrong. After all the royal feathers he had ruffled, the conventions he had overturned, maybe Gemma did not have the strength and courage required to be his wife and a royal princess.

'Of course,' he said.

He bowed stiffly in her direction, turned on his heel and strode away from her.

Gemma watched Tristan walk away with that mix of military bearing and athletic grace she found so attractive. It struck her how resolute he looked, in the set of his shoulders, the strength of his stride.

He was walking out of her life.

Her hand went to her heart at the sudden shaft of pain.

What a massive mistake she had just made.

He must think she didn't care. And that couldn't be further from how she felt.

The truth hit her with a force that left her breathless. This wasn't about her not understanding the conventions of being a princess, being nervous of making the wrong kind of curtsy. It was about her fearing that she wasn't good enough for Tristan. Deep down, she was terrified he would discover her inadequacies and no longer want her. This was all about her being afraid of getting hurt. She had behaved like a spineless wimp. A spineless, *stupid* wimp.

Through all the time she'd shared with Tristan, fragmented as it had been, he had been unequivocal about what he felt for her. He had tricked her onto the *Argus* because he had been so taken with her. He had confessed to a *coup de foudre.* He had left her with his phone because he had wanted to stay in touch. *He had changed the law of his country so they could be together.*

It was *she* who had resisted him from the get go—she who had backed off. *She* who had insisted they break all contact. If he hadn't left those messages on the phone, would she have even found the courage to call him?

And now the man who was truly her once-in-a-lifetime love had left her. He was already out of sight.

She had to catch him—had to explain, had to beg for another chance. To prove to him she would be the best of all possible princesses for him.

But he was already gone.

She ran after him. Became hopelessly confused as she hit one dead end after the other. Clawed against a bolted gate in her frustration. Then she remembered the ancient walkway he had taken her to on that first afternoon. The place where he went to think.

She peered up at the battlement walls. Noted the slits through which his ancestors had shot their arrows. Noticed the steps that wound towards the walkway. And picked up her speed.

He was there. Standing in the same arched lookout where she'd stood, admiring that magnificent view of the lake. His hands were clasped behind his back, and he was very still.

It struck her how solitary he seemed in his dark business suit. How *lonely.* Tristan was considered one of the most eligible young men in the world. Handsome, charming, intelligent and kind. Yet all he wanted was her. And she had let him down.

She swore under her breath, realised she'd picked up a Montovian curse word. And that it hadn't been as quiet as she'd thought.

He whipped around. Unguarded, she saw despair on his face—and an anger he wasn't able to mask. Anger at *her.*

'Gemma. How did you find me here?'

What if he wouldn't forgive her?

'I followed my heart,' she said simply.

Without a word Tristan took the few steps to reach her and folded her in his arms. She burrowed against his chest and shuddered her deep, heartfelt relief. *This was where she belonged.*

Then she pulled back from his arms so she could look up into his face. 'Tristan, I'm so sorry. I panicked. Was afraid I'd let you down. I lost sight of what counts—us being together.'

'You can *learn* to be a princess. All the help you need is here. From me. From my sister…my mother. The people who only wish you happiness.'

'I can see that now. You stepped up to be crown prince. I can step up to be crown princess. *I can do it.* But, Tristan, I love you so much and—'

He put his hand over her mouth to silence her. 'Wait. Don't you remember when we were at your grandmother's cottage? You instructed me not to say the L word until I was able to propose.'

'I do remember.' Even then she'd been putting him off. She felt hot colour flush her cheeks. 'When it comes to proposing, is it within the Montovian royal code of conduct for the woman to do the asking?'

'There's nothing I know of that forbids it,' he said.

'Okay, then,' she said. 'I'll do it. Tristan, would you—?'

'Just because you *can* propose, it doesn't mean I want you to. This proposal is mine.'

'I'm willing to cede proposing rights to you,' she said. She spread out her hands in mock defeat.

He took them both in his, looked down into her face. Her heart turned over at the expression in the blue eyes that had so captivated her from the beginning.

'Gemma, I love you. I love you more than you can imagine. 'Will you be my wife, my princess, my queen? Will you marry me, Gemma?'

'Oh, yes, Tristan. *Yes* to wife. *Yes* to princess. *Yes* to queen. There is nothing I want more than to marry you and love you for the rest of my life.'

Tristan kissed her long and sweetly, and she clung to him. How could she ever have thought she could exist without him?

'There's one more thing,' he said.

He reached into his inner pocket and drew out a small velvet box.

She tilted her head to one side. 'I thought…'

'You thought what?'

'Natalia implied that part of the deal at the crown prince's birthday is that he publicly slips the ring on his betrothed's finger.'

'It has always been the custom. But I'm the Prince of Change, remember? I *had* intended to follow the traditional way. Now I realise that proposing to you in front of an audience of strangers would be too overwhelming for you—and too impersonal. This is a private moment—*our* moment.'

He opened the box and took out an enormous, multicarat cushion-cut diamond ring. She gasped at its splendour.

'I ordered the ring as soon as my father agreed to change the rule about royals marrying outside the nobility. I never gave up hope that you would wear it.'

He picked up her left hand. She noticed his hand was less than steady as he slid the ring onto her third finger.

'I love you, Gemma Harper—soon to be Gemma, crown princess of Montovia.'

'More importantly, soon to be your wife,' she said.

She held up her hand, twisting and turning it so they could admire how the diamond caught the light.

'It's magnificent, and I shall never take it off,' she said. She paused. 'Natalia said it was customary to propose with the prince's grandmother's ring?'

'That's been the custom, yes,' he said. 'But I wanted to start our own tradition, with a ring that has significance only to us. Your ring. Our life. Our way of ruling the country when the time comes.'

'Already I see how I can take my place by your side.'

'*Playboy Prince Meets His Match*?' he said, his voice husky with happiness.

'*Mystery Redhead Finds Her Once-in-a-Lifetime Love...*' she murmured as she lifted her face for his kiss.

CHAPTER NINETEEN

As Gemma swept into the castle ballroom on Tristan's arm, she remembered what Natalia had told her. 'The more you look like a princess, the more you'll be treated like one.'

She knew she looked her best. But was it *princess* best?

The exquisite ballgown in shades of palest pink hugged her shape in a tight bodice, then flared out into tiers of filmy skirts bound with pink silk ribbon. Tiny crystals sewn randomly onto the dress gleamed in the light of the magnificent chandeliers under which guests were assembled to celebrate the crown prince's thirtieth birthday.

The dress was the most beautiful she had ever imagined wearing. She loved the way it swished around her as she walked. Where in Sydney would she wear such a gown? Back home she might devise the *menu* for a grand party like this—she certainly wouldn't be the crown prince's guest of honour. What was that old upstairs/downstairs thing? Through her engagement to Tristan—still unofficial—she had been rapidly elevated to the very top stair.

The dress was modest, its bodice topped with sheer silk chiffon and sleeves. Natalia had advised her that a princess of Montovia was expected to dress stylishly yet modestly. She must never attract attention for the wrong reasons, be the focus of critical press or be seen to reflect badly on the throne.

So many rules to remember. Would she ever be able to relax again?

'You are the most beautiful woman in the room,' Tristan murmured in her ear. 'There will be much envy when I announce you as my chosen bride.'

'As long as I'm the most beautiful woman in your eyes,' she murmured back.

'You will always be that,' he said.

The thing was, she believed him. She felt beautiful when she was with him—whether she was wearing a ballgown or an apron.

Yet even knowing she looked like a princess in the glorious gown, with her hair upswept and diamonds borrowed from the queen—*she had borrowed jewellery from a queen!*—she still felt her stomach fall to somewhere near the level of her silver stilettoes when she looked into the room. So many people, so many strange faces, so much priceless jewellery.

So many critical eyes on her.

Would they see her as an interloper?

Immediately Tristan stepped closer. 'You're feeling intimidated, aren't you?'

She swallowed hard against a suddenly dry throat. 'Maybe,' she admitted.

In this glittering room, full of glittering people, she didn't know a soul except for Tristan and his family. And she was hardly on a first-name basis with the king and queen.

'Soon these faces will become familiar,' Tristan said. 'Yes, there are courtiers and officials and friends of my parents. But many of these guests are my personal friends—from school, the military, from university. They are so looking forward to meeting you.'

'That's good to hear,' she said, grateful for his consideration. Still, it was unnerving.

Thank heaven she hadn't been subjected to a formal receiving line. That would come at their formal engagement party, when she'd have the right to stand by Tristan's side as his fiancée. This was supposedly a more informal affair. With everyone wearing ballgowns and diamonds. Did Montovians actually *ever* do informal?

'Let me introduce you to someone I think you will like very much,' Tristan said.

He led her to a tall, thin, grey-haired man and his plump, cheery-faced wife. He introduced the couple as Henry and Anneke Blair.

'Henry was my English tutor,' Tristan said.

'And it was a privilege to teach you, Your Highness,' Henry said.

'Your English is perfect,' said Gemma.

'I was born and bred in Surrey, in the UK,' said Henry, with a smile that did not mock her mistake.

'Until he came to Montovia to climb mountains and fell in love with a local girl,' said his wife. 'Now he speaks perfect Montovian, too.'

Henry beamed down affectionately at his wife. So an outsider *could* fit in.

'Gemma is keen to learn Montovian,' said Tristan. 'We were hoping—'

'That I could tutor your lovely fiancée?' said Henry. He smiled at Gemma—a kind, understanding smile. 'It would be my pleasure.'

'And I would like very much to share with you the customs and history of the Montovian people,' said Anneke. 'Sometimes a woman's point of view is required.'

Gemma felt an immense sense of relief. She couldn't hope to fit in here, to gain the people's respect, if she couldn't speak the language and understand their customs. 'I would like lessons every day, please,' she said. 'I want to be fluent as soon as possible. And to understand the way Montovian society works.'

Tristan's smile told her she had said exactly the right thing.

Tristan had been right, Gemma thought an hour later. Already some of the faces in the crowd of birthday celebration guests were familiar. More importantly, she sensed a swell of goodwill towards her. Even among the older guests—whom she might have expected would want to adhere to the old ways—there was a sense that they cared for Tristan and wanted him to be happy. After so much tragedy in the royal family, it seemed the Montovians were hungry for a story with a happy ending and an excuse for gaiety and celebration.

She stood beside Tristan on a podium as he delivered a charming and witty speech about how he had fallen so hard for an Australian girl, he had worked to have the law changed so they could be together, only to find that she was of noble birth after all.

The audience obviously understood his reference to water nymphs better than she did, judging by the laughter. It was even more widespread when he repeated his speech in Montovian. She vowed that by the time his thirty-first birthday came around she would understand his language enough to participate.

She noticed the king had his head close to a tall, middle-aged woman, chatting to her with that air of familiarity only long-time couples had, and realised she must be his mistress. Elsewhere, the queen looked anxious in the company of a much younger dark-haired man. Even from where she stood, Gemma realised the man had a roving eye.

How many unhappy royal marriages had resulted from the old rules?

Then Tristan angled his body towards her as he spoke. 'It is the custom that if a crown prince of Montovia has not married by the age of thirty he is obliged to announce his engagement on the night of his birthday celebration. In fact, as you know, he is supposed to propose to his future bride in front of his assembled guests. I have once again broken with tradition. To me, marriage is about more than tradition and alliances. It is about love and a shared life and bringing children up out of the spotlight. I felt my future wife deserved to hear me ask for her hand in marriage in private.'

In a daze, Gemma realised she was not the only person in the room to blink away tears. Only now did she realise the full depth of what Tristan had achieved in this conservative society in order to ensure they could spend their lives together.

He took her hand in his and turned them back so they both faced the guests. The chandeliers picked up the facets in her diamond ring so it glinted into tiny shards of rainbow.

'May I present to you, my family and friends, my chosen bride: Gemma Harper-Clifford—future crown princess of Montovia.'

There was wild applause from an audience she suspected were usually rather more staid.

Her fiancé murmured to her. 'And, more importantly, my wife and the companion of my heart.'

'*Crown Prince Makes Future Bride Shed Tears of Joy…*' she whispered back, holding tightly to his hand, wanting never to let it go.

EPILOGUE

Three months later

IF TRISTAN HAD had his way, he would have married Gemma in the side chapel of the cathedral the day after he'd proposed to her.

However, his parents had invoked their roles as king and queen to insist that some traditions were sacrosanct and he would break them at his peril.

His mother had actually made mention of the medieval torture room in the dungeon—still intact and fully operational—should her son imagine he could elope or in any other way evade the grand wedding that was expected of him. And Tristan hadn't been 100 per cent certain she was joking.

A royal wedding on the scale that was planned for the joining in holy matrimony of Tristan, crown prince of Montovia, and Gemma Harper-Clifford, formerly of Sydney, Australia, would usually be expected to be a year in the planning.

Tristan had negotiated with all his diplomatic skills and open chequebook to bring down the planning time to three months.

But he had been so impatient with all the rigmarole required to get a wedding of this scale and calibre off the ground that Gemma had quietly taken it all away from him. She'd proceeded to organise the whole thing with remarkable efficiency and grace.

'I am a Party Queen, remember?' she'd said, flushed with a return of her old confidence. 'This is what I *do*. Only may I say it's a heck of a lot easier when the groom's family own both the cathedral where the service is to take place *and* the castle where the reception is to be held. Not to mention having a limitless budget.'

Now he stood at the high altar of the cathedral, dressed in the full ceremonial military uniform of his Montovian regiment, its deep blue tunic adorned with gold braid and fringed epaulettes. Across his chest he wore the gold-trimmed blue sash of the royal family and the heavy rows of medals and insignia of the crown prince.

Beside him stood his friend Jake Marlowe as his best man, two of his male cousins and an old school friend.

Tristan peered towards the entrance to the cathedral, impatient for a glimpse of his bride. She'd also invoked tradition and moved into his parents' apartment for the final three days before the day of their wedding. He had no idea what her dress—ordered on a trip to Paris she'd made with Natalia—would look like.

Seemed she'd also embraced the tradition of being ten minutes late for the ceremony…

Then he heard the joyous sound of ceremonial trumpets heralding the arrival of the bride, and his heart leapt. He was surprised it didn't set his medals jangling.

A tiny flower girl was the first to skip her way down the seemingly endless aisle, scattering white rose petals along the red carpet. Then Gemma's bridesmaids—his sister, Princess Natalia, Party Queens Andie and Eliza and Gemma's cousin Jane—each in gowns of a different pastel shade, glided down.

The trumpets sounded again, and the huge cathedral organ played the traditional wedding march. At last Gemma, flanked by her mother on one side and her Clifford grandfather on the other—both of whom were going to 'give her away'—started her slow, graceful glide down the aisle towards him.

Tristan didn't see the king and queen in the front pew, nor the hundreds of guests who packed the cathedral, even though the pews were filled with family, friends and invited dignitaries from around the world, right down to the castle servants in the back rows. And the breathtaking flower arrangements might not have existed as far as Tristan was concerned.

All he saw was Gemma.

Her face was covered by a soft, lace-edged veil that fell to her waist at the front and at the back to the floor, to join the elaborate train that stretched for metres behind her, which was attended by six little girls from the cathedral school. Her full-skirted, long-sleeved dress was both magnificent and modest, as was appropriate for a Montovian bride. She wore the diamond tiara worn by all royal brides, and looked every inch the crown princess.

As she got closer he could see her face through the haze of the veil, and he caught his breath at how beautiful she was. Diamonds flashed at her ears—the king and queen's gift to her. And on her wrist was his gift to her—a diamond-studded platinum bracelet, from which hung a tiny platinum version of the wooden spoon she had wielded at their first meeting.

His bride.

The bride he had chosen and changed centuries of tradition for so he could ensure she would become his wife.

Tristan. There he was, waiting for her at the high altar, with the archbishop and the two bishops who would perform the ceremony behind him. She thought her heart would stop when she saw how handsome he looked in his ceremonial uniform. And the love and happiness that made his blue eyes shine bright was for her and only her. It was a particular kind of joy to recognise it.

She had never felt more privileged. Not because she was

marrying into a royal family, but because she was joining her life with the man she loved. The *coup de foudre* of love at first sight for the mysterious Mr Marco had had undreamed-of repercussions.

She felt buoyed by goodwill and admiration for the way she was handling her new role in the royal family. And she was surrounded by all the people she loved and who loved her.

There was a gasp from the congregation when she made her vows in fluent Montovian. When Tristan slid the gold band onto her ring finger, and she and the man she adored were pronounced husband and wife, she thought her heart would burst from happiness.

After the service they walked down the aisle as a new royal couple to the joyful pealing of the cathedral bells. They came out onto the top of the steps of the cathedral to a volley of royal cannons being fired—which, Gemma could not help thinking, was something she had never encountered at a wedding before. And might not again until their own children got married.

Below them the town square was packed with thousands of well-wishers, who cheered and threw their hats in the air. *Their subjects.* It might take a while for an egalitarian girl from Australia to truly grasp the fact that she had *subjects*, but Tristan would help her with all the adjustments she would have to make in the years to come. With Tristan by her side, she could face anything.

Tension was building in the crowd below them and in the guests who had spilled out of the cathedral behind them. The first royal kiss of the newly wed prince and his princess was what they wanted.

She looked up at Tristan, saw his beloved face smiling down at her. They kissed.

The crowd erupted, and she was almost blinded by the lights from a multitude of camera flashes. They kissed again, to the almost hysterical delight of the crowd. A third kiss and she was almost deafened by the roar of approval.

Tristan had warned her that lip-readers would be planted in the audience, to see what they might say to each other in this moment. Why not write the headlines for them?

'*Prince Weds Party Planner*?' Tristan whispered.

'*And They Live Happily Ever After…*' she murmured as, together with her husband, she turned to wave to the crowd.

* * * * *

The Bridesmaid's Baby Bump

Dear Reader,

Have you ever had a lovely, smart, loyal friend who never seems to have a lot of luck with men? She's always the bridesmaid, never the bride—or if she was the bride it didn't end well. Your friend is so wonderful she deserves love and happiness and you just wish you could find Mr. Right for her.

Eliza Dunne is that girl—and the great thing about being an author is I was able to create for her the perfect man in gorgeous billionaire Jake Marlowe. But their happy-ever-after ending doesn't come easily in *The Bridesmaid's Baby Bump.* Both Eliza and Jake have secrets and hidden hurts that make it quite an up-and-down journey for each to realize the other is their once-in-a lifetime love. When they do, I think you'll be cheering for them both!

Eliza is one of three partners in a successful party-planning business, Party Queens. We've met her briefly in Andie's story, *Gift-Wrapped in Her Wedding Dress*, then Gemma's story, *Crown Prince's Chosen Bride*. As I wrote those books, I was getting to know Eliza and looking forward to writing her story.

Eliza was bridesmaid and Jake best man at two weddings and I wanted the next wedding to be theirs. I so hope you enjoy meeting Eliza and Jake as they head toward their own trip down the aisle!

Warm regards,

Kandy

To my wonderful editor, Laura McCallen, whose insight and encouragement help me make my books the best they can be. Thank you, Laura!

CHAPTER ONE

ELIZA DUNNE FELT she had fallen into a fairytale as Jake Marlowe waltzed her around the vast, glittering ballroom of a medieval European castle. Hundreds of other guests whirled around them to the elegant strains of a chamber orchestra. The chatter rising and falling over the music was in a mix of languages from all around the world. Light from massive crystal chandeliers picked up the gleam of a king's ransom in jewellery and the sheen of silk in every colour of the rainbow.

Eliza didn't own any expensive jewellery. But she felt she held her own in a glamorous midnight-blue retro-style gown with a beaded bodice, nipped-in waist and full skirt, her dark hair twisted up with diamante combs, sparkling stilettos on her feet. Jake was in a tuxedo that spoke of the finest Italian tailoring.

The excitement that bubbled through her like the bubbles from expensive champagne was not from her fairytale surroundings but from her proximity to Jake. Tall, imposing, and even more handsome than the Prince whose wedding they had just witnessed, he was a man who had intrigued her from the moment she'd first met him.

Their dance was as intimate as a kiss. Eliza was intensely aware of where her body touched Jake's—his arm around her waist held her close, her hand rested on his broad shoulder, his cheek felt pleasantly rough against the smoothness of her own. She felt his warmth, breathed in his scent—spicy and fresh and utterly male—with her eyes closed, the better to savour the intoxicating effect it had on her senses. Other couples danced around them but she was scarcely aware of their presence—too lost in the rhythm of her private dance with him.

She'd first met Jake nearly two years ago, at the surprise wedding of her friend and business partner Andie Newman to *his* friend and business partner Dominic Hunt. They'd been best man and bridesmaid and had made an instant connection in an easy, friends of friends way.

She'd only seen him once since, at a business function, and they'd chatted for half the night. Eliza had relived every moment many times, unable to forget him. He'd been so unsettlingly *different*. Now they were once more best man and bridesmaid at the wedding of mutual friends.

Her other business partner, Gemma Harper, had just married Tristan, Crown Prince of Montovia. That afternoon she and Jake, as members of the bridal party, had walked slowly down the aisle of a centuries-old cathedral and watched their friends make their vows in a ceremony of almost unimaginable splendour. Now they were celebrating at a lavish reception.

She'd danced a duty dance with Tristan, then with Dominic. Jake had made his impatience obvious, then had immediately claimed her as his dance partner. The room was full of royalty and aristocrats, and Gemma had breathlessly informed her which of the men was single, but Eliza only wanted to dance with Jake. This was the first chance she'd had to spend any real time with the man who had made such a lasting impression on her.

She sighed a happy sigh, scarcely realising she'd done so.

Jake pulled away slightly and looked down at her. Her breath caught in her throat at the slow-to-ignite smile that lit his green eyes as he looked into hers. With his rumpled blond hair, strong jaw and marvellous white teeth he was as handsome as any actor or model—yet he seemed unaware of the scrutiny he got from every woman who danced by them.

'Having fun?' he asked.

Even his voice, deep and assured, sent shivers of awareness through her.

'I don't know that *fun* is quite the right word for something so spectacular. I want to rub my eyes to make sure I'm not dreaming.' She had to raise her voice over the music to be heard.

'It's extraordinary, isn't it? The over-the-top opulence of a royal wedding… It isn't something an everyday Australian guy usually gets to experience.'

Not quite an everyday guy. Eliza had to bite down on the words. At thirty-two, Jake headed his own technology solutions company and had become a billionaire while he was still in his twenties. He could probably fund an event like this with barely a blip in his bank balance. But on the two previous occasions when she'd met him, for all his wealth and brilliance and striking good looks, he had presented as notably unpretentious.

'I grew up on a sheep ranch, way out in the west of New South Wales,' she said. 'Weddings were more often than not celebrated with a barn dance. This is the stuff of fairytales for a country girl. I've only ever seen rooms like this in a museum.'

'You seem like a sophisticated city girl to me. Boss of the best party-planning business in Sydney.' Jake's green eyes narrowed as he searched her face. 'The loveliest of the Party Queens.' His voice deepened in tone.

'Thank you,' she said, preening a little at his praise, fighting a blush because he'd called her lovely. 'I'm not the boss, though. Andie, Gemma and I are equal partners in Party Queens.'

Eliza was Business Director, Andie looked after design and Gemma the food.

'The other two are savvy, but you're the business brains,' he said. 'There can be no doubt about that.'

'I guess I am,' she said.

She was not being boastful in believing that the success of Party Queens owed a lot to her sound financial management. The business was everything to her and she'd given her life to it since it had launched three years ago.

'Tristan told me Gemma organised the wedding herself,' Jake said. 'With some long-distance help from you and Andie.'

'True,' said Eliza.

Jake—the 'everyday Aussie guy'—was good friends with the Prince. They'd met, he'd told her, on the Montovian ski-fields years ago.

'Apparently the courtiers were aghast at her audacity in breaking with tradition.'

'Yet look how brilliantly it turned out—another success for Party Queens. My friend the Crown Princess.' Eliza shook her head in proud wonderment. 'One day she'll be a real queen. But for Gemma it isn't about the royal trappings, you know. It's all about being with Tristan—she's so happy, so in love.'

Eliza couldn't help the wistful note that crept into her voice. That kind of happiness wasn't for her. Of course she'd started out wanting the happy-ever-after love her friends had found. But it had proved elusive. So heartbreakingly elusive that, at twenty-nine, she had given up on hoping it would ever happen. She had a broken marriage behind her, and nothing but dating disasters since her divorce. No way would she get married again. She would not risk being trapped with a domineering male like her ex-husband, like her father. Being single was a state that suited her, even if she did get lonely sometimes.

'Tristan is happy too,' said Jake. 'He credits me for introducing him to his bride.'

Jake had recommended Party Queens to his friend the Crown Prince when Tristan had had to organise an official function in Sydney. Tristan had been incognito when Gemma had met him and they'd fallen in love. The resulting publicity had been off the charts for Party Queens, and Eliza would always be grateful to Jake for putting the job their way.

Jake looked down into her face. 'But you're worried about what Gemma's new status means for your business, aren't you?'

'How did you know that?' she asked, a frown pleating her forehead.

'One business person gets to read the signs in another,' he said. 'It was the way you frowned when I mentioned Gemma's name.'

'I didn't think I was so transparent,' she said, and realised she'd frowned again. 'Yes, I admit I *am* concerned. Gemma wants to stay involved with the business, but I don't know how that can work with her fifteen thousand kilometres away from our headquarters.' She looked around her. 'She's moved into a different world and has a whole set of new royal duties to master.'

Eliza knew it would be up to her to solve the problem. Andie and Gemma were the creatives; she was the worrier, the plotter, the planner. The other two teased her that she was a control freak, let her know when she got too bossy, but the three Party Queens complemented each other perfectly.

Jake's arm tightened around her waist. 'Don't let your concern ruin the evening for you. I certainly don't want to let it ruin mine.'

His voice was deep and strong and sent a thrill of awareness coursing through her.

'You're right. I just want to enjoy every moment of this,' she said.

Every moment with him. She closed her eyes in bliss when he tightened his arms around her as they danced. He was the type of man she had never dreamed existed.

The Strauss waltz came to an end. 'More champagne?' Jake asked. 'We could drink it out on the terrace.'

'Excellent idea,' she said, her heart pounding a little harder at the prospect of being alone with him.

The enclosed terrace ran the length of the ballroom, with vast arched windows looking out on the view across the lit-up castle gardens to the lake, where a huge pale moon rode high in the sky. Beyond the lake were snow-capped mountains, only a ghostly hint of their peaks to be seen under the dim light from the moon.

There was a distinct October chill to the Montovian air. It seemed quite natural for Jake to put his arm around her as Eliza gazed out at the view. She welcomed his warmth, still hyper-aware of his touch as she leaned close to his hard strength. There must be a lot of honed muscle beneath that tuxedo.

'This place hardly seems real,' she said, keeping her voice low in a kind of reverence.

'Awesome in the true sense of the word,' he said.

Eliza sipped slowly from the flute of champagne. Wine was somewhat of a hobby for her, and she knew this particular vintage was the most expensive on the planet, its cost per bubble astronomical. She had consulted with Gemma on the wedding wine list. But she was too entranced with Jake to be really aware of what she was drinking. It might have been lemon soda for all the attention she paid it.

He took the glass from her hand and placed it on an antique table nearby. Then he slid her around so she faced him. He was tall—six foot four, she guessed—and she was glad she was wearing stratospheric heels. She didn't like to feel at a disadvantage with a man—even this man.

'I've waited all day for us to be alone,' he said.

'Me too,' she said, forcing the tremor out of her voice.

How alone? She had a luxurious guest apartment in the castle all to herself, where they could truly be by themselves. No doubt Jake had one the same.

He looked into her face for a long moment, so close she could feel his breath stir her hair. His eyes seemed to go a deeper shade of green. *He was going to kiss her.* She found her lips parting in anticipation of his touch as she swayed towards him. There was nothing she wanted more at this moment than to be kissed by Jake Marlowe.

Yet she hesitated. Whether she called it the elephant in the room, or the poisoned apple waiting to be offered as in the fairy-tale, there was something they had not talked about all day in the rare moments when they had been alone. Something that had to be said.

With a huge effort of will she stepped back, folded her arms in front of her chest, took a deep breath. 'Jake, has anything changed since we last spoke at Tristan's party in Sydney? Is your divorce through?'

He didn't immediately reply, and her heart sank to the level of her sparkling shoes. 'Yes, to your first question. Divorce proceedings are well under way. But to answer your second question: it's not final yet. I'm still waiting on the decree nisi, let alone the decree absolute.'

'Oh.' It was all she could manage as disappointment speared through her. 'I thought—'

'You thought I'd be free by now?' he said gruffly.

She chewed her lip and nodded. There was so much neither of them dared say. Undercurrents pulled them in the direction of possibilities best left unspoken. Such as what might happen between them if he wasn't still legally married…

It was his turn to frown. 'So did I. But it didn't work out like that. The legalities… The property settlements…'

'Of course,' she said.

So when will *you be free?* She swallowed the words before she could give impatient voice to them.

He set his jaw. 'I'm frustrated about it, but it's complex.'

Millions of dollars and a life together to be dismantled. Eliza knew all about the legal logistics of that, but on a much smaller scale. There were joint assets to be divided. Then there were emotions, all twisted and tangled throughout a marriage of any duration, that had to be untangled—and sometimes torn. Wounds. Scars. All intensely personal. She didn't feel she could ask him any more.

During their first meeting Jake had told her his wife of seven years wanted a divorce but he didn't. At their second meeting he'd said the divorce was underway. Eliza had sensed he was ambivalent about it, so had declined his suggestion that they keep in touch. Her attraction to him was too strong for her ever to pretend she could be 'just friends' with him. She'd want every chance to act on that attraction.

But she would not date a married man. She wouldn't kiss a married man. Even when he was nearly divorced. Even when he was Jake Marlowe. No way did she want to be caught up in any media speculation about being 'the other woman' in his divorce. And then there was the fact that her ex had cheated on her towards the end of their marriage. She didn't know Jake's wife. But she wouldn't want to cause her the same kind of pain.

Suffocating with disappointment, Eliza stepped back from him. She didn't have expectations of any kind of relationship with him—just wanted a chance to explore the surprising connection between them. Starting with a kiss. Then…? Who knew?

She cleared her throat. 'I wish—' she started to say.

But then an alarm started beeping, shrill and intrusive. Startled, she jumped.

Jake glanced down at his watch, swore under his breath. 'Midnight,' he said. 'I usually call Australia now, for a business catch-up.' He switched off the alarm. 'But not tonight.'

It seemed suddenly very quiet on the terrace, with only faint strains of music coming from the ballroom, distant laughter from a couple at the other end of the terrace. Eliza was aware of her own breathing and the frantic pounding of her heart.

'No. Make your call. It's late. I have to go.'

She doubted he'd guessed the intensity of her disappointment, how much she'd had pinned on this meeting—and she didn't want him to see it on her face. She turned, picked up her long, full skirts and prepared to run.

Then Jake took hold of her arm and pulled her back to face him. 'Don't go, Eliza. Please.'

* * *

Jake watched as Eliza struggled to contain her disappointment. She seemed to pride herself on having a poker face. But her feelings were only too apparent to him. And her disappointment had nothing on his.

'But I have to go,' she said as she tried to pull away from him. 'You're still married. We can't—'

'Act on the attraction that's been there since the get go?'

Mutely, she nodded.

Their first meeting had been electric—an instant *something* between them. For him it had been a revelation. A possibility of something new and exciting beyond the dead marriage he had been struggling to revive. Eliza had been so beautiful, so smart, so interesting—yet so unattainable. The second time they'd met he'd realised the attraction was mutual. And tonight he'd sensed in her the same longing for more that he felt.

But it was still not their time to explore it. She'd made it very clear the last time they'd met that she could not be friends with a married man—and certainly not more than friends. He'd respected her stance. As a wealthy man he'd met more than a few women with dollar signs flashing in their eyes who had held no regard for a man's wedding vows—or indeed their own.

When Tristan had asked him to be best man at his wedding he'd said yes straight away. The bonus had been a chance to see Eliza again. In her modest lavender dress she'd been the loveliest of the bridesmaids, eclipsing—at least in his admittedly biased eyes—even the bride. Tonight, in a formal gown that showed off her tiny waist and feminine curves, she rivalled any of the royalty in the ballroom.

'This is not what I'd hoped for this evening,' he said.

'Me neither.' Her voice was barely louder than a whisper as she looked up to him.

He caught his breath at how beautiful she was. Her eyes were a brilliant blue that had him struggling to describe them—like sapphires was the closest he could come. They were framed by brows and lashes as black as her hair, in striking contrast to her creamy skin. Irish colouring, he suspected. He knew nothing about her heritage, very little about her.

Jake thirsted to know more.

He—a man who had thought he could never be interested in another woman. Who had truly thought he had married for life. He'd been so set on hanging on to his marriage to a woman who didn't want to be married any more—who had long outgrown him and he her—that he hadn't let himself think of any other. Until he'd met Eliza. And seen hope for the future.

He cursed the fact that the divorce process was taking so long. At first he'd delayed it because he'd hoped he could work things out with his soon-to-be ex-wife. Even though she'd had become virtually a stranger to him. Then he'd discovered how she'd betrayed him. Now he was impatient to have it settled, all ties severed.

'A few months and I'll be free. It's so close, Eliza. In fact it's debatable that I'm not single again already. It's just a matter of a document. Couldn't we—?'

He could see her internal debate, the emotions flitting across her face. Was pleased to see that anticipation was one of them. But he was not surprised when she shook her head.

'No,' she said, in a voice that wasn't quite steady. 'Not until you're legally free. Not until we can see each other with total honesty.'

How could he fault her argument? He admired her integrity. Although he groaned his frustration. Not with her, but with the situation.

He pulled her close in a hug. It was difficult not to turn it into something more, not to tilt her face up to his and kiss her. A campaign of sensual kisses and subtle caresses might change her mind—he suspected she wanted him as much as he wanted her. But she was right. He wasn't ready—in more ways than one.

'As soon as the divorce is through I'll get in touch, come

see you in Sydney.' He lived in Brisbane, the capital city of Queensland, about an hour's flight north.

Scarcely realising he was doing so, he stroked the smooth skin of her bare shoulders, her exposed back. It was a gesture more of reassurance than anything overtly sexual. He couldn't let himself think about Eliza and sex. Not now. Not yet. Or he'd go crazy.

Her head was nestled against his shoulder and he felt her nod. 'I'd like that,' she said, her voice muffled.

He held her close for a long, silent moment. Filled his senses with her sweet floral scent, her warmth. Wished he didn't have to let her go. Then she pulled away. Looked up at him. Her cheeks were flushed pink, which intensified the blue of her eyes.

'I've been in Montovia for a week. I fly out to Sydney tomorrow morning. I won't see you again,' she said.

'I have meetings in Zurich,' he said. 'I'll be gone very early.'

'So…so this is goodbye,' she said.

He put his fingers to the soft lushness of her mouth. 'Until next time,' he said.

For a long moment she looked up at him, searching his face with those remarkable eyes. Then she nodded. 'Until next time.'

Without another word Eliza turned away from him and walked away down the long enclosed terrace that ran along the outside of the ballroom. She did not turn back.

Jake watched her. Her back was held erect, the full skirts of her deep blue dress with its elaborately beaded bodice nipped into her tiny waist swishing around her at each step. He watched her until she turned to the right through an archway. Still she didn't look back, although he had his hand ready to wave farewell to her. Then she disappeared out of sight.

She left behind her just the lingering trace of her scent. He breathed it in to capture its essence. Took a step to go after her, then halted himself. He had no right to call her back a second time. He groaned and slammed his hand against the ancient stone wall.

For a long time he looked out through the window to the still lake beyond. Then he looked back to the ballroom. Without Eliza to dance with there was no point in returning. Besides, he felt like an impostor among the glittering throng. His role as best man, as friend to the Prince, gave him an entrée to their world. His multi-million-dollar houses and string of prestige European cars made him look the part.

Would they welcome him so readily into their elite company if they knew the truth about his past? Would Eliza find him so appealing if she knew his secrets?

He took out his phone and made his business call, in desperate need of distraction.

CHAPTER TWO

Six months later

ELIZA NOTICED JAKE MARLOWE the instant he strode into the business class lounge at Sydney's Kingsford Smith Airport. Tall, broad-shouldered, with a surfer's blond hair and tan, his good looks alone would attract attention. The fact that he was a billionaire whose handsome face was often in the media guaranteed it. Heads turned discreetly as he made his way with his easy, athletic stride towards the coffee station.

He was half a room away from her, but awareness tingled down Eliza's spine. A flush of humiliation warmed her cheeks. She hadn't seen him or heard from him since the wedding in Montovia, despite his promise to get in touch when his divorce was through. And here he was—on his way out of Sydney.

Jake had been in her hometown for heaven knew how long and hadn't cared to get in touch. She thought of a few choice names for him but wouldn't let herself mutter them, even under her breath. Losing her dignity over him was not worth it.

Over the last months she'd gone past disappointed, through angry, to just plain embarrassed that she'd believed him. That she'd allowed herself to spin hopes and dreams around seeing him again—finally being able to act on that flare of attraction between them. An attraction that, despite her best efforts to talk herself out of it, had flamed right back to life at the sight of him. She'd failed dismally in her efforts to extinguish it. He looked just as good in faded jeans and black T-shirt as he looked in a tuxedo. Better, perhaps. Every hot hunk sensor in her body alerted her to that.

But good looks weren't everything. She'd kidded herself that Jake was something he wasn't. Sure, they'd shared some interesting conversations, come close to a kiss. But when it boiled down to it, it appeared he was a slick tycoon who'd known how to spin the words he'd thought would please her. And she'd been sucker enough to fall for it. Had there been *anything* genuine about him?

Jake had put her through agony by not getting in touch when he'd said he would. She never wanted that kind of emotional turmoil in her life again. Especially not now, when Party Queens was in possible peril. She needed all her wits about her to ensure the future of the company that had become her life.

Perhaps back then she'd been convenient for Jake—the bridesmaid paired with the best man. An instant temporary couple. Now he was single and oh-so-eligible he must have women flinging themselves at him from all sides. Even now, as she sneaked surreptitious glances at him, a well-dressed woman edged up close to him, smiling up into his face.

Jake laughed at something she said. Eliza's senses jolted into hyper mode. *He looked so handsome when he laughed.* Heck, he looked so handsome whatever he did.

Darn her pesky libido. Her brain could analyse exactly what she didn't want in a man, but then her body argued an opposing message. She'd let her libido take over at Gemma's wedding, when she'd danced with Jake and let herself indulge in a fantasy that there could be something between them one day. But she prided herself on her self-control. Eliza allowed herself a moment to let her eyes feast on him, in the same way she would a mouthwatering treat she craved but was forbidden to have. Then she ducked her head and hid behind the pale pink pages of her favourite financial newspaper.

Perhaps she hadn't ducked fast enough—perhaps she hadn't masked the hunger in her gaze as successfully as she'd thought. Or perhaps Jake had noticed her when he came in as readily as she had noticed him.

Just moments later she was aware of him standing in front of her, legs braced in a way that suggested he wasn't going anywhere. Her heart started to thud at a million miles an hour. As she lowered the newspaper and looked up at him she feigned surprise. But the expression in his green eyes told her she hadn't fooled him one little bit.

She gathered all her resolve to school her face into a mask of polite indifference. He could not know how much he'd hurt her. Not *hurt*. That gave him too much power. *Offended.* His divorce had been splashed all over the media for the last three months. Yet there'd been no phone call from him. What a fool she'd been to have expected one. She'd obviously read way too much into that memorable 'next time' farewell.

Eliza went to get up but he sat down in the vacant seat next to her and angled his body towards her. In doing so he brushed his knee against her thigh, and she tried desperately not to gasp at his touch. Her famed self-control seemed to wobble every which way when she found herself within touching distance of Jake Marlowe.

He rested his hands on his thighs, which brought them too close for comfort. She refused to let herself think about how good they'd felt on her body in that close embrace of their dance. She could not let herself be blinded by physical attraction to the reality of this man.

'Eliza,' he said.

'Jake,' she said coolly, with a nod of acknowledgment.

She crossed her legs to break contact with his. Made a show of folding her newspaper, its rustle satisfyingly loud in the silence between them.

There was a long, awkward pause. She had no intention of helping him out by being the first one to dive into conversation. Not when he'd treated her with such indifference. Surely the thread of friendship they'd established had entitled her to better.

She could see he was looking for the right words, and at any other time she might have felt sorry for this intelligent, successful man who appeared to be struggling to make conversation. Would have fed him words to make it easier for him. But she knew how articulate Jake could be. How he had charmed her. This sudden shyness must be all part of his game. It seemed he felt stymied at seeing her by accident when he'd so obviously not wanted to see her by intent.

She really should hold her tongue and let him stumble through whatever he had to say. But she knew there wasn't much time before her flight would be called. And this might be her only chance to call him on the way he had broken his promise.

Of course it hadn't been a *promise* as such. But, spellbound by the magic of that royal wedding in Montovia, she had believed every word about there being a 'next time', when he was free. She'd never believed in fairytales—but she'd believed in *him.*

Even though the lounge chairs were spaced for privacy in the business class lounge—not crammed on top of each other like at the airport gate, where she was accustomed to waiting for a flight—she was aware that she and Jake were being observed and might possibly be overheard. She would have to be discreet.

She leaned closer to him and spoke in an undertone. 'So whatever happened to getting in touch? I see from the media that your divorce is well and truly done and delivered. You're now considered to be the most eligible bachelor in the country. You must be enjoying that.'

Jake shifted in his seat. Which brought his thigh back in touch with her knee. She pointedly crossed her legs again to break the contact. It was way too distracting.

'You couldn't be more wrong.' He cleared his throat. 'I want to explain.'

Eliza didn't want to hear his half-hearted apologies. She glanced at her watch. 'I don't think so. My flight is about to be called.'

'So is mine. Where are you headed?'

It would be childish to spit, *None of your business,* so she refrained. 'Port Douglas.'

She'd been counting the days until she could get up to the resort in far north-east tropical Queensland. From Sydney she was flying to Cairns, the nearest airport. She needed to relax—to get away from everyday distractions so she could get her head around what she needed to do to ensure Party Queens' ongoing success.

Jake's expression, which had bordered on glum, brightened perceptibly. 'Are you on Flight 321 to Cairns? So am I.'

Eliza felt the colour drain from her face. It couldn't be. It just *couldn't* be. Australia was an enormous country. Yet she happened to be flying to the same destination as Jake Marlowe. What kind of cruel coincidence was that?

'Yes,' she said through gritted teeth.

Port Douglas was a reasonably sized town. The resort she was booked into was pretty much self-contained. She would make darn sure she didn't bump into him.

Just then they called the flight. She went to rise from her seat. Jake put his hand on her arm to detain her. She flinched.

He spoke in a fierce undertone. 'Please, Eliza. I know it was wrong of me not to have got in touch as I said I would. But I had good reason.'

She stared at him, uncertain whether or not to give him the benefit of the doubt. He seemed so sincere. But then he'd seemed so sincere at the wedding. Out there on the terrace, in a place and at a time that hardly seemed real any more. As if it *had* been a fairytale. How could she believe a word he said?

'A phone call to explain would have sufficed. Even a text.'

'That wouldn't have worked. I want you to hear me out.'

There was something about his request that was difficult to resist. She wanted to hear what he had to say. Out of curiosity, if nothing else. Huh! Who was she kidding? How could she *not* want to hear what he had to say? After six months of wondering why the deafening silence?

She relented. 'Perhaps we could meet for a coffee in Port Douglas.' At a café. Not her room. Or his. For just enough time to hear his explanation. Then she could put Jake Marlowe behind her.

'How are you getting to Port Douglas from Cairns?' he asked.

'I booked a shuttle bus from the airport to the resort.'

His eyebrows rose in such disbelief it forced from her a reluctant smile.

'Yes, a shuttle bus. It's quite comfortable—and so much cheaper than a taxi for an hour-long trip. That's how we non-billionaires travel. I'm flying economy class, too.'

When she'd first started studying in Sydney, cut off from any family support because she'd refused to toe her father's line, she'd had to budget for every cent. It was a habit she'd kept. Why waste money on a business class seat for a flight of less than three hours?

'Then why…?' He gestured around him at the exclusive waiting area.

'I met a friend going through Security. She invited me in here on her guest pass. She went out on an earlier flight.'

'Lucky for me—otherwise I might have missed you.'

She made a *humph* kind of sound at that, which drew a half-smile from him.

'Contrary to what you might think, I'm very glad to see you,' he said, in that deep, strong voice she found so very appealing.

'That's good to hear,' she said, somewhat mollified. Of course she was glad to see him too—in spite of her better judgement. How could she deny even to herself that her every sense was zinging with awareness of him? She would have to be very careful not to be taken in by him again.

'Are you going to Port Douglas on business or pleasure?'

'Pleasure,' she said, without thinking. Then regretted her response as a flush reddened on her cheeks.

She had fantasised over pleasure with *him*. When it came to Jake Marlowe it wasn't so easy to switch off the attraction that had been ignited at their very first meeting. She would have to fight very hard against it.

It had taken some time to get her life to a steady state after her divorce, and she didn't want it tipping over again. When she'd seen the media reports of Jake's divorce, but hadn't heard from him, she'd been flung back to a kind of angst she didn't welcome. She cringed when she thought about how often she'd checked her phone for a call that had never come. It wasn't a situation where she might have called *him*. And she hated not being in control—of her life, her emotions. Never did she want to give a man that kind of power over her.

'I mean relaxation,' she added hastily. 'Yes, relaxation.'

'Party Queens keeping you busy?'

'Party Queens always keeps me busy. Too busy right now. That's why I'm grabbing the chance for a break. I desperately need some time away from the office.'

'Have you solved the Gemma problem?'

'No. I need to give it more thought. Gemma will always be a director of Party Queens, for as long as the company exists. It's just that—'

'Can passengers Dunne and Marlowe please make their way to Gate Eleven, where their flight is ready for departure?'

The voice boomed over the intercom.

Eliza sat up abruptly, her newspaper falling in a flurry of pages to the floor. Hissed a swearword under her breath. 'We've got to get going. I don't want to miss that plane.'

'How about I meet you at the other end and drive you to Port Douglas?'

Eliza hated being late. For anything. Flustered, she hardly heard him. 'Uh…okay,' she said, not fully aware of what she might be letting herself in for. 'Let's go!'

She grabbed her wheel-on cabin bag—her only luggage—and half-walked, half-ran towards the exit of the lounge.

Jake quickly caught up and led the way to the gate. Eliza had to make a real effort to keep up with his long stride. They made the flight with only seconds to spare. There was no time to say anything else as she breathlessly boarded the plane through the cattle class entrance while Jake headed to the pointy end up front.

Jake had a suspicion that Eliza might try to avoid him at Cairns airport. As soon as the flight landed he called through to the garage where he kept his car to have it brought round. Having had the advantage of being the first to disembark, he was there at the gate to head Eliza off.

She soon appeared, head down, intent, so didn't see him as he waited for her. The last time he'd seen her she'd been resplendent in a ballgown. Now she looked just as good, in cut-off skinny pants that showed off her pert rear end and slim legs, topped with a form-fitting jacket. Deep blue again. She must like that colour. Her dark hair was pulled back in a high ponytail. She might travel Economy but she would look right at home in First Class.

For a moment he regretted the decision he'd made to keep her out of his life. Three months wasted in an Eliza-free zone. But the aftermath of his divorce had made him unfit for female company. Unfit for *any* company, if truth be told.

He'd been thrown so badly by the first big failure of his life that he'd gone completely out of kilter. Drunk too much. Made bad business decisions that had had serious repercussions to his bottom line. Mistakes he'd had to do everything in his power to fix. He had wealth, but it would never be enough to blot out the poverty of his childhood, to assuage the hunger for more that had got him into such trouble. He had buried himself in his work, determined to reverse the wrong turns he'd made. But he hadn't been able to forget Eliza.

'Eliza!' he called now.

She started, looked up, was unable to mask a quick flash of guilt.

'Jake. Hi.'

Her voice was higher than usual. Just as sweet, but strained. She was not a good liar. He stored that information up for later, as he did in his assessments of clients. He'd learned young that knowledge of people's weaknesses was a useful tool. Back then it had been for survival. Now it was to give him a competitive advantage and keep him at the top. He could not let himself slide again.

'I suspected you might try and avoid me, so I decided to head you off at the pass,' he said.

Eliza frowned unconvincingly. 'Why would you do that?'

'Because you obviously think I'm a jerk for not calling you after the divorce. I'm determined to change your mind.' He didn't want to leave things the way they were. Not when thoughts of her had intruded, despite his best efforts to forget her.

'Oh,' she said, after a long pause. 'You could do that over coffee. Not during an hour's drive to Port Douglas.'

So she'd been mulling over the enforced intimacy of a journey in his car. So had he. But to different effect.

'How do you know I won't need an hour with you?'

She shrugged slender shoulders. 'I guess I don't. But I've booked the shuttle bus. The driver is expecting me.'

'Call them and cancel.' He didn't want to appear too high-handed. But no way was she going to get on that shuttle bus. 'Come on, Eliza. It will be much more comfortable in my car.'

'Your rental car?'

'I have a house in Port Douglas. And a car.'

'I thought you lived in Brisbane?'

'I do. The house in Port Douglas is an escape house.'

He took hold of her wheeled bag. 'Do you need to pick up more luggage?'

She shook her head. 'This is all I have. A few bikinis and sundresses is all I need for four days.'

Jake forced himself not to think how Eliza would look in a bikini. She was wearing flat shoes and he realised how petite she was. Petite, slim, but with curves in all the right places. She would look sensational in a bikini.

'My car is out front. Let's go.'

Still she hesitated. 'So you'll drop me at my resort hotel?'

Did she think he was about to abduct her? It wasn't such a bad idea, if that was what it took to get her to listen to him. 'Your private driver—at your service,' he said with a mock bow.

She smiled that curving smile he found so delightful. The combination of astute businesswoman and quick-to-laughter Party Queen was part of her appeal.

'Okay, I accept the offer,' she said.

The warm midday air hit him as they left the air-conditioning of the terminal. Eliza shrugged off her jacket to reveal a simple white top that emphasised the curves of her breasts. She stretched out her slim, toned arms in a movement he found incredibly sensual, as if she were welcoming the sun to her in an embrace.

'Nice and hot,' she said with a sigh of pleasure. 'Just what I want. Four days of relaxing and swimming and eating great food.'

'April is a good time of year here,' he said. 'Less chance of cyclone and perfect conditions for diving on the Great Barrier Reef.'

The garage attendant had brought Jake's new-model four-by-four to the front of the airport. It was a luxury to keep a car for infrequent use. Just as it was to keep a house up here that was rarely used. But he liked being able to come and go whenever he wanted. It had been his bolthole through the unhappiest times of his marriage.

'Nice car,' Eliza said.

Jake remembered they'd talked about cars at their first meeting. He'd been impressed by how knowledgeable she was. Face it—he'd been impressed by *her*. Period. No wonder she'd been such a difficult woman to forget.

He put her bag into the back, went to help her up into the passenger's seat, but she had already swung herself effortlessly up. He noticed the sleek muscles in her arms and legs. Exercise was a non-negotiable part of her day, he suspected. Everything about her spoke of discipline and control. He wondered how it would be to see her come to pieces with pleasure in his arms.

Jake settled himself into the driver's seat. 'Have you been to Port Douglas before?' he asked.

'Yes, but not for some time,' she said. 'I loved it and always wanted to come back. But there's been no time for vacations. As you know, Party Queens took off quickly. It's an intense, people-driven business. I can't be away from it for long. But I need to free my head to think about how we can make it work with Gemma not on the ground.'

Can't or *didn't want to* be away from her job? Jake had recognised a fellow workaholic when he'd first met her.

'So you're familiar with the drive from Cairns to Port Douglas?'

With rainforest on one side and the sea on the other, it was considered one of the most scenic drives in Australia.

'I planned the timing of my flight to make sure I saw it in daylight.'

'I get the feeling very little is left to chance with you, Eliza.'

'You've got it,' she said with a click of her fingers. 'I plan, schedule, timetable and organise my life to the minute.'

She was the total opposite of his ex-wife. In looks, in personality, in attitude. The two women could not be more different.

'You don't like surprises?' he asked.

'Surprises have a habit of derailing one's life.'

She stilled, almost imperceptibly, and there was a slight hitch to her voice that made him wonder about the kind of surprises that had hit her.

'I like things to be on track. For me to be at the wheel.'

'So by hijacking you I've ruined your plans for today?'

His unwilling passenger shrugged slender shoulders.

'Just a deviation. I'm still heading for my resort. It will take the same amount of time. Just a different mode of transportation.' She turned her head to face him. 'Besides. I'm on vacation. From schedules and routine as much as from anything else.'

Eliza reached back and undid the tie from her ponytail, shook out her hair so it fell in a silky mass to her shoulders. With her hair down she looked even lovelier. Younger than her twenty-nine years. More relaxed. He'd like to run his hands through that hair, bunch it back from her face to kiss her. Instead he tightened his hands on the steering wheel as she settled back in her seat.

'When you're ready to tell me why I had to read about your divorce in the gossip columns rather than hear it from you,' she said, 'I'm all ears.'

CHAPTER THREE

JAKE WAS VERY good at speaking the language of computers and coding. At talking the talk when it came to commercial success. While still at university he had come up with a concept for ground-breaking software tools to streamline the digital workflow of large businesses. His friend Dominic Hunt had backed him. The resulting success had made a great deal of money for both young men. And Jake had continued on a winning streak that had made him a billionaire.

But for all his formidable skills Jake wasn't great at talking about emotions. At admitting that he had fears and doubts. Or conceding to any kind of failure. It was one of the reasons he'd got into such trouble when he was younger. Why he'd fallen apart after the divorce. No matter how much he worked on it, he still considered it a character flaw.

He hoped he'd be able to make a good fist of explaining to Eliza why he hadn't got in touch until now.

He put the four-by-four into gear and headed for the Captain Cook Highway to Port Douglas. Why they called it a highway, he'd never know—it was a narrow two-lane road in most places. To the left was dense vegetation, right back to the distant hills. To the right was the vastness of the Pacific Ocean, its turquoise sea bounded by narrow, deserted beaches, broken by small islands. In places the road ran almost next to the sand. He'd driven along this road many times, but never failed to be impressed by the grandeur of the view.

He didn't look at Eliza but kept his eyes on the road. 'I'll cut straight to it,' he said. 'I want to apologise for not getting in touch when I said I would. I owe you an explanation.'

'Fire away,' Eliza said.

Her voice was cool. The implication? *This had better be good.*

He swallowed hard. 'The divorce eventually came through three months ago.'

'I heard. Congratulations.'

He couldn't keep the cynical note from his voice. 'You *congratulate* me. Lots of people congratulated me. A divorce party was even suggested. To celebrate my freedom from the ball and chain.'

'Party Queens has organised a few divorce parties. They're quite a thing these days.'

'Not *my* thing,' he said vehemently. 'I didn't want congratulations. Or parties to celebrate what I saw as a failure. The end of something that didn't work.'

'Was that because you were still…still in love with your wife?'

A quick glance showed Eliza had a tight grip on the red handbag she held on her lap. He hated talking about stuff like this. Even after all he'd worked on in the last months.

'No. There hadn't been any love there for a long time. It ended with no anger or animosity. Just indifference. Which was almost worse.'

He'd met his ex when they were both teenagers. They'd dated on and off over the early years. Marriage had felt inevitable. He'd changed a lot; she hadn't wanted change. Then she'd betrayed him. He'd loved her. It had hurt.

'That must have been traumatic in its own way.' Eliza's reply sounded studiously neutral.

'More traumatic than I could have imagined. The process dragged on for too long.'

'It must have been a relief when it was all settled.'

Again he read the subtext to her sentence: *All settled, but you didn't call me.* It hinted at a hurt she couldn't mask. Hurt caused by *him.* He had to make amends.

'I didn't feel relief. I felt like I'd been turned upside down and wasn't sure where I'd landed. Couldn't find my feet. My ex and I had been together off and on for years, married for seven. Then I was on my own. It wasn't just her I'd lost. It was a way of life.'

'I understand that,' she said.

The shadow that passed across her face hinted at unspoken pain. She'd gone through divorce too. Though she hadn't talked much about it on the previous occasions when they had met.

He dragged in a deep breath. *Spit it out. Get this over and done with.* 'It took a few wipe-out weeks at work for me to realise going out and drinking wasn't the way to deal with it.'

'It usually isn't,' she said.

He was a guy. A tough, successful guy. To him, being unable to cope with loss was a sign of weakness. Weakness he wasn't genetically programmed to admit to. But the way he'd fallen to pieces had lost him money. That couldn't be allowed to happen again.

'Surely you had counselling?' she said. 'I did after my divorce. It helped.'

'Guys like me don't do counselling.'

'You bottle it all up inside you instead?'

'Something like that.'

'That's not healthy—it festers,' she said. 'Not that it's any of my business.'

The definitive turning point in his life had not been his divorce. That had come much earlier, when he'd been aged fifteen, angry and rebellious. He'd been forced to face up to the way his life was going, the choices he would have to make. To take one path or another.

Jake didn't know how much Eliza knew about Dominic's charity—The Underground Help Centre in Brisbane for homeless young people—or Jake's involvement in it. A social worker with whom both Dominic and Jake had crossed paths headed the charity. Jim Hill had helped Jake at a time when he'd most needed it. He had become a friend. Without poking or prying, he had noticed Jake's unexpected devastation after his marriage break-up, and pointed him in the right direction for confidential help.

'Someone told me about a support group for divorced guys,' Jake said, with a quick, sideways glance to Eliza and in a tone that did not invite further questions.

'That's good,' she said with an affirmative nod.

He appreciated that she didn't push it. He still choked at the thought he'd had to seek help.

The support group had been exclusive, secret, limited to a small number of elite men rich enough to pay the stratospheric fees. Men who wanted to protect their wealth in the event of remarriage, who needed strategies to avoid the pitfalls of dating after divorce. Jake had wanted to know how to barricade his heart as well as his bank balance.

The men and the counsellors had gone into lockdown for a weekend at a luxury retreat deep in the rainforest. It had been on a first-name-only basis, but Jake had immediately recognised some of the high-profile men. No doubt they had recognised him too. But they had proved to be discreet.

'Men don't seem to seek help as readily as women,' Eliza said.

'It was about dealing with change more than anything,' he said.

'Was that why you didn't get in touch?' she said, with an edge to her voice. 'You changed your mind?'

Jake looked straight ahead at the road. 'I wasn't ready for

another relationship. I needed to learn to live alone. That meant no dating. In particular not dating *you.*'

Her gasp told him how much he'd shocked her.

'*Me?* Why?'

'From the first time we met you sparked something that told me there could be life after divorce. I could see myself getting serious about you. I don't want serious. But I couldn't get you out of my head. I had to see you again.'

To be sure she was real and not some fantasy that had built up in his mind.

Eliza didn't even notice the awesome view of the ocean that stretched as far as the eye could see. Or the sign indicating the turn-off to a crocodile farm that would normally make her shudder. All she was aware of was Jake. She stared at him.

'*Serious?* But we hardly knew each other. Did you think I had my life on hold until you were free so I could bolt straight into a full-on relationship?'

Jake took his eyes off the road for a second to glance at her. 'Come on, Eliza. There was something there between us. Something more than a surface attraction. Something we both wanted to act on.'

'Maybe,' she said.

Of course there had been something there. But she wasn't sure she wanted to admit to it. Not when she'd spent all that time trying to suppress it. Not when it had the potential to hurt her. Those three months of seeing his divorce splashed over the media, of speculation on who might hook up with the billionaire bachelor had hurt. He had said he'd get in touch. Then he hadn't. How could she trust his word again? She couldn't afford to be distracted from Party Queens by heartbreak at such a crucial time in the growth of her business.

The set of his jaw made him seem very serious. 'I didn't want to waste your time when I had nothing to offer you. But ultimately I had to see you.'

'Six months later? Maybe you should have let *me* be the one to decide whether I wanted to waste my time or not?' She willed any hint of a wobble from her voice.

'I needed that time on my own. Possibly it was a mistake not to communicate that with you. I was married a long time. Now I'm single again at thirty-two. I haven't had a lot of practice at this.'

Eliza stared in disbelief at the gorgeous man beside her in the driver's seat. At his handsome profile with the slightly crooked nose and strong jaw. His shoulders so broad they took up more than his share of the car. His tanned arms, strong and muscular, dusted with hair that glinted gold in the sunlight coming through the window of the car. His hands— Best she did not think about those hands and how they'd felt on her bare skin back in magical Montovia.

'I find that difficult to buy,' she said. 'You're a really good-looking guy. There must be women stampeding to date you.'

He shrugged dismissively. 'All that eligible billionaire stuff the media likes to bang on about brings a certain level of attention. Even before the divorce was through I had women hounding me with dollar signs blazing in their eyes.'

'I guess that kind of attention comes with the territory. But surely not *everyone* would be a gold-digger. You must have dated *some* genuine women.'

She hated the thought of him with another woman. Not his ex-wife. That had been long before she'd met him. But Eliza had no claim on him—no right to be jealous. For all his fine talk about how he hadn't been able to forget her, the fact remained she was only here with him by accident.

Jake slowly shook his head. 'I haven't dated anyone since the divorce.' He paused for a long moment, the silence only broken by the swish of the tyres on the road, the air blowing from the air-conditioning unit. Jake gave her another quick, sideward glance. 'Don't you get it, Eliza? There's only one woman who interests me. And she's sitting here, right beside me.'

Eliza suddenly understood the old expression about having all the wind blown out of her sails. A stunned, 'Oh…' was all she could manage through her suddenly accelerated breath.

Jake looked straight ahead as he spoke, as if he was finding the words difficult to get out. 'The support group covered dating after divorce. It suggested six months before starting to date. Three months was long enough. The urge to see you again became overwhelming. I didn't get where I am in the world by following the rules. All that dating-after-divorce advice flew out the window.'

Eliza frowned. 'How can you *say* that? You left our seeing each other again purely to chance. If we hadn't met at the airport—'

'I didn't leave anything to chance. After six months of radio silence I doubted you'd welcome a call from me. Any communication needed to be face to face. I flew down to Sydney to see you. Then met with Dominic to suss out how the land lay.'

'You *what*? Andie didn't say anything to me.'

'Because I asked Dominic not to tell her. He found out you were flying to Port Douglas this morning. I couldn't believe you were heading for a town where I had a house. Straight away I booked onto the same flight.'

Eliza took a few moments to absorb this revelation. 'That was very cloak and dagger. What would have happened if you hadn't found me at the airport?'

He shrugged those broad shoulders. 'I would have abducted you.' At her gasp he added, 'Just kidding. But I *would* have found a way for us to reconnect in Port Douglas. Even if I'd had to call every resort and hotel I would have tracked you down. I just had to see you, Eliza. To see if that attraction I'd felt was real.'

'I… I don't know what to say. Except I'm flattered.'

There was a long beat before he spoke. 'And pleased?'

The tinge of uncertainty to his voice surprised her.

'Very pleased.'

In fact her heart was doing cartwheels of exultation. She was so dizzy that the warning from her brain was having trouble getting through. Jake tracking her down sounded very romantic. So did his talk of abduction. But she'd learned to be wary of the type of man who would ride roughshod over her wishes and needs. Like her domineering father. Like her controlling ex. She didn't know Jake very well. It must take a certain kind of ruthlessness to become a billionaire. She couldn't let her guard down.

'So, about that coffee we talked about…?' he said. 'Do you want to make it lunch?'

'Are you asking me on a *date*, Jake?' Her tone was deliberately flirtatious.

His reply was very serious. 'I realise I've surprised you with this. But be assured I've released the baggage of my marriage. I've accepted my authentic self. And if you—'

She couldn't help a smile. 'You sound like you've swallowed the "dating after divorce" handbook.'

His brows rose. 'I told you I was out of practice. What else should I say?'

Eliza started to laugh. 'This is getting a little crazy. Pull over, will you, please?' she said. She indicated a layby ahead with a wave of her hand.

Jake did so with a sudden swerve and squealing of tyres that had her clutching onto the dashboard of the car. He skidded to a halt under the shade of some palm trees.

Still laughing, Eliza unbuckled her seatbelt and turned to face him. 'Can I give you a dating after divorce tip? Don't worry so much about whether it's going to lead to something serious before you've even gone on a first date.'

'Was that what I did?'

She found his frown endearing. How could a guy who was one of the most successful entrepreneurs in the country be having this kind of trouble?

'You're over-thinking all this,' she said. 'So am I. We're making it so much harder than it should be. In truth, it's simple. There's an attraction here. You're divorced. I'm divorced. We don't answer to anyone except ourselves. There's nothing to stop us enjoying each other's company in any way we want to.'

He grinned in that lazy way she found so attractive. 'Nothing at all.'

'Shall we agree not to worry about tomorrow when we haven't even had a today yet?'

Eliza had been going to add *not even a morning.* But that conjured up an image of waking up next to Jake, in a twist of tangled sheets. Better not think about mornings. Or nights.

Jake's grin widened. 'You've got four days of vacation. I've got nothing to do except decide whether or not to offload my house in Port Douglas.'

'No expectations. No promises. No apologies.'

'Agreed,' he said. He held out his hand to shake and seal the deal.

She edged closer to him. 'Forget the handshake. Why don't we start with a kiss?'

CHAPTER FOUR

JAKE KNEW THERE was a dating after divorce guideline regarding the first physical encounter, but he'd be damned if he could think about that right now. Any thoughts other than of Eliza had been blown away in a blaze of anticipation and excitement at the invitation in her eyes—a heady mix of sensuality, impatience and mischief.

It seemed she had forgiven him for his broken promise. He had a second chance with her. It was so much more than he could have hoped for—or probably deserved after his neglect.

He hadn't told her the whole truth about why he hadn't been in touch. It was true he hadn't been able to forget her, had felt compelled to see her again. He was a man who liked to be in the company of one special woman and he'd hungered for her. But not necessarily to commit to anything serious. Not now. Maybe not ever again. Not with her. Not with any woman. However it seemed she wasn't looking for anything serious either. Four days without strings? That sounded like a great idea.

She slid a little closer to him from her side of the car. Reached down and unbuckled his seat belt with a low, sweet laugh that sent his awareness levels soaring. When her fingers inadvertently trailed over his thigh he shuddered and pulled her kissing distance close.

He focused with intense anticipation on her sweet mouth. Her lips were beautifully defined, yet lush and soft and welcoming. She tilted her face to him, making her impatience obvious. Jake needed no urging. He pressed his mouth against hers in a tender kiss, claiming her at last. She tasted of salt—peanuts on the plane, perhaps?—and something sweet. Chocolate? Sweet and sharp at the same time. Like Eliza herself—an intriguing combination.

She was beautiful, but his attraction had never been just to her looks. He liked her independence, her intelligence, her laughter.

The kiss felt both familiar and very different. Within seconds it was as if *her* kiss was all he'd ever known. Her lips parted under his as she gave a soft sigh of contentment.

'At last,' she murmured against his mouth.

Kissing Eliza for the first time in the front seat of a four-by-four was hardly ideal. Jake had forgotten how awkward it was to make out in a car. But having Eliza in his arms was way too exciting to be worrying about the discomfort of bumping into the steering wheel or handbrake. She held his face between her hands as she returned his kiss, her tongue sliding between his lips to meet his, teasing and exploring. He was oblivious to the car, their surroundings, the fact that they were parked in a public layby. He just wanted to keep kissing Eliza.

Was it seconds or minutes before Eliza broke away from him? That kind of excitement wasn't easily measured. Her cheeks were flushed, her eyes shades brighter, her lips swollen and pouting. She was panting, so it took her some effort to control her voice. 'Kissing you was all I could think about that night in the castle.'

'Me too,' he said.

Only his thoughts had marched much further than kissing. That last night he hadn't been able to sleep, taunted by the knowledge she was in the apartment next to his at the castle, overwhelmed by how much he wanted her. Back then his married state had been an obstacle. Now there was nothing stopping them from acting on the attraction between them.

He claimed her mouth again, deeper, more demanding. There'd been enough talking. He was seized with a sense of urgency to be with her while he could. He wasn't going to 'overthink' about where this might lead. Six months of pent-up longing for this woman erupted into passion, fierce and hungry.

As their kiss escalated in urgency Jake pulled her onto his lap, one hand around her waist, the other resting against the side of the car to support her. He bunched her hair in his hand and tugged to tilt her face upward, so he could deepen the kiss, hungry for her, aching for more. The little murmurs of pleasure she made deep in her throat drove him crazy with want.

His hands slid down her bare arms, brushed the side curves of her breasts, the silkiness of her top. She gasped, placed both hands on his chest and pushed away. She started to laugh—that delightful, chiming laughter he found so enchanting.

'We're steaming up the windows here like a coupled of hormone-crazed adolescents,' she said, her voice broken with laughter.

'What's wrong with being hormone-crazed *adults*,' he said, his own voice hoarse and unsteady.

'Making out in a car is seriously sexy. I don't want to stop,' she said, moaning when he nuzzled against the delicious softness of her throat, kissing and tasting.

The confined area of the car was filled with her scent, heady and intoxicating. 'Me neither,' he said.

Eliza was so relaxed and responsive she took away any thought of awkwardness. He glanced over to the back seat. There was more room there. It was wider and roomier.

'The back seat would be more comfortable,' he said.

He kissed her again, manoeuvring her towards the door. They would have to get out and transfer to the back, though it might be a laugh to try and clamber through the gap between the front seats. Why not?

Just then another car pulled into the layby and parked parallel to the four-by-four. Eliza froze in his arms. Their mouths were still pressed together. Her eyes communicated her alarm.

'That puts paid to the back seat plan,' he said, pulling away from her with a groan of regret.

'Just as well, really,' Eliza said breathlessly.

She smoothed her hair back from her face with her fingers and tucked it behind her ears. Even her ears were lovely—small and shell-like.

'The media would love to catch their most eligible bachelor being indiscreet in public.'

He scowled. 'I hate the way they call me a *bachelor*. Surely that's a term for someone who has never been married?'

'*Most eligible divorcé* doesn't quite have the same headline potential, does it?' she said.

'I'd rather not feature in *any* headlines,' he growled.

'You might just have to hit yourself with the ugly stick, then,' she said. 'Handsome and rich makes you a magnet for headlines. You're almost too good to be true.' She laughed. 'Though if you scowl like that they might forget about calling you the most eligible guy in the country.'

Jake exaggerated the scowl. He liked making her laugh. 'Too good to be true, huh?'

'Now you look cute,' she said.

'*Cute?* I do *not* want to be called cute,' he protested.

'Handsome, good-looking, hot, smokin', babelicious—'

'Stop right there,' he said, unable to suppress a grin. 'You don't call a guy *babelicious*. That's a girl word. Let me try it on you.'

'No need,' she protested. 'I'm not the babelicious type.'

'I think you are—if I understand it to mean sexy and desirable and—' Her mock glare made him stop. 'How about lovely, beautiful, sweet, elegant—?'

'That's more than enough,' she said. 'I'll take elegant. Audrey Hepburn's style is my icon. Not that I'm really tall enough to own *elegant*. But I try.'

'You succeed, let me assure you,' he said.

'Thank you. I like *smokin'* for you,' she said, her eyes narrowing as she looked him over.

Her flattering descriptive words left him with a warm feeling. No matter how he'd tried to put a brave face on it, the continued rejection by his ex had hurt. She'd found someone else, of course. He should have realised earlier, before he'd let his ego get so bruised. The admiration in Eliza's eyes was like balm to those bruises. He intended to take everything she offered.

'I'd rather kiss than talk, wouldn't you?' he said.

He'd rather do so much more than kiss.

'If you say so,' she said with a seductive smile.

They kissed for a long time, until just kissing was not enough. It was getting steamy in the car—and not in an exciting way. It was too hot without the air-conditioning, but they couldn't sit there with the engine on.

The windows really were getting fogged up now. Visibility was practically zero. Eliza swiped her finger across the windscreen. Then spelled out the word KISSING. 'It's very obvious what's going on in here.'

He found her wicked giggle enchanting.

'More so now you've done that,' he said.

Spontaneity wasn't something he'd expected from cool and controlled Eliza. He ached to discover what other surprises she had in store for him.

'We really should go,' she said breathlessly. 'How long will it take to get to Port Douglas?'

'Thirty minutes to my place,' he said.

She wiggled in her seat in a show of impatience. 'Then put your foot to the floor and get us there ASAP, will you?'

Jake couldn't get his foot on the accelerator fast enough.

Eliza had a sense she was leaving everything that was everyday behind her as the four-by-four effortlessly climbed the steep driveway which led from the street in Port Douglas to Jake's getaway house. His retreat, he'd called it. As she slid out of the high-set car she gaped at the magnificence of the architectural award-winning house nestled among palm trees and vivid tropical gardens. Large glossy leaves in every shade of green contrasted with riotous blooms in orange, red and yellow. She breathed in air tinged with salt, ginger and the honey-scented white flowers that grew around the pathway.

This was his second house. No, his third. He'd told her he had a penthouse apartment in one of the most fashionable waterfront developments in Sydney, where his neighbours were celebrities and millionaires. His riverfront mansion in Brisbane was his home base. There were probably other houses too, but she'd realised early on that Jake wasn't the kind of billionaire to boast about his wealth.

Then Jake was kissing her again, and she didn't think about houses or bank balances or anything other than him and the way he was making her feel. He didn't break the kiss as he used his fingerprints on a sensor to get into the house—nothing so mundane as a key—and pushed open the door. They stumbled into the house, still kissing, laughing at their awkward progress but refusing to let go of each other.

Once inside, Eliza registered open-plan luxury and an awesome view. Usually she was a sucker for a water view. But nothing could distract her from Jake. She'd never wanted a man more than she wanted him. Many times since the wedding in Montovia she'd wondered if she had been foolish in holding off from him. There would be no regrets this time—no 'if only'. She didn't want him to stop...didn't want second thoughts to sneak into her consciousness.

In the privacy of the house their kisses got deeper, more demanding. Caresses—she of him and he of her—got progressively more intimate. Desire, warm and urgent, thrilled through her body.

She remembered when she'd first met Jake. He'd flown down to Sydney to be best man for Dominic at the surprise wedding

Dominic had organised for Andie. Eliza had been expecting a geek. The athletic, handsome best man had been the furthest from her image of a geek as he could possibly have been. She'd been instantly smitten—then plunged into intense disappointment to find he was married.

Now she had the green light to touch him, kiss him, undress him. *No holds barred.*

'Bedroom?' he murmured.

He didn't really have to ask. There had been no need for words for her to come to her decision of where to take this mutually explosive passion. Their kisses, their caresses, their sighs had communicated everything he needed to know.

She had always enjoyed those scenes in movies where a kissing couple left a trail of discarded clothing behind them as they staggered together towards the bedroom. To be taking part in such a scene with Jake was like a fantasy fulfilled. A fantasy that had commenced in the ballroom of a fairytale castle in Europe and culminated in an ultra-modern house overlooking a tropical beach in far north Australia.

They reached his bedroom, the bed set in front of a panoramic view that stretched out over the pool to the sea. Then she was on the bed with Jake, rejoicing in the intimacy, the closeness, the confidence—the wonderful new entity that was *them*.

Eliza and Jake.

CHAPTER FIVE

ELIZA DIDN'T KNOW where she was when she woke up some time later. In a super-sized bed and not alone. She blinked against the late-afternoon sunlight streaming through floor-to-ceiling windows with a view of palm trees, impossibly blue sky, the turquoise sea beyond.

Jake's bedroom.

She smiled to herself with satisfaction. Remembered the trail of discarded clothes that had led to this bed. The passion. The fun. The ultimate pleasure. Again and again.

He lay beside her on his back, long muscular limbs sprawled across the bed and taking up much of the space. The sheets were tangled around his thighs. He seemed to be in a deep sleep, his broad chest rhythmically rising and falling.

She gazed at him for a long moment and caught her breath when she remembered what a skilled, passionate lover he'd proved to be. Her body ached in a thoroughly satisfied way.

Beautiful wasn't a word she would normally choose to describe a man. But he *was* beautiful—in an intensely masculine way. The tawny hair, green eyes—shut tight at the moment—the sculpted face, smooth tanned skin, slightly crooked nose. His beard had started to shadow his jaw, dark in contrast to the tawny blond of his hair.

There were some things in life she would never, ever forget or regret. Making love with Jake was one of them. Heaven knew where they went from here, but even if this was all she ever had of him she would cherish the memory for the rest of her days. In her experience it was rare to want someone so intensely and then not be disappointed. Nothing about making love with Jake disappointed her.

Eliza breathed in the spicy warm scent of him; her own classic French scent that was her personal indulgence mingled with it so that it became the scent of *them*. Unique, memorable, intensely personal.

She tentatively stretched out a leg. It was starting to cramp under his much larger, heavier leg. Rolling cautiously away, so her back faced him, she wondered where the bathroom was, realised it was en suite and so not far.

She started to edge cautiously away. Then felt a kiss on her shoulder. She went still, her head thrown back in pleasure as Jake planted a series of kisses along her shoulder to land a final one in her most sensitive spot at the top of her jaw, below her ear. She gasped. They had so quickly learned what pleased each other.

Then a strong arm was around her, restraining her. 'You're not going anywhere,' he said as he pulled her to him.

She turned around to find Jake lying on his side. His body was so perfect she gasped her admiration. The sculptured pecs, the flat belly and defined six-pack, the muscular arms and legs… He was without a doubt the hottest billionaire on the planet.

Eliza trailed her hand over the smooth skin of his chest. *'Smokin',*' she murmured.

He propped himself up on his other elbow. Smiled that slow smile. 'Okay?' he asked.

'Very okay,' she said, returning his smile and stretching like one of her cats with remembered pleasure. 'It was very sudden. Unexpected. So soon, I mean. But it was good we just let it happen. We didn't get a chance to over-think things. Over-analyse how we felt, what it would mean.'

'Something so spontaneous wasn't in my dating after divorce guidebook,' he said with that endearing grin.

His face was handsome, but strong-jawed and tough. That smile lightened it, took away the edge of ruthlessness she sensed was not far from the surface. He couldn't have got where he had by being Mr Nice Guy. That edge excited her.

'Lucky you threw it out the window, then,' she said. 'I seriously wonder about the advice in that thing.'

'Best thing I ever did was ignore it,' he said.

He kissed her lightly on the shoulder, the growth of his beard pleasantly rough. She felt a rush of intense triumph that she was here with him—finally. With her finger she traced around his face, exploring its contours, the feel of his skin, smooth in parts, rough with bristle in others. Yes, she could call this man *beautiful*.

He picked up a strand of her hair and idly twisted it between his fingers. 'What did you do to get over *your* divorce?'

The question surprised her. It wasn't something she really wanted to remember. 'Became a hermit for a while. Like you, I felt an incredible sense of failure. I'm not used to failing at things. There was relief though, too. We got married when I was twenty-four. I'd only known him six months when he marched me down the aisle. Not actually an aisle. He'd been married before so we got hitched in the registry office.'

'Why the hurry?'

'He was seven years older than me. He wanted to start a family. I should have known better than to be rushed into it. Big mistake. Turned out I didn't know him at all. He showed himself to be quite the bully.'

She had ended up both fearing and hating him.

'Sounds like you had a lucky escape.'

'I did. But it wasn't pleasant at the time. No break-up ever is, is it? No matter the circumstances.'

Jake nodded assent. 'Mine dragged on too long.'

'I know. I was waiting, remember.'

'It got so delayed at the end because her new guy inserted himself into the picture. He introduced an element of ugliness and greed.'

Ugliness. Eliza didn't want to admit to Jake how scary *her* marriage had become. There hadn't been physical abuse, but she had endured some serious mental abuse. When she'd found herself getting used to it, even making excuses for Craig because she'd hated to admit she'd made a mistake in marrying him, she'd known it was time to get out. The experience had wounded her and toughened her. She'd vowed never again to risk getting tied up in something as difficult to extricate herself from as marriage.

'It took me a while to date again,' she said. 'I'd lost faith in my judgement of men. Man, did I date a few duds. And I turned off a few guys who were probably quite decent because of my interrogation technique. I found myself trying to discover anything potentially wrong about them before I even agreed to go out for a drink.'

Jake used her hair to tug her gently towards him for a quick kiss on her nose before he released her. 'You didn't interrogate me,' he said.

'I didn't need to. You weren't a potential date. When we first met at Andie and Dominic's wedding you were married. I could chat to you without expectation or agenda. You were an attractive, interesting man but off-limits.'

He picked up her hand, began idly stroking first her palm and then her fingers. Tingles of pleasure shot through her body right down to her toes. Nothing was off-limits now.

'You were so lovely, so smart—and so accepting of me,' he said. 'It was a revelation. You actually seemed interested in what I had to say.'

As his ex hadn't been? Eliza began to see how unhappy Jake

had been. Trapped in a past-its-use-by-date marriage. Bound by what seemed to have been misplaced duty and honour.

'Are you kidding me?' she said. 'You're such a success story and only a few years older than me. I found you fascinating. And a surprise. All three Party Queens had been expecting a stereotype geek—not a guy who looked like an athlete. You weren't arrogant either, which was another surprise.'

'That was a social situation. I can be arrogant when it comes to my work and impatient with people who don't get it.'

His expression hardened and she saw again that underlying toughness. She imagined he would be a demanding boss.

'I guess you have to be tough to have got where you are—a self-made man. Your fortune wasn't handed to you.'

'I see you've done your research?'

'Of course.' She'd spent hours on the internet, looking him up—not that'd she'd admit to the extent of her 'research'. 'There's a lot to be found on Jake Marlowe. The media loves a rags-to-riches story.'

'There were never rags. Clothes from charity shops, yes, but not rags.' The tense lines of his mouth belied his attempt at a joke. 'My mother did her best to make life as good for me as she could. But it wasn't easy. Struggle Street is not where I ever wanted to stay. Or go back to. My ex never really got that.'

'You married young. Why?' There hadn't been a lot in the online information about his early years.

He replied without hesitation. 'Fern was pregnant. It was the right thing to do.'

'I thought you didn't have kids?'

'I don't. She lost the baby quite early.'

'That's sad…' Her voice trailed away. *Very* sad. She would not—could not—reveal how very sad the thought made her. How her heart shrank a little every time she thought about having kids.

'The pregnancy was an accident.'

'Not a ploy to force your hand in marriage?' She had always found the 'oldest trick in the book' to be despicable.

'No. We'd been together off and on since my last year of high school. Marriage was the next step. The pregnancy just hurried things along. Looking back on it, though, I can see if she hadn't got pregnant we might not have ended up married. It was right on the cusp, when everything was changing. Things were starting to take off in a big way for the company Dominic and I had started.'

'You didn't try for a baby again?'

'Fern didn't want kids. Felt the planet was already over-populated. That it was irresponsible to have children.'

'And you?' She held her breath for his answer.

During her infrequent forays into dating she'd found the children issue became urgent for thirty-somethings. For women there was the very real fact of declining fertility. And men like her ex thought they had biological clocks too. Craig had worried about being an old dad. He'd been obsessed with being able to play active sports with his kids. Boys, of course, in particular. Having come from a farming family, where boys had been valued more than girls, that had always rankled with her.

Jake's jaw had set and she could see the hard-headed businessman under the charming exterior.

'I've never wanted to have children. My ex and I were in agreement about not wanting kids.'

'What about in the future?'

He shook his head. 'I won't change my mind. I don't want to be a father. *Ever.*'

'I see,' she said, absorbing what he meant. What it meant to her. It was something she didn't want to share with him at this stage. She might be out of here this afternoon and never see him again.

'My support group devoted a lot of time to warnings about women who might try and trap a wealthy, newly single guy into marriage by getting pregnant,' he said.

'Doesn't it take two to get a woman pregnant?'

'The odds can be unfairly stacked when one half of the equation lies about using contraception.'

Eliza pulled a face. 'Those poor old gold-diggers again. I don't know *any* woman I could label as a gold-digger, and we do parties through all echelons of Sydney society. Are there really legions of women ready to trap men into marriage by getting pregnant?'

'I don't know about legions, but they definitely exist. The other guys in that group were proof of that. It can be a real problem for rich men. A baby means lifetime child support—that's a guaranteed income for a certain type of woman.'

'But surely—'

Jake put up a hand at her protest. 'Hear me out. Some of those men were targeted when they were most vulnerable. It's good to be forewarned. I certainly wouldn't want to find myself caught in a trap like that.'

'Well, you don't have to worry about me,' she said. In light of this conversation, she *had* to tell him. 'I can't—'

He put a finger over her mouth. She took it between her teeth and gently nipped it.

'Be assured I don't think of you like that,' he said. 'Your fierce independence is one of the things I like about you.'

'Seriously, Jake. Listen to me. I wouldn't be able to hold you to ransom with a pregnancy because…because…' How she hated admitting to her failure to be able to fulfil a woman's deepest biological purpose. 'I… I can't have children.'

He stilled. 'Eliza, I'm sorry. I didn't know.'

'Of course you didn't know. It's not something I blurt out too often.' She hated to be defined by her infertility. Hated to be pitied. *Poor Eliza—you know she can't have kids?*

'How? Why?'

'I had a ruptured appendix when I was twelve years old. No one took it too seriously at first. They put my tummy pains down to something I ate. Or puberty. But the pain got worse.

By the time they got me to hospital—remember we lived a long way from the nearest town—the appendix had burst and septicaemia had set in.'

Jake took her hand, gripped it tight. 'Eliza, I'm so sorry. Couldn't the doctors have done something?'

'I don't know. I was twelve and very ill. Turned out I was lucky to be alive. Unfortunately no one told me, or my parents, what damage it had done to my reproductive system—the potential for scar tissue on the fallopian tubes. I wasn't aware of the problem until I tried to have a baby and couldn't fall pregnant. Only then was I told that infertility is a not uncommon side effect of a burst appendix.'

He frowned. 'I really don't know what to say.'

'What *can* you say? Don't try. You can see why I don't like to talk about it.'

'You said your ex wanted to start a family? Is that why you split?'

'In part, yes. He was already over thirty and he really wanted to have kids. His *own* kids. Adoption wasn't an option for him. I wanted children too, though probably later rather than sooner. I never thought I wouldn't be able to have a baby. I always believed I would be a mother. And one day a grandmother. Even a great-grandmother. I'll miss out on all of that.'

'I'm sorry, Eliza,' he said again.

She couldn't admit to him—to anyone—her deep, underlying sense of failure as a woman. How she grieved the loss of her dream of being a mother, which had died when the truth of her infertility had been forced into her face with the results of scans and X-rays.

'They don't test you until after a year of unsuccessfully trying to get pregnant,' she said. 'Then the tests take a while. My ex couldn't deal with it. By that stage he thought he'd invested enough time in me.'

Jake spat out a number of choice names for her ex. Eliza didn't contradict him.

'By that stage he'd proved what a dreadful, controlling man he was and I was glad to be rid of him. Still, my sense of failure was multiplied by his reaction. He actually used the word "barren" at one stage. How old-fashioned was that?'

'I'd call it worse than that. I'd call it cruel.'

'I guess it was.' One of a long list of casual cruelties he'd inflicted on her.

Eliza hadn't wanted to introduce such a heavy subject into her time with Jake, those memories were best left buried.

'Where did you meet this jerk—your ex, I mean—and not know what he was really like? Online?'

'At work. I told you when I first met you how I started my working life as an accountant at a magazine publishing company. I loved the industry, and jumped at the chance to move into the sales side when it came up. My success there and my finance background gave me a good shot at a publisher's role with another company. He was my boss at the new company.'

'You married the boss?'

'The classic cliché,' she said. 'But what made him a good publisher made him a terrible husband. Now, I don't want to waste another second talking about him. He's in my past and staying there. I moved to a different publishing company—and a promotion—and never looked back. Then when the next magazine I worked on folded—as happens in publishing—Andie, Gemma and I started Party Queens.'

'And became the most in-demand party-planners in Sydney,' he said.

Sometimes it seemed to Eliza as if her brief marriage had never happened. But the wounds Craig had left behind him were still there. She'd been devastated at the doctor's prognosis of infertility caused by damaged fallopian tubes. Craig had only thought about what it meant to *him*. Eliza had realised she couldn't live with his mental abuse. But she still struggled with doubt and distrust when it came to men.

Thank heaven she'd had the sense to insist they signed a pre-nup. He'd had no claim on her pre-marriage apartment, and she'd emerged from the marriage financially unscathed.

'I suppose your "dating after divorce" advice included getting a watertight pre-nup before any future nuptials?' she said. 'I'm here to suggest it's a good idea. To add to all his faults, my ex proved to be an appalling money-manager.'

'Absolutely,' he said. 'That was all tied up with the gold-digger advice.'

Eliza laughed, but she was aware of a bitter edge to her laughter. 'I interrogated all my potential dates to try and gauge if they were controlling bullies like my ex. You're on the lookout for gold-diggers. Are we too wounded by our past experiences just to accept people for what they appear to be?'

Jake's laugh added some welcome levity to the conversation. 'You mean the way you and I have done?' he said.

Eliza thought about that for a long moment. Of course. That was exactly what they'd done. They'd met with no expectation or anticipation.

'Good point,' she conceded with an answering smile. 'We just discovered we liked each other, didn't we? In the old-fashioned boy-meets-girl way. The best man and the bridesmaid.'

'But then had to wait it out until we could pursue the attraction,' he said.

She reached out and placed her hand on his cheek, reassuring herself that he really was there and not one of the dreams she'd had of him after she'd got home from Montovia. 'And here we are.'

When it came to a man, Eliza had never shut down her good sense to this extent. She wasn't looking any further ahead than right here, right now. She'd put caution on the back burner and let her libido rule and she intended to enjoy the unexpected gift of time with this man she'd wanted since she'd first met him.

Jake went to pull her closer. Mmm, they could start all over again… Just then her stomach gave a loud, embarrassing rumble. Eliza wished she could crawl under the sheets and disappear.

But Jake smiled. 'I hear you. My stomach's crying out the same way. It's long past lunchtime.'

As he got up from the bed the sheet fell from him. Naked, he walked around the room with a complete lack of inhibition. He was magnificent. Broad shoulders tapered down to a muscled back and the most perfect male butt, his skin there a few shades lighter than his tan elsewhere. He was just gorgeous. The prototype specimen of the human male. She felt a moment's regret for humanity that his genes weren't going to be passed on to a new generation. That combination of awesome body and amazing brain wouldn't happen too often.

She had nothing to be ashamed of about her own body—she worked out and kept fit. But she suddenly felt self-conscious about being naked and tugged the sheets up over her chest. It was only this morning that she'd encountered him at the airport lounge. She wasn't a one-night stand kind of person. Or hadn't been up until now. *Until Jake.*

He slung on a pale linen robe. 'I'll go check what food there is in the kitchen while you get dressed.'

Eliza remembered their frantic dash into the bedroom a few hours before. 'My bag with my stuff in it—it's still in the car.'

'It's in the dressing room,' said Jake, pointing in the direction of the enormous walk-in closet. 'I went out to the car after you fell asleep. Out like a light and snoring within seconds.'

Eliza gasped. 'I do *not* snore!' *Did* she? It was so long since she'd shared a bed with someone she wouldn't know.

'Heavy breathing, then,' Jake teased. 'Anyway, I brought your bag in and put it in there.'

'Thank you,' said Eliza.

The bathroom was as luxurious as the rest of the house. All natural marble and bold, simple fittings like in an upscale hotel. She quickly showered. Then changed into a vintage-inspired white sundress with a full skirt and wedge-heeled white sandals she'd bought just for the vacation.

Standing in front of the mirror, she ran a brush through

the tangles of her hair. Then scrutinised her face to wipe the smeared mascara from under her eyes. Thank heavens for waterproof—it hadn't developed into panda eyes. She slicked on a glossy pink lipstick.

Until now she hadn't planned on wearing make-up at all this vacation. But hooking up with Jake had changed all that. Suddenly she felt the need to look her most feminine best. She wanted more than a one-night stand. Four days stretched out ahead of her in Port Douglas and she hoped she'd spend all of them with Jake. After that—who knew?

CHAPTER SIX

JAKE WAITED IMPATIENTLY for Eliza to get dressed and join him in the living area. He couldn't believe she was here in his house with him. It was more than he could have hoped for when he'd intercepted her at the airport.

He welcomed the everyday sounds of running taps, closing doors, footsteps tapping on the polished concrete floors. Already Eliza's laughter and her sweet scent had transformed the atmosphere. He'd like to leave that sexy trail of clothing down the hallway in place as a permanent installation.

This house was a prize in a property portfolio that was filled with magnificent houses. But it seemed he had always been alone and unhappy here. There had been many opportunities for infidelity during the waning months of his marriage but he'd never taken them up. He'd always thought of himself as a one-woman man.

That mindset had made him miserable while he'd refused to accept the demise of his marriage. But meeting Eliza, a woman as utterly different from his ex as it was possible to be, had shown him a different possible path. However he hadn't been ready to set foot on that path. Not so soon after the tumult and turmoil that had driven him off the rails to such detriment to his business.

Extricating himself from a marriage gone bad had made him very wary about risking serious involvement again. He'd stayed away from Eliza for that very reason—she did not appear to be a pick-her-up-and-put-her-down kind of woman, and he didn't want to hurt her. Or have his own heart broken. Ultimately, however, he'd been *compelled* to see her again—despite the advice from his divorce support group and his own hard-headed sense of self-preservation.

She'd told him he'd been over-thinking the situation. Too concerned about what *might* happen before they'd even started anything. Then she'd gifted him with this no-strings interlude. *No expectations or promises, no apologies if it didn't work out.* What more could a man ask for?

Eliza had surprised and enthralled him with her warm sensuality and lack of inhibition. He intended to make the most of her four days in Port Douglas. Starting by ensuring that she spent the entire time of her vacation with him.

He sensed Eliza's tentative entry into the room from the kitchen before he even heard her footsteps. He looked up and his breath caught at the sight of her in a white dress that was tight at her waist and then flared to show off her slim figure and shapely legs.

He gave a wolf whistle of appreciation. 'You're looking very babelicious.'

Her eyes narrowed in sensual appraisal as she slowly looked him up and down. 'You don't look too smokin' bad yourself,' she said.

He'd quickly gone into one of the other bathrooms, showered and changed into shorts and a T-shirt.

'Comfortable is my motto,' he said. He dragged at his neck as if at an imaginary necktie. 'I hate getting trussed up in a suit and tie.'

'I don't blame you. I feel sorry for guys in suits, sweltering in the heat of an Australian summer.'

'It's a suit-free zone at *my* company headquarters.' A tech company didn't need to keep corporate dress rules.

'I enjoy fashion,' she said. 'After a childhood spent in jeans and riding boots—mostly hand-me-downs from my brothers—I can't get enough girly clothes.'

'Your dress looks like something from my grandma's wardrobe,' he said. Then slammed his hand against his forehead 'That didn't come out quite as I meant it to. I meant from when my grandma was young.'

'You mean it has a nice vintage vibe?' she said. 'I take that as a compliment. I love retro-inspired fashion.'

'It suits you,' he said. He thought about saying that he preferred her in nothing at all. Decided it was too soon.

She looked around her. 'So this is your vacation house? It's amazing.'

'Not bad, is it?'

The large open-plan rooms, with soaring ceilings, contemporary designer furniture, bold artworks by local artists, were all designed to showcase the view and keep the house cool in the tropical heat of far north Queensland. As well as to withstand the cyclones that lashed at this area of the coast with frequent violence.

'He says, with the modest understatement of a billionaire…' she said.

Jake liked her attitude towards his wealth. He got irritated by people who treated him with awe because of it. Very few people knew the truth about his past. How closely he'd courted disaster. But a mythology had built up around him and Dominic—two boys from nowhere who had burst unheralded into the business world.

He had worked hard, but he acknowledged there had been a certain element of luck to his meteoric success. People referred to him as a genius, but there were other people as smart as he—smarter, even—who could have identified the same need for ground-breaking software. He'd been in the right place at the right time and had been savvy enough to recognise it and act on it—to his and Dominic's advantage. Then he'd had the smarts to employ skilled programmers to get it right. Come to think of it, maybe there *was* a certain genius to that. Especially as he had replicated his early success over and over again.

'I found some gourmet pizzas in the freezer,' he said. 'I shoved a couple of them in the oven. There's salad too.'

'I wondered what smelled so good,' she said. 'Breakfast seems a long time ago.'

'We can eat out for dinner. There are some excellent restaurants in Port Douglas—as you no doubt know.'

'Yes…' she said. Her brow pleated into a frown. 'But I need to check in at my resort. I haven't even called them. They might give my room to someone else.'

'Wouldn't you rather stay here?' he asked.

Her eyes narrowed. 'Is that a trick question?'

'No tricks,' he said. 'It's taken us a long time—years—to get the chance to spend time together. Why waste more time to-ing and fro-ing from a resort to here? This is more private. This is—'

'This is fabulous. Better than any resort. Of course I'd like to stay here. But is it too soon to be—?'

'Over-thinking this?'

'You're throwing my own words right back at me,' she said, with her delightful curving smile.

Her eyes seemed to reflect the colour of the sea in the vista visible through the floor-to-ceiling windows that looked out over the beach to the far reaches of the Pacific Ocean. He didn't think he'd ever met anyone with eyes of such an extraordinary blue. Eyes that showed what she was feeling. Right now he saw wariness and uncertainty.

'I would very much like to have you here with me,' he said. 'But of course it's entirely your choice. If you'd rather be at your resort I can drive you there whenever you want.'

'No! I… I want to be with you.'

'Good,' he said, trying to keep his cool and not show how gratified he was that he would have her all to himself. 'Then stay.'

'There's just one thing,' she said hesitantly. 'I feel a little… uncomfortable about staying here in a house you shared with your ex-wife. I notice there aren't any feminine touches in the bathroom and dressing room. But I—'

'She's never visited here,' he said. 'I bought this house as my escape when things started to get untenable in my marriage. That was not long before I met you at Dominic's wedding.'

'Oh,' she said.

'Does that make you feel better?' he asked.

She nodded. 'Lots better.'

He stepped closer, placed his hands on her shoulders, looked into her eyes. 'You're the only woman who has stayed here. Apart from my mother, who doesn't count as a woman.'

'I'm sure she'd be delighted to know that,' Eliza said, strangling a laugh.

'You know what I mean.' Jake felt more at home with numbers and concepts than words. Especially words evoking emotion and tension.

'Yes. I do. And I'm honoured to be the first.'

He took her in his arms for a long, sweet kiss.

The oven alarm went off with a raucous screech. They jumped apart. Laughed at how nervous they'd seemed.

'Lunch is ready,' he said. He was hungry, but he was tempted to ignore the food and keep on kissing Eliza. Different hungers required prioritising.

But Eliza had taken a step back from him. 'After we eat I need to cancel my resort booking,' she said. 'I'll have to pay for today, of course, but hopefully it will be okay for the other days. Not that I care, really. After all I—'

'I'll pay for any expense the cancellation incurs.'

He knew straight away from her change of expression that he'd made a mistake.

'You will *not* pay anything,' she said. 'That's my responsibility.'

Jake backed down straight away, put up his hands as if fending off attack. That was one argument he had no intention of pursuing. He would make it up to her in other ways—make sure she didn't need to spend another cent during her stay. He would organise everything.

'Right. I understand. My credit cards will remain firmly in my wallet unless you give me permission to wield them.'

She pulled a rueful face. 'Sorry if I overreacted. My independence is very important to me. I get a bit prickly when it's threatened. I run my own business and my own life. That's how I like it. And I don't want to ever have to answer to anyone again—for money or anything else.'

'Because of your ex-husband? You described him as controlling.'

'To be honest, he's turned me off the entire concept of marriage. And before him I had a domineering father who thought he had the right to rule my life even after I grew up.'

Jake placed his hand on her arm. 'Hold it right there. Don't take offence—I want to hear more. But right now I need food.' His snack on the plane seemed a long time ago.

She laughed. 'I grew up with three brothers. I know the rules. Number one being never to stand between a hungry man and his lunch.'

Jake grinned his relief at her reply. 'You're right. The pizza will burn, and I'm too hungry to wait to heat up more.'

'There are *more*?'

'The housekeeper has stocked the freezer with my favourite foods. She doesn't live in. I like my privacy too much for that. But she shops for me as well as keeps the house in order.'

'Unlimited pizza? Sounds good to me.'

From the look of her slim body, her toned muscles, he doubted Eliza indulged in pizza too often. But at his height and activity level he needed to eat a lot. There had been times when he was a kid he'd been hungry. Usually the day before his mother's payday, when she'd stretched their food as far as it would go. That would never happen again.

He headed for the oven. 'Over lunch I want to hear about that country upbringing of yours,' he said. 'I grew up here in Queensland, down on the Gold Coast. Inland Australia has always interested me.'

'Trust me, it was *not* idyllic. Farming is tough, hard work. A business like any other. Only with more variables out of the farmer's control.'

She followed him through the kitchen to the dining area, again with a view of the sea. 'I was about to offer to set the table,' she said. 'But I see you've beaten me to it.'

'I'm domesticated. My mother made sure of that. A single mum working long hours to keep a roof over our heads couldn't afford to have me pulling less than my weight,' he said.

That was when he'd chosen to *be* at home, of course. For a moment Jake wondered what Eliza would think of him if he revealed the whole story of his youth. She seemed so moralistic, he wondered if she could handle the truth about him. Not that he had any intention of telling her. There was nothing he'd told her already that couldn't be dug up on an online search—and she'd already admitted to such a search. The single mum. The hard times. His rise to riches in spite of a tough start. The untold story was in a sealed file never to be opened.

'It must have been tough for her. Your mother, I mean.'

'It was,' he said shortly. 'One of the good things about having money is that I can make sure she never has to worry again.' As a teenager he'd been the cause of most of her worries. As an adult he tried to make it up to her.

'So your mother lets you take care of her?'

'I don't give her much of a choice. I owe her so much and I will do everything I can to repay her. I convinced her to let me buy her a house and a business.'

'What kind of business did you buy for her?'

Of course Eliza would be interested in that. She was a hard-headed businesswoman herself.

'She worked as a waitress for years. Always wanted her own restaurant—thought she could do it better. Her café in one of the most fashionable parts of Brisbane is doing very well.' Again, this was nothing an online search wouldn't be able to find.

'There's obviously a family instinct for business,' she said.

He noted she didn't ask about his father, and he didn't volunteer the information.

'There could be something in that,' he said. 'She's on vacation in Tuscany at the moment—doing a residential Italian cooking course and having a ball.'

Eliza smiled. 'Not just a vacation. Sounds like it's work as well.'

'Isn't that the best type of work? Where the line between work and interest isn't drawn too rigidly?'

'Absolutely,' she said. 'I always enjoyed my jobs in publishing. But Party Queens is my passion. I couldn't imagine doing anything else now.'

'From what I hear Party Queens is so successful you never will.'

'Fingers crossed,' she said. 'I never take anything for granted, and I have to be constantly vigilant that we don't slip down from our success.'

She seated herself at the table, facing the view. He swooped the pizza onto the table with an exaggerated flourish, like he'd seen one of his mother's waiters do. 'Lunch is served, *signorina,*' he said.

Eliza laughed. 'You're quite the professional.'

'A professional heater-upper of pizza?'

'It isn't burned, and the cheese is all bubbly and perfect. You can take credit for *that*.'

Jake sat down opposite her. He wolfed down three large slices of pizza in the time it took Eliza to eat one. 'Now, tell me about life on the sheep ranch,' he said. And was surprised when her face stilled and all laughter fled from her expression.

Eliza sighed as she looked across the table at Jake. Her appetite for pizza had suddenly deserted her. 'Are you sure you want to hear about that?'

Did she want to relive it all for a man who might turn out to be just a fling? He'd told her something of the childhood that must have shaped the fascinating man he had become. But it was nothing she didn't already know. She really didn't like revisiting *her* childhood and adolescence. Not that it had been abusive, or anything near it. But she had been desperately unhappy and had escaped from home as soon as she could.

'Yes,' he said. 'I want to know more about you, Eliza.'

His gaze was intense on her face. She didn't know him well enough to know what was genuine interest and what was part of a cultivated image of charm.

'Can I give you the short, sharp, abbreviated version?' she said.

'Go ahead,' he said, obviously bemused.

She took a deep, steadying breath. 'How about city girl at heart is trapped in a rural backwater where boys are valued more than girls?'

'It's a start.'

'You want more?'

He nodded.

'Okay…smart girl with ambition has hopes ridiculed.'

'Getting there,' he said. 'What's next?'

'Smart girl escapes to city and family never forgives her.'

'Why was that?' He frowned.

She knew there was danger now—of her voice getting wobbly. 'No easy answer. How about massive years-long drought ruins everything?' She took in another deep breath. 'It's actually difficult to make light of such disaster.'

'I can see that,' he said.

She wished he'd say there was no need to go on, but he didn't.

'Have you ever seen those images of previously lush green pastures baked brown and hard and cracked? Where farmers have to shoot their stock because there's no water, no feed? Shoot sheep that have not only been bred on your land so you care about their welfare, but also represent income and investment and your family's daily existence?'

'Yes. I've seen the pictures. Read the stories. It's terrible.'

'That was my family's story. Thankfully my father didn't lose his land or his life, like others did, before the rains eventually came. But he changed. Became harsher. Less forgiving. Impossible to live with. He took it out on my mother. And nothing *I* could do was right.'

Jake's head was tilted in what seemed like real interest. 'In what way?'

'Even at the best of times life in the country tends to be more traditional. Men are outdoors, doing the hard yakka—do you have that expression for hard work in Queensland?'

'Of course,' he said.

'Men are outside and women inside, doing the household chores to support the men. In physical terms it makes a lot of sense. And a lot of country folk like it just the way it's always been.'

'But you didn't?'

'No. School was where I excelled—maths and legal studies were my forte. My domestic skills weren't highly developed. I just wasn't that interested. And I wasn't great at farm work either, though I tried.' She flexed her right arm so her bicep showed, defined and firm. 'I'm strong, but not anywhere near as strong as my brothers. In my father's eyes I was useless. He wouldn't even let me help with the accounts; that was not my business. In a time of drought I was another mouth to feed and I didn't pull my weight.'

She could see she'd shocked Jake.

'Surely your father wouldn't really have thought that?' he said.

She remembered he'd grown up without a father.

'I wanted to be a lawyer. My father thought lawyers were a waste of space. My education was a drain on the farm. Looking back, I can see now how desperate he must have been. If he'd tried to communicate with me I might have understood. But he just walked all over me—as usual.'

'Seems like I've got you to open a can of worms. I'm sorry.'

She shrugged. 'You might as well hear the end of it. I was at boarding school. One day when I was seventeen I was called to the principal's office to find my father there to take me home so I could help my mother. For good. It was my final year of high school. I wasn't to be allowed to sit my end-of-school exams.'

Jake frowned. 'You're right—your dad must have been desperate. If there was no money to feed stock, school fees would have been out of the question.'

'For *me*. Not for my younger brother. My father found the fees for *him*.' She couldn't keep the bitterness from her voice. 'A boy who was never happier than when he was goofing off.'

'So the country girl went home? Is that how the story ended?'

She shook her head. 'Thankfully, no. I was a straight-A student—the school captain.'

'Why does that not surprise me?' said Jake wryly.

'The school got behind me. There was a scholarship fund. My family were able to plead hardship. I got to sit my final exams.'

'And blitzed them, no doubt?'

'Top of the state in three out of five subjects.'

'Your father must have been proud of you then.'

'If he was, he never said so. I'd humiliated him with the scholarship, and by refusing to go home with him.'

'Hardly a humiliation. Half of the eastern states were in one of the most severe droughts in Australia's history. Even *I* knew that at the time.'

'Try telling *him* that. He'd call it pride. I'd call it pig-headed stubbornness. The only thing that brought me and my father together was horses. We both loved them. I was on my first horse before I was two years old. The day our horses had to go was pretty well the end of any real communication between me and my father.'

There was real sympathy in his green eyes. 'You didn't have to shoot—?'

'We were lucky. A wonderful horse rescue charity took them to a different part of the state that wasn't suffering as much. The loss hit my father really hard.'

'And you too?'

She bowed her head. 'Yes.'

Jake was quiet for a long moment before he spoke again. 'You don't have to talk about this any more if you don't want to. I didn't realise how painful it would be for you.'

'S'okay,' she said. 'I might as well gallop to the finish.' She picked up her fork, put it down again, twisted a paper serviette between her fingers. 'Country girl wins scholarship to university in Sydney to study business degree. Leaves home, abandoning mother to her menfolk and a miserable marriage. No one happy about it but country girl…' Her voice trailed away.

Jake got up from the table and came to her side. He leaned down from behind her and wrapped big, strong muscular arms around her. 'Country girl makes good in the big city. That's a happy ending to the story.'

'I guess it is,' she said, leaning back against him, enjoying his strength and warmth, appreciating the way he was comforting her. 'My life now is just the way I want it.'

Except she couldn't have a baby. Underpinning it all was the one area of her life she'd been unable to control, where the body she kept so healthy and strong had let her down so badly.

She twisted around to look up at him. 'And Day One of my vacation is going perfectly.'

'So how about Days Two, Three and Four?' he said. 'If you were by yourself at your resort what would you be doing?'

'Relaxing. Lying by the pool.'

'We can do that here.'

'Swimming?'

'The pool awaits,' he said, gesturing to the amazing wet-edge pool outside the window, its aquamarine water glistening in the afternoon sunlight.

'That water is calling to me,' she said, twisting herself up and out of the chair so she stood in the circle of his arms, looking up at him. She splayed her hands against his chest, still revelling in the fact she could touch him.

For these few days he was hers.

His eyes narrowed. 'I'm just getting to know you, Eliza. But I suspect there's a list you want to check off before you fly home—you might even have scheduled some activities in to your days.'

'List? Schedules?' she said, pretending to look around her. 'Have you been talking to Andie? She always teases me about the way I order my day.'

'I'm not admitting to anything,' he said. 'So there *is* a list?'

'We-e-ell…' She drew out the word. 'There *are* a few things I'd like to do. But only if you want to do them as well.'

'Fire away,' he said.

'One: go snorkelling on the Great Barrier Reef. Two: play golf on one of the fabulous courses up here. Then—'

Jake put up one large, well-shaped hand in a halt sign. 'Just wait there. Did I hear you say "play golf"?'

'Uh, yes. But you don't have to, of course. I enjoy golf. When I was in magazine advertising sales it was a very useful game to play. I signed a number of lucrative deals after a round with senior decision-makers.'

He lifted her up and swooped her around the room. 'Golf! The girl plays *golf*. One of my favourite sports.'

'You being a senior decision-maker and all,' she said with a smile.

'Me being a guy who likes to swing a club and slam a little white ball,' he said.

'In my case a neon pink ball. I can see it better on the fairway,' she said.

'She plays with a pink ball? Of *course* she does. Are you the perfect woman, Eliza Dunne?' He sounded more amused than mocking. 'I like snorkelling and diving too. Port Douglas is the right place to come for that. All can be arranged. Do you want to start checking off your list with a swim?'

'You bet.'

He looked deep into her face. Eliza thrilled to the message in his green eyes.

'The pool is very private. Swimsuits are optional.'

Eliza smiled—a long, slow smile of anticipation. 'Sounds very good to me.'

CHAPTER SEVEN

ELIZA SOON REALISED that a vacation in the company of a billionaire was very different from the vacation she had planned to spend on her own. Her own schedule of playing tourist and enjoying some quiet treatments in her resort spa had completely gone by the board.

That was okay, but she hadn't had any time to plan her strategy to keep the company thriving without the hands-on involvement of Gemma, Crown Princess of Montovia—and that worried her. Of course Princess Gemma's name on the Party Queens masthead brought kudos by the bucketload—and big-spending clients they might otherwise have struggled to attract. However, Gemma's incredible skills with food were sorely missed. Party Queens was all Eliza had in terms of income and interest. She needed to give the problem her full attention.

But Jake was proving the most enthralling of distractions.

She had stopped insisting on paying for her share of the activities he had scheduled for her. Much as she valued her independence, she simply couldn't afford a vacation Jake-style. Her wish to go snorkelling on the Great Barrier Reef had been granted—just her and Jake on a privately chartered glass-bottom boat. Their games of golf had been eighteen holes on an exclusive private course with a waiting list for membership. Dinner was at secluded tables in booked-out restaurants.

Not that she was complaining at her sudden elevation in lifestyle, but there was a nagging feeling that she had again allowed herself to be taken over by a man. A charming man, yes, but controlling in his own quietly determined way.

When she'd protested Jake had said he was treating her, and wanted to make her vacation memorable. It would have seemed churlish to disagree. Just being with him was memorable enough—there was no doubt he was fabulous company. But she felt he was only letting her see the Jake he wanted her to see—which was frustrating. It was almost as if there were two different people: pre-divorce Jake and after-divorce Jake. After she'd spilled about her childhood, about her fears for the business, she'd expected some reciprocal confidences. There had been none but the most superficial.

On the afternoon of Day Four, after a long walk along the beach followed by a climb up the steep drive back home, Eliza was glad to dive into Jake's wet-edge pool. He did the same.

After swimming a few laps she rested back against him in the water, his arms around her as they both kicked occasionally to keep afloat. The water was the perfect temperature, and the last sunlight of the day filtered through the palm trees. Tropical birds flew around the trees, squawking among themselves as they settled for the evening. In the distance was the muted sound of the waves breaking on the beach below.

'This is utter bliss,' she said. 'My definition of heaven.'

The joy in her surroundings, in *him*, was bittersweet as it was about to end—but she couldn't share that thought with Jake. *This was just a four-day fling.*

'In that case you must be an angel who's flown down to keep me company,' he said.

'That's very poetic of you,' she said, twisting her head to see his face.

He grinned. 'I have my creative moments,' he replied as he dropped a kiss on her forehead.

It was a casual kiss she knew didn't mean anything other than to signify their ease with the very satisfying physical side of this vacation interlude.

'I could see *you* with a magnificent set of angel man wings, sprouting from your shoulder blades,' she said. 'White, tipped with gold.' *And no clothes at all.*

'All the better to fly you away with me,' he said. 'You must have wings too.'

'Blue and silver, I think,' she mused.

She enjoyed their light-hearted banter. After three days with him she didn't expect anything deeper or more meaningful. He was charming, fun, and she enjoyed being with him.

But he wasn't the Jake Marlowe who had so intrigued her with hints of hidden depths when she'd first met him. That Jake Marlowe had been as elusive as the last fleeting strains of the Strauss waltz lilting through the corridor as she had fled that ballroom in Montovia. She wondered if he had really existed outside her imagination. Had she been so smitten with his fallen angel looks that she'd thought there was more there for her than physical attraction?

'We did an angel-themed party a few months ago,' she said. 'That's what made me think about the wings.'

'You feasted on angel food cake, no doubt?'

'A magnificent celestial-themed supper was served,' she said. 'Star-shaped cookies, rainbow cupcakes, cloud-shaped meringues. Gemma planned it all from Montovia and Andie made sure it happened.'

The angel party had worked brilliantly. The next party, when Gemma had been too caught up with her royal duties to participate fully in the planning, hadn't had quite the same edge. Four days of vacation on, and Eliza was still no closer to finding a solution to the lack of Gemma's hands-on presence in the day-to-day running of the company. Party Queens was heading to crisis point.

'Clever Gemma,' said Jake. 'Tristan told me she's shaken up all the stodgy traditional menus served at the castle.'

'I believe she has,' Eliza said. 'She's instigated cooking programmes in schools, too. They're calling her the people's princess, she told me. Gemma's delighted.'

'No more than Tristan is delighted with Gemma.'

Gemma and Tristan had found true love. Whereas *she* had found just a diverting interlude with Jake. After the royal wedding both Gemma and Andie had expressed high hopes for romance between the best man and the bridesmaid. Eliza had denied any interest. But deep in Eliza's most secret heart she'd entertained the thought too. She couldn't help a sense of regret that it so obviously wasn't going to happen.

Idly, Eliza swished her toes around in the water. 'They call these wet-edge pools infinity pools, don't they? Because they stretch out without seeming to end?'

'That's right,' he said.

'In some way these four days of my vacation seemed to have gone on for ever. In another they've flown. Only this evening left.'

'Can you extend your break? By another day, perhaps?'

She shook her head. 'There's still the Gemma problem to solve. And there are some big winter parties lined up for the months ahead. I have back-to-back appointments for the day after I get back. Some of which took me weeks to line up.'

'That's what happens when you run a successful business,' he said.

'As you know only too well,' she said. Party Queens was insignificant on the corporate scale compared to *his* company.

'I'd have trouble squeezing in another day here, too,' Jake said. 'I'm out of the country a lot these days. Next week I fly to Minnesota in the United States, to meet with Walter Burton on a joint venture between him and Dominic in which I'm involved. My clients are all around the world. I'll be in Bangalore in India the following week. Singapore the week after that.'

'Are you ever home?' Her voice rose.

'Not often, these days. My absences were a bone of contention with my ex. She was probably right when she said that I didn't give her enough time.'

Eliza paused. 'It doesn't sound like you have any more time now.'

Jake took a beat to answer. 'Are you any different? Seems to me you're as career-orientated as I am. How much room does Party Queens leave for a man in your life?'

'Not much,' she admitted. She felt bad that she had fielded so many phone calls while she'd been with him. But being a party planner wasn't a nine-to-five weekday-only enterprise. 'The business comes first, last and in between.'

It could be different! she screamed silently. *For the right man.* But was she being honest with herself? Could Jake be the right man?

'Seems to me we're both wedded to our careers,' he said slowly. 'To the detriment of anything else.'

'That's not true,' she said immediately. Then thought about it. 'Maybe. If neither of us can spare another day to spend here together when it's been so perfect.'

'That tells *me* something,' he said, his voice guarded.

Eliza swallowed hard against the truth of his words. The loss of *what might have been* hurt.

'It could be for the best,' she said, trying to sound matter of fact, but inwardly weeping over a lost opportunity.

She didn't know him any better than on Day One. His body, yes. His heart and soul—no. Disappointment stabbed deep that Jake hadn't turned out to be the man she'd expected him to be when he'd been whirling her around that fairytale ballroom.

Why had she ever hoped for more? When she thought about it, the whole thing with Jake hadn't seemed quite real. From the moonlit terrace in Montovia to the way he'd intercepted her at the airport and whisked her away to this awesome house perched high above the beach, it had all had an element of fantasy.

Jake held her for a long moment without replying. She could feel the thudding of his heart against her back. The water almost stilled around them, with only the occasional slap against the tiled walls of the pool. She had a heart-stopping feeling he was saying goodbye.

Finally he released her, then swam around her so he faced her, with her back to the edge of the pool. His hair was dark with water and slick to his head. Drops of water glistened on the smooth olive of his skin. Her heart contracted painfully at how handsome he looked. At how much she wanted him.

But although they got on so well, both in bed and out of it, it was all on the surface. Sex and fun. Nothing deeper had developed. She needed something more profound. She also needed a man who cared enough to make time to see her—and she him.

'Do you really think so?' he asked.

'Sometimes things are only meant to be for a certain length of time,' she said slowly. 'You can ruin them by wanting more.'

Jake's heart pounded as he looked down into Eliza's face. She'd pushed her wet hair back from her face, showing the perfect structure of her cheekbones, the full impact of her eyes. Water from the pool had dripped down over her shoulders to settle in drops on the swell of her breasts. The reality of Eliza in a bikini had way exceeded his early fantasies.

Eliza was everything he'd hoped she'd be and more. She was an extraordinary woman. They were compatible both in bed and out. They even enjoyed the same sports. But she'd been more damaged by her divorce than he had imagined. Not to mention by the tragedy of her inability to have a baby.

The entire time he'd felt he had to tread carefully around her, keeping the conversation on neutral topics, never digging too deep. For all her warmth and laughter and seeming openness, he sensed a prickly barrier around her. And then there was her insistence on answering her phone at all but their most intimate of moments. Eliza seemed so determined to keep her independence—there appeared little room for compromise. And if there was one lesson he'd learned from his marriage it was that compromise was required when two strong personalities came together as a couple.

She was no more ready for a serious relationship than he was.

Day Four was practically done and dusted—and so, it seemed, was his nascent relationship with Eliza.

And yet… He couldn't tolerate the thought of this being a final goodbye. There was still something about her that made him want to know more.

'We could catch up again some time, when we find ourselves in each other's cities,' he said.

'Absolutely.'

She said it with an obviously forced enthusiasm that speared through him.

'I'd like that.'

She placed her hand on his cheek, cool from the water, looked into his eyes. It felt ominously like a farewell.

'Jake, I'm so glad we did this.'

He had to clear his throat to speak. 'Me too,' he managed to choke out. There was a long pause during which the air seemed heavy with words unsaid before he spoke again. 'We have mutual friends. One day we might get the chance to take up where we left off.'

'Yes,' she said. 'That would be nice.'

Nice? Had all that passion and promise dwindled to *nice?*

Maybe that was what happened in this brave new world of newly single dating. Jake couldn't help a nagging sense of doubt that it should end like this. Had they missed a step somewhere?

'Jake, about our mutual friends…?' she said.

'Yes?' he said.

'I didn't tell them I'd met you here. Can Dominic be discreet?'

'He doesn't know we caught up with each other either.'

'Shall we keep it secret from them?' she asked. 'It would be easier.'

'As far as they're concerned we went our separate ways in Port Douglas,' he said.

He doubted Dominic would be surprised to hear it had turned out that way. He had warned Jake that, fond as he was of Eliza, she could be 'a tough little cookie'. Jake had thought there was so much more to her than that. Perhaps Dominic had been right.

'That's settled, then,' she said. There was an air of finality to her words.

Eliza swam to the wide, shallow steps of the pool, waded halfway up them, then turned back. Her petite body packed a powerfully sexy punch in her black bikini. High, firm breasts, a flat tummy and narrow waist flaring into rounded hips and a perfectly curved behind. Perhaps he'd read too much into this episode. *It was just physical—nothing more.* A fantasy fulfilled.

'I need to finish packing,' she said. 'Then I can enjoy our final dinner without worrying.'

That was it? 'Eliza, don't go just yet. I want to tell you—'

She paused, turned back to face him. Their gazes met for a long moment in the dying light of the day. Time seemed to stand still.

'I've booked a very good restaurant,' he said.

'I'll… I'll look forward to it,' she said. She took the final step out of the pool. 'Don't forget I have an early start in the morning.'

'I'll be ready to drive you to Cairns,' he said.

He dreaded taking that journey in reverse with her, when the journey here from the airport had been so full of promise and simmering sensuality. Tomorrow's journey would no doubt be followed by a stilted farewell at the airport.

'That's so good of you to offer,' she said with excess politeness. 'But I didn't cancel my return shuttle bus trip. It would be easier all round if we said goodbye here tomorrow morning.'

'You're sure, Eliza?' He made a token protest.

'Absolutely sure,' she said, heading towards the house without a backward glance.

Jake watched her, his hands fisted by his sides. He fancied blue angel wings unfurling as she prepared to fly right out of his life.

It was stupid of him ever to have thought things with Eliza could end any other way.

CHAPTER EIGHT

TEN WEEKS LATER Eliza sat alone in her car, parked on a street in an inner western suburb of Sydney, too shaken even to think about driving away from an appointment that had rocked her world. She clutched her keys in her hand, too unsteady to get the key into the ignition.

Eliza hated surprises. She liked to keep her life under control, with schedules and timetables and plans. Surprises had derailed her life on more than one occasion. Most notably the revelation that her burst appendix had left her infertile. But in this case the derailment was one that had charged her with sheer bubbling joy in one way and deep, churning anxiety in the other.

She was pregnant.

'It would take a miracle for you to get pregnant.'

Those had been her doctor's words when Eliza had told her of her list of symptoms. Words that had petered out into shock at the sight of a positive pregnancy test.

That miracle had happened in Port Douglas, with Jake—most likely the one time there had been a slip with their protection. Eliza hadn't worried. After all, she couldn't get pregnant.

Seemed she could.

And she had.

She laid her hand on her tummy, still flat and firm. But

there was a tiny new life growing in there. *A baby.* She could hardly believe it was true, still marvelled at the miracle. But she had seen it.

Not *it*.

Him or her.

The doctor had wanted an ultrasound examination to make absolutely sure there wasn't an ectopic pregnancy in the damaged tube.

Active—like me, had been Eliza's first joyous thought when she'd seen the image of her tiny baby, turning cartwheels safe and sound inside her womb. Her second thought had been of loneliness and regret that there was no one there to share the miraculous moment with her. But she wanted this more than she had ever wanted anything in her life.

Her baby.

Eliza realised her cheeks were wet with tears. Fiercely, she scrubbed at her eyes.

Her third thought after the initial disbelief and shock had been to call Jake and tell him. There was absolutely no doubt he was the father.

His baby.

But how could she? He'd made it very clear he didn't *ever* want to be a father.

Dear heaven, she couldn't tell him.

He would think she was one of the dollar signs flashing gold-diggers he so despised. What had he said?

'A baby means lifetime child support—that's a guaranteed income for a certain type of woman.'

She dreaded the scorn in his eyes if she told him.

You know I told you I couldn't have a baby? Turns out I'm pregnant. You're going to be a daddy.

And what if he wanted her not to go forward with the pregnancy? No way—ever—would that be an option for her.

How on earth had this happened?

'Nature can be very persistent,' her doctor had explained.

'The tube we thought was blocked must not have been completely blocked. Or it unblocked itself.'

It really was a miracle—and one she hugged to herself.

She was not daunted by the thought of bringing the baby up by herself. Not that she believed it would be easy. But she owned her own home—a small terraced house in Alexandria, not far from the converted warehouse that housed the Party Queens headquarters. And Party Queens was still doing well financially, thanks to her sound management and the talent and drive of her business partners. And a creative new head chef was working out well. The nature of the business meant her hours could be flexible. Andie had often brought baby Hugo in when he was tiny, and did so even now, when he was a toddler. Eliza could afford childcare when needed—perhaps a nanny. Though she was determined to raise her child herself, with minimal help from nannies and childminders.

Her impossible dream had come true. *She was going to be a mother.* But the situation with her baby's father was more of a nightmare.

Eliza rested her head on her folded arms on top of the steering wheel, slumped with despair. *Pregnant from a four-night stand.* By a man she hadn't heard from since he'd walked her down the steep driveway that led away from his tropical hideaway and waved her goodbye.

Now he'd think she'd tried to trap him.

'I certainly wouldn't want to find myself caught in a trap like that,' he'd said, with a look of horror on his handsome face.

Eliza raised her head up off her folded arms. Took a few deep, steadying breaths. She wouldn't tell Jake. Nor would she tell her best friends about her pregnancy. Not yet. Not when both their husbands were friends with Jake.

If her tummy was this flat now, hopefully she wouldn't show for some time yet. Maybe she could fudge the dates. Or say the baby had been conceived by donor and IVF. The fact that Jake lived in Brisbane would become an advantage once she couldn't hide her pregnancy any longer. He wouldn't have to see her and her burgeoning bump.

But what if the baby looked like Jake? People close to Jake, like Andie and Dominic, would surely twig to the truth. *What if...what if...what if?* She covered her ears with her hands, as if to silence the questions roiling in her brain. But to no effect.

Was it fair *not* to tell him he was going to be a father? If she didn't make any demands on him surely he wouldn't believe she was a gold-digger? Maybe he would want to play some role in the baby's life. She wouldn't fight him if he did. It would be better for the baby. The baby who would become a child, a teenager, a person. A person with the right to know about his or her father.

It was all too much for her to deal with. She put her hand to her forehead, then over her mouth, suddenly feeling clammy and nauseous again.

The sickness had been relentless—so had the bone-deep exhaustion. She hadn't recognised them as symptoms of pregnancy. Why would she when she'd believed herself to be infertile?

Instead she had been worried she might have some terrible disease. Even when her breasts had started to become sensitive she had blamed it on a possible hormonal disturbance. She'd believed she couldn't conceive right up until the doctor's astonished words: *'You're pregnant.'*

But why would Jake—primed by both his own experience with women with flashing dollar signs in their eyes and the warnings of what sounded like a rabid divorce support group—believe her?

She was definitely in this on her own.

Eliza knew she would feel better if she could start making plans for her future as a single mother. Then she would feel more in control. But right now she had to track down the nearest bathroom. No wonder she had actually lost weight rather than put it on, with this morning, noon and night sickness that was plaguing her.

Party Queens was organising a party to be held in two weeks' time—the official launch of a new business venture of Dominic's in which Jake held a stake. No doubt she would see him there. But she would be officially on duty and could make their contact minimal. Though it would be difficult to deal with. And not just because of her pregnancy. She still sometimes woke in the night, realising she had been dreaming about Jake and full of regrets that it hadn't worked out between them.

CHAPTER NINE

THE NEARER JAKE got to Dominic's house in Sydney for the launch party, the drier his mouth and the more clammy his hands on the wheel of the European sports car he kept garaged there. Twelve weeks since he'd seen Eliza and he found himself feeling as edgy as an adolescent. Counting down the minutes until he saw her again.

The traffic lights stayed on red for too long and he drummed his fingers impatiently on the steering wheel.

For most of the time since their four-day fling in Port Douglas he'd been out of the country. *But she'd rarely been out of his mind.* Jake didn't like admitting to failure—but he'd failed dismally at forgetting her. From the get-go he'd had trouble accepting the finality of their fling.

The driveway up to his house in Port Douglas had never seemed so steep as that morning when he had trudged back up it after waving Eliza off on the shuttle bus. He'd pushed open his door to quiet and emptiness and a sudden, piercing regret. Her laughter had seemed to dance still on the air of the house.

No matter how much he'd told himself he was cool about the way his time had gone with her, he hadn't been able to help but think that by protecting himself he had talked himself out of something that might have been special. Cheated himself of the chance to be with a woman who might only come along once in a lifetime.

He'd had no contact with her at all since that morning, even though Party Queens were organising this evening's launch party. Dominic had done all the liaising with the party planners. Of course he had—he was married to the Design Director.

By the time he reached Dominic's house, Jake was decidedly on edge. He sensed Eliza's presence as soon as he was ushered through the door of Dominic's impressive mansion in the waterfront suburb of Vaucluse. Was it her scent? Or was it that his instincts were so attuned to Eliza they homed in on her even within a crowd? He heard the soft chime of her laughter even before he saw her. Excitement and anticipation stirred. Just seeing Eliza from a distance was enough to set his heart racing.

He stood at a distance after he'd found her, deep in conversation with a female journalist he recognised. This particular journalist had been the one to label Dominic—one of the most generous men Jake had ever known—with the title of 'Millionaire Miser'.

Andie and Party Queens had organised a party on Christmas Day two years ago that had dispelled *that* reputation. Planning that party was how Andie had met Dominic. And a week after Christmas Dominic had arranged a surprise wedding for Andie. Jake had flown down from Brisbane to be best man, and that wedding was where he'd met Eliza for the first time.

Jake looked through the wall of French doors that opened out from the ballroom of Dominic's grand Art Deco house to the lit-up garden and swimming pool beyond. He remembered his first sight of Eliza, exquisite in a flowing pale blue bridesmaid's dress, white flowers twisted through her dark hair. She had laughed up at him as they'd shared in the conspiracy of it all: the bride had had no idea of her own upcoming nuptials.

Jake had been mesmerised by Eliza's extraordinary blue eyes, captivated by her personality. They had chatted the whole way through the reception. He'd been separated from Fern at that stage, but still trying to revive something that had been long dead. Not wanting to admit defeat. Eliza had helped him see how pointless that was—helped him to see hope for a new future just by being Eliza.

Now she wasn't aware that he was there, and he watched her as she chatted to the journalist, her face animated, her smile at the ready. She was so lovely—and not just in looks. He couldn't think of another person whose company he enjoyed more than Eliza's. *Why had he let her go?*

He couldn't bear it if he didn't get some kind of second chance with her. He'd tried to rid himself of the notion that he was a one-woman man. After all, a billionaire bachelor was spoiled for choice. He didn't have to hunt around to find available woman—they found *him*. Theoretically, he could date a string of them—live up to his media reputation. Since Port Douglas he'd gone out with a few women, both in Australia and on his business travels. Not one had captured his interest. None had come anywhere near Eliza.

Tonight she looked every inch the professional, but with a quirky touch to the way she was dressed that was perfectly appropriate to her career as a party planner. She wore a full-skirted black dress, with long, tight, sheer sleeves, and high-heeled black stilettos. Her hair was twisted up behind her head and finished with a flat black velvet bow. What had she called her style? Retro-inspired? He would call the way she dressed 'ladylike'. But she was as smart and as business-savvy as any guy in a suit and necktie.

Did she feel the intensity of his gaze on her? She turned around, caught his eye. Jake smiled and nodded a greeting, not wanting to interrupt her conversation. He was shocked by her reaction. Initially a flash of delight lightened her face, only to be quickly replaced by wariness and then a conscious schooling of her features into polite indifference.

Jake felt as if he had been kicked in the gut. *Why?* They'd parted on good terms. He'd even thought he'd seen a hint of tears glistening in her eyes as she'd boarded the shuttle bus in Port Douglas. They'd both been aware that having mutual friends would mean they'd bump into each other at some stage. She must have known he would be here tonight—he was part of the proceedings.

He strode towards her, determined to find out what was going on. Dismissing him, she turned back to face the journalist. Jake paused mid-stride, astounded at her abruptness. Then it twigged. Eliza didn't want this particular newshound sniffing around for an exclusive featuring the billionaire bachelor and the party planner.

Jake changed direction to head over to the bar.

He kept a subtle eye on Eliza. As soon as she was free he headed towards her, wanting to get her attention before anyone else beat him to it.

'Hello,' he said, for all the world as if they weren't anything other than acquaintances with mutual friends. He dropped a kiss on her cool, politely offered cheek.

'Jake,' Eliza said.

This was Eliza the Business Director of Party Queens speaking. Not Eliza the lover, who had been so wonderfully responsive in his arms. Not Eliza his golfing buddy from Port Douglas, nor Eliza his bikini-clad companion frolicking in the pool.

'So good that you could make it down from Brisbane,' the Business Director said. 'This is a momentous occasion.'

'Indeed,' he said.

Momentous because it was the first time they'd seen each other after their four-day fling? More likely she meant it was momentous because it was to mark the occasion not only of the first major deal of Dominic's joint venture with the American billionaire philanthropist Walter Burton, but also the setting up the Sydney branch of Dominic's charity, The Underground Help Centre, for homeless young people.

'Walter Burton is here from Minnesota,' Eliza said. 'I believe you visited with him recently.'

'He flew in this morning,' he said.

Jake had every right to be talking to Eliza. He was one of the principals of the deal they were celebrating tonight. Party Queens was actually in *his* employ.

However, when that pushy journalist's eyes narrowed with interest and her steps slowed as she walked by him and Eliza, Jake remembered she'd been in Montovia to report on the royal wedding. As best man and bridesmaid, he and Eliza had featured in a number of photo shoots and articles. If it was rumoured they'd had an affair—and that was all it had been—it would be big tabloid news.

He gritted his teeth. There was something odd here. Something else. Eliza's reticence could not be put down just to the journalist's presence.

Jake leaned down to murmur in her ear, breathed in her now familiar scent, sweet and intoxicating. 'It's good to see you. I'd like to catch up while I'm in Sydney.'

Eliza took a step back from him. 'Sorry—not possible,' she said. She gave an ineffectual wave to indicate the room, now starting to fill up with people. The action seemed extraordinarily lacking in Eliza's usual energy. 'This party is one of several that are taking up all my time.'

So what had changed? Work had always seemed to come first with Eliza. Whereas *he* was beginning to see it shouldn't. That there should be a better balance to life.

'I understand,' he said. But he didn't. 'What about after the party? Catch up for coffee at my apartment at the wharf?' He owned a penthouse apartment in a prestigious warehouse conversion right on the harbour in inner eastern Sydney.

Eliza's lashes fluttered and she couldn't meet his eyes. 'I'm sorry,' she said again. 'I… I'm not in the mood for company.'

Jake was too flabbergasted to say anything. He eventually found the words. 'You mean not in the mood for *me*?'

She lifted her chin, looked up at him. For once he couldn't

read the expression in those incredible blue eyes. Defiance? Regret? *Fear?* It both puzzled and worried him.

'Jake, we agreed to four days only.'

The sentence sounded disconcertingly well-rehearsed. A shard of pain stabbed him at her tone.

'We left open an option to meet again, did we not?' He asked the question, but he thought he could predict the answer.

She put her hand on her heart and then indicated him in an open-palmed gesture that would normally have indicated togetherness. 'Me. You. We tried it. It…it didn't work.'

The slight stumble on her words alerted him to a shadow of what looked like despair flitting across her face. *What was going on?*

'I don't get it.' Jake was noted for his perseverance. He wouldn't give up on Eliza easily.

A spark of the feisty Eliza he knew—or thought he knew—flashed through.

'Do I have to analyse it? Isn't it enough that I just don't want to be with you again?'

He didn't believe her. Not when he remembered her unguarded expression when she'd first noticed him this evening. There was something not right here.

Or was he being arrogant in his disbelief that Eliza simply didn't want him in her life? That the four days had proved he wasn't what she wanted? Was he falling back into his old ways? Unable to accept that a woman he wanted no longer wanted *him*? That wanting to persevere with Eliza was the same kind of blind stubbornness that had made him hang on to a marriage in its death throes—to the ultimate misery of both him and his ex-wife? Not to mention the plummeting profit margins of his company—thankfully now restored.

'Is there someone else?' he asked.

A quick flash of something in her eyes made him pay close attention to her answer.

'Someone else? No. Not really.'

'What do you mean "not really"?'

'Bad choice of words. There's no other man.'

He scrutinised her face. Noticed how pale she looked, with dark shadows under her eyes and a new gauntness to her cheekbones. Her lipstick was a red slash against her pallor. More colour seemed to leach from her face as she spoke.

'Jake. There's no point in going over this. It's over between us. Thank you for understanding.' She suddenly snatched her hand to her mouth. 'I'm afraid I have to go.'

Without another word she rushed away, heading out of the ballroom and towards the double arching stairway that was a feature of the house.

Jake was left staring after her. Dumbfounded. Stricken with a sudden aching sense of loss.

He knew he had to pull himself together as he saw Walter Burton heading for him. He pasted a smile on his face. Extended his hand in greeting.

The older man, with his silver hair and perceptive pale eyes, pumped his hand vigorously. 'Good to see you, Jake. I'm having fun here, listening to people complain that it's cold for June. Winter in Sydney is a joke. I'm telling them they don't know what winter is until they visit Minnesota in February.'

'Of course,' Jake said.

He was trying to give Walter his full attention, but half his mind was on Eliza as he looked over the heads of the people who now surrounded him, nodded vaguely at guests he recognised. *Where had she gone?*

Walter's eyes narrowed. 'Lady trouble?' he observed.

'Not really,' Jake said. He didn't try to deny that Eliza was his lady. Dominic and Andie had had to stage a fake engagement because of this older man's moral stance. He found himself wishing Eliza really was his lady, with an intensity that hurt so much he nearly doubled over.

'Don't worry, son, it'll pass over,' Walter said. 'They get that way in the first months. You know…a bit erratic. It gets better.'

Jake stared at him. 'What do you mean?'

'When a woman's expecting she—'

Jake put up his hand. 'Whoa. I don't know where you're going with this, Walter. Expecting? Not Eliza. She…she can't have children.' And Eliza certainly didn't *look* pregnant in that gorgeous black dress.

'Consider me wrong, then. But I've had six kids and twice as many grandkids.' Walter patted his rather large nose with his index finger. 'I've got an instinct for when a woman's expecting. Sometimes I've known before she was even aware herself. I'd put money on it that your little lady is in the family way. I'm sorry for jumping the gun if she hasn't told you yet.'

Reeling, Jake managed to change the subject. But Walter's words kept dripping through his mind like the most corrosive of acids.

Had she tricked him? His fists clenched by his sides. Eliza? A scheming gold-digger? Trying to trap him with the oldest trick in the book? She had sounded so convincing when she'd told him about the burst appendix and her subsequent infertility. Was it all a lie? If so, what else had she lied about?

He felt as if everything he'd believed in was falling away from him.

Then he was hit by another, equally distressing thought. If she wasn't pregnant, was she ill?

One thing was for sure—she was hiding something from him. And he wouldn't be flying back to Brisbane until he found out what it was.

CHAPTER TEN

JAKE USUALLY NEVER had trouble sleeping. But late on the night of the launch party, back in his waterfront apartment, he tossed and turned. The place was luxurious, but lonely. He'd had high hopes of bringing Eliza back here this evening. To talk, to try and come to some arrangement so he could see more of her. If they'd ended up in bed that would have been good too. He hadn't been with anyone else since her. Had recoiled from kissing the women he'd dated.

Thoughts of his disastrous encounter with her kept him awake for what seemed like most of the night. And then there was Walter's observation to nag at him. Finally, at dawn, he gave up on sleep and went for a run. Vigorous physical activity helped his thought processes, he'd always found.

In the chill of early morning he ran up past the imposing Victorian buildings of the New South Wales Art Gallery and through the public green space of The Domain.

He paused to do some stretches at the end of the peninsula at Mrs Macquarie's Chair—a bench cut into a sandstone slab where it was reputed a homesick early governor's wife had used to sit and watch for sailing ships coming from Great Britain. The peaceful spot gave a panoramic view of Sydney Harbour: the 'coat hanger' bridge and the white sails of the Opera

House. Stray clouds drifting around the buildings were tinted pink from the rising sun.

Jake liked Sydney and thought he could happily live in this city. Brisbane seemed all about the past. In fact he was thinking about moving his company's headquarters here. He had wanted to talk to Eliza about that, to put forward the idea that such a move would mean he'd be able to see more of her if they started things up between them again. Not much point now.

The pragmatic businessman side of Jake told him to wipe his hands of her and walk away. Eliza had made it very clear she didn't want him around. A man who had graduated from a dating after divorce workshop would know to take it on the chin, cut his losses and move on. After all, they'd only been together for four days, three months ago.

But the more creative, intuitive side of him, which had guided him through decisions that had made him multiple millions, wouldn't let him off that easily. Even if she'd lied to him, tricked him, deceived him—and that was only a suspicion at this stage—he had a strong feeling that she needed him. And he needed to find out what was going on.

He'd never got a chance to chat with her again at the party—she had evaded him and he'd had official duties to perform. But he'd cancelled his flight back to Brisbane, determined to confront her today.

Jake ran back home, showered, changed, ate breakfast. Predictably, Eliza didn't reply to his text and her phone went to voicemail. He called the Party Queens headquarters to be told Eliza was working at home today. Okay, so he would visit her at home—and soon.

He hadn't been to Eliza's house before, but he knew where it was. Investment-wise, she'd been canny. She'd bought a worker's terraced cottage in an industrial area of the inner city just before a major push to its gentrification. The little house, attached on both sides, looked immaculately restored and maintained. Exactly what he'd expect from Eliza.

It sat on one level, with a dormer window in the roof, indicating that she had probably converted the attic. External walls were painted the colour of natural sandstone, with windows and woodwork picked out in white and shades of grey. The tiny front garden was closed off from the sidewalk by a black wrought-iron fence and a low, perfectly clipped hedge.

Jake pushed open the shiny black gate and followed the black-and-white-tiled path. He smiled at the sight of the front door, painted a bold glossy red to match the large red planter containing a spiky-leaved plant. Using the quaint pewter knocker shaped like a dragonfly, he rapped on the door.

He heard footsteps he recognised as Eliza's approaching the door. They paused while, he assumed, she checked out her visitor through the peephole. Good. He was glad she was cautious about opening her door to strangers.

The pause went on for rather too long. Was she going to ignore him? He would stay here all day if he had to. He went to rap again but, with his hand still on its knocker, the door opened and she was there.

Jake didn't often find himself disconcerted to the point of speechlessness. But he was too shocked to greet her.

This was an Eliza he hadn't seen before: hair dishevelled, face pale and strained with smudges of last night's make-up under her eyes. But what shocked him most was her body. Dark grey yoga pants and a snug pale grey top did nothing to disguise the small but definite baby bump. Her belly was swollen and rounded.

Eliza's shoulders slumped, and when she looked up at him her eyes seemed weary and dulled by defeat. In colour more denim than sapphire.

She took a deep breath and the rising of her chest showed him that her breasts were larger too. The dress she'd worn the previous night had hidden everything.

'Yes, I'm pregnant. Yes, it's yours. No, I won't be making any claims on you.'

Jake didn't mean to blurt out his doubt so baldly, but out it came. 'I thought you couldn't conceive.'

'So did I. That I'm expecting a baby came as a total surprise.' She gestured for him to follow her. 'Come in. Please. This isn't the kind of conversation I want to have in the street.'

The cottage had been gutted and redesigned into an open usable space, all polished floors and white walls. It opened out through a living area, delineated by carefully placed furniture, to a kitchen and eating area. Two black cats lay curled asleep on a bean bag, oblivious to the fact that Eliza had company. At the back, through a wall of folding glass doors, he saw a small courtyard with paving and greenery. A staircase—more sculpture than steps—led up to another floor. The house was furnished in a simple contemporary style, with carefully placed paintings and ornaments that at another time Jake might have paused to examine.

'I need to sit down,' Eliza said, lowering herself onto the modular sofa, pushing a cushion behind her back, sighing her relief.

'Are you okay?' Jake asked, unable to keep the concern from his voice. A sudden urge to protect her pulsed through him. But it was as if there was an invisible barrier flashing *Don't Touch* around her. The dynamic between them was so different it was as if they were strangers again. He hated the feeling. Somehow he'd lost any connection he'd had with her, without realising how or why.

She gave that same ineffectual wave she'd made the night before. It was as if she were operating at half-speed—like an appliance running low on battery. 'Sit down. Please. You towering over me is making me feel dizzy.'

She placed her hand on her bump in a protective gesture he found both alien and strangely moving.

He sat down on the sofa opposite her. 'Morning sickness?' he asked warily. He wasn't sure how much detail he'd get in reply. And he was squeamish about illness and female things—very squeamish.

'I wish,' she said. 'It's non-stop nausea like I couldn't have imagined. All day. All night.' She closed her eyes for a moment and shook her head before opening them again. 'I feel utterly drained.'

Jake frowned. 'That doesn't sound right. Have you seen your doctor?'

'She says some women suffer more than others and nausea is a normal part of pregnancy. Though it's got much worse since I last saw the doctor.' She grimaced. 'But it's worth it. Anything is worth it. I never thought I could have a baby.'

'So what happened? I mean, how—?'

She linked her hands together on her lap. 'I can see doubt in your eyes, Jake. I didn't lie to you. I genuinely believed I was infertile. Sterile. Barren. All those things my ex called me, as if it was my fault. But I'm not going to pretend I'm anything but thrilled to be having this baby. I… I don't expect you to be.'

Jake had believed in Eliza's honesty and integrity. She had sounded so convincing when she'd told him about her ruptured appendix and the damage it had caused. Her personal tragedy. And yet suddenly she was pregnant. Could a man be blamed for wanting an explanation?

'So what happened to allow—?' He couldn't find a word that didn't sound either clinical or uncomfortably personal.

'My doctor described it as a miracle. Said that a microscopic-sized channel clear in a sea of scar tissue must have enabled it to happen. I can hardly believe it myself.' A hint of a wan smile tilted the corners of her mouth. 'Though the nausea never allows me to forget.'

'Are you sure—?'

She leaned forward. 'Sure I'm pregnant? Absolutely. Up until my tummy popped out it was hard to believe.' She stilled. Pressed her lips together so hard they became colourless. 'You didn't mean that, did you? You meant am I sure the baby is yours.'

Her eyes clouded with hurt. Jake knew he had said inextricably the wrong thing. Though it seemed reasonable for him to want to be sure. He *still* thought it was reasonable to ask. They'd had a four-day fling and he hadn't heard a word from her since.

'I didn't mean—'

Her face crumpled. 'Yes, you did. For the record, I'll tell you there was no one else. There had been no one else for a long time and has been no one since. But feel free to ask for a DNA test if you want proof.'

He moved towards her. 'Eliza, I—'

Abruptly she got up from the sofa. Backed away from him. 'Don't come near me. Don't touch me. Don't quote your dating after divorce handbook that no doubt instructs you about the first question to ask of a scheming gold-digger trying to trap you.'

'Eliza, I'm sorry. I—'

She shrugged with a nonchalance he knew was an absolute sham.

'You didn't know me well at Port Douglas,' she said. 'I could have bedded a hundred guys over the crucial time for conception for all you knew. It's probably a question many men would feel justified in asking under the circumstances. But not *you* of *me*. Not after I'd been straightforward with you. Not when we have close friends in common. A relationship might not have worked for us. But I thought there was mutual respect.'

'There was. There is. Of course you're upset. Let me—'

'I'm not *upset*. I'm *disappointed*, if anything. Disappointed in *you*. Again, for the record, I will not ask anything of you. Not money. Not support. Certainly not your name on the birth certificate. I am quite capable of doing this on my own. *Happy* to do this on my own. I have it all planned and completely under control. You can just walk out that door and forget you ever knew me.'

Jake had no intention of leaving. If indeed this baby was his—and he had no real reason to doubt her—he would not evade his responsibilities. But before he had a chance to say anything further Eliza groaned.

'Oh, no. Not again.'

She slapped her hand over her mouth, pushed past him and ran towards the end of the house and, he assumed, the bathroom.

He waited for what seemed like a long time for her to do what she so obviously had to do. Until it began to seem too long. Worried, he strode through the living room to find her. That nagging sense that she needed him grew until it consumed him.

'Eliza! Answer me!' he called, his voice raw with urgency.

'I… I'm okay.' Her voice, half its usual volume, half its usual clarity, came from behind a door to his left.

The door slowly opened. Eliza put one foot in front of the other in an exaggerated way to walk unsteadily out. She clutched the doorframe for support.

Jake sucked in a breath of shock at how ashen and weak she looked. Beads of perspiration stood out on her forehead. He might not be a doctor, but every instinct told him this was not right. 'Eliza. Let me help you.'

'You…you're still here?' she said. 'I told you to leave.'

'I'm not going anywhere.'

'There…there's blood.' Her voice caught. 'There shouldn't be blood. I… I don't know what to do. Can you call Andie for me, please?'

Jake felt gutted that he was right there and yet not the first person she'd sought to help her.

She wanted him gone.

No way was he leaving her.

He took her elbow to steady her. She leaned into him and he was stunned at how thin she'd become since he'd last held her in his arms. Pregnant women were meant to put *on* weight, not lose it. *Something was very wrong.*

Fear grabbed his gut. He mustn't let her sense it. Panic would make it worse. She felt so fragile, as if she might break if he held her too hard. Gently he lifted her and carried her to a nearby chair. She moaned as he settled her into it.

She cradled her head in her hands. 'Headache. Now I've got a headache.' Her voice broke into a sob.

Jake realised she was as terrified as he was. He pulled out his phone.

'Call Andie…' Her voice trailed away as she slumped into the chair.

He supported her with his body as he started to punch out a number with fingers that shook. 'I'm not calling Andie. I'm calling an ambulance,' he said, his voice rough with fear.

CHAPTER ELEVEN

WHEN ELIZA WOKE up in a hospital bed later that day, the first thing she saw was Jake sprawled in a chair near her bed. He was way too tall for the small chair and his long, blue-jeans-clad legs were flung out in front of him. His head was tilted back, his eyes closed. His hair looked as if he'd combed it through with his hands and his black T-shirt was crumpled.

She gazed at him for a long moment. Had a man ever looked so good? Her heart seemed to skip a beat. Last time she had seen him asleep he had been beside her in his bed at Port Douglas on Day Three. She had awoken him with a trail of hungry little kisses that had delighted him. Now here he was in a visitor's chair in a hospital room. She was pregnant and he had doubts that the baby was his. How had it come to this?

Eliza had only vague memories of the ambulance trip to the hospital. She'd been drifting in and out of consciousness. What she did remember was Jake by her side. Holding her hand the entire time. Murmuring a constant litany of reassurance. *Being there for her.*

She shifted in the bed. A tube had been inserted in the back of her left hand and she was attached to a drip. Automatically her hand went to her tummy. She was still getting used to the new curve where it had always been flat.

Jake opened his eyes, sat forward in his chair. 'You're awake.' His voice was underscored with relief.

'So are you. I thought you were asleep.' Her voice felt croaky, her throat a little sore.

He got up and stood by her bed, looked down to where her hand remained on her tummy. The concern on his face seemed very real.

'I don't know what you remember about this morning,' he said. 'But the baby is okay. *You're* okay.'

'I remember the doctor telling me. Thank heaven. And seeing the ultrasound. I couldn't have borne it if—'

'You'd ruptured a blood vessel. The baby was never at risk.'

She closed her eyes, opened them again. 'I felt so dreadful. I thought I must be dying. And I was so worried for the baby.'

'Severe dehydration was the problem,' he said.

She felt at a disadvantage, with him towering so tall above her. 'I can see how that happened. I hadn't even been able to keep water down. The nausea was so overwhelming. It's still there, but nothing like as bad.'

'Not your everyday morning sickness, according to your doctor here. An extreme form known as *Hyperemesis gravidarum*. Same thing that put the Duchess of Cambridge in hospital with her pregnancies, so a nurse told me.'

He sounded both knowledgeable and concerned. Jake here with her? The billionaire bachelor acting nurse? How had this happened?

'A lot of the day is a blur,' she said. 'But I remember the doctor telling me that. No wonder I felt so bad.'

'You picked up once the doctors got you on intravenous fluids.'

She raised her left wrist and looked up at the clear plastic bag hooked over a stand above. 'I'm still on them, by the looks of it.'

'You have to stay on the drip for twenty-four hours. They said you need vitamins and nutrients as well as fluids.'

Eliza reeled at the thought of Jake conversing with the doctors, discussing her care. It seemed surreal that he should be here, like this. 'How do you know all this? In fact, how come you're in my room?' Eliza didn't want to sound ungrateful. But she had asked him to leave her house. Though it was just as well he hadn't, as it had turned out.

'I admitted you to the hospital. They asked about my relationship to you. I told them I was your partner and the father of the baby. On those terms, it's quite okay for me to be in your room.'

'Oh,' she said. She slumped back on the pillows. Their conversation of this morning came flooding back. How devastated she'd felt when he'd asked if she sure he was the father. 'Even though you don't actually think the baby is yours?' she said dully.

He set his jaw. 'I never said that. I believed you couldn't get pregnant. You brushed me off at the party. Didn't tell me anything—refused to see me. Then I discovered you were pregnant. It's reasonable I would have been confused as to the truth. Would want to be sure.'

'Perhaps,' she conceded.

It hurt that his first reaction had been distrust. But she had no right to feel a sense of betrayal—they'd had a no-strings fling. They'd been lovers with no commitment whatsoever. And he was a man who had made it very clear he never wanted children.

'I believe you when you say the baby is mine, Eliza. It's unexpected. A shock. But I have no reason to doubt you.'

Eliza was so relieved at his words she didn't know what to say and had to think about her response. 'I swear you *are* the father. I would never deceive you about something so important.'

'Even about the hundred other men?' he said, with a hint of a smile for the first time.

She managed a tentative smile in return. 'There was only ever you.'

'I believe you,' he said.

'You don't want DNA testing to be certain? Because I—'

'No,' he said. 'Your word is enough.'

Eliza nodded, too overcome to say anything. She knew how he felt about mercenary gold-diggers. But the sincerity in his eyes assured her that he no longer put her in that category. If, indeed, he ever had. Perhaps she had been over-sensitive. But that didn't change the fact that he didn't want to be a father.

'I don't want to be a father—ever.'

How different this could have been in a different universe—where they were a couple, had planned the child, met the result of her pregnancy test with mutual joy. But that was as much a fantasy as those frozen in time moments of him whirling her around in a waltz, when the future had still been full of possibilities for Eliza and Jake.

Now here he was by her bedside, acting the concerned friend. She shouldn't read anything else into his care of her. Jake had only done for her what he would have done for any other woman he'd found ill and alone.

Eliza felt a physical ache at how much she still wanted him. She wondered—not for the first time—if she would *ever* be able to turn off her attraction to him. But physical attraction wasn't enough—no matter how good the sex. A domineering workaholic, hardly ever in the same country as her, was scarcely the man she would have chosen as the father of her child. Though his genes were good.

'Thank you for calling the ambulance and checking me in to the hospital,' she said. 'And thank you for staying with me. But can I ask you one more thing, please?' *Before we say goodbye.*

'Of course,' he said.

'Can you ask the hospital staff to fix their mistake with my room?' She looked around her. The room was more like a luxurious hotel suite than a hospital room. 'I'm not insured for a private room. They'll need to move me to a shared ward.'

'There's been no mistake,' he said. 'I've taken responsibility for paying your account.'

Eliza stared at him. '*What?* You can't do that,' she said.

'As far as the hospital is concerned I am the baby's father. I pay the bills.'

Eliza gasped. This wasn't right. She needed to keep control over her pregnancy and everything involved with it. 'That was a nice gesture, but I can't possibly accept your offer,' she said.

'You don't have a choice,' he said. 'It's already done.'

Eliza had never felt more helpless, lying in a hospital bed tied up to a drip and monitors. It wasn't a feeling she was used to. 'Jake, please don't make me argue over this.' She was feeling less nauseous, but she'd been told she had to avoid stress and worry as well as keep up fluids and nourishment. 'What happened to you keeping your credit cards in your wallet when it comes to me?'

'You can't have it both ways, Eliza. You want me to acknowledge paternity? That means I take financial responsibility for your care. It's not negotiable.'

This was the controlling side of Jake that had made her wary of him for more than a no-strings fling. 'You don't make decisions for me, Jake. I will not—'

At that moment a nurse came into the room to check on Eliza's drip and to take her temperature and blood pressure. Jake stepped back from the bed and leaned against the wall to let the nurse get on with what she needed to do.

'She's looking so much better now than when you brought her in,' the nurse said.

'Thankfully,' said Jake. 'I was very worried about her.'

Eliza fumed. The nurse was addressing Jake and talking about her as if she was some inanimate object. 'Yes, I *am* feeling much better,' she said pointedly to the nurse. But Jake's smile let her know he knew exactly what was going on—and found it amusing. Which only made Eliza fume more.

'That's what we want to hear,' said the nurse with a cheerful smile, seemingly oblivious to the undercurrents.

She was no doubt well meaning, but Eliza felt she had to

assert herself. It was *her* health. *Her* baby. Under *her* control. 'When can I go home?' Eliza asked.

The nurse checked her chart. 'You have to be on the intravenous drip for a total of twenty-four hours.'

'So I can go home tomorrow morning?'

'If the doctor assesses you as fit to be discharged. Of course you can't leave by yourself, and there has to be someone at home to care for you.'

'That's okay,' said Jake, before Eliza could say anything. 'I'll be taking her home and looking after her.'

The nurse smiled. 'That's settled, then.'

'No, it's not. I—' Eliza protested.

'Thank you,' said Jake to the nurse.

Eliza waited until the nurse had left the room. 'What was that about?' she hissed.

Jake moved back beside her bed. 'I'll be picking you up when you're discharged from hospital tomorrow. We can talk about whether you'd like me to stay with you for a few days or whether I organise a nurse.'

She had to tilt her head back to confront him. 'Or how about I look after myself?' she said.

'That's not an option,' said Jake. 'Unless you want to stay longer in hospital. *Hyperemesis gravidarum* is serious. You have to keep the nausea under control and get enough nourishment for both your health and your baby's sake. You know all this. The doctor has told you that you're still weak.'

'That doesn't mean *you* have to take over, Jake.'

Eliza felt she was losing control of the situation and she didn't like it one bit. At the same time she didn't want to do anything to risk harming the baby.

'You have another choice,' he said. 'You could move in with Andie. She's offered to have you to stay with her and Dominic.'

'You've spoken to Andie? But she doesn't know—'

'That you're pregnant? She does now. You asked me to call her this morning. So I did while you were asleep.'

'What did she say?' Andie would not appreciate being left out of the loop.

'She was shocked to find out you and I had had an affair and you'd kept it from her. And more than a little hurt that you didn't take her into your confidence about your pregnancy.'

'I would have, but I didn't want her telling…'

'Telling me?'

'That's right.'

'If I'd flown back to Brisbane this morning instead of coming to see you would you have *ever* told me?' His mouth was set in a grim line.

'I wasn't thinking that far ahead. I just didn't want you to think I was trying to trap you into something you didn't want. You were so vehement about gold-diggers. I… I couldn't bear the thought of seeing disgust in your eyes when you looked at me.'

'You will *never* see disgust in my eyes when it comes to you, Eliza,' he said. 'Disbelief that you would try to hide this from me, but not disgust. We have mutual friends. I would have heard sooner or later.'

'I would rather it had been later. I didn't want you trying to talk me out of it.'

The look of shock on his face told her she might have said the wrong thing.

'I would never have done that,' he said.

She realised how out-of-the-blue her situation had been for him. And how well he was handling it.

'I wasn't to know,' she said. 'After all, we hardly know each other.'

For a long moment Jake looked into her face—searching for what she didn't know.

Finally he spoke. 'That's true. But there should be no antagonism between us. Here isn't the time or the place to discuss how we'll deal with the situation on an ongoing basis.' He glanced down at his watch. 'Andie will be here to visit you soon. I'm going to go. I'll see you in the morning.'

Eliza's feelings were all over the place. She didn't know whether she could blame hormones for the tumult of her emotions. No way did she want Jake—or any other man—controlling her, telling her what to do with her life. But she had felt so safe and comforted with him by her side today. Because while her pregnancy had changed the focus of everything, it didn't change the attraction she'd felt for Jake from the get-go. He had been wonderful to her today. She wished she could beg him to stay.

'Before you leave, let me thank you again for your help today, Jake. I can't tell you how much I appreciate you being with me.'

'You're welcome,' he said. 'I'm just glad you're okay. And so glad I called by to your house this morning.'

She sat up straighter in an attempt to bring him closer. Put out her hand and placed it on his arm. 'I'm sorry,' she said. 'Not sorry about the baby—my miracle baby. But sorry our carefree fling had such consequences and that we've been flung back together again in such an awkward situation.'

'No need to apologise for that,' he said gruffly.

Jake kept up the brave front until he was out of the hospital and on the pavement. He felt totally strung out from the events of the last day. Everything had happened so quickly. He needed time to think it through and process it.

Thank heaven he hadn't encountered Andie on the way out. He'd liked Andie from the moment Dominic had first introduced him to her, on the day of their surprise wedding. Each time he met his friend's wife he liked her more. Not in a romantic way—although she was undoubtedly gorgeous. He liked the way Andie made his best friend so happy after the rotten hand life had dealt Dominic when it came to love. If Jake had had a sister, he would have wanted her to be just like Andie.

But Andie told it how it was. And Eliza was her dearest

friend, whom she would defend with every weapon at hand. Jake wouldn't have appreciated a face-to-face confrontation with her on the steps of the hospital. Not when he was feeling so on edge. Not after the conversation he'd already had with her on the phone.

When he'd called to tell her Eliza was in hospital Andie been shocked to hear the reason. Shocked and yet thrilled for Eliza, as she knew how much her friend had wanted to have children but had thought she couldn't conceive.

'This is a miracle for her!' Andie had exclaimed, and had promptly started to sob on the phone. Which had been further proof—not that he'd needed it—that Eliza had not been lying. Then, in true sisterly fashion, Andie had hit Jake with some advice. Advice he hadn't thought he'd needed but he'd shut up and listened.

'Don't you hurt her, Jake,' she'd said, her voice still thick with tears. 'I had no idea you two had had a...a thing. Eliza is Party Queens family. *You're* family. She thinks she's so strong and independent, but this pregnancy will make her vulnerable. She's not some casual hook-up girl. You can't just write a cheque and walk away.'

'It's not like that—' he'd started to protest. But the harsh truth of it, put into words, had hit him like blows to the gut.

Eliza was connected to his life through his best friends, Dominic and Tristan, and their wives. He could argue all he liked that their fling had been a mutually convenient scratching of the itch of their attraction. But that sounded so disrespectful to Eliza. In his heart he knew he'd wanted much more time with her. Which was why he had been considering a move to Sydney. But Eliza's pregnancy had put everything on a very different footing.

Andie had continued. 'Oh, what the heck? This is none of my business. You're a big boy. *You* figure out what Eliza needs. And give it to her in spades.'

Jake was beginning to see what Eliza needed. And also what

he needed. He'd never been so scared than when she'd passed out on the chair while they were waiting for the ambulance to arrive. In a moment of stricken terror he'd thought he was going to lose her. And it had hit him with the power of a sledgehammer hurtling towards his head how much she had come to mean to him—as a friend as well as a lover. Suddenly a life without Eliza in it in some way had become untenable.

But the phone call with Andie wasn't what had him still staggering, as if that sledgehammer really had connected. It was the baby.

First he'd been hit with the reality of absorbing the fact that Eliza was expecting a baby—and the realisation that it had irrevocably changed things between them. Then he'd been stricken by seeing Eliza so frighteningly ill. But all that had been eclipsed by the events at the hospital.

Once the medical team had stabilised Eliza with fluids—she'd been conscious enough to refuse any anti-nausea medication—they'd wheeled her down, with him in attendance, to have an ultrasound to check that all was well with her developing foetus.

The technician had covered Eliza's bump with a jelly—cold, and it had made her squeal—and then pressed an electronic wand over her bump. The device had emitted high-frequency soundwaves that had formed an image when they'd come into contact with the embryo.

Up until the moment when the screen had come alive with the image, the pregnancy had been an abstract thing to Jake. Even—if he were to be really honest with himself—an *inconvenient* thing. But there on the screen had appeared a *baby.* Only about six centimetres at this stage, the radiographer had explained, but a totally recognisable baby. With hands and feet and a *face.*

To the palpable relief of everyone in the room, a strong and steady amplified heartbeat had been clearly audible. The baby had been moving around and showing no signs of being affected by Eliza's inability to keep down so very little food over the last weeks. It had looked as if it was having a ball, floating in the amniotic fluid, secure in Eliza's womb.

Jake had felt as if his heart had stopped beating, and his lungs had gone into arrest as, mesmerised, he'd watched that image. He was a man who never cried but he'd felt tears of awe and amazement threatening to betray him. He hadn't been able to look at Eliza—the sheer joy shining from her face would have tipped him over. Without seeming to be aware she was doing it, she had reached for his hand and gripped it hard. All he'd been able to do was squeeze it back.

This was a real baby. A child. A *person.* Against all odds he and Eliza had created a new life.

What he had to do had become very clear.

CHAPTER TWELVE

THE NEXT DAY Eliza was surprised at how weak she still felt as Jake helped her up the narrow, steep stairs to her bedroom in the converted attic of her house. She usually bounded up them.

'Just lean on me,' he said.

'I don't want to lean on anyone,' she said, more crossly than she had intended.

Forcing herself to keep her distance from this gorgeous man was stressful. Even feeling weak and fatigued, she still fancied him like crazy. But way back in Port Douglas she'd already decided that wasn't enough. Just because she was pregnant it didn't change things.

'Sometimes you have to, Eliza.'

She knew he wasn't only referring to her taking the physical support his broad shoulders offered.

'You can't get through this on your own.'

There was an edge of impatience to his voice she hadn't heard before. Looking after her the way he'd done yesterday, and now today, wasn't part of their four-day fling agreement. That had been about uncomplicated fun and uninhibited sex. Now he must feel he was stuck with her when she was unwell. He couldn't be more wrong. She didn't need his help.

'I appreciate your concern, truly I do,' she said. 'You've been so good to me. But I'm not on my own. I have friends. My GP is only a block away. I spoke to her yesterday after you left the hospital. Both she and the practice nurse can make home visits if required.'

'You need to be looked after,' he said stubbornly.

Eliza's heart sank as she foresaw them clashing over this. She had been perturbed at how Jake had taken over her vacation—how much more perturbing was the thought that he might take over her life?

Eliza reached the top of the stairs. Took the few steps required to take her to her bed and sat down on the edge with a sigh of relief.

'I'd prefer to look after myself,' she said. 'I'm quite capable of it, you know.'

'It didn't look that way to me yesterday.' He swore under his breath. 'Eliza, what might have happened if I hadn't got here when I did? What if you'd passed out on the bathroom floor? Hit your head on the way down?'

She paused for a long moment. 'It's a very scary thought. I will never be able to thank you enough for being there for me, Jake. Why *did* you come to my house when you did?'

'The obvious. I didn't get why you blanked me at the party and I wanted an explanation.'

Her chin lifted. 'Why did you feel you were owed an explanation? We had a fling. I didn't want to pick up from where we left off. Enough said.'

'Now you're pregnant. That makes it very different. From where I stand, it doesn't seem like you're doing a very good job of looking after yourself.'

Her hackles rose. 'This is all very new to me. It's a steep learning curve.' Eliza took a deep, calming breath. She couldn't let herself get too defensive. Not when Jake had pretty much had to pick her up from the floor.

'There's a lot at stake if you don't learn more quickly,' he said.

She gritted her teeth. 'Don't you think I *know* that? While

I was lying there in that hospital bed I kept wondering how I had let myself get into that state.'

'I suspect you thought the sickness was a natural part of pregnancy. That you had to put up with the nausea. Perhaps if you'd told your friends you were pregnant they might have seen what you were going through wasn't normal and that you were headed into a danger zone.'

Eliza wasn't sure whether he was being sympathetic or delivering a reprimand. 'When did you get to know so much?' she said, deciding to err on the side of offered sympathy. The direction of where this conversation was beginning to go scared her. It almost sounded as though it might lead into an accusation that she was an incompetent mother—before she'd even give birth.

'Since yesterday, when the hospital doctor explained it,' he said with a shrug of his broad shoulders. 'I learned more than I ever thought I'd need to know about that particular complication.'

How many men would have just dropped her at the hospital and run? She was grateful to Jake—but she did *not* want him to take over.

'I've learned a lot too,' she said. 'If I keep on top of the nausea, and don't let myself get dehydrated, that shouldn't happen again. I admit this has given me a real shock. I had no reason to think I wouldn't fly through pregnancy with my usual good health. But the doctors have given me strategies to deal with it. Including more time in the hospital on a drip if required. I'll be okay.'

He shook his head. 'I wish I could believe that. But I suspect you'll be back at Party Queens, dragging a drip on its stand along behind you, before you know it.'

That forced a reluctant smile from her. But he wasn't smiling and her smile quickly faded. He was spot-on in his assessment of her workaholic tendencies. Though she didn't appreciate his lack of faith in her ability to look after herself.

'Jake, trust me—I won't over-extend myself. Miracles don't

come along too often in a person's life.' She placed her hand protectively on her bump. 'Truth is, this is almost certainly my only chance to have a baby. I won't jeopardise anything by being foolish. Believe me—if I need help, I'll ask for it.'

Asking for help didn't come easily to her. Because with accepting help came loss of control. One of her biggest issues in management training had been learning to delegate. Now it looked as if she might have to learn to give over a degree of control in her private life too. To doctors, nurses, other health professionals. Because she had to consider her baby as well as herself. But she would not give control over to a man.

For a converted attic in a small house, the bedroom was spacious, with an en suite shower room and a study nook as well as sleeping quarters. But Jake was so tall, so broad-shouldered, he made the space seem suddenly cramped.

How she wished things could be different. Despite all that had happened desire shimmered through her when she feasted her eyes on him, impossibly handsome in black jeans and a black T-shirt. Jake, here in her bedroom, was looking totally smokin'.

Then there was her—with lank hair, yesterday's clothes, a big wad of sterile gauze taped to the back of her hand where the drip had been, and a plastic hospital ID band still around her wrist. Oh, and pregnant.

Jake paced the length of the room and back several times, to the point when Eliza started to get nervous without really knowing why. He stood in front of the window for a long moment with his back to her. Then pivoted on his heel to turn back to face her.

'We have to get married,' he said, without preamble.

Eliza's mouth went dry and her heart started to thud. She was so shocked all she could do was stare up at him. '*What?*' she finally managed to choke out. 'Where did *that* come from?' She pulled herself up from the bed to face him, though her shaky knees told her she really should stay seated.

'You're pregnant. It's the right thing to do.'

He looked over her head rather than directly at her. There was no light in his eyes, no anticipation—nothing of the expression she might expect from a man proposing marriage.

'Get married because I'm pregnant?'

She knew she was just repeating his statement but she needed time to think.

'We have to get married,' he'd commanded. There had been no joy, no feeling, certainly no talk of love—and that hurt more than it should have. Not that *love* had ever come into their relationship. Worse, there had been no consultation with her. She'd rank it more as a demand than a proposal. And demands didn't sit well with her.

What would she have done if he had actually proposed? With words of affection and hope? She couldn't think about that. That had never been part of their agreement.

'You being pregnant is reason enough,' he said.

'No, it isn't. You know I don't want to marry again. Even if I did, we don't know each other well enough to consider such a big step.'

The irony of it didn't escape her. They knew each other well enough to make a baby. Not well enough to spend their lives together.

She shook her head. 'I can't do it, Jake.'

The first time she'd married for love—or what she'd thought was love—and it had been a disaster. Why would marrying for less than love be any better? Marrying someone she'd known for such a short time? An even shorter time than she'd known her ex.

'Your pregnancy changes everything,' Jake said. His face was set in severe lines.

'It does. But not in that way.'

'You're having a baby. *My* baby. I want to marry you.'

'Why? For my reputation? Because of the media?'

There was a long pause before he spoke. 'To give the baby a father,' he said. 'The baby deserves to have two parents.'

That was the last reason she would have anticipated from him and it took her aback for a moment. She put her hand to her heart to try and slow its sudden racing. 'Jake, that's honourable of you. But it's not necessary for you to marry me. If you want to be involved with the baby I'm happy—'

'I want the baby to have my name,' he said. 'And a good life.'

'*I* can give him or her a good life. You don't have to do this. We knew marriage wasn't an option for us.'

'It's important to me, Eliza.'

She noticed his fists, clenched by his sides. The tension in his voice. There was something more here—something that belied the straightforwardness of his words.

'You married your ex-wife because she was pregnant,' she said. 'I don't expect that. Really I don't. Please stop pacing the room like a caged lion.'

Her knees felt suddenly too weak to support her. She wanted to collapse back onto the bed. Instead she sat down slowly, controlled, suddenly fearing to show any weakness. Jake was a man used to getting what he wanted. Now it seemed he wanted *her.* Correction. He wanted her for the baby she was carrying. *His baby.*

'Why, Jake? You said you never wanted to be a father. Why this sudden interest?'

Jake sat down on the bed beside her, as far away from her as he could without colliding with the bedhead. He braced both hands on his knees. Overlying Eliza's nervousness was a pang of mingled longing and regret. Back in Port Douglas they wouldn't have been sitting side by side on a bed, being careful not to touch. They would have been making love by now, lost in a breathtaking world of intimacy and mutual pleasure. *Lovemaking that had created a miracle baby.*

'Seeing the baby on the ultrasound affected me yesterday,' he said now. 'The pregnancy which, up until then had been an abstract thing, became very real for me.'

Eliza noticed how weary he looked, with shadows under his

eyes, lines she hadn't noticed before etched by his mouth. She wondered how much sleep he'd had last night. Had he been awake half the night, wrangling with the dilemma she had presented him with by unexpectedly bearing his baby?

'It affected me too.'

She remembered she had been so overcome that she had gripped his hand—so tightly it must have hurt him. Then she had intercepted a smiling glance from the nurse. She and Jake must have looked quite the proud parents-to-be. If only that sweet nurse had known the less than romantic truth.

'You didn't see a scan when your ex—Fern—was pregnant?' she asked Jake.

'She didn't believe in medical intervention of any kind.'

'But an ultrasound isn't like an X-ray. It's safe and—'

'I know that. But that's beside the point. The point is I saw a little person yesterday. A tiny baby who is going to grow up to be a boy, like I was, or a girl like you were. We didn't plan it. We didn't want—'

She put up a hand in a halt sign, noticed her hand wasn't quite steady. 'Stop right there. You mightn't want it—I mean him or her… I hate calling my baby "it"—but I *do* want him or her. Very much.'

'I'm aware of how much you want the baby. Of the tragedy it was for you to discover you couldn't conceive. But the fact is I didn't want children. I would never have chosen to embark on a pregnancy with you. You know that.'

His words stung. Not just because of his rejection of her but because of her baby, unwanted by its father. No way would she have chosen a man she scarcely knew—a man who didn't want kids—as the father of her baby.

'I know we had a deal for four days of no-strings fun,' she said. 'Mother Nature had other ideas. Trust me—I wouldn't have *chosen* to have a child this way either.'

He indicated her bump. 'This is no longer just about me or about you; it's about another person at the start of life. And it's *my* responsibility. This child deserves a better life than you can give it on your own.'

If that wasn't an insult from an arrogant billionaire, she didn't know what was.

She forced herself to sound calm and reasonable. 'Jake, I might not be as wealthy as you, but I can give my child a more than decent life, thank you very much. I'm hardly a pauper.'

'Don't delude yourself, Eliza. You can't give it anything *like* what I have the resources to provide.'

Perspiration beaded on her forehead and she had to clasp her hands to stop them from trembling. It wasn't just that she was still feeling weak. She had a sudden, horrible premonition that she was preparing to do battle for her own child.

So quickly this had turned adversarial. From a proposal to a stand-off. She couldn't help but think how different this would be if she and Jake were together on this. As together and in tune as they had been in bed. Instead they were sitting here, apart on the bed, glaring at each other—she the mother, he the inadvertent sperm donor who wanted to take things further than he had any right to do.

'I can—and will—give this child a good life on my own,' she said. 'He or she will have everything they need.'

Jake was so wealthy. He could buy anything he wanted. What was he capable of doing if he wanted to take her child from her?

'Except its father's name,' he said.

Eliza was taken aback. She'd expected him to talk about private schooling, a mansion, travel, the best of everything as far as material goods went. Not the one intangible thing she could not provide.

'Is *that* what this is about?' she said. 'Some patriarchal thing?'

'What is that meant to mean?' He stared at her as if she'd suddenly sprouted horns. 'This is about making my child legitimate. Giving it its rightful place in the world.'

My child. How quickly he had claimed her baby as his own.

'Legitimate? What does *that* mean these days?' she asked.

He gave a short, sharp bark of laughter she'd never heard from him before. 'I went through hell as a kid because I was illegitimate. Life for a boy with no father was no fun at all.' His mouth set in a grim line.

'That was thirty years ago, Jake,' she said, trying not to sound combative about an issue that was obviously sensitive for him. 'Attitudes have changed now.'

'Have they really? I wonder… I walked the walk. Not just the bullying from the kids, but the sneering from the adults towards my mother, the insensitivity of the schoolteachers. Father's Day at school was the worst day of the year. The kids all making cards and gifts for their dads… Me with no one. I don't want to risk putting my child through what I went through.'

He traced the slight crookedness of his nose with his index finger. The imperfection only made him more handsome, Eliza had always thought.

'Surely it wasn't such a stigma then?' she asked.

He scowled. 'You have no idea, do you?' he said. 'Born into a family with a father who provided for you. Who gave you his name. His protection.'

Eliza felt this was spiralling away from her. Into something so much deeper than she'd realised. 'No, I don't. Have any idea, I mean.'

One of her first memories was of her father lifting her for the first time up onto a horse's back, with big, gentle hands. How proud he'd been of her fearlessness. No matter what had come afterwards, she had that. Other scenes of her father and her with their beloved horses jostled against the edges of her memory.

Jake's face was set into such grim lines he almost looked ugly. 'Every time I got called the B-word I had to answer the insult with my fists. My mother cried the first time I came home with a broken nose. She soon ran out of tears. Until the day I got big enough to deliver some broken noses of my own.'

Eliza shuddered at the aggression in his voice, but at the same time her heart went out to that little boy. 'I didn't realise how bad it was not to have a dad at home.'

'It's a huge, aching gap.'

His green eyes were clouded with a sadness that tore at her.

'Not one I want my own child to fall into.'

'Why wasn't your father around?'

'Because he was a selfish pig of a man who denied my existence. Is that a good enough answer?'

The bitterness in his voice shocked Eliza. She imagined a dear little boy, with a shock of blond hair and green eyes, suffering a pain more intense than that of any broken nose. She yearned to comfort him but didn't know what she could say about such a deep-seated hurt. At the same time she had to hold back on her feelings of sympathy when it came to Jake. She had to be on top of her game if Jake was going to get tough.

He sighed. Possibly he didn't realise the depth of anguish in that sigh.

She couldn't stop herself from placing her hand over his. 'I'm sorry, Jake. It was his loss.'

He nodded a silent acknowledgment.

Back in Port Douglas she had yearned for Jake to share his deeper side with her. Now she'd been tossed into its dark depths and she felt she was drowning in a sea of hurts and secrets, pulled every which way by conflicting currents. On top of her nausea, and her worries about handling life as a single mother, she wasn't sure she had the emotional fortitude to deal with this.

'Do you know anything about your father?'

About the man who was, she realised with a shock, her unborn child's grandfather. Jake's mother would be his or her grandmother. Through their son or daughter she and Jake would be connected for the rest of their lives—whether they wanted to be or not.

'It's a short, ugly story,' he said, his mouth a grim line. 'My mother was a trainee nurse at a big Brisbane training hospital. She was very pretty and very naïve. He was a brilliant, handsome doctor and she fell for him. She didn't know he was engaged to a girl from a wealthy family. He seduced her. She fell pregnant. He didn't want to know about it. She got booted out of her job in disgrace and slunk home to her parents at the Gold Coast.'

The father handsome, the mother pretty… Both obviously intelligent… For the first time a thought flashed through Eliza's head. Would the baby look like her or like Jake? Be as smart? It wasn't speculation she felt she could share with him.

'That's the end of it?' she said. 'What about child support?'

'Not a cent. He was tricky. My mother's family couldn't afford lawyers. She wanted nothing to do with him. Just to get on with her life. My grandparents helped raise me, though they didn't have much. It was a struggle.'

Poor little Jake. Imagine growing up with *that* as his heritage. Before the drought her parents had loved to tell the story of how they had met at an agricultural show—her dad competing in the Western riding, her mum winning ribbons for her scones and fruitcake. She wondered if they remembered it now. Would her child want to know how she and his or her dad had met? How would she explain why they weren't together?

'You never met him?' she asked.

'As a child, no.' Jake's mouth curled with contempt. 'But when media reports started appearing on the "young genius" who'd become a billionaire, he came sniffing around, looking for his long-lost son.'

'What did you do?'

'Kicked him to the kerb—like he'd sent my mother packing.'

Eliza shuddered at the strength of vengeful satisfaction in his voice. Jake would make a formidable enemy if crossed.

Jake got up from the bed. It was hard to think straight, sitting so close to Eliza She looked so wan and frail, somehow even more beautiful. Her usual sweet, floral scent had a sharp overtone of hospital from the bandage on her hand, which reminded him of what she had been through. He would never forget that terrifying moment when he'd thought she had stopped breathing.

He fought a powerful impulse to fold her in his arms and hold her close. She needed him, and yet he couldn't seem to make her see that. He wanted to look after her. Make sure she and the baby had everything they needed. If his own father had looked after his mother the way he wanted to look after Eliza, how different his life might have been. Yet he sensed a battle on his hands even to get access to his child.

He hadn't intended to confide in her about his father. Next thing he'd be spilling the details of his criminal record. Of his darkest day of despair when he'd thought he couldn't endure another minute of his crappy life. But he'd hoped telling her something of his past might make her more amenable to the idea of getting married to give their child a name.

'I'm asking you again to marry me, Eliza. Before the baby is born. So it—'

'Can you please not call the baby *it*? Try *he* or *she*. This is a little person we're talking about here. I thought you got that?'

He felt safer calling the baby *it*. Calling it *he* or *she* made it seem too real. And the more real it seemed, the more he would get attached. And he couldn't let himself get too attached if Eliza was going to keep the baby from him.

He didn't know a lot about custody arrangements for a child with single parents—though he suspected he was soon to know a whole lot more. But he doubted the courts were much inclined to give custody of a newborn to anyone other than its mother. No matter how much money he threw at the best possible legal representation. Once it got a little older that would be a different matter. His child would not grow up without a father the way he had.

'I want you to marry me before the baby is born so *he* or *she* is legitimate,' he said.

She glared at him. 'Jake, I've told you I don't want to get

married. To you or to anyone else. And if I did it would be because I was in love with my husband-to-be.'

Jake gritted his teeth. He had married before for love and look where it had got him. 'That sounds very idealistic, Eliza. But there can be pragmatic reasons to marry, too. There have been throughout history. To secure alliances or fortunes. Or to gain property or close a business deal. Or to legitimise a child.'

Slowly she shook her head. A lock of her hair fell across her eyes. She needed a haircut. She'd obviously been neglecting herself. Why couldn't she see that she needed someone to look after her? *Vulnerable.* That was what Andie had called her. Yet Eliza just didn't seem to see it.

Her eyes narrowed. 'I wish you could hear how you sound, Jake. Cold. Ruthless. This isn't a business deal we're brokering. It's our lives. You. Me. A loveless marriage.'

'A way to ensure our child is legitimate.'

'What about a way to have a woman squirming under a man's thumb? That was *my* experience of marriage. And I have no desire to experience it again.'

'Really?' he said. 'I wouldn't want to see you squirming. Or under my thumb.' Jake held up his fingers in a fist, his thumb to the side. 'See? It's not nearly large enough to hold you down.'

It was a feeble attempt at levity and he knew it. But this was the most difficult conversation he had ever had. The stakes were so much higher than in even the most lucrative of potential business deals.

'I don't know whether to take that as an insult or not. I'm not *that* big.'

'No, you're not. In fact you're not big enough. You've lost weight, Eliza. You need to gain it. I can look after you as well as the baby.'

Her chin lifted in the stubborn way he was beginning to recognise.

'I don't *want* to be looked after. I can look after both myself and my baby on my own. You can see him or her, play a role in their life. But I most certainly don't want to *marry* you.'

'You're making a mistake, Eliza. Are you sure you don't want to reconsider?'

'You can't force me to marry you, Jake.'

'But I can make life so much easier for you if you do,' he said.

'Love is the only reason to marry. But love hasn't entered the equation for us. For that reason alone, I can't marry you.'

'That's your final word?'

She nodded.

He got up. 'Then you'll be hearing from my lawyer.'

Eliza's already pale face drained of every remaining scrap of colour. *'What?'*

She leapt up from the bed, had to steady herself as she seemed to rock on her feet as if she were dizzy. But she pushed aside his steadying hand and glared at him.

'You heard me,' he said. 'I intend to seek custody.'

'You can't have custody over an unborn child.' Her voice was high and strained.

'You're about to see what I can do,' he said.

He turned on his heel, strode to the top of the stairs. Flimsy stairs. Too dangerous. She couldn't bring up a child in this house. He ignored the inner voice that told him this house was a hundred times safer and nicer than the welfare housing apartment he'd grown up in. *Nothing but the best for his child.*

She put up her hand in a feeble attempt to stop him. 'Jake. You can't go.'

'I'm gone, Eliza. I suggest you get back to bed and rest. An agency nurse will be arriving in an hour. I've employed her to look after you for the next three days, as per doctor's orders. I suggest you let her in and allow her to care for you. Otherwise you might end up back in hospital.'

He swung himself on to the top step.

'I'll see you in court.'

CHAPTER THIRTEEN

So it had come to this. Eliza placed her hand protectively on her bump as she rode the elevator up to the twenty-third floor of the prestigious building in the heart of the central business district of Sydney, where the best law firms had their offices. She hadn't heard from Jake for three weeks. All communication had been through their lawyers. Except for one challenging email.

Now she was headed to a meeting with Jake and his lawyers to finalise a legal document that spelled out in detail a custody and support agreement for the unborn Baby Dunne.

She must have paled at the thought of the confrontation to come, because her lawyer gave her arm a squeeze of support. Jake had, of course, engaged the most expensive and well-known family law attorney in Sydney to be on his side of the battle lines.

He'd sent her an email.

Are you sure you can afford not to marry me, Eliza? Just your lawyer's fees alone will stop you in your tracks.

What he didn't realise, high up there in his billionaire world, where the almighty dollar ruled, was that not everybody could be bought. She had an older cousin who was a brilliant family lawyer. And Cousin Maree was so outraged at what Jake was doing that she was representing Eliza *pro bono*. Well, not quite for free. Eliza had agreed that Party Queens would organise the most spectacular twenty-first birthday party possible for Maree's daughter.

Now, Maree squeezed her arm reassuringly. 'Chin up. Just let me do the talking, okay?'

Eliza nodded, rather too numbed at the thought of what she was about to face to do anything else *but* keep quiet.

She saw Jake the moment she entered the large, traditionally furnished meeting room. Her heart gave such a jolt she had to hold on for support to the back of one of the chairs that were ranged around the boardroom table. He was standing tall, in front of floor-to-ceiling windows that looked out on a magnificent mid-morning view of Sydney Harbour. The Bridge loomed so closely she felt she could reach out and touch it.

Jake was wearing a deep charcoal-grey business suit, immaculately tailored to his broad shoulders and tapered to his waist. His hair—darker now, less sun-streaked—crept over his collar. No angel wings in sight—rather the forked tail and dark horns of the demon who had tormented her for the last three weeks with his demands.

At the sound of her entering the room Jake turned. For a split second his gaze met hers. There was a flash of recognition—and something else that was gone so soon she scarcely registered it. But it could have been regret. Then the shutters came down to blank his expression.

'Eliza,' he said curtly, acknowledging her presence with a brief nod in her direction.

'Jake,' she said coolly, despite her inner turmoil.

Her brain, so firmly in charge up until now, had been once more vanquished by her libido—she refused to entertain for even one second the thought that it might be her heart—which flamed into life at the sight of the beautiful man who had been her lover for those four, glorious days. So treacherous her libido, still to clamour for this man. Her lover who had become her enemy—the hero of her personal fairytale transformed into the villain.

Eliza let Jake's lawyer's assistant pull out the chair for her. Before she sat she straightened her shoulders and stood proud. Her tailored navy dress with its large white collar was tucked and pleated to accommodate and show off her growing bump. She hoped her silent message was loud and clear—*she* was in possession of the prize.

But at the same time as she displayed the ace in her hand she felt swept by a wave of inexplicable longing for Jake to be sharing the milestones of her pregnancy with her. She hadn't counted on the loneliness factor of single motherhood. There was a vague bubbling sensation that meant the baby was starting to kick, she thought. At fifteen weeks it was too soon for her to be feeling vigorous activity; she knew that from the 'what to expect' pregnancy books and websites she read obsessively. But she had a sudden vision of Jake, resting his hand on her tummy, a look of expectant joy on his face as he waited to feel the kicking of their baby's tiny feet.

That could only happen in a parallel universe. Jake had no interest in her other than as an incubator.

She wondered, too, if he had really thought ahead to his interaction with their son or daughter? His motivation seemed purely to be making up for the childhood he felt he'd lost because of his own despicable father. To try to right a family wrong and force a certain lifestyle on her whether she liked it or not.

What if their child—who might be equally as smart and stubborn as his or her parents—had other ideas about how he or she wanted to live? He or she might be as fiercely independent as both her, Eliza, and the paternal grandmother—Jake's mother.

Would she ever get to meet his mother? Unlikely. Unless she was there when Eliza handed over their child for Jake's court-prescribed visits.

That was not how it was meant to be. She ached at the utter *wrongness* of this whole arrangement.

Jake settled in to a chair directly opposite her, his lawyer to his right. That was *his* silent statement, she supposed. Confrontation, with the battlefield between them. *Bring it on,* she thought.

It was fortunate that the highly polished dark wooden table was wide enough so there was no chance of his knees nudging hers, her foot brushing against his when she shifted in her seat. Because, despite all the hostility, her darn libido still longed for his touch. It was insane—and must surely be blamed on the up-and-down hormone fluctuations of pregnancy.

Maree cleared her throat. 'Shall we start the proceedings? This is very straightforward.'

Maree had explained all this to her before, but Eliza listened intently as her cousin spoke, at the same time keeping her gaze firmly fixed on Jake's face. He gave nothing away—not the merest flicker of reaction. He ran his finger along his collar and tugged at his tie—obviously uncomfortable at being 'trussed up'. But she guessed he'd wanted to look like an intimidating billionaire businessman in front of the lawyers.

Maree explained how legally there could not be any formal custody proceedings over an unborn child. However, the parties had agreed to prepare a document outlining joint custody to present to a judge after the event of a live birth.

Eliza had known that particular phrase would be coming and bit her lip hard. She caught Jake's eye, and his slight nod indicated his understanding of how difficult it was for her to hear it. Because its implication was that something could go wrong in the meantime. Her greatest fear was that she would lose this miracle baby—although her doctor had assured her the pregnancy was progressing very well.

Jake's hands were gripped so tightly together that his knuckles showed white—perhaps he feared it too. He had been so brilliant that day he'd taken her to hospital.

Eliza was looking for crumbs to indicate that Jake wasn't the enemy, that this was all a big misunderstanding. That brief show of empathy from him might be it. Then she remembered why she was here in the first place. To be coerced into signing an agreement she didn't want to sign.

She was being held to a threat—hinted at rather than spoken out in the open—that if she didn't co-operate Jake would use his influence to steer wealthy clients away from Party Queens. Right at a time when her ongoing intermittent nausea and time away from work, plus the departure of their new head chef to a rival firm, meant her beloved company—and her livelihood—was tipping towards a precipice. What choice did she have?

Maree continued in measured tones, saying that both parties acknowledged Jake Marlowe's paternity, so there would be no need for a court-ordered genetic test once the baby was born. She listed the terms of the proposed custody agreement, starting with limited visits by the father while the child was an infant, progressing to full-on division of weekends and vacations. The baby's legal name would be Baby Dunne-Marlowe—once the sex was known a first name satisfactory to both parents would be agreed upon.

Then Jake's lawyer took over, listing the generous support package to be provided by Mr Marlowe—all medical expenses paid, a house to be gifted in the child's name and held in trust by Mr Marlowe, a trust fund to be set up for—

Eliza half got up from her chair. She couldn't endure this sham a second longer. 'That's enough. I know what's in the document. Just give it to me and I'll sign.'

She subsided in her chair. Bent her head to take Maree's counsel.

'Are you sure?' her cousin asked in a low voice. 'You don't want further clarification of the trust fund provisions? Or the—?'

'No. I just want this to be over.'

The irony of it struck her. Jake had been worried about gold-diggers. Now he was insisting she receive money she didn't want, binding her with ties that were choking all the joyful anticipation of her pregnancy. She tried to focus on the baby. That precious little person growing safe and happy inside her. Her unborn child was all that mattered.

She avoided looking at Jake as she signed everywhere the multiple-paged document indicated her signature was required, stabbing the pen so hard the paper tore.

Jake followed Eliza as she departed the conference room, apparently so eager to get away from him that she'd broken into a half-run. She was almost to the bank of elevators, her low-heeled shoes tapping on the marble floor, before he caught up with her.

'Eliza,' he called.

She didn't turn around, but he was close enough to hear her every word.

'I have nothing to say to you, Jake. You've got what you wanted, so just go away.'

Only she didn't say *go away.* She used far pithier language.

She reached the elevator and jabbed the elevator button. Once, twice, then kept on jabbing it.

'That won't get it here any faster,' he said, and immediately regretted the words. *Why had he said something so condescending?* He cursed his inability to find the right words in moments of high tension and emotion.

She turned on him, blue eyes flashing the brightest he'd seen them. Bright with threatening tears, he realised. Tears of anger—directed at *him.*

'Of course it won't. But I live in hope. Because the sooner I can get away from you, the better. Even a second or two would help.' She went back to jabbing the button.

Her baby bump had grown considerably since he'd last seen her. She looked the picture of an elegant, perfectly groomed businesswoman. The smart, feisty Eliza he had come to— Come to what? Respect? Admire? Something more than that. Something, despite all they'd gone through, he couldn't put a name to.

'You look well,' he said. *She looked more beautiful than ever.*

With a sigh of frustration she dropped her finger from the elevator button. Aimed a light kick at the elevator door. She turned to face him, her eyes narrowed with hostility.

'Don't try and engage me in polite chit-chat. Just because you've forced me to sign a proposed custody agreement it doesn't mean you own me—like you're trying to own my baby.'

You didn't own children—and you couldn't force a woman to marry you. Belatedly he'd come to that realisation.

Jake didn't often admit to feeling ashamed. But shame was what had overwhelmed him during the meeting, as he'd watched the emotions flickering over Eliza's face, so easy to read.

He'd been a teenage troublemaker—the leader of a group of other angry, alienated kids like himself. Taller and more powerful than the others, he'd used his off-the-charts IQ and well-developed street-smarts to control and intimidate the gang—even those older than him.

He'd thought he'd put all that long behind him. Then in that room, sitting opposite Eliza—proud, brave Eliza—it had struck him in the gut like a physical blow. He'd behaved as badly towards her as he had in his worst days as a teenage gang leader. Jim Hill would be ashamed of him—but not as ashamed as he was of himself.

'I'm sorry, Eliza. I didn't mean it to go this far.'

She blinked away the threatening tears. 'You played dirty, Jake. I wouldn't marry you, so you brought in the big guns. I would have played fair with you. Visitation rights. Even the Dunne-Marlowe name. For the sake of our baby. I was *glad* you wanted to play a role in our child's life. But I wasn't in a space for making life-changing decisions right then. I'd just got out of hospital.'

How had he let this get so far? 'I was wrong. I should have—'

'Now the document is signed you think you can placate me?

Forget it. Don't you see? You're so concerned about giving this child your name, you're bequeathing to him or her something much worse. A mother who resents her baby's father. Who hates him for the way she's had to fight against him imposing his will on her, riding roughshod over her feelings.'

Now he was on the ground, being kicked from all sides. And the blows were much harder than those Eliza had given the elevator door.

'*Hate?* That's a strong word.'

'Not strong enough for how I feel about you,' she said, tight-lipped. 'I reckon you've let the desire to win overcome all your common sense and feelings of decency.'

Of course. He'd been guilty of *over-thinking* on a grand scale. 'I just want to do the right thing by our child,' he said. 'To look after it and to look after you too, Eliza. You need me.'

She shook her head. 'I don't need you. At one stage I wanted you. And...and I... I could have cared for you. When you danced me around that ballroom in Montovia I thought I was on the brink of something momentous in my life.'

'So did I,' he said slowly.

'Then there was Port Douglas. Leaving you seemed so *wrong.* We had something *real.* Only we were so darn intent on protecting ourselves from hurt we didn't recognise it and we walked away from it. The baby gave us a second chance. To be friends. Maybe more than friends. But we blew that too.'

'There must be such a thing as a third chance,' he said.

She shook her head so vehemently it dislodged the clip that was holding her hair off her face and she had to push it back into place with hands that trembled.

'No more chances. Not after what happened in that room today. You won't break me. I will never forgive you. For the baby's sake, I'll be civil. It would be wrong to pump our child's mind with poison against his or her father. Even if I happen to think he's a...a bullying thug.' Her cheeks were flushed scarlet, her eyes glittered.

Now he'd been kicked to a pulp—bruised black and blue all over. Hadn't the judge used a similar expression when sentencing him to juvenile detention? The words *bully* and *thug* seemed to be familiar. But that had been so long ago. He'd been fifteen years of age. Why had those tendencies he'd thought left well and truly behind him in adolescence surfaced again?

Then it hit him—the one final blow he hadn't seen coming. It came swinging again like that sledgehammer from nowhere to slam him in the head. This wasn't about Eliza needing him—it was about *him* needing *her*. Needing her so desperately he'd gone to crazy lengths to try to secure her.

Just then the elevator arrived.

'At last,' Eliza said as she stepped towards it. She had to wait until a girl clutching a bunch of legal folders to her chest stepped out.

'Eliza.'

Jake went to catch her arm, to stop her leaving. There was so much he had to say to her, to explain. But she shrugged off his hand.

'Please, Jake, no more. I can't take it. I'll let you know when the baby is born. As per our contract.'

She stood facing him as the elevator doors started to slide slowly inward. The last thing he saw of her was a slice of her face, with just one fat, glistening tear sliding down her cheek.

Jake stood for a long time, watching the indicator marking the elevator's progress down the twenty-three floors. He felt frozen to that marble floor, unable to step backwards or forwards.

When the elevator reached the ground floor he turned on his heel and strode back to his meeting. He needed to rethink his strategy. Jake Marlowe was not a man who gave up easily.

CHAPTER FOURTEEN

THE LAST PLACE Eliza expected to be a week after the lawyers' meeting with Jake was on an executive jet flying to Europe. Despite the gravity of the reason for her flight, it was a welcome distraction.

Gemma had called an emergency meeting of the three Party Queens directors. Eliza's unexpected pregnancy had tipped the problem of an absentee director into crisis point. And because Gemma was Crown Princess, as well as their Food Director, she had sent the Montovian royal family's private jet to transport Eliza and Andie from Sydney to Montovia for the meeting.

Just because Gemma *could*, Eliza had mused with a smile when she'd got the summons, along with the instructions for when a limousine would pick her up to take her to the airport where she would meet Andie.

Dominic had decided to come along for the flight, too. He and Andie's little boy Hugo was being looked after by his doting grandma and grandpa—Andie's parents.

Eliza was very fond of Andie's husband. But despite the luxury of the flight—the lounge chair comfort of leather upholstery, the crystal etched with the Montovian royal coat of arms, the restaurant-quality food, the hotel-style bathrooms—she hadn't been able to relax because of the vaguely hostile emanations coming her way from Dominic.

Jake was Dominic's best male friend. The bonds between them went deep. According to the legend of the two young billionaires they went way back, to when they'd been in their first year at university. Together, they had built fortunes. Created a charitable foundation for homeless kids. And cemented that young friendship into something adult and enduring.

In the air, somewhere over Indonesia, Dominic told Eliza in no uncertain terms that Jake was unhappy and miserable. He couldn't understand why Eliza wouldn't just marry Jake and put them *all* out of their misery.

Dominic got a sharp poke in the ribs from his wife's elbow for *that* particular opinion. He was referring to the fact that sympathies had been split down the middle among the other two Party Queens and their respective spouses.

Andie and Gemma were on her side—though they'd been at pains to state that they weren't actually *taking* sides. Neither of her friends saw why Eliza should marry a man she didn't love just to give her baby Jake's name when he or she was born. Nor did they approve of the domineering way Jake had tried to force the issue.

Dominic and Tristan, however, thought differently.

Dominic had an abusive childhood behind him—tough times living on the streets. He'd told Eliza she was both crazy and unwise not to jump straight into the safety net Jake was offering.

Tristan, a hereditary Crown Prince, also couldn't see the big deal. There was only one way forward. The baby carried Jake's blood. As far as Tristan was concerned, Gemma had told Eliza, Jake was doing the correct and honourable thing in offering Eliza marriage. Eliza must do the right thing and accept. That from a man who had changed the laws of his country regarding marriage so he could marry for love and make Gemma his wife.

Both men had let Eliza know that they saw her stance as stubborn in the extreme, and contributing to an unnecessary rift between very close friends. They stood one hundred per cent by their generous and maligned buddy Jake. The women could not believe how blindly loyal their husbands were to the *bullying thug* that was Jake.

Of course Eliza was well aware that neither Andie nor Gemma had ever called Jake that in front of Dominic or Tristan. They were each way too wise to let problems with their mutual friends interfere with their own blissfully happy marriages to the men they adored. Besides, as Andie told Eliza, they actually still liked Jake a lot. They just didn't like the way he'd treated her.

'Although Jake *is* very generous,' Andie reminded her.

'Of course he is—exceedingly generous,' said Eliza evenly.

Inside she was screaming: *And sexy and kind and even funny when he wants to be.* As if she needed to be reminded of his good points when they were all she seemed to think about these days.

She kept remembering that time in the ambulance, as she'd drifted in and out of consciousness and the man who had never let go of her hand had murmured reassurance and encouragement all the way to the hospital. The man who'd chartered a private boat for her because she'd said she wanted to dive on the Great Barrier Reef. The man who hadn't needed angel wings to send her soaring to heaven when they'd made love.

Eliza wished, not for the first time, that she hadn't actually called Jake a bullying thug—or told Andie she'd called him that. That day she'd got all the way to the bottom of the building on the elevator and seriously considered going all the way back up to apologise. Then realised, as she had just told him she hated him, that it might not be the best of ideas.

'Do you ever regret not marrying him?' Andie asked. 'You would never have to worry about money again.'

'No,' Eliza replied firmly. 'Because I don't think financial security is a good enough reason to marry—not for me, anyway. Not when I'm confident I'll always be able to earn a good living.'

What she couldn't admit—not even to her dearest friend Andie, and certainly not to Dominic—was that these weeks away from Jake had made her realise how much she had grown to care for him. That along with all the other valid reasons for her not to marry Jake there was one overwhelming reason—she couldn't put herself through the torture of a pragmatic arrangement with a man she'd begun to realise she was half in love with but who didn't love her.

By the end of the long-haul flight to Montovia—Australia to Europe being a flight of some twenty-two hours—Eliza was avoiding Dominic as much as she could within the confines of the private jet. Andie was okay. Eliza didn't think she had a clue about how much Eliza was beginning to regret the way she had handled her relationship with Jake. But she didn't want to share those thoughts with anyone.

She hoped she and Dominic would more easily be able to steer clear of each other in the vast expanses of the royal castle. Avoiding Tristan might not be so easy.

The day after she'd landed in Montovia, Eliza sat in Gemma's exquisitely decorated office in the Crown Prince's private apartment at the castle. A 'small' room, it contained Gemma's desk and a French antique table and chairs, around which the three Party Queens were now grouped. Under the window, which looked out onto the palace gardens, there was a beautiful chaise longue that Eliza recognised from her internet video conversations with Gemma.

What a place for three ordinary Aussie girls to have ended up for a meeting, Eliza couldn't help thinking.

The three Party Queens were more subdued than usual, with the future of the company they had started more as a lark than any seriously considered business decision now under threat. It was still considered the best party planning business in Sydney, but it was at a crossroads—Eliza had been pointing that out with increasing urgency over the last months.

'I thought it would be too intimidating for us to meet in the castle boardroom,' auburn-haired Gemma explained once they were all settled. 'Even after we were married it took me a while before I could overcome my nerves enough to make a contribution there.'

Andie laughed. 'This room is so easy on the eye I might find it difficult to concentrate from being too busy admiring all the treasures.'

'Not to mention the distraction of the view out to those beautiful roses,' Eliza said.

It felt surreal to be one day in the late winter of Australia, the next day in the late summer of Europe.

'Okay, down to business,' said Gemma. 'We all know Party Queens is facing some challenges. Not least is the fact that I now live here, while the business is based in Sydney.'

'Which makes it problematical when your awesome skills with food are one of the contributing factors to our success,' said Eliza.

'True,' said Andie. 'Even as Creative Director, there are limitations to what I can do in terms of clever food ideas. Those ideas need to be validated by a food expert to tell me if they can be practical.'

Gemma nodded. 'I can still devise menus from here. And I can still test recipes myself, as I like to do.' The fact that Gemma had been testing a recipe for a white chocolate and citrus mud cake when she had first met Tristan, incognito in Sydney, had been fuel for a flurry of women's magazine articles. More so when the recipe had become the royal wedding cake. 'But the truth is both the time difference between Montovia and Sydney and my royal duties make a hands-on presence from me increasingly difficult.'

Eliza swallowed hard against a dry throat. 'Does that mean you want to resign from the partnership, Gemma?'

'Heavens, no,' said Gemma. 'But maybe I need to look at my role in a different way.'

'And then there's your future as a sole parent to consider, Eliza,' said Andie.

'Don't think I haven't thought of the challenges that will present,' Eliza said.

'Think about those challenges and multiply them a hundred times,' said Andie, and put up her hand to stop the protest Eliza was already formulating. 'Being a parent is tough, Eliza. Even tougher without a pair of loving hands from the other parent to help you out.'

Eliza gritted her teeth. She was sure Andie had meant 'the other parent' in abstract terms. But of course she could only think of Jake in that context.

'I understand that, Andie,' she said. 'And my bouts of extreme nausea showed me that even with the best workaholic will in the world there are times when the baby will have to come before the business.'

Andie raised her hand for attention. 'May I throw into the mix the fact that Dominic and I would like another baby? With two children, perhaps more, I might have to scale down my practical involvement as well.'

'It's good to have everything on the table,' said Eliza. 'No doubt a royal heir might factor into *your* future, Gemma.'

'I hope so,' said Gemma with a smile. 'We're waiting until a year after the wedding to think about that. I need to learn how to be a princess before I tackle motherhood.'

'Now we've heard the problems, I'm sure you've come armed with a plan to solve them, Eliza,' said Andie.

This kind of dilemma was something Eliza was more familiar with than the complications of her relationship with Jake. She felt very confident on this turf. 'Of course,' she said. 'The business is still very healthy, so option one is to sell Party Queens.'

She was gratified at the wails of protest from Gemma and Andie.

'It *is* a viable option,' she continued. 'There are two possible buyers—'

'No,' said Andie.

'No,' echoed Gemma.

'How could the business be the same without us?' said Andie, with an arrogant flick of her blonde-streaked hair. 'We *are* the Party Queens.'

'Good,' said Eliza. 'I feel the same way. The other proposal is to bring in another level of management in Sydney. Gemma would become a non-executive director, acting as ongoing adviser to a newly appointed food manager.'

Gemma nodded. 'Good idea. I have someone in mind. I've worked with her as a consultant and she would be ideal.'

Eliza continued. 'And Andie would train a creative person to bring on board so she can eventually work part-time. I'm thinking Jeremy.'

Freelance stylist Jeremy had been working with them since the beginning—long forgiven for his role in the disastrous Christmas tree incident that had rocked Andie and Dominic's early relationship.

Andie frowned. 'Jeremy is so talented… He's awesome. And he's really organised. But he's not a Party Queen.' She paused. 'Actually, he's a queen of a different stripe. I think he'd love to come on board.'

'Which brings us to *you*, Eliza,' said Gemma.

Eliza heaved a great sigh, reluctant to be letting go. 'I'm thinking I need to appoint a business manager to deal with the day-to-day finances and accounting.'

'Good idea.' Andie reached out a hand to take Eliza's. 'But you, out of all of us, might have a difficult time relinquishing absolute control over the business we started,' she said gently.

'I… I get that,' Eliza said.

Gemma smiled her friendship and understanding. 'Will you be able to give a manager the freedom to make decisions independent of you? Not hover over them and micro-manage them? Like watching a cake rise in the oven?'

Eliza bowed her head. 'I really am a control freak, aren't I?'

Andie squeezed her hand. 'You said it, not me.'

'I reckon your control freak tendencies are a big part of Party Queens's success,' said Gemma. 'You've really kept us on track.'

'But they could also lead to its downfall if I don't loosen the reins,' said Eliza thoughtfully.

'It's a matter of believing someone can do the job as well as you—even if they do it differently,' said Andie.

'Of accepting help because you need it,' said Gemma.

Her friends were talking about Party Queens. But, seen through the filter of her relationship with Jake, Eliza saw how she might have done things very differently. She'd fought so hard not to relinquish control over her life, over her baby—over her heart—she hadn't seen what Jake could bring to her. Not just as a father but as a life partner. Maybe she had driven him to excessive control on his side because she hadn't given an inch on hers.

In hindsight, she realised she might have thought more about compromise than control. When it came to giving third chances, maybe it should have been *her* begging *him* for a chance to make it right.

CHAPTER FIFTEEN

DINNER AT THE royal castle of Montovia was a very formal affair. Luckily Eliza had been warned by Gemma to pack appropriate clothes. From her experiences of dinners at the castle before the wedding she knew that meant a dress that would be appropriate for a ball in Sydney. Thank heaven she still fitted into her favourite vintage ballgown in an empire style in shimmering blue that was very flattering to her pregnant shape.

Still, when she went down to dinner in the private section of the palace that was never opened to the public, she was astounded to see the level of formality of the other guests. She blinked at the dazzle of jewellery glinting in the lights from the chandeliers. It took her a moment to realise they were all members of Tristan and Gemma's bridal party. Tristan's sister Princess Natalia, his cousin with his doctor fiancée, she and Andie, other close friends of Tristan's. Natalia waved when she caught her eye.

'It's a wedding reunion,' Andie said when Eliza was seated beside her at the ornate antique banqueting table.

'So I see. Did you know about it?' Eliza asked.

'No. Gemma didn't either. Apparently when Tristan knew we were coming to visit he arranged it as a surprise. He invited everyone, and these are the ones who could make it. Obviously we're the only Australians.'

'What a lovely thing for him to do,' Eliza said.

Gemma was glowing with happiness.

'Very romantic,' said Andie. 'Gemma really struck husband gold with Tristan, in more ways than one.'

It was romantic in a very heart-wrenching way for Eliza. Because the most important member of the wedding party was not here—the best man, Jake.

Bittersweet memories of her last visit to the castle came flooding back in a painful rush. During the entire wedding she'd been on the edge of excitement, longing for a moment alone with him. How dismally it had all turned out. Except for the baby. Her miracle baby. Why couldn't it be enough to have the baby she'd yearned for? Why did she ache to have the father too?

What with being in a different time zone, Eliza was being affected by more than a touch of jet-lag. She also had to be careful about what she ate. The worst, most debilitating attacks of nausea seemed to have passed, but she still had to take care. She just picked at course after course of the magnificent feast—in truth she had no appetite. As soon as it was polite to do so she would make her excuses and go back up to her guest suite—the same luxurious set of rooms she'd been given on her last visit.

After dessert had been cleared Tristan asked his guests to move into the adjoining reception room, where coffee was to be served. There were gasps of surprise as the guests trooped in, at the sight of a large screen on one wall, with images of the wedding projected onto it. The guests burst into spontaneous applause.

Eliza stared at the screen. There was Gemma, getting ready with her bridesmaids. And Eliza herself, smiling as she patted a stray lock of Gemma's auburn hair back into place. The images flashed by. Andie. Natalia. The Queen placing a diamond tiara on Gemma's head.

Then there were pictures at the cathedral. The cluster of tiny flower girls. The groomsmen. The best man—Jake—standing at the altar with Tristan. Jake was smiling straight at the first bridesmaid coming up the aisle. *Her.* She was smiling back at him. It must have been so obvious to everyone what was going on between them. And here she was—without him. But pregnant with his baby.

Her hand went to her heart when she saw a close-up of Jake saying something to Tristan. The image was so large he seemed life-size. Jake looked so handsome her mouth went dry and her heart started to thud so hard she had to take deep breaths to try and control it.

She couldn't endure this. It was cruel. No one would realise if she slipped away. They were all too engrossed with the photographs.

She turned, picked up her long skirts.

And came face to face with Jake.

It was as if the image of him that had so engrossed her on the screen had come to life. Was she hallucinating? With a cautious hand, she reached out and connected with warm, solid Jake. He was real all right. She felt the colour drain from her face. He was wearing a similar tuxedo as he was in the photo, but his smile was more reticent. *He was unsure of his welcome from her.*

'Jake…' she breathed, unable to say another thing. She felt light-headed and swayed a little. *Please. Not now.* She couldn't pass out on him again.

'You need some fresh air,' he said, and took her arm.

She let him look after her. *Liked* that he wanted to look after her. Without protest she let him lead her out of the room and then found her voice—though not any coherent words to say with it.

'What…? How…?'

'I was in London when Tristan called me about the wedding party reunion. I got here as soon as I could when I heard you were in Montovia.'

Eliza realised he was leading her onto the same terrace where they'd parted the last time they'd been in Montovia. Not quite the same view—it must be further down from that grand ballroom—and not a full moon over the lake either. But a new moon—a crescent moon that gave her a surge of hope for a new start.

She took another deep, steadying breath. Looked up at him and hoped he saw in her eyes what she was feeling but was unable to express.

'Jake, I'm asking for a third chance. Will you give it to me?'

Jake prided himself on being able to read Eliza's expressions. But he couldn't put a label on what he saw shining from her eyes. He must be reading into it what he longed to see, not what was really there. But he took hope from even that glimmering of emotion.

'Of course I give you a third chance,' he said hoarsely. He'd give her a million chances if they brought her back to him. 'But only if you'll give *me* a third chance.'

'Third chance granted,' she said, a tremulous edge to her voice.

He pulled her into his arms and held her close, breathed in her sweet scent. She slid her arms around his back and pressed closer with a little sigh. He smiled at the feel of her slender body, with the distinct curve of his baby resting under her heart. *His baby. His woman.* Now he had to convince her—not coerce her—into letting him be her man.

He looked over her head to the dark night sky, illuminated only by a sliver of silver moon, and thanked whatever power it was that had given him this chance to make good the wrongs he'd done her.

'I've missed you,' he said, not sure how to embellish his words any further.

'I've missed you too. Terribly.'

He'd flown back to Brisbane after she'd left him at the lawyer's office. His house had seemed empty—his life empty. He'd longed to be back with Eliza in her little house, with the red front door and the dragonfly doorknocker. Instead he'd tied her down to a contract to ensure his child's presence in his life and in doing so had driven her away from him.

Over and over he'd relived his time with her in Port Douglas. The passion and wonder of making love with her. Thought of the real reason he wanted to spend millions to relocate his company to Sydney. The overwhelming urge to protect her he'd felt as he'd held her hand in the ambulance and soothed her fears she might lose the baby she'd longed for. *His baby.* The incredible gift he'd been able to give her. The baby was a bonus. Eliza was the prize. But he still had to win her.

Eliza pulled away from his arms but stayed very close.

'Jake, I don't hate you—really, I don't.' The words tumbled out of her as if she had been saving them up. 'And I don't think you're a bullying thug. I… I'm really sorry I called you that.'

He'd always known he'd have to tell her the truth about his past some time—sooner rather than later. Her words seemed to be a segue into it. There was a risk that she would despise him and walk away. But he had to take that risk. If only because she was the mother of his child.

He cleared his throat. 'You're not the first person to call me a bully and a thug,' he said.

She frowned. 'What do you mean?'

'When I was fifteen years old I came up in front of the children's court and was charged with a criminal offence. The magistrate used just those words.'

'Jake!'

To his relief, there was disbelief in her voice, in the widening of her eyes, but not disgust.

'I was the leader of a gang of other young thugs. We'd stolen a car late one night and crashed it into a shopfront. I wasn't driving, but I took responsibility. The police thought it was a ram-raid—that we'd driven into the shop on purpose. In fact it was an accident. None of us could drive properly. We didn't have a driver's licence between us—we were too young. With the pumped-up pride of an adolescent male, I thought it was cooler to be charged with a ram-raid than admit to being an idiot. It was my second time before the court so I got sentenced to a spell in juvenile detention.'

Eliza kept close, didn't back away from him in horror. 'You? In a gang? I can't believe it. Why?'

'Things weren't great at home. My grandfather, who was the only father I'd ever known, had died. My mother had a boyfriend I couldn't stand. I was angry. I was hurting. The gang was a family of sorts, and I was the kingpin.'

'Juvenile detention—that's jail, isn't it?'

'A medium security prison for kids aged from eleven to sixteen.'

She shuddered. 'I still can't believe I'm hearing this. How awful for you.'

He gritted his teeth. 'I won't lie. It *was* awful. There were some really tough kids in there.'

'Thank heaven you survived.' Her voice was warm with compassion.

She placed her hand on his cheek. He covered it with his own.

'My luck turned with the care officer assigned to me. Jim Hill. He saw I was bored witless at school and looking for diversion.'

'The school hadn't realised you were a genius?'

'They saw me as a troublemaker. Jim really helped me with anger management, with confidence-building. He showed me I had choices.' Jake smiled at the memory. 'He knew I hungered for what I didn't have, after growing up poor. Jim told me I had the brains to become a criminal mastermind or to make myself a fortune in the commercial world. The choice was mine. When my detention was over he worked with my mother to get me moved to a different school in a different area, further down the coast. The new school put me into advanced classes that challenged me. I chose to take the second path. You know the rest.'

Eliza's eyes narrowed. 'Jim Hill? The name sounds familiar.'

'He heads up The Underground Help Centre. You must have met him at the launch party.'

'So you introduced him to Dominic?'

'Jim introduced *me* to Dominic. Dominic was under his care too. But that's Dominic's story to tell. Thanks to Jim, Dominic and I already knew each other by the time we started uni. We both credit Jim for getting our lives on track. That's why we got him on board to help other young people in trouble like we were.'

'How have you managed to keep this under wraps?'

'Juvenile records are sealed when a young offender turns eighteen. I was given a fresh start and I took it. Now you know the worst about me, Eliza.'

Jake was such a tall, powerfully built man. And yet at that moment he seemed to Eliza as vulnerable as his fifteen-year-old self must have been, standing before a magistrate, waiting to hear his sentence.

She leaned up and kissed him on his cheek. It wasn't time yet for any other kind of kiss. Not until they knew where this evening might take them. Since they'd last stood on this terrace together they'd accumulated so much more baggage. Not to mention a baby bump.

'That's a story of courage and determination,' she said. 'Can you imagine if someone ever made a movie of your life story?'

'Never going to happen,' he growled.

'Well, it will make a marvellous story to tell your child one day.'

'Heavily censored,' he said, with a hint of the grin she had got so fond of.

She slowly shook her head. 'I wish you'd told me before. It helps me understand you. And I've been struggling to understand you, Jake.'

To think she had thought him superficial. He'd just been good at hiding his wounds.

He took both her hands in his and drew her closer. 'Would it have made a difference if I'd told you?'

'To help me see why you're so determined to give your child a name? Yes. To make me understand why you're so driven? Yes. To make me love you even more, knowing what you went through? Yes. And I—'

'Stop right there, Eliza,' he said, his voice hoarse. 'Did you just say you love me?'

Over the last days she'd gotten so used to thinking how much she loved him, she'd just blurted out the words. She could deny it. But what would be the point?

She looked up into his face, saw not just good looks but also his innate strength and integrity, and answered him with honesty. 'Yes, Jake, I love you. I fell in love with you… I can't think when. Yes, I can. Here. Right here on this terrace. No. Earlier than that. Actually, from the first moment. Only you weren't free. And then there was Port Douglas, and I got all tied up in not wanting to get hurt again, and…'

She realised he hadn't said anything further and began to feel exposed and vulnerable that she'd confessed she'd fallen in love with a man who had never given any indication that he might love *her*.

She tried to pull away but he kept a firm grip on her hands. 'I… I know you don't feel the same, Jake, so I—'

'What makes you say that? Of *course* I love you. I fell in love with you the first time I was best man to your bridesmaid. We must have felt it at the same moment. You in that blue bridesmaid's dress, with white flowers in your hair…'

'At Andie's wedding?' she said, shaking her head in wonder.

'At Dominic's wedding,' he said at the same time.

He drew her closer. This man who wanted to care for her, look after her, miraculously seemed to love her.

'You laughed at something I said and looked up at me with those incredible blue eyes and I fell right into them.'

'I remember that moment,' she said slowly. 'It felt like time suddenly stopped. The wedding was going on all around me, and all I could think of was how smitten I was with you.'

'But I was too damn tied up with protecting myself to let myself recognise it,' he said.

'Just as well, really,' she said. 'I wasn't ready for something so life-changing then. And you certainly weren't.'

'You could look at it that way. Or you could see that we wasted a lot of time.'

'Then the baby complicated things.'

'Yes,' he said.

The spectre of that dreadful contract hovered between them.

'Your pregnancy brought out my old fears,' he said. 'I'd chosen not to be a father because I don't know *how* to be a father. I had no role model. My uncle lived in the Northern Territory and I rarely saw him. My grandfather tried his best to be a male influence in my life but he was quite old, and suffering from the emphysema that eventually killed him.'

She nodded with realisation. 'You were *scared* to be a father.'

'I was *terrified* I'd be a bad father.'

'Do you still think that way?'

'Not so much.'

'Why?'

'Because of you,' he said. 'I know you're going to be a brilliant mother, Eliza. That will help me to be the best father I can be to our child.'

'Thank you for the vote of confidence,' she said a little shakily. 'But I'll have to *learn* to be a mother. We'll *both* have to learn to be parents. And I know our daughter will have the most wonderful daddy who—'

'Our *daughter*?'

Eliza snatched her hand to her mouth. 'I haven't had a chance to tell you. I had another ultrasound last week.'

For the first time Jake placed his hand reverently on her bump. 'A little girl…' he said, his voice edged with awe. 'My daughter.'

For a long moment Eliza looked up at Jake, taking in the wonder and anticipation on his face.

'So…so where does that leave us?' she asked finally.

'I'm withdrawing my offer of marriage,' he said.

'*What?*'

Jake looked very serious. 'It was more a command than a proposal. I want to do it properly.'

'Do *what* properly?'

But she thought she might know what. Hope flew into her mind like a tiny bird and flew frantically around, trilling to be heard.

'Propose,' he said.

Jake cradled her face in his big, strong hands. His green eyes looked intently down into hers.

'Eliza, I love you. Will you marry me? Do me the honour of becoming my wife?'

She didn't hesitate. 'Yes, Jake, yes. Nothing would make me happier than to be your wife. I love you.'

Now was the time to kiss. He gathered her into his arms and claimed her mouth. She wound her arms around his neck and kissed him back, her heart singing with joy. She loved him and she wanted him and now he was hers. No way would she be alone in that palatial guest apartment tonight.

Jake broke away from the kiss. Then came back for another brief kiss, as if he couldn't get enough of her. He reached inside his jacket to an inside pocket. Then pulled out a small embossed leather box and flipped it open.

Eliza was too stunned to say anything, to do anything other than stare at the huge, perfect solitaire diamond on a fine platinum band, glinting in the faint silver light of the new moon. He picked up her hand and slipped the ring onto the third finger of her left hand. It fitted perfectly.

'I love it,' she breathed. 'Where did you get—?'

'In London.'

'But—'

'I was planning to propose in Sydney. But then Tristan invited me here.'

'Back to where it started.'

He kissed her again, a kiss that was tender and loving and full of promise.

'Can we get married as soon as possible?' he asked.

She paused. 'For the baby's sake?'

'To make you my wife and me your husband. This is about us committing to each other, Eliza. Not because you're pregnant. The baby is a happy bonus.'

'So what happens about the contract once we're married?'

'That ill-conceived contract? After I left you at the elevator I went back to the meeting room and tore my copy up. Then I fired my lawyer for giving me such bad advice.'

She laughed. 'I put my copy through the shredder.'

'We'll be brilliant parents without any need for that,' he said.

'I love you, Jake,' she said, rejoicing in the words, knowing she would be saying them over and over again in the years to come.

'I love you too, Eliza.' He lowered his head to kiss her again.

'Eliza, are you okay? We were worried—'

Andie's voice made both Eliza and Jake turn.

'Oh,' said Andie. Then, *'Oh...'* again, in a very knowing way.

Gemma was there too. She smiled. 'I can see you're okay.'

'Very okay,' Eliza said, smiling her joy. She held out her left hand and splayed her fingers, the better to display her ring. 'We're engaged. For real engaged.'

Andie and Gemma hugged her and Jake, accompanying their hugs with squeals of excitement and delight. Then Dominic and Tristan were there, slapping Jake on the back and hugging her, telling her they were glad she'd come to her senses and that they hoped she realised what a good man she'd got.

'Oh, I realise, all right,' she said, looking up at Jake. 'I couldn't think of a better man to be my husband and the father of my child.'

'You got the best man,' said Jake with a grin.

CHAPTER SIXTEEN

THE BEAUTY OF having your own party planning business, Eliza mused, was that it was possible to organise a wedding in two weeks flat without cutting any corners.

Everything was perfect, she thought with satisfaction on the afternoon of her wedding day. They'd managed to keep her snaring of 'the Billionaire Bachelor' under the media radar. So she and Jake were getting the quiet, intimate wedding they both wanted without any intrusion from the press.

It had been quite a feat to keep it quiet. After all, not only was the most eligible bachelor in Australia getting married, but the guest list of close family and friends included royalty.

Andie had found a fabulous waterfront house at Kirribilli as their venue. The weather was perfect, and the ceremony was to be held on the expansive lawns that stretched right down to the harbour wall, with the Opera House and Sydney Harbour Bridge as backdrop.

It really was just as she wanted it, Eliza thought as she stood with her father at the end of the veranda. Andie had arranged two rows of elegant white bamboo chairs to form an aisle. Large white metal vases filled with informal bunches of white flowers marked the end of each row of seats.

Now, the chairs were all filled with guests, heads turned,

waiting for the bride to make her entrance. Everyone she cared about was there, including Jake's mother, whom she'd liked instantly.

Ahead, Jake stood flanked by his best man, Dominic, and his groomsman Tristan, at one side of the simple white wedding arch completely covered in white flowers where the celebrant waited. On the other side stood her bridesmaids, Andie and Gemma. A jazz band played softly. When it struck up the chords of the traditional 'Wedding March', it was Eliza's cue to head down the aisle. On the back of a white pony named Molly—her father's wedding gift to her.

Her vintage-inspired, full-skirted tea-length gown hadn't really been chosen with horseback-riding in mind. But when her father had reminded her of how as a little girl she had always wanted to ride to her wedding on her pony, she had fallen for the idea. Andie had had hysterics, but eventually caved in.

'I really hope we can carry this off, Dad,' Eliza said now, as her father helped her up into the side saddle.

'Of course you can, love,' he said. 'You're still the best horsewoman I know.'

Amazing how a wedding and a baby could bring families together, she thought. Her father had mellowed and their rift had been healed—much to her mother's joy. Now Eliza was seated on Molly and her father was leading the pony by a lead-rope entwined with white ribbons down the grassy aisle. There was no 'giving away' of the bride as part of the ceremony. She and Jake were giving themselves to each other.

Her entrance was met with surprised delight and the sound of many cameras clicking.

Jake didn't know about her horseback entrance—she'd kept it a secret. 'Brilliant,' he whispered as he helped her off Molly and into his arms. 'Country girl triumphs.'

But once the novelty of her entrance was over, and her father had led Molly away, it was all about Jake and her.

They had written the words of the ceremony themselves,

affirming their love and respect for each other and their commitment to a lifetime together as well as their anticipation of being parents. Her dress did nothing to disguise her bump—she hadn't wanted to hide the joyous presence of their miracle baby.

Everything around her seemed to recede as she exchanged her vows with Jake, looking up into his face, his eyes never leaving hers. Their first kiss as husband and wife went on for so long their friends starting applauding.

'I love you,' she whispered, just for his ears.

'For always and for ever,' he whispered back.

* * * * *

Keep reading for an excerpt of
The Sicilian Doctor's Proposal
by Sarah Morgan.
Find it in the
The Diamond Inheritance anthology,
out now!

PROLOGUE

'I DON'T BELIEVE in love. And neither do you.' Alice put her pen down and stared in bemusement at her colleague of five years. Had he gone mad?

'That was before I met Trish.' His expression was soft and far-away, his smile bordering on the idiotic. 'It's finally happened. Just like the fairy-tales.'

She wanted to ask if he'd been drinking, but didn't want to offend him. 'This isn't like you at all, David. You're an intelligent, hard-working doctor and at the moment you're talking like a—like a…' *A seven-year-old girl?* No, she couldn't possibly say that. 'You're not sounding like yourself,' she finished lamely.

'I don't care. She's the one. And I have to be with her. Nothing else matters.'

'Nothing else matters?' On the desk next to her the phone suddenly rang, but for once Alice ignored it. 'It's the start of the summer season, the village is already filling with tourists, most of the locals are struck down by that horrid virus, you're telling me you're leaving and you don't think it matters? Please, tell me this is a joke, David, please tell me that.'

Even with David working alongside her she was working flat out to cope with the demand for medical care at the moment. It wasn't that she didn't like hard work. Work was her life. *Work had saved her.* But she knew her limits.

David dragged both hands through his already untidy hair. 'Not leaving exactly, Alice. I just need the summer off. To be with Trish. We need to decide on our future. We're in love!'

Love. Alice stifled a sigh of exasperation. Behind every stupid action was a relationship, she mused silently. She should know that by now. She'd seen it often enough. Why should David be different? Just because he'd *appeared* to be a sane, rational human being—

'You'll hate London.'

'Actually, I find London unbelievably exciting,' David confessed. 'I love the craziness of it all, the crowds of people all intent on getting somewhere yesterday, no one interested in the person next to them—' He broke off with an apologetic wave of his hand. 'I'm getting carried away. But don't you ever feel trapped here, Alice? Don't you ever wish you could do something in this village without the whole place knowing?'

Alice sat back in her chair and studied him carefully. She'd never known David so emotional. 'No,' she said quietly. 'I like knowing people and I like people knowing me. It helps when it comes to understanding their medical needs. They're our responsibility and I take that seriously.'

It was what had drawn her to the little fishing village in the first place. And now it felt like home. And the people felt like family. *More than her own ever had.* Here, she fitted. She'd found her place and she couldn't imagine living anywhere else. She loved the narrow cobbled streets, the busy harbour, the tiny shops selling shells and the trendy store selling surfboards and wetsuits. She loved the summer when the streets were crowded with tourists and she loved the winter when the beaches were empty and lashed by rain. For a moment she thought of London with its muggy, traffic-clogged streets and then she thought of her beautiful house. The house overlooking the broad sweep of the sea. The house she'd lovingly restored in every spare moment she'd had over the past five years.

It had given her sanctuary and a life that suited her. A life that was under her control.

'Since we're being honest here…' David took a deep breath and straightened, his eyes slightly wary. 'I think you should consider leaving, too. You're an attractive, intelligent woman but you're never going to find someone special buried in a place like this. You never meet anyone remotely eligible. All you think about is work, work and work.'

'David, I don't want to meet anyone.' She spoke slowly and clearly so that there could be no misunderstanding. 'I love my life the way it is.'

'Work shouldn't be your life, Alice. You need love.' David stopped pacing and placed a hand on his chest. 'Everyone needs love.'

Something inside her snapped. 'Love is a word used to justify impulsive, irrational and emotional behaviour,' she said tartly, 'and I prefer to take a logical, scientific approach to life.'

David looked a little shocked. 'So, you're basically saying that I'm impulsive, irrational and emotional?'

She sighed. It was unlike her to be so honest. *To reveal so much about herself.* And unlike her to risk hurting someone's feelings. On the other hand, he was behaving very oddly. 'You're giving up a great job on the basis of a feeling that is indefinable, notoriously unpredictable and invariably short-lived so yes, I suppose I am saying that.' She nibbled her lip. 'It's the truth, so you can hardly be offended. You've said it yourself often enough.'

'That was before I met Trish and discovered how wrong I was.' He shook his head and gave a wry smile. 'You just haven't met the right person. When you do, everything will make sense.'

'Everything already makes perfect sense, thank you.' She

reached for a piece of paper and a pen. 'If I draft an advert now, I just might find a locum for August.'

If she was lucky.

And if she wasn't lucky, she was in for a busy summer, she thought, her logical brain already involved in making lists. The village with its pretty harbour and quaint shops might not attract the medical profession but it attracted tourists by the busload and her work increased accordingly, especially during the summer months.

David frowned. 'Locum?' His brow cleared. 'You don't need to worry about a locum. I've sorted that out.'

Her pen stilled. 'You've sorted it out?'

'Of course.' He rummaged in his pocket and pulled out several crumpled sheets of paper. 'Did you really think I'd leave you without arranging a replacement?'

Yes, she'd thought exactly that. All the people she'd ever known who'd claimed to be 'in love' had immediately ceased to give any thought or show any care to those around them.

'Who?'

'I have a friend who is eager to work in England. His qualifications are fantastic—he trained as a plastic surgeon but had to switch because he had an accident. Tragedy, actually.' David frowned slightly. 'He was brilliant, by all accounts.'

A plastic surgeon?

Alice reached for the papers and scanned the CV. 'Giovanni Moretti.' She looked up. 'He's Italian?'

'Sicilian.' David grinned. 'Never accuse him of being Italian. He's very proud of his heritage.'

'This man is well qualified.' She put the papers down on her desk. 'Why would he want to come here?'

'You want to work here,' David pointed out logically, 'so perhaps you're just about to meet your soulmate.' He caught her reproving look and shrugged. 'Just joking. Everyone is entitled to a change of pace. He was working in Milan, which might explain it but, to be honest, I don't really know why he wants to come here. You know us men. We don't delve into details.'

Alice sighed and glanced at the CV on her desk. He'd probably only last five minutes, but at least he might fill the gap while she looked for someone to cover the rest of the summer.

'Well, at least you've sorted out a replacement. Thanks for that. And what happens at the end of the summer? Are you coming back?'

David hesitated. 'Can we see how it goes? Trish and I have some big decisions to make.' His eyes gleamed at the prospect. 'But I promise not to leave you in the lurch.'

He looked so happy, Alice couldn't help but smile. 'I wish you luck.'

'But you don't understand, do you?'

She shrugged. 'If you ask me, the ability to be ruled by emotion is the only serious flaw in the human make-up.'

'Oh, for goodness' sake.' Unexpectedly, David reached out and dragged her to her feet. 'It's out there, Alice. Love. You just have to look for it.'

'Why would I want to? If you want my honest opinion, I'd say that love is just a temporary psychiatric condition that passes given sufficient time. Hence the high divorce rate.' She pulled her hands away from his, aware that he was gaping at her.

'A temporary psychiatric condition?' He gave a choked laugh and his hands fell to his sides. 'Oh, Alice, you *have* to be joking. That can't really be what you believe.'

Alice tilted her head to one side and mentally reviewed all the people she knew who'd behaved oddly in the name of love. There were all too many of them. Her parents and her sister included. 'Yes, actually.' Her tone was flat as she struggled with feelings that she'd managed to suppress for years. Feeling suddenly agitated, she picked up a medical journal and scanned the contents, trying to focus her mind on fact. Facts were safe and comfortable. Emotions were dangerous and uncomfortable. 'It's exactly what I believe.'

Her heart started to beat faster and she gripped the journal more tightly and reminded herself that her life was under her control now. She was no longer a child at the mercy of other people's emotional transgressions.

David watched her. 'So you still don't believe love exists? Even seeing how happy I am?'

She turned. 'If you're talking about some fuzzy, indefinable emotion that links two people together then, no, I don't think that exists. I don't believe in the existence of an indefinable emotional bond any more than I believe in Father Christmas and the tooth fairy.'

David shook his head in disbelief. 'But I *do* feel a powerful emotion.'

She couldn't bring herself to put a dent in his happiness by saying more, so she stepped towards him and took his face in her hands. 'I'm pleased for you. Really I am.' She reached up and kissed him on the cheek. 'But it isn't "love". She sat back down and David studied her with a knowing, slightly superior smile on his face.

'It's going to happen to you, Alice.' He folded his arms across his chest and his tone rang with conviction. 'One of these days you're going to be swept off your feet.'

'I'm a scientist,' she reminded him, amusement sparkling in her blue eyes as they met the challenge in his. 'I have a logical brain. I don't believe in being swept off my feet.'

He stared at her for a long moment. 'No. Which is why it's likely to happen. Love strikes when you're not looking for it.'

'That's measles,' Alice said dryly, reaching for a pile of results that needed her attention. 'Talking of which, little Fiona Ellis has been terribly poorly since her bout of measles last winter. I'm going to check up on her today. See if there's anything else we can do. And I'm going to speak to Gina, the health visitor, about our MMR rates.'

'They dipped slightly after the last newspaper scare but I

thought they were up again. The hospital has been keeping an eye on Fiona's hearing,' David observed, and Alice nodded.

'Yes, and I gather there's been some improvement. All the same, the family need support and we need to make sure that no one else in our practice suffers unnecessarily.' She rose to her feet and smiled at her partner. 'And that's what we give in a small community. Support and individual care. Don't you think you'll miss that? In London you'll end up working in one of those huge health centres with thousands of doctors and you probably won't get to see the same patient twice. You won't know them and they won't know you. It will be completely impersonal. Like seeing medical cases on a production line.'

She knew all the arguments, of course. She understood that a large group of GPs working together could afford a wider variety of services for their patients—psychologists, chiropodists—but she still believed that a good family doctor who knew his patients intimately was able to provide a superior level of care.

'You'll like Gio,' David said, strolling towards the door. 'Women always do.'

'As long as he does his job,' Alice said crisply, 'I'll like him.'

'He's generally considered a heartthrob.' There was a speculative look on his face as he glanced towards her. 'Women go weak at the knees when he walks into a room.'

Great. The last thing she needed was a Romeo who was distracted by everything female.

'Some women are foolish like that.' Alice stood up and reached for her jacket. 'Just as long as he doesn't break more hearts than he heals, then I really don't mind what he does when he isn't working here.'

'There's more to life than work, Alice.'

'Then go out there and enjoy it,' she advised, a smile on her face. 'And leave me to enjoy mine.'